"What's wrong?" The knight asked, eyes trying to pierce the darkness.

"I don't know, but the pack lizards are upset, and a bird flew off, screeching," Davorin said. He thought he saw the thief pivot towards him, but he wasn't concerned by that right now.

"Could be nothing?" The scholar suggested, not sounding very hopeful, even as she tried to move closer to the fire.

"Not a muddy chance. When animals panic, you need to be alert." The thief picked up a heavy stick. "There!" She pointed.

Sir Jors let out a string of swears creative enough to impress even the thief before apologizing. "Unicorns."

Those Who Go Do Not Return

H. J. Harding

Whimsy and Wonder Publishing

Library of Congress Control Number: 2018675309
Printed in the United States of America

To my family, who had to listen over the years as I agonized over this one. To my readers, who allow me to keep doing this.

Contents

Chapter One

The Gathering

Or

"I have to work with *Them*?"

Lakara, adept scholar, did not initially pay much attention to the messenger that would change her life. A messenger direct from the king was rare, but was always the purview of the head archivist, not a mere adept. More annoyed than interested in the spreading whispers of rumor and wild speculation, Lakara tried to tune out her surroundings to focus on the tome she was copying. The whispers died as the head archivist paused in front of her workstation.

"Lakara can answer His Majesty's questions. Lakara, go with this messenger and see the king."

"The... king?" A personal audience with the king? That was all but unheard of for one of her status and would either prove to be very good or very, very bad. Why would the head archivist suggest *her*? Lakara was no one. She hadn't even known the head archivist knew her name.

"Yes, the king. And it's better not to keep him waiting." He looked down at her with an irritated glance.

Lakara jumped to her feet and immediately began to cap her ink. No, it would not be wise to keep the king waiting. Thankfully, the day had barely broken and she hadn't had time to gather the ink stains that were inevitable no matter how careful one was.

"Just, go! Someone else can finish up here." She couldn't tell if the snap in his voice was anger or agitation. Possibly both. Lakara gave a quick bow and followed the messenger who took off at a walk that was uncomfortably brisk for her.

"This way, Scholar." The green-clad attendant said. Green meant he was foreign-born. Probably from Salardis. He didn't have the right coloring for a Trovian, and Graldish was a long way from any other country.

As one of the king's scholars, Lakara knew the history of the kingdom better than she knew her name but she had never seen the throne room. Nor had she seen the previous one, which King Zikkar had considered too small and converted into a ballroom.

The new throne room was twice the size of the old one, with more than a ton of gold molded onto the walls, studded with jewels that gleamed and sparkled in the torchlight. Eighteen columns of ivory, bedecked by silver, lined the path, one pair for each of the gods. The room even had carpet! With silk from Salardis, costing over ten thousand gold doruts. The dais itself and the runner leading up to it were pure silk, while the rest of the room had silk mixed with the finest wool. But the jewel of the room was the throne itself. Even for the room, it was massive. Solid gold, with silk cushions. An intricate unicorn, one hoof pressed onto the head of a pack lizard, stood engraved in the back of the chair, able to be seen even with the king seated. The entire room had caused taxes to be doubled for ten years to pay for it all. The throne alone took two years of taxes. It was a marvel.

Like the messenger, Lakara made sure not to stand on the runner. That was for nobles, ambassadors, and the like. Always aware of palace hierarchy, the extravagant finery made her feel very self-conscious, perhaps more than was warranted. After all, didn't she wear the red and blue robes of the king's scholars? She even had the silver embroidery that only the adepts could wear. That put her higher than the attendants, equal to most of the magicians, and just below the lower-ranked nobles. Still not high enough to dare step foot on that carpet.

"The scholar, Lakara," the messenger announced with a bow, before stepping away, leaving her face-to-face with her king for the very first time. Lakara struck a deep bow and said nothing.

"You, Scholar! Tell me what you know of the Jewel of Ishni."

Lakara racked her brain for everything she knew of the legend. "A somewhat obscure story in our histories. It was claimed, hundreds of years ago, that the Jewel of Ishni was a bauble that possessed no power of its own, yet was so coveted by many of the gods, that the All-Knowing, All-Father, took the jewel and hid it somewhere that only a mortal could go. It is rumored that even the other gods do not know where it is. AKAF gave each of them a clue to incorporate into one of their temples. Legend has it that if a mortal were to find the gem, he could probably trade it to the god of his choice for, well, almost anything."

"Could you find these clues?"

"Well, it would be a matter of comparing records to figure out which temples the clues were supposedly in..." Lakara stared into space as she pondered it. "It should be possible. Though many have tried in the past and fai—"

"Excellent." King Zikkar pointed to a table in the corner. "That is all the information we have on the Jewel of Ishni. Start going through it and figure out which temples the clues are in."

"Y...yes, your Majesty." Lakara bowed deeply and scurried over to the table, not daring to ask why she was supposed to be going through the various scrolls, tomes, and books in the king's throne room instead of in the nice, quiet library.

"Call in Sir Jors," The king ordered.

It wasn't a name she knew, though 'Sir' implied either a knight or one of the lower-ranked nobles. Nor was that her immediate concern. Taking one of the pieces of paper she had been given for notes, Lakara quickly made a list of what characteristics the temples' hiding clues should have.

Each of the gods had many temples, some had a temple or shrine in every city. But each of the gods also had major temples. However, what counted as a major temple varied over the centuries. Since the clues, if they existed, were given centuries ago, the temples would have to be ancient ones.

Her attention was diverted as a new person, presumably Sir Jors, arrived. A knight wearing leather armor approached the dais, also not walking on the runner, clasped his fist to his chest, and knelt before the king. His shield had the crest of the kingdom on it, indicating at least ten years of service; but neither his blond hair nor beard appeared touched by gray. The armor was probably a family heirloom, in the same style used in the Wars which ended over a hundred years ago.

Lakara noticed these things then went back to cross-referencing if the legend had first been written down four or five hundred years ago. It would make a difference as to which temples were possibilities.

"Excellent. Sir Jors, I have a special task for you."

"Sire, I live to serve."

"I know you do. Have you heard of the Jewel of Ishni?"

Lakara had been trying to ignore them, but this caught her attention. Perhaps this would explain what she was doing here and why the king was interested.

"I am familiar—"

"Excellent. This scholar here," King Zikkar turned to her.

"Um, Lakara, Sire."

"Yes, her." He turned his attention back to Sir Jors, "is an expert on the jewel. I'm sending an expedition. You will be in charge of making sure everyone gets there and back safely."

"Expedition, your Majesty?" The knight asked, voice thick with trepidation. Lakara didn't think she could speak at all. Expert? She wasn't an expert in this. No one was. Oh, she had hand-copied at least two of these books, but that didn't make her an expert. Did he really expect her to figure out which temples the clues were in, something that had been debated for centuries, in one afternoon?

"To find the jewel, of course," King Zikkar said, as if it were obvious.

Utter silence. The dungeons held several who had forgotten that King Zikkar did not tolerate criticism. He continued, "If you succeed, you will be inducted into the Order of Paladins. Now, go to the armory and make preparations for, oh, four or five. I'll have them sent to you when they are ready."

"As you wish, your Majesty."

"One more thing, Sir Jors. Your... 'condition' has rendered you a liability in the past. Fail again and you *won't* get another chance."

He seemed to wince, but she may have imagined it. "As you say, Sire."

"Of course. You are dismissed."

There was semi-quiet again as Lakara concentrated on listing all the temples that would have been built within fifty years before or a hundred years after the first reference of the Jewel of Ishni legend. Then she would remove the ones that no longer existed and try to concentrate on which were probably the most important at the time they were built. It was possible that one of the temples that held a clue would have been destroyed, but wouldn't the deity that planted the clue there make sure to prevent that? And if it was truly destroyed, then no one was going to find it anyway. Lakara was so deep in her work that she missed who the king had summoned to come next. Until he arrived.

Master Davorin was the best necromancer in the kingdom, having raised three skeletons at the same time to qualify as King's Necromancer. Probably close in age to the knight, the necromancer was very much his opposite. He seemed surrounded by black. Black hair, kept long and tied back, clean shaven, and his robe, which could not be more than a year old if that, was black and purple with gold embroidery that proclaimed him to be the king's personal necromancer. From her angle, Lakara couldn't see the solid black eyes, iris and pupil, the unmistakable sign of a necromancer.

Ignoring the finery of the room, Master Davorin stood square on the runner and gave a half bow. "You called for me, Sire?"

"Yes, I have a task that requires your... particular talents. When I want the best, I make sure to send the best."

"Of course, Sire."

"Excellent. This scholar here," King Zikkar waved a hand in her direction, causing Master Davorin to actually look at her for the first time. Lakara stifled a shudder at those inky void eyes and gave as best a curtsey as she could while seated. He sneered and tilted his head marginally. The king continued, "is an expert on the Jewel of Ishni. I want you to go on the expedition to find the jewel and bring it here. I'm sure it is well within the reach of a man with your talents. Succeed and you will be richly rewarded."

The necromancer had started to open his mouth, closed it, and opened it again. "As your Majesty wishes."

"Good. Now, gather your supplies and head to the armory to be outfitted for your journey."

Master Davorin gave another half-bow and left. Lakara went back to her work. If the king wanted an expedition sent out soon, then she had to hurry to figure out where they would have to go. It wasn't like they could stop and ask directions once they left.

Lakara had her list mostly settled when the guards entered, dragging a young woman wearing cheap brown clothing. The woman was in chains and had the complexion of one who spent a lot of time outside or had some Trovian ancestry. Possibly both. Time in the sun wouldn't have given her hair that black, and Trovians were rare in the country and almost always worked outside jobs. Neither of which were favored in this circle.

The guards gave the runner a wide berth as they hauled the woman to the front and forced her to the ground in front of the dais. King Zikkar sneered down at her. "You stand condemned of theft. And not just any theft, but theft against your sovereign king. Nevertheless, I am not without mercy."

The thief scoffed and was kicked by one of the guards. King Zikkar cleared his throat. "As I said. You rejected my first offer, but I will offer you mercy once more." Lakara thought she saw the thief roll her eyes but couldn't be sure. "I find myself needing one of your... *skills*. I am sending an expedition to find the Jewel of Ishni. Now, one as low-bred and uneducated as yourself may have never heard of—"

"The one where the clues are scattered all over the continent, making you visit the Endless Grasslands, the Ocean of Sand, the Mountains of Death, the Swamp of Despair, the Sea of Tears, the Forests of Gloom, and the Dead Lands? That Jewel of Ishni?"

King Zikkar's face froze in a strained smile. "Er, yes. That

Jewel of Ishni."

"Pass. I'm better off here."

The thief had a point. Punishment for theft varied depending on status, value of the items stolen, and the whims of the king; but generally ranged from a fine, time in the stocks, time in the dungeon, or in extreme cases, loss of a hand.

"If you insist, I'll have no choice but to have you executed for treason in two days."

"What? Are you out of your mind?!" The thief leaped to her feet with as much grace as a woman wearing a quarter of her weight in chains could scrounge up. Which, to be honest, was more than Lakara would have thought possible. She didn't stay upright long, as the guards quickly shoved her back down. "OW!"

"Yes, it has been decided that attempting to steal from your king is treason." King Zikkar turned to his most trusted advisor, the only one who was permitted to sit on a chair on the dais itself. "Lord Sartik, please be so kind as to remind me what we do to lowborn *trash* like this when accused of treason?"

"I believe they are hung, drawn, and quartered, Sire," Lord Sartik answered, smirking.

The thief paled and even Lakara winced. The woman carefully rose to her knees, watching the guards warily. "On second thought, I've heard the Mountains of Death are lovely. When do we leave?"

Was it Lakara's imagination, or did the king look disappointed by her answer? "Very well. Take the chains off her, except for her hands. Those can be removed later." The guards started unlocking the shackles while the king continued. "Make no mistake, your team will have orders to discipline or even kill you if you cause trouble or try to escape. Failure would not be wise."

The woman looked at the king, with boldness that Lakara would never have dared. "And if we succeed, Sire?"

"Then you will be pardoned."

"Is that all?"

"You overspeak, Thief," Lord Sartik snarled. "The king is being most generous."

She didn't move or respond, as if she hadn't heard him.

King Zikkar sat up, paying more attention. "And what would you have? Should you succeed."

"If we succeed, we find the jewel and bring it back, alive, I want to be a lady. In my own rights. Not because you married me off to one of your lords."

Lord Sartik gaped at her, and Lakara wondered at her audacity. The guards apparently did too, as one went to strike her. King Zikkar laughed and waved him off. "Very well. If you succeed, I will consider your request. Take her away."

The guards forced the thief into a bow before dragging her from the room. Lord Sartik waited until the door closed before turning to the king. "Sire, I hesitate to point out something I'm certain you have already considered, but about the thief's request..."

"Rest easy. I said I would consider her request and I have. Impossible! Nobles are nobility for a reason. Throwing in *scum* like that would ruin everything."

Lakara tried not to react to the profanity, but wasn't entirely successful, drawing the king's attention.

"Tell no one what we discussed. Anything you hear in here is to be considered secret. Do you understand?"

"Y... yes, Sire."

"Excellent. Did you determine which temples?"

"Almost. I have a list of the fifteen most likely. The temple of AKAF in this city may have some more information allowing me to narrow the list down."

King Zikkar nodded. "Very well, then that will be the first step on your quest."

"M... my quest? Sire?"

"Of course, I can't send out the expedition without the expert! How would they get anywhere? Gather the resources you'll need and meet your team in the armory. They'll need you to take charge."

Not just go, but be in charge? How was this happening? Licking her lips, Lakara tried to continue, "With all due respect, your Majesty, I do not believe I am any more an expert on the Jewel of Ishni than any other scholar and I have absolutely no leadership experience. Perhaps you would be better off sending a different scholar?"

"Nonsense. You've already managed to figure out what temples to visit or will have soon. The Head Archivist is planning to retire soon. This could be just what you need to take his place."

Her? The Head Archivist? By birth, she had already advanced as far as she could go. But if the king himself wanted her as Head Archivist, who could possibly say no? Besides, refusal could end up with her seeing the inside of the dungeons. "I shall do my best, Sire."

"Excellent. There's your group. Watch the thief carefully. If she resists after you get the jewel, cut off her hands and feet and leave her in the wilderness. Watch all your group, actually. Gather what you need and go to the armory. These attendants will help you carry your supplies. I want you started by nightfall. Tell no one your goal. Make sure the others know as well."

"Yes, your Majesty." Lakara followed the blue-clad attendants in a daze. Blue tunics meant they had been born in the palace. Like her and her parents. What would they think about their scholar daughter leading an expedition?

***

Sir Jors surveyed the weapons in the armory, waiting for the rest to arrive. A team or four or five. Not the most promising, especially if one of the numbers was the scholar or one like her. Ideally, a team that small, traveling over such distant and varied terrain would contain a healer, preferably a magical one; a ranger who was trained in javelin, preferably one who knew a lot about pack lizards, in addition to one or two standard fighters such as himself. Since he himself specialized in the sword, perhaps a master of spear or staff. Axe wouldn't be bad either, especially when one considered the terrain they were likely to face, but like him, they would be short-range. At least one paladin would be preferred, but the paladins outranked him and would be in charge if there was one in the group. If the scholar was also multilingual, preferably trained in diplomacy; then this might just work. He had seen similar strike teams work in battle, with luck, a civilian task would work similarly. As long as everyone had some training in some weapon, they could work on sharpening and honing skills as they traveled.

He was pulled from his thoughts as the palace guards shoved a chained woman into the room. "Here, thief." The woman spun with the motion so that she not only kept her balance but was able to face the door and Sir Jors at the same time. "You take responsibility for her?" The guard asked.

Sir Jors backed up a step. "She is part of the expedition?" He hadn't expected a thief.

"Says the king."

"Then, yes. I suppose I do."

The woman looked at them. "I'll need my pack. The one taken from me when I was arrested."

"What makes you think you have any right to demand anything?" The guard growled.

"You want a thief? Then I need my tools. I need my hands, too." She held up her chained wrists.

Sir Jors spoke up before the guard could hit her. He never could stand to see a woman struck. "She makes a valid point. I have charge of her."

The woman looked penetratingly at him, unreadable emotions flashing in her amber eyes.

"I'll get the pack. We'll undo the manacles when I get back." The guard left.

Sir Jors took a moment to evaluate her as if she were a threat, very aware that she was doing the same. She had been caught as a thief, but that may have been simply bad luck on her part. He wouldn't ask her age, but she had to be between twenty and thirty. To have survived that long, she would have to have skills or very good luck. Her hands had a few calluses that he didn't recognize, probably from the tools of her trade. While she didn't have the muscle definition of a farm girl, she wasn't far off. This was a woman who knew hard work and didn't shrink from it. Judging from her shoes, she also did a lot of traveling. So, a roaming thief rather than one who stuck to a city. Yes, there were sling calluses. She could hunt, at least to some extent. Probably knew her way around a knife too. For self-defense, if nothing else. Not an immediate threat, but it would be unwise to forget that this woman was a survivor who was coerced into a task she likely wanted nothing to do with.

"I am Sir Jors of Vaslisina. What's your name?"

"Kita." She didn't volunteer anything else, and he didn't ask. She may not have any other name.

He eyed the wall of weapons. Handing her a weapon seemed unwise, but there would be plenty of dangers on the way, where they would need every able fighter. Well, he'd let her keep her sling and maybe, after there had been some time to develop trust and some sort of bond, he could make sure to pass her a blade or something if need be.

As long as the other members were better equipped and trained fighters, this was still workable. Just as he was thinking that, Davorin, the palace necromancer entered the room with a sneer. Turning to the attendants following him, he gave orders to have his packs, at least five by the look of things, taken to wherever the pack lizards might be.

Sir Jors couldn't help but notice that though the necromancer bore no pack himself, his breath sped a little too rapidly, not used to the exertion. Of what? Packing bags and walking from his tower to the armory? Or perhaps carrying the extra weight of such a soft life. The only calluses on the man came from book and quill. If handed a weapon, he'd probably hurt himself with it.

Still, Davorin was a natural magician. A necromancer, no less. That was not to be underestimated. After all, it was a battle between necromancers that turned a once-fertile country into the Dead Lands centuries ago. Not that Sir Jors had heard anything to suggest that Davorin was anywhere near that level. He also couldn't help the thought that he'd trade even the country's most powerful necromancer for an apprentice healer.

Davorin scowled as he looked around the room. "You were assigned to find the jewel?"

Sir Jors flushed. What did the necromancer know? Had he heard? Beyond that, why would he be forced to work with a necromancer? It was forbidden for paladins. But he wasn't a paladin yet.

The thief leaned against the wall, looking no more impressed with the necromancer than he was with her. "Unfortunately. Why does he want *you* dead?"

"What? Do you know who I am?" Davorin rose to his full height, looming almost a head taller than the woman, but still shorter than Sir Jors himself.

"A necromancer, from the looks of it. One the king clearly has no use for if he's assigning you a suicide mission for something that doesn't exist." She didn't bother looking up at him, choosing to study her hands.

"Hold your tongue, She-whelp. I can curse you where you stand," Davorin snarled. "I am the best necromancer in the land!"

"Out of how many? Five?" She asked, still not looking at him.

"Three, actually. Bartlow the necromancer lives in the Great Temple of Shadow Master in Chiswat to train others. He's ninety-five. Virn the necromancer lives in the city of Wris. He is believed to be even older. Which means Master Davorin is also the youngest known necromancer." The scholar from the throne room joined them, an attendant leading her. She sounded like she was speaking automatically.

"Your packs, Scholar Lakara?" The attendant asked when Lakara didn't do anything for a moment.

"Oh! Right. Thank you. I need these taken to where the rest of the supplies will be." She handed over two packs, which the attendant took in addition to the large sack he had slung over a shoulder. From what he knew about scholars, which admittedly wasn't much, it would be almost entirely books and papers, with little practical supplies.

If this woman had ever been more than twenty miles from the palace or handled anything sharper than a pen knife, he would eat his shield. Her shoes would fall apart before they had been on the road a week if they didn't find her a pair of traveling boots. The best he could think of was that she didn't carry the extra weight of the necromancer and seemed at least willing to do her share of work.

"The pack lizards await in the north courtyard. They will be ready to leave when you are." The attendant bowed to her, before giving another, shallower bow to the room in general and leaving. The message was clear. The scholar was the one in charge.

"Good, everyone's here." She gave a smile. He had seen that smile once before. It was the same smile he had seen on his brother, Anor, when he had been unexpectedly given control of a band of men and had no idea what he was doing.

Judging from Davorin's sneer and Kita's wince and head shake, Sir Jors wasn't the only one who noticed. Eyeing the wall of weapons, Sir Jors found himself doubting he would ever return to see them again.

***

Davorin stood back, watching the pack lizards be loaded up. It was a job for attendants, far below his station. Except, the pack lizards would have to be unburdened, unharnessed, and repacked many, many times on a journey of this length. But Davorin was clearly the highest-ranked of their group. Surely, *he* wouldn't be expected to saddle the things.

He had never actually been this close to one before. The ten-foot-long lizard came up to his knees at the shoulders and was eyeing him in a way that showed off its sharp teeth. It was currently red, but most could change their colors, so that meant nothing. A black tongue darted out, licking an eye that looked a lot like his. Davorin stepped back involuntarily.

Fortunately, the scholar had a much worse reaction, crying out and jumping back. No one noticed his response. So far, he was finding little to no motivation to want to get closer to the beasts. The one eyeing him stretched out a foot causing long claws to scrape stone with a *scrrrt*. No motivation at all.

Well, he would just have to make sure he wasn't the one leading it. Or its partner. Apparently, between his supplies, the scholar's tomes, the knight's armor and weapons, and food, tents, and general supplies, they'd need two lizards. Any more and they would probably need three. At least the thief didn't have anything but a shoulder pack that she insisted on carrying herself. Fine with him, that's what her class was for.

They would be leaving soon, so Davorin turned to Trois, his personal attendant, for last instructions and orders. While he would prefer to have the man accompany him, that wouldn't be feasible. "I expect everything to be in good order when I return. My rooms tidy, my pigeons in good health, and so forth."

"Yes, Master Davorin."

"Good. I should be displeased if I have problems to straighten out when I return. Be certain no one goes near my magic books. They are not to be handled by the untrained. Some will attempt to kill anyone who glances at their pages." And those weren't even the most dangerous.

Trois blanched but nodded again. "I will be most certain, Master Davorin."

Excellent. Trois was a good man; one he didn't want to lose to a life-draining book. Davorin nodded in dismissal and watched Trois leave before turning back to his... fellow travelers. This was not going to be fun.

It was borderline insulting, actually. Blow to his ego it might be, Davorin could, silently, admit that he wouldn't be the best choice to lead an expedition. As long as someone who *knew* what they were doing *was* in charge. The scholar clearly was no leader. The knight was of no rank or consequence, and the thief didn't show any respect at all. To anyone, as far as Davorin could tell.

Besides, it had been years since he had walked more than a few hundred feet at once. Already today, Davorin had probably walked more in one day than he had in at least a year, and they hadn't left the palace yet. This was going to be miles and miles and miles, over rough terrain. Rough, dangerous terrain. He held back a shiver.

"So, Scholar, where to first?" The thief asked. She had finally gotten her hands free and was currently tempting the pack lizards to bite one off as she rubbed the beast's eye ridge.

The scholar had been staring in horrified fascination but shook herself free. "Um, well, we need to visit nine temples to get the clues. I *think* I've mostly narrowed down which ones. If I'm right, the nearest one would be, er, the temple of AKAF in this city. And I think the temple has the information I need to finish my list. We could visit while the final preparations are being completed?"

"A good plan," The knight agreed. The thief shrugged but rose to her feet and moved away from the lizards. Davorin quickly followed. They weren't leaving him alone with the beasts.

The Great Temple of AKAF was even older than the city of Corvis. The initial temple was built over seven hundred years ago, but it was expanded and added onto a few hundred years later. It was the largest building in the city except for the palace itself, but unlike temples built within the last three hundred years, it was designed simply, like a fort. AKAF was a practical god who had always allowed his penitents to take shelter in his temples during emergencies. According to legend, AKAF had claimed that the whole of the world could not contain him and the temples were more for the people anyway. Therefore, sacrifices should not be beyond their ability to give, and the temple should be a place of refuge.

As always, the temple thronged with petitioners, worshipers, and priests. Even the outer courtyard was so full that the four of them stopped short, hesitant to join the crowd. If he were wearing his normal robes, there would be no issue. People made way for a necromancer, even if he didn't have the royal patronage. But they were ordered not to tell anyone who they were or what they had gone out to do.

Having to fight through the crowd like commoners; it was humiliating! But perhaps it wouldn't be necessary. "Well, Scholar," Davorin slurred the title. "Do the legends tell us what we're looking for? Or where?"

The scholar, maybe he should actually try to learn his companions' names, bit her bottom lip while playing with her hair, a brown tangle that managed to be neither straight nor curly, and had been hastily tied back in a knot that was probably supposed to resemble the fashion of court ladies, five years ago. It made him think of dried-out reeds. "There is supposed to be some symbol that pulls the clues together. But the books in the palace don't say what it is."

"So where do we start?" The knight asked. He was the only one not wearing one of the provided traveler's robes, having decided to wear his travel armor, a leather monstrosity that was worn in and out in places. Why he was wearing it now, instead of waiting until they left the city, Davorin neither knew nor cared enough to ask.

"The library. If we can get there." The scholar eyed the crowd dubiously.

"Oh, for..." The thief snapped out, but apparently decided against swearing in a temple. Unlike the others, she actually looked better in a travel robe. While standard palace issue travel robes had only enchantments for waterproofing and durability, Davorin didn't doubt the travel robe was finer than anything the woman had ever owned. Shaking her head impatiently, causing the black braid of her hair to go swishing, the thief spoke. "Come on." She snaked her way through the crowd like it wasn't there. The rest of them weren't so lucky.

They were separated almost immediately. A man jostled him, causing Davorin to shove him away. The man turned to say something, possibly push back, when he saw Davorin's eyes. The necromancer could tell the exact moment that happened because the peasant paled and backed away silently.

Normally, Davorin wouldn't let it go so easily, but he could see the Shadows. The black mists had started to surround the peasant. Shadow Master would collect him within days. Davorin wondered if the man knew. Perhaps that was why he was here, to pray for healing, though why he would come here instead of to Aloses's shrine, he didn't know. It might even work. Perhaps.

He turned away, concentrating on getting out of the crowd before he saw more. No one ever thought about that part, if they even knew. As a necromancer, he had a connection to Shadow Master, who collected the dead. He knew when someone would die, often before they knew. No one else could see or feel the shadows; reaching out, beckoning. No one else could hear the whispers of the dead whenever other noises didn't drown them out. Lucky ones.

Then he was out of the courtyard, standing between the knight and the scholar, staring at the thief who sat on the steps of the temple, eating a pomegranate. "Took you long enough."

"If you run off..." The scholar warned.

"I didn't run off. I just went ahead. Now, suppose we ask the Head Priest what he knows of the Jewel of Ishni?"

"Where did you get that pomegranate?" Davorin demanded. He knew for a fact that she hadn't had that when she left them.

"That merchant. Only one bronze duc." She nodded her

head to one of the merchants selling flowers and fruits. Seeing them looking, the man started energetically waving his wares. Davorin turned away quickly, seeing the others do the same. You couldn't encourage the merchants at all, or they wouldn't let you leave.

"Those are meant for the symbolic sacrifices," The knight pointed out gravely.

She shrugged, unconcerned. "I'm hungry. Somehow, I think AKAF will understand. Besides, I got these too." She waved a handful of cheap candles. "We'll each light one for a safe journey after we talk to the priest. Mu...ss, if you ask, he might even bless the quest."

"You can't swear in a temple," The scholar hissed.

"I didn't. I only nearly did."

Davorin shook his head. "Loath as I am to admit it, the she-whelp has a point. Let's talk to the priest and leave." He should have thought of the candles. He was a devout follower of the gods, whereas this thief was actually eating a temple pomegranate! "You can't take that inside."

The thief shrugged, pulled a cloth from her pack, wrapped what was left of the pomegranate in it, and slipped the whole thing back into her bag. Davorin gave her a wide berth, but for some reason, she was not struck down dead as she entered the temple.

Four travelers demanding to speak to the Head Priest would probably not have gotten very far, except that one of the neophytes, a woman with the silver fingernails of an enchanter, recognized the scholar and agreed to intercede. The Head Priest, regaled in white and silver, greeted them in person once they had been escorted to a quiet area.

"A most curious group," he said, looking them over. "Still, AKAF works in mysterious ways. How may I aid you?"

The scholar came forward and curtseyed. "Good Priest, forgive my impertinence. I'm the Scholar Lakara, and I have come to ask what information you have on the Jewel of Ishni."

The priest looked them over carefully. "I see. Interesting. You should know, copies of everything we have in our library also exist in yours."

"Everything?" Asked the thief.

Before someone could shut her up, the priest smiled. "Well, *almost* everything. There are a few fragments. I suppose there is no harm in letting you see them, provided you are careful."

Davorin wasn't quite sure how he went from standing in the hallway to sitting at a table in the priest's private library, studying fragments of writing that were older than the kingdom itself. Unfortunately, because of the age, these were pre-Graldian, even pre-Restor. Many of the older books, especially magic books were written in Restor, and Davorin was confident in his ability in the language. But no, this was Vesrop, far older still. Some claimed Vesrop was the language of the gods. Davorin didn't know about that, but he did know it was the oldest known language in the land.

Vesrop was *not* a language he knew well, and the knight and thief didn't seem to know any at all, though he would be more surprised if they did. The scholar knew the most, but even she was far from expert. Muttering under her breath, she copied every page exactly, just as he was doing, but she was trying to translate at the same time.

Finally, they had everything copied down. Sitting back, the scholar rubbed at her forehead. "I'm pretty sure I've figured out which temples we need. And I think I found something significant."

The thief turned away from the window she had been staring out of. No one had asked her to copy anything. The knight had tried, but he didn't have the right hand for it. "What do you have?" He asked.

"I found references to the jewel, and information about the symbol. One that was used to mark the clues in the temples."

"That helps," the thief said. "What kind of symbol?"

"This." She drew a square, topped by a circle with a diamond inside. "I don't know the significance, but that's the symbol." She hesitated but continued. "I'm not positive, but I *think* this tells what the clue here is. It says we need to go to the Heart of Earth."

"And that means, what, exactly?" The thief asked, sounding less than impressed.

"Not sure. But when we do find out, I'm sure we'll all think it was obvious." The scholar smiled hopefully.

"Heart of Earth," the knight mused. "I seem to recall something. When I was young, my grandfather told me something about each of the compass points being once named for an element."

"Yes, they were," Davorin answered. "That could be it. Water was east, fire was south, wind was west, and earth was north."

"Which would mean we head north? Well, good. We have to go that way anyway. Most of the temples are north of here." Scholar nodded to herself as she collected the copied fragments with an air of distraction.

"So, what else is bothering you?" The thief asked, rolling the candles in her hands.

"What? Nothing. Nothing is wrong. I'm sure I'm mistranslating." The scholar wouldn't look at anyone.

"Mistranslating what?" The knight asked gravely. "If

there is an issue, we all need to know."

She caved. "I'm sure I'm mistaken. But one of the comments. About the quest for the jewel. It said that those who go, do not return."

"How… reassuring." Davorin stood and stretched, trying to hide his shivers. "I suggest you get better at translating, and soon. I imagine the other clues will likely be in Vesrop as well." It took all he had to keep his voice steady and the fear off his face.

***

Kita didn't bother to offer to help with the research, and it didn't seem like anyone expected her to. She couldn't read, let alone read ancient, forgotten languages; nor did she really care whether they found the filthy jewel or not. Muddy thing probably didn't even exist. But it was go on this dirty trip or be executed. If they did find it, then the king might just have her executed anyway.

Still, there were hundreds, maybe thousands, of miles between Corvis and the last of the temples if the legends were right about anything. Surely, somewhere along the way, she could find an opportunity to escape. Not now, of course. They'd be watching her too closely. But time would cause carelessness. As long as she was alert, the chance would come.

And they didn't know about Whisper. As long as she could keep him hidden, she'd have an advantage they didn't know about. Hiding him would get harder, but between the two of them, they'd work it out.

She had spotted him while the others were buried in their inky puzzles. Not so close that anyone had noticed, but close enough that she could feel him, close enough she could Borrow him. Not that she could in front of the others. Borrowing was illegal here. But, so was theft. They wouldn't figure it out. They couldn't figure it out.

Torn from her thoughts when the scholar finished, Kita was *not* impressed by the nonsense riddle or the vague threat. If the warning was accurate, it was probably because addled people tried to use nonsense riddles to find something that didn't exist and wound up far over their heads. 'Heart of Earth', indeed. Maybe it meant north. Maybe it meant it was buried in a hole of dirt! Maybe it meant nothing at all.

The scholar believed. Believed that if she was smart, if she tracked down all the clues correctly, then they could succeed. Probably believed everything she read in a book. Kita couldn't even count the number of people like her that she had seen taken advantage of because they believed the wrong person, the wrong source. Too loyal for her own good. Too sure of her own intelligence. But those books would fail her sooner or later. When that happened, she'd either double down on her beliefs, sure *she* made a mistake somewhere, or fall into despair. Could be useful, if Kita stuck around that long.

The necromancer probably believed. But Kita doubted he was doing this strictly because the king said so. Maybe he hoped to use the jewel himself, or maybe he counted on a reward from the king. If things got hard enough, and judging from the luxury he seemed used to, that might not take long, he might be tempted to give up. As much as he seemed to hate her, and as much as she hated arrogant rich people like him; he could be her best ally. Even if he never knew it.

The knight would be her biggest threat. Like the scholar, he seemed to be influenced mostly by loyalty to the king. Unlike her, he wouldn't be as easily misled. He was also used to hardship and travel. Kita had seen the two javelins packed away and had no desire to see how skilled he was with them. She could probably outrun him. She didn't want to find out if she could outrun his javelin. On the plus side, he had treated her with almost uncommon courtesy so far and had shown no desire to lord his position over anyone below him. Which would be her, as the scholar was in charge of the expedition and the necromancer probably outranked knights.

To her mild surprise, they did use her candles to pray for a safe journey after getting a blessing from the Head Priest. She hadn't been sure if they would. After all, they were purchased by a thief, and a part Trovian thief at that. Though they seemed more concerned about getting the favor of the gods than she was. Kita had enough to do with finding food to worry about what the gods wanted as long as they didn't smite her down. But she did feel a little better having a priest pray for them.

Allowed to use one of the back entrances to the temple, they were able to avoid the crowds that her *companions* had struggled with before and were soon back at the palace courtyard. The pack lizards were fully loaded up, and the yard was empty except for the lizards and two attendants to mind them. Both left as soon as Kita and the group arrived. Despite the fact that it was a few hours after noon, it was clear that they were meant to leave at once, rather than waiting the night and starting in the morning. Not much of a sendoff.

From the corner of her eye, Kita spotted Whisper hovering about. It was time to leave Corvis. Good. She had been here long enough. Even if she hadn't been caught thieving, Kita would have been moving on about now or soon. Her mother had called her a Rover. One who couldn't stand to be in one place for long. Sometimes it was a problem, but now it might be to her advantage.

The scholar and the necromancer didn't leave the palace much, if at all. The knight would have more endurance and stamina, but he also wore armor. Not the heaviest kind, true, but it would still weigh him down. If she were able to slip away unseen, she might be able to stay ahead long enough for him to give up. Or she could get somewhere he couldn't. But that was for later.

Sir Jors took the halter of the first lizard, then looked to the rest of them to see who would take the other. Both the scholar and the necromancer immediately stepped back, with the scholar's hands flinching away. Which was better than the necromancer who stuck his hands behind his back. Kita shook her head. Pathetic. "I'll lead her," she offered.

The knight nodded reluctantly. "We'll switch out later. I'm sure everyone will have to take their share."

The scholar opened her mouth but swallowed whatever she was going to say. "R...Right. We, um, need to head to Wris next. The temple of Pirette."

Goddess of craft. Patron to scholars if Kita was correct. Perhaps that was why she wanted to go there next. "You said we're going north. Wris is south."

The scholar nodded. "Yes, that temple is the furthest south we need to go. After that, we head north."

Kita accepted the information with a shrug. It *would* be a little odd if all the temples were in a nice straight line with them at the end. It would be nice, but a little odd.

As ready as she was to leave the city and its filthy scum of a king, the rest seemed more reluctant. Mud, had they all even left the city before? Still, did they have to stand there staring at the gates? Kita was ready to leave!

With everyone watching her, the scholar swallowed hard and walked to the open gates. As she reached the threshold, she turned and looked back at them. "We go on. To Wris."

Chapter Two

The Journey Begins

Or

"Are we there yet?"

For the first hour, the trip was almost pleasant. The day was bright and warm without being hot. It was a little exciting being out of the city. Lakara had never left Corvis before. In fact, she had rarely left the palace. Surely, she would learn new things. The scholar's code rang in her ears, 'Never forget how little you know.' Best of all, everyone was quiet.

Sir Jors and the thief scanned their surroundings at frequent intervals, though only the thief bothered looking towards the sky. What she expected to see, Lakara had no idea, but didn't ask. More interestingly, the thief had dark glasses. Lakara was familiar with glasses, of course. Many of the older scholars used them. But they were a relatively new invention, really only becoming accessible to most scholars in the last fifteen years. How could she have a pair, and what was the purpose of having a dark set?

Master Davorin had taken off his traveling cloak, revealing his necromancer robes. It made Lakara uneasy, but it shouldn't make a difference as long as no one saw them.

They weren't supposed to be recognized. Though, to be fair, she had identified herself by name *and* asked about the jewel while they were at the temple. Then again, she had been recognized; so lying about her name, even if she dared do that in a temple, would have done no good. Well, surely it wouldn't be a problem while they were still in the city.

Anyway, the first hour was almost pleasant. Then it got hotter. And her feet started to hurt. And time to relieve herself would not go amiss. And Master Davorin started grumbling. And one of the lizards tried to eat a bird.

Lakara stifled a groan as she realized that it would be a two-day journey to Wris. At least. But she couldn't complain; she was supposed to be the leader. So, she would keep on, even though her feet ached, clearly these slippers were not made for walking; and even though the sun was causing her to... become moist; and...

Sir Jors turned. "We should take a brief rest."

Lakara was ready to drop from relief, but forced herself to ask, "Are you sure? We've barely started."

"It's a long journey. We should pace ourselves and not overburden the lizards. Rest for about ten minutes, drink some water, eat a little bread. That's how we travel in the army."

"Besides, you two look like you're about to pass out," The thief said. To prove the massive unfairness of the world, she looked like she could go on for several more hours without a problem.

They pulled off the road into a dell that gave them some shade. The ground was wet, but Lakara found a decent boulder to sit on. The lizards were unharnessed so they could forage. Water was passed around, along with a loaf of bread and some smoked cod. The thief offered to share her pomegranate, but no one else wanted to risk the wrath of AKAF by eating a sacrificial fruit. Deciding against trying to relieve herself just yet, Lakara gave in to her curiosity.

"Um," She broke off, realizing she hadn't learned the thief's name yet, and didn't want to address her as 'thief' to her face. Fortunately, speaking was enough to get the other woman's attention. "Where did you get the dark glasses?"

"They belonged to my father."

"Oh? Your father was a scholar?"

"No."

That gave her more questions than answers. "Why are they dark?"

"To protect my eyes from the sun."

What a marvelous idea. Why had she never heard of that? A closer look revealed that the glasses were far older than Lakara had initially thought, very battered and scratched. Probably older than fifteen years. How very odd.

"We should move on," Sir Jors suggested. "We have a long way to travel."

He stood up. Turning to the nearest lizard, which was currently blue, he started to put the harness on it. The thief jumped to her feet, stretched out, and started harnessing the other lizard, currently green. Lakara forced back a shudder at the small pile of feathers and fur near the lizards' mouths.

"There has to be a better way to travel," Master Davorin grumbled, as he stood and took a few shaky steps. "One that doesn't require as much walking."

"I've heard rumors that across the ocean they've actually learned to tame unicorns," Sir Jors said, leading them back to the road.

"Unicorns? Those are messy mean," the thief objected. "Who would *want* to get close enough to tame them?"

Sir Jors shrugged. "Wild lizards aren't exactly gentle either. They were domesticated."

"How much could a unicorn carry?" Lakara asked. "I

can't see them as very strong." She didn't say anything about the thief's swearing.

"They say that they can actually carry a man in full armor," Sir Jors answered.

"Not as much as a pack lizard, but riding would probably be preferable to walking," Master Davorin mused.

"Fine, when we see a pack of wild unicorns, you can tame a few of them for us." The thief tossed her head as she looked around, dark glasses glinting in the sun.

Master Davorin bristled. "She-whelp, if you don't watch your tongue—"

"Kita, why don't you take point for a while?" Sir Jors cut in. "I'll take the harness. Just don't go so far we can't see you."

The thief, apparently named 'Kita', shrugged and handed over the rope. Soon she was a few hundred feet ahead of them.

"Are you sure that's wise?" Lakara asked.

"She won't run off. Not here. We have all the supplies and there's no cover. And maybe, just maybe, we should attempt to get through this journey without trying to kill each other," Sir Jors suggested in a mild voice.

"Why are you taking that spawn's side?" Master Davorin snarled.

"I'm not. I'm simply assuming that an intelligent, mannered, high-born man like yourself can demonstrate the manners and attitude needed to get along. Perhaps Kita can learn from our examples. Or at least get bored of trying to provoke a response."

Master Davorin pondered that. "I suppose you may have a point."

"Excellent. Who knows, perhaps she wasn't even trying

to be rude but believed that a skilled practitioner such as yourself truly could tame unicorns."

Before anyone could respond to that, Kita let out a high-pitched whistle, which actually resembled a grass quail cry, and stood still with one hand raised. Sir Jors dropped the harnesses and ran to her. The lizards paused before ambling after him, while Lakara and Master Davorin held back, wondering what to do. Slowly, they followed after them.

Sir Jors, stopped conversing with the thief, turned, and headed back. "The road is out. Blocked off with obstacles in the way. Kita thinks, and I agree, that someone might be waiting to ambush travelers. We're going to have to take a detour."

"I thought you said there was no cover," Lakara said. Bandits. She hadn't even thought about them.

"No trees or anything, but there are dips and valleys in the grass that you can't see until you're right on top of them," Kita said. "I know of a few."

"I suppose you would, wouldn't you? You're just like them." Master Davorin sniffed.

"I'm a thief, not a bandit!"

Sir Jors stepped between them. "A detour then. Problem is, we don't know exactly where these bandits are, if they are there."

"I can find out," Kita said.

"Of course, you could," Master Davorin accused.

"Good. Why don't you go with her?" Sir Jors said, turning to the necromancer, who promptly turned white. "That way she isn't defenseless if spotted, and she's less tempted to run." Rummaging around in one of the packs, he found what was either a long dagger or a short sword and offered it to Master Davorin.

"Why me?"

"Because I would make too much noise, and Lakara doesn't know how to fight."

"*He'll* make too much noise *and* he doesn't know how to fight," Kita protested.

"Are you sure this is a good idea?" Lakara asked. "Maybe we could..." She trailed off realizing she didn't have a single idea that could help.

"Enough. *You* may be in charge of the expedition, but *I* am in charge of its safety. This is the best idea we have." Turning to the two, he continued, "If you argue on the way, you will probably be overheard. If so, we may not get there in time to save you."

"Fine," Kita snapped. "But you had better stay back."

***

Kita worked on melding herself into the grass. The trick to moving in grass without being seen was to keep the grass from swaying, giving you away. It was noisy and movement in grass could be visible at a far distance.

I am the wind. Nothing more, nothing less. I cannot be seen. I can barely be heard. I am the wind. Slowly, low to the ground, a little bit at a time, she moved. Not a rustle betrayed her.

About fifteen yards behind her, the lummox of a necromancer crashed through the grass, alerting everyone in the proximity to his exact location. She left him behind and lay on the ground. Closing her eyes, she mentally called for Whisper. He was ecstatic at her beckons. She had been so careful not to summon him for the past few days, ever since she got arrested.

Asking permission, she Borrowed his eyes. Even under the circumstances, she couldn't help but feel ecstasy at the feeling of flight, the wind rushing around her/their wings. As asked, the hawk flew over the area several times.

There was that stupid necromancer, who had clearly gotten himself lost already. There she was, barely visible in the grass. There, on the road, were the knight and scholar. Following the road, she could see the boulders blocking the path. He/they circled around and around again. There. There were the bandits. Three of them. They were waiting in a deep hollow, about fifteen feet to the right of the road. Reluctantly, she released her hold on Whisper, going back to herself.

The necromancer was far enough back that he couldn't see her and wouldn't know where she had gone or what she had done. But Sir Jors had taken her pack before she left, so she couldn't just run now. Slowly, carefully, she backtracked, finding the necromancer and pulling him back to the road.

Once they caught up to the other two, Kita quickly filled in what she had seen, without mentioning how. With a little luck, they wouldn't think to ask, assuming she was simply good enough to sneak up and see them without being seen. She might be, but no point in taking the risk if she didn't have to.

"Three, hmm?" Sir Jors stroked his beard. "We could probably handle three if we had to, but I'd prefer not testing that. Best to go around them."

"Is it?" The necromancer asked. "We know about this hazard. We don't know what other hazards we could run into while trying to avoid this one."

"Quagmires, other bandits, unicorns, snakes, wild cats…" The scholar looked to be giving herself a nervous fit just thinking about the dangers before the knight cut her off.

"Then does anyone have any other ideas? Kita, I imagine you would know some about bandits and how to get around them. What would you do?"

If anyone else had said that; she would have snapped.

But so far, the knight had been decent towards her. Even now, he spoke like it was a simple fact, not a judgment. "Bandits, and thieves, are usually looking for an easy target. The way they are hiding, it's so that if a strong group comes through, they can stay put, and not be in danger. So, if we want to walk past them, we need to not look like an easy target."

"Perhaps, but I may be the only one who can truly fight," Sir Jors said, "unless you'd care to summon something to drive them off?" He looked at the necromancer, who had gotten even pastier.

"Th... the arts are, are not to be used like *that*."

"Odd, history shows several instances of necromancers using their powers for self-defense or defense of their country," Lakara said, sounding confused.

Before he could answer that, probably with another lie, Kita broke in. "How many sets of armor do you have?"

***

Sir Jors did not like this plan. It had too many elements of chance in it and it depended on Kita being honest with them. On the other hand, unless she wanted to die, it was probably in her best interest to make sure they survived at the moment. Unless she actually, personally, knew these bandits, everything was guesswork. If she did know them, then they had another set of problems.

In any case, this was the best plan they had, and he wasn't going to badmouth it to the others. They had to believe it would succeed. Sometimes, that extra bit of confidence made all the difference.

Walking ahead of them was Kita, leading both pack lizards. As she came to the rocks piled in the road, she slowed as if surprised, before encouraging the lizards to climb over the obstacle. Since pack lizards were known for their ability to climb sheer cliff faces, this pile of rocks was no trouble for them. Kita didn't seem to be slowed down significantly either. Good thing to know.

She got to the top safely, and stayed there, looking around and waiting. No one came out of the underbrush. Perhaps they weren't willing to take on a woman wearing a visible sword and leading two trained lizards, as everyone knew they could be vicious when threatened.

Or perhaps it was the second party that caused them to hold back. The one that held back just far enough that anyone attempting to attack one could be flanked by the other. The party that appeared to consist of two armored knights, and one visibly armed necromancer.

They followed their supposed servant, also pretending surprise at the obstacle before walking around the rocks to the left. Once on the other side, they walked on about twenty feet and waited for Kita to meet them with the lizards.

Before they had actually seen the blockage, Lakara had suggested removing the rocks so that other people could get through. She changed her mind when it was pointed out that her disguise wouldn't be successful that long, and that at least with the rocks there, others had a little warning that there could be trouble.

Now seeing the rocks up close, Sir Jors was glad they had talked her down. The boulders were huge and would take hours to move. They couldn't afford to stay here that long with bandits watching their every move.

His nerves were on high alert the whole time, but no matter how much he watched and listened, there was never a rustle in the grass to the right. He didn't think the bandits had been fooled by their 'surprise' for a heartbeat, but that part didn't matter. As long as they didn't attack. It wasn't until they were at least a mile away that he felt himself relax at all. "It worked."

"Of course it did," Kita said, sounding smug, even as she smacked one of the lizards away from trying to eat her skirt. "It's all about looking strong."

"Can I take off the armor now?" Lakara asked. The poor woman had been forced to be silent since putting it on. Sir Jors had the armor of a close-range fighter. Women in the army were rare and almost always spear or javelin wielders who had a completely different type of armor. No one wanted to take a chance on the bandits knowing the difference.

"Yes, why don't we take another rest here? You can take off the armor, and I'll collect the weapons."

The break was quickly agreed to, though Kita seemed reluctant to pass back the sword he had lent her. Too bad. He didn't trust her with a weapon yet. He didn't trust any of them with a weapon yet. Though for the other two, it was that he didn't trust them not to hurt themselves. Still, she didn't argue with him. In fact, she spent most of the break leaning into the grassy slope, eyes shut, not responding to anything. He left her alone. Everyone reacts to nerves in a different way, and she had been the one in the most danger. He filed it away as 'interesting' and concentrated on helping Lakara out of the armor before she hurt herself or damaged something.

No one was particularly talkative. They had been lucky, this time. But there would be a lot more dangers out there. This break was a little longer than the last one, letting everyone have some water and refresh themselves, but soon enough, they were heading out again. Sir Jors hoped they could make at least another ten miles before nightfall.

They made five. Barely. "We really should stop here. It's starting to get dark, and this is a decent spot for a camp. Isn't it?" Lakara said, looking around.

Sir Jors would give her some credit; it wasn't a *bad* spot.

They were near one of the many creeks that dotted the Endless Grasslands, so they had fresh water. There was no sign of rain, so it was unlikely to flood. It would be cold and setting up the tent might be a little tricky, but it could work. "I don't know of a better spot nearby, or where the nearest traveler's hut is, so this will have to do."

"I do," Kita said.

"Oh, where?" Davorin asked, looking dubiously around.

"Nearest traveler's hut is another seven miles down the road." She smirked and started clearing a space for the fire as the others groaned. Sir Jors shook his head. There was no way the other two could do another seven miles tonight.

"Then we'll make do here. We'll have to keep watch. Best way to do that is probably to split the night in thirds," Sir Jors said.

"Which should I take?" Kita asked.

"Oh, like we'll trust you on watch?" Davorin asked. "You'd probably slit our throats while we slept."

"I'm no murderer, you diseased bone mage."

"Enough!" Lakara snapped. "I'm accustomed to waking up early. May I have the third watch?"

"That works," Sir Jors said. Turning to the necromancer, he asked, "Do you want first watch?"

"Me?"

"Three shifts, and you don't trust Kita to do it."

"Suits me. I get a full night's sleep," Kita said, from the ground, trying to build a fire.

"Fine, I'll take first watch," Davorin bit out.

"It's easier than second," Sir Jors said. "You'll probably get more sleep at any rate."

"Are we going to have to do this every night?" Lakara asked.

"Most of them. Perhaps not when we are at an inn. Though it is generally wise to be alert at many of them as well," Sir Jors answered. It was an established rule of travel and campaigning. Unfortunately, in a group this small, it was going to be harder to keep watch without wearing everyone down. Especially if they didn't dare have one member take her turn. Sir Jors didn't think Kita would kill them in their sleep, but he seriously doubted she would be there in the morning if they gave her that opportunity.

Kita jumped back from her spot on the ground. His hand was reaching for his sword as he turned, relaxing when he saw that she was only jumping out of the way of the fire she had finally stoked to completion. Her sudden success must have startled the woman.

The rest of the group was quick to take advantage of the fire. Light and heat were comforting in the dark damp of the grasslands. Dinner had been sent with them, and they had enough meat and bread for four or five days. They could buy some more in Wris, but it would probably be a good idea to teach some of the others a few hunting skills. Which would help sharpen their weapons skills in case of other threats.

This was both a familiar and strange experience to Sir Jors, sitting around the fire with traveling companions. He had always considered it the best part of travel. It was said that you only knew a person when you had shared a hundred fires with them. The stories that got told, the songs that were sung, the contests and challenges of bravery and strength. There was noise, there was spirit, there was life.

Here, there was none of that. Everyone was quiet, watching each other suspiciously, no one willing to give away parts of themselves. Sir Jors shook his head but didn't say anything. It wasn't a surprise, but it was a disappointment.

The scholar, Lakara, was the first to want to sleep, probably because she'd be getting up the earliest. However, she had clearly never pitched a tent before. In fact, Sir Jors found himself unwilling to swear that she had ever seen a tent before. Kita pulled herself out of whatever trance she had been in to snicker at the lost expression on the scholar's face.

Lakara's eyes narrowed. "Considering we're sharing a tent, you had better hope I figure this out or come and help me. Have you ever set up a tent before?"

"No. But I have made lean-tos. And I've seen it done." She pulled out all the necessary parts and examined them for a moment before starting to arrange everything, directing the scholar where to plant the stakes while she set up the frame.

Sir Jors knew he ought to offer to help the women. But it had been a few years since he had made his own tent, instead of his squire making it for him. He didn't want to tell them he could do it and then embarrass himself. Besides, they seemed to be doing fine.

Indeed, they had a tent up quickly and retired to bed. Knowing that second shift meant the least sleep, Sir Jors decided it was a good idea to emulate them. Of course, if he thought the scholar had no idea what she was doing, then she was an absolute genius compared to the necromancer. He just stared at the tent stakes as if they were strange artifacts from ancient, distant civilizations. "This is servant's work."

"There aren't any servants here," Sir Jors pointed out. "And keep your voice down. The women have retired already."

Davorin eyed the whole thing with distaste. "But a man of my standing—"

"Is only a few degrees higher than I am. I can sleep without a tent and have done so many times. You will probably prefer having at least *some* shelter when your watch is over."

While not enthusiastic about the idea, Davorin agreed to help then. Eventually, they had a… *serviceable* shelter ready. Well, they would get better with practice. "Wake me about two." Sir Jors slipped into the tent, loosened his armor and tunic, put his sword to the side, and lay down. He hoped that sleep actually came quickly this time, even as he knew it probably wouldn't.

***

Davorin shivered as the night noises, mostly unfamiliar sounds, washed over him. The whispers of the dead were louder than usual with nothing to drown it out. Who knew what was out here? More bandits, vicious beasts, things that would creep upon him quietly to drag him to Shadow Master's domain. The dirty knight hadn't even left him a sword to defend himself with if they did get attacked.

He moved closer to the fire, hoping to warm up. It was bright and cheerful, allowing him to see at least a few feet around him. Other than that, all was dark. Even the sky seemed to be denying him stars. Davorin started to add some more dried grass to the flames when he froze as a thought occurred to him.

The fire was the only thing visible for miles. If anything nasty was out there, it would see the fire and know people were there. Animals might avoid it, but people, bandits, would see it. What if they came?

Fool! That was why he was keeping watch, so they would have a warning if someone came. But how would he see them? Other than the fire, there was practically no light. Having the fire might let him see a few feet, but it meant sacrificing any night vision he could possibly have. Maybe the knight knew a way around that, but if he did, he hadn't informed the rest of them.

One of the pack lizards stirred before subsiding back to

sleep. Davorin's heart rate peaked before starting to settle. The lizards were here, and they probably had better hearing than he did. If they were calm, then everything should be fine. Or did lizards hear?

A sudden noise almost wrung a scream from him, but he swallowed it down. Especially when he saw the source of the noise, a small hawk now perched on a stone not far from him. Once the wave of fear passed, Davorin smiled. He liked birds.

"Hello, friend. What are you doing out so late?" He didn't expect an answer, and truly might have run screaming into the night if he had gotten one. But hearing his own voice reassured him and helped drown out both the night noises and the whispers of the dead.

The bird tilted his head and looked at him. Not scared by his talk, but not necessarily trusting him either.

"There aren't many trees around here. Where do you roost?" The grasslands had a few stunted trees, useful for little more than firewood and fruit, and poor at that. Most wooden implements came from other areas. Sometimes the islands, but not often. "But if you've been here a while, then you must know some good spots."

The bird looked around the camp and made a small cry.

"Hush, hush. Do not wake the others." Davorin thought a minute. "I think I may have some food I can give you." As long as he didn't take too much, no one should notice.

Evidently, his feathered friend knew the word 'food', as he promptly had the raptor's full attention. Rummaging through the pack as quickly as possible, Davorin found some beef. "It's cooked. Not how you would prefer it, but it's what I have," he said, ripping off a bite's worth.

Davorin lightly tossed the morsel, not expecting the bird to come to him. The hawk caught the meat in the air before pinning it to the rock and tearing it. The necromancer laughed quietly, keeping an eye on the lizards. They were big enough to eat a hawk this size, and he didn't want that to happen. But the lizards were still asleep.

"Someone owns you. Or did recently. That's the only reason you'd accept my company, and my food, so readily. Either that, or you're starving. I doubt that one. You look well fed and your feathers are in fine condition."

Davorin tossed another bit of meat and leaned back to watch. "No, I wager on an owner. One who cares for you as well as I do my pigeons. So, where is your owner, Hawk?"

Hawk looked at him, as if asking if more meat was forthcoming. Shaking his head, Davorin pulled another piece loose. He was about to throw it when he changed his mind, holding it out instead. "Will you take it from my hand, Hawk?"

The bird eyed him for a bit before flying forward, to Davorin's surprise and pleasure. He took the meat but flew back with it, instead of staying perched on Davorin. Perhaps it was just as well. His robe wasn't made to withstand a raptor's claws. Even when handling his pigeons, he had worn a special robe. One that could be easily cleaned, or at least it didn't matter if it wasn't clean, and thick enough to protect him from claws and beaks.

After finishing, the hawk looked to him for more. "No more. It wouldn't be good for you." He received an indignant bird screech for his concern. "Hush. Do not wake the others. Someone might decide you would make a decent meal."

The hawk gave a quieter cry before taking flight. Davorin didn't have time to be disappointed when Sir Jors exited their tent. "Who are you talking to?"

"No one. It isn't two yet."

"No, but I can't sleep. I'll take my watch now."

Davorin nodded. The hawk was away and safe. Probably knew of Sir Jors moving about before Davorin did. "Very well."

Chapter Three

Arrival at Wris

Or

"Civilization... almost"

Against all odds, they had made it. They hadn't killed each other or died by the various hazards on the road. Unfortunately, Sir Jors stifled a sigh at the thought, the trip to Wris was one of the shortest legs of their journey.

They arrived shortly before sunset. It took very little discussion for a unanimous agreement to rent space at an inn and deal with everything else in the morning. Propriety would dictate that the women have their own room if feasible, but that might not be the wisest idea. Some tavern owners took advantage of customers they considered vulnerable, such as women or solitary travelers. Besides, while Kita hadn't made anything that could be considered an escape attempt yet, she might be more willing to try in a city. Though calling Wris a city was being generous.

Long ago, when his grandfather's grandfather was a boy, Wris had been a thriving city built on a major crossroads. Three nearby port towns brought merchants from far and wide. The nation's capital was Brawy, about three days south and Wris was a popular stopping point for people traveling between Brawy and Corvis.

Then Trovian pirates started to roam the oceans, with better and more numerous ships than the Graldians could muster. With few supplies to make more ships, especially with water-based trade choked off, Graldish and mostly Salardis, turned to almost exclusively land-based trade routes, which were only slightly safer than water, but couldn't be stopped as easily. When the capital was switched to Corvis, Brawy fell into decline. Wris was no longer a major crossroads and it showed.

Sir Jors carefully led the group around what must have been Beggar's Quarters. "Don't make eye contact. Don't let anyone get too close." If they gave money to one, they'd never be able to leave alive.

Kita had no trouble. Few tried to approach her at all, and those that did fell back before they got close. Sir Jors couldn't see quite what she was doing, but it seemed to be some kind of hand signal. Since most of the people who saw the signal didn't bother the rest of the group, he left it alone.

Davorin had more trouble, since his clothing was obviously better, but between his foul temper and whatever Kita had done, most people left him alone quickly. Especially once someone saw his eyes and whispers of, "Necromancer" permeated the air.

The scholar, Lakara, was another story. She couldn't stop staring and they knew she'd be an easy target. She was swarmed until Sir Jors risked rudeness by putting a hand on her back and steering her away. He didn't take a full breath until they were past.

"How... how can they live like that?" The scholar sounded close to tears. "No shelter, most of them probably haven't bathed in... years!"

"Probably haven't eaten in days either," Kita said, looking at the darkening sky. "They live like that because they have no choice. It's like that or like me."

Sir Jors blinked at that. It hadn't occurred to him that it was very possible that Kita had lived like that before. Possibly even recently. His surprise made him a little too blunt. "You're too clean."

Kita glared at him, before relaxing with a shrug. "They made me clean up before I was dragged before the king. Besides, the job's hard enough without everyone being able to smell you a mile upwind. I did everything in my power to stay at least clean enough that I could pass for a servant. Soap is small, easy to grab. Cheap enough I could buy it sometimes. Couple times, I could even make it."

Lakara looked horrified and even the necromancer seemed ill at ease. Sir Jors felt like apologizing, but wasn't sure what to apologize for, or even if she would take it if he offered. "We need to find an inn."

"I agree," Kita answered quickly. "I don't know Wris. Do you?"

"No, but I know someone from here." One of his former soldiers had settled down as an innkeeper in Wris after losing a leg.

Tiw gave his old leader a brave smile while promising them two rooms for two gold doruts, while the lizards were tended in the pen. Sir Jors looked around the inn. Dinner was cheap rabbit stew with no identifiable spices, the tables and benches were poor quality wood, only two customers were visible in the hall, and Tiw's jacket was generously patched. Tiw was giving them a discount he could ill afford. "Three if we can break fast in the morning."

The smile got wider. "Of course."

Sir Jors took the candle offered as he made a mental point to encourage the group to spend at least one more night here. The rooms offered, while not fine, were clean, safe, and private, which would be enough. He saw the women settled first, making sure the windows were barred and telling them to bar the door. It would be rude to directly tell Lakara to make sure Kita didn't try to leave, but he did warn them both to be careful and try not to sleep too deeply. He trusted Tiw, but who knew about his other patrons.

Once he knew the women would be fine, Sir Jors went to his own room where the necromancer was already eyeing the room with distaste. "This is —"

"Better than sleeping outside," Sir Jors said. "It's the best we're going to get here, so there's no point in complaining."

"Surely there are better inns here."

"One, I wouldn't count on that. Two, even if there were, we couldn't use them and remain discreet and unnoticed. Like we were ordered."

Davorin bristled but didn't argue. "Must we keep watch?"

"No, not tonight. But don't sleep too deeply if you can help it. I'm barring the door and recommend barring the windows." Inn or not, Sir Jors didn't plan to let his guard down. He could sleep comfortably enough in his trousers and with his sword near at hand. "There's a basin of water for washing. Since we don't know when we'll get another chance, you may wish to take advantage of it."

The soap was coarse and not pleasantly scented, but it would get them clean. As he expected, the necromancer wanted that. Sir Jors let him go first, using the water when he was done.

Davorin slipped to sleep not long after, obviously tired from the journey. Sir Jors was tired as well, but sleep proved more elusive. Not that that was anything new. Still, he had been lucky so far. Vicaw had not touched him with visions nor had sleep forced itself upon him. But neither had he managed to fall asleep easily when he tried. What an odd and troubling relationship he had with sleep.

The others didn't seem to know. No one had mentioned

it and he hadn't had any trouble yet. Could he keep it up? Tiw knew. He would have to talk to his former soldier before he mentioned anything to one of the others.

But was it right to keep his condition a secret? What if it endangered the others? It could, easily. Lakara was in charge, he should probably inform her at the very least. But she seemed overwhelmed enough without adding one more hazard that she had no control over. On the other hand, security of the group was his job. How could he hide one of the biggest dangers? When sleep finally claimed him, he was no closer to an answer than when he began.

***

Clean, oh, it was amazing to be clean again. It was all Lakara could do not to collapse in pleasure. She had never gotten so unclean before or gone so long without washing. Her work as a scholar required her to maintain high standards of cleanliness.

It felt so nice to be clean that she could be generous enough to ignore the thief practically laughing at her while waiting for her own turn to get clean. She could ignore that the water was cold, that the soap stank, and that they would be getting unclean again tomorrow. None of that mattered in the face of actually getting clean.

"So, tomorrow we see the temple of Pirette?" Kita asked, glaring at the windows. Something she had been doing periodically since they had been barred.

"Yes. While today the major temple for Pirette is in Glacdon, once upon a time, this was the biggest temple. Oh, it was famous in its day. People came across land and sea to visit it. Because Pirette is the goddess of craft and learning, all the craftsmen and scholars hold her in high regard and a lot of extra effort was put into her temple. I transcribed a scroll into a book about the temples once and it described the building thoroughly. They built twenty-five marble pillars, one for each of her valued attributes. There are three golden fountains, the floors are made of jade and silver, the censers for fine incense are amber, and there's even ivory stairwells. We could still get sea ivory back then."

Even the thief looked impressed at that. "And now?"

Lakara stepped back. "What do you mean 'and now'?"

"You said it was famous. You saw what the city looks like. Even the richer parts of the city are poorer than Corvis. Do you honestly believe people would be satisfied living like this if they knew there was wealth beyond their wildest dreams just miles away?"

"But... but it's a temple! You can't steal from the gods!"

"*I* never have. But I'm not as muddy desperate as some. Believe me, when you can't remember what you ate last or know when you'll eat again, the possible wrath of some god or other feels a lot less worrying than avoiding Shadow Master."

Lakara stuttered for a minute trying to figure out a way to rebut her. Surely no one would dare do such a thing. "I... I'm going to bed." She would have to watch the thief carefully in the temple.

To her dismay, the thief turned out to have a point. The great temple to Pirette, while a masterpiece of engineering centuries ago, had fallen into a sad state of disuse. Much of the silver had tarnished and what she could see of the ivory had yellowed. The temple had been allowed to become unclean and pieces were missing. Evidently, some had decided that enough money was worth risking the wrath of the goddess.

There were few priests and priestesses, and many of them looked well-fed enough that Kita muttered they had probably been helping themselves to some of the temple's wealth. Lakara didn't want to believe her, but what if she was right?

"Suppose we just find the message we need and leave?" Sir Jors suggested, breaking up another argument before it started. He rubbed at his eyes, which seemed red. Lakara briefly wondered how much sleep he had gotten. He had been up, taking care of the lizards and getting news, before any of the others.

Searching for the symbol and trying to keep an eye on the thief at the same time was difficult. But Lakara was certain that she didn't want to be on a dangerous expedition with one who would rob the gods. They had enough hazards to face. Some made the mistake of thinking that Pirette was not vengeful as she rarely acted immediately or directly. But further reading would show the wise that Pirette was extremely thorough in her vengeance even if it took a long time in coming. And thorough meant that it wasn't always limited to the wrongdoer alone.

The thief was eyeing the high walls and ceiling. At least she couldn't steal anything up that high. "I think I see it."

Lakara jolted and abruptly felt abashed. Here she had been doubting the woman and Kita had been putting in more effort than she had. "Where?"

"There. Isn't that it? The symbol?" She pointed to something half hidden in the shadows. Kita must have good eyes. Lakara could barely see anything.

Neither could anyone else. Eventually, they talked a priest into lighting one of the chandeliers near that area. He did so reluctantly, giving them enough light to see that Kita had been right about the symbol. Finding the clue was a little harder because reading words that high up was more difficult than finding a symbol. But find it they did. Lakara and Master Davorin made sure to copy it exactly.

The first words she was able to translate were 'solid' and

'sky'. A solid something something sky? A solid something to the sky? A something solid to the sky?

"Will you be making an offering today?" The priest who lit the chandelier asked them, making it clear that only the lowest of godless heathens would come to the temple and *not* make an offering.

"Yes, we need some incense for clarity and four candles for insight," Lakara asked instantly. As a scholar, Pirette was her patron goddess. One did not neglect one's patron deity when attempting the impossible.

"Very good," the priest answered. "Will you also be making a donation for the rebuilding of the temple?"

Lakara looked around. The temple could certainly use it, but how far would their money stretch? "We are on a journey and our funds are limited. Should we return safely, I will certainly come and make a donation in gratitude." That would only be right and proper.

The priest seemed to scowl at that, but he did get the incense and candles, lit them, and left them to their prayers.

"He was disappointed we didn't give him more money," Kita said. "Probably planned to take some of it. Or all of it."

"Kita! He's a priest!" Lakara said, scandalized.

"You aren't upset I said that. You're upset that you think I might be right."

"Kita, are you finished praying?" Sir Jors cut in.

The thief quieted and at very least stood silently while the others made their prayers. Lakara wasn't going to try to guess if she had prayed herself. The prayers worked; they had barely gone down the outer steps of the temple when Lakara stopped and looked at her notes again. "Of course! Shout. A solid shout to the sky."

"What is *that* supposed to mean?" Master Davorin grumbled.

Lakara bit her lip but didn't say anything as her excitement at figuring out the word was dashed. She didn't know what the clue meant, only what it said.

"Hopefully, we will figure it out before we get there," Sir Jors said. "Did you wish to visit Necromancer Virn while we are here?"

Master Davorin drew back. "No, no I don't think so. I've not met the man before, and we are supposed to be inconspicuous."

"Fine. I believe it would be best to purchase supplies here, to equip us for the next leg of the journey." Sir Jors frowned. "Where *is* the next leg of our journey to?"

Lakara looked at her notes. "Oh, we need to go to the temple of Vicaw in Tediz. But I think there may be a town or two we can stop at on the way. Have you been to the Great temple of Vicaw?" She asked the knight. After all, the goddess of victory should be his patron goddess. It only made sense that he would have visited her chief temple at least once.

"I have. For my dedication to the knighthood," Sir Jors answered. "Tediz is at least five to seven days from here. Seven if we stick to the roads, five if we cross the country. Either way, the terrain will get rougher. Yes, we'll need more supplies."

He was probably right, but the last thing Lakara wanted was to even think about more travel. Master Davorin appeared to be in similar shape. "Should we all go to the market?" Lakara asked, hoping the answer was no.

Sir Jors eyed the group, probably noticing how much they didn't want to go. "No, I doubt it would take all of us. Though I could use some assistance."

"I'll come," Kita said, tossing her head so her braid

swished. "No point being cooped up in a stuffy inn all day."

Lakara had to keep herself from gaping. Staying in the inn was exactly what she wanted to do. Maybe even getting a little more sleep.

Sir Jors gave a rueful smile. "You may think differently by the next town. Anyone else wish to come?"

"No, I don't imagine you will require my assistance," Master Davorin answered.

She was the leader; she really should be helping. But, oh, she was stiff and sore. The thought of going back to the inn and stretching out on the bed, maybe another wash, was so very tempting. "Do you *need* more help?"

He thought for a moment. "No, I believe the two of us can manage. We'll just walk you back to the inn first."

"Good. I can study the maps, perhaps find a good route. Or I can study the clues we have so far." Then she would be helping without having to leave the inn. Why, oh why, hadn't she brought a book on Vesrop? When she realized the clue in the temple of AKAF was in Vesrop, once back at the palace, she could have gone to the library and found something on Vesrop. As long as no one spotted her and reported to the king that she was delaying the expedition. That... well, that could be bad.

Sir Jors nodded. "An excellent plan. While we are all together, I would like to make a suggestion. Unless anyone has an objection, I think it might be best to stay another night in Wris, allowing us to get an early start tomorrow morning."

No one objected. Least of all, Lakara. She had barely slept at all the first night in the open and the second hadn't been much better. A real bed and a door that could be locked were so much more useful in aiding peaceful slumber than strange sounds and cold, hard, rocky ground.

The only thing she had to worry about in the inn was the

thief. But Kita wasn't a cutthroat. She wouldn't attack Lakara in her sleep. Right?

***

Davorin locked the door as soon as he got to his room. It would mean getting up to unlock it when the knight came back but until then he would rather just keep everyone out. Right now, he was alone. Not surrounded by crowds of people, any of whom might be a thief or a cutthroat. Not forced to pander to the sway of the scrum. He was alone, and he was safe.

Then suddenly, he was neither.

The shadows converged to reveal the shade. What the unfortunate may have been in life, be it man, woman, or child, was no longer evident. A permanent shade, one bound to the mortal plain until the death of the necromancer who bound them. Probably it had been bound for decades, possibly longer than Davorin had been alive.

"What... what do you want? I didn't call you!" He backed away a step or two. He could *probably* drive off or banish any normal shade. But one bound to another necromancer? That got trickier.

"My Master sends greetings and asks your purpose," the shade spoke in a flat voice with no intonation. The words didn't matter to it, nor the answer. Only that it fulfilled its purpose.

"Passing through. We'll be on our way tomorrow." Perhaps that would be enough to assuage the other necromancer. Davorin really didn't want to have to compete with him. He could probably win, he was the strongest necromancer in the land, supposedly. Not that he wanted to put it to the test. Even if he did, what would he gain? Wris was a mudhole compared to Corvis.

"Who shall I say is passing through his territory?" A

suggestion of eyes in a mostly featureless face stared through him.

"I am Master Davorin, King's Necromancer." Left unsaid was the implication that very bad things would happen to Virn should anything untoward happen to Davorin in Virn's city. Probably, anyway. Surely, King Zikkar would be furious should something happen to him. Even if the king did think that Davorin's talents and abilities were somehow necessary for this expedition.

The shade nodded and dissolved back into the shadows. Davorin let out a slow breath and sat quickly on the bed. Too much exercise and excitement. It wasn't good for him. That was why his heart thrummed and his legs felt like they might give out. Even his hands were shaking slightly. Perhaps it was linked to lack of sleep. He certainly hadn't slept well since they left the castle. Maybe a nap would be just the thing to help his nerves.

Davorin cringed as the whispers of the dead got louder. Two shades appeared before him. It took everything he had in him not to flinch. He couldn't look weak. Not here and not now. "What do you need now?" Yes, better to sound annoyed. Never show fear, never show weakness. Not that he felt either of those, of course.

"Our Master sends his greetings to Davorin, King's Necromancer," The shades spoke in tandem. Why not? Any personality, drive, or desire they might have had would have faded long ago. Which meant it was entirely Virn's fault that he was greeted without his proper title since they would repeat exactly what they were told. "Our Master has a message for you."

"Well, what is it?" The sooner they delivered their message the sooner they would leave.

"Be careful, King's Necromancer. Power isn't always

what or where you think it is and death is never more than a step or two away. Especially for us."

What in the name of the gods was that supposed to mean? "Yes, well, thank your master for the message. I shall consider myself duly warned."

One shade opened its mouth, but to Davorin's shock and surprise, the voice that came through wasn't the voice of a shade, but the voice of a very old man. Virn, himself. It had to be. Davorin hadn't even known that was possible. "You naïve pup. You think you have power and authority. Oh, the *King's Necromancer*. How fancy. You have no idea."

"I will thank you to keep your opinions to yourself, Virn. You forget yourself." Davorin drew himself to his full height.

"I know more about you than you do. You wear borrowed authority. Power you have, you are afraid to wield. The power you do wield is so much weaker than you think. Wait, you will see. If Shadow Master spares you long enough."

"We'll see what the king thinks about that. And about what he thinks of threats to his court," Davorin pointed out. King Zikkar could be touchy about taking offense.

He laughed. "I'll waste no more words on you. You still don't understand. You choose not to understand. Pass through Wris. Do not tarry. Death is close to you, *Master* Davorin, and I'd rather it not find you in my city."

Before Davorin could answer that or demand an apology for the insult, the shades were gone. He was alone once more. But this time, he wouldn't swear to being safe.

***

Kita waited while the knight satisfied himself that their other companions would be as safe as possible while they separated. Clearly, he took his responsibility for the safety of the party seriously. She would have to keep that in mind when she made her escape.

That was a worry for another time, however. Today, Kita was going shopping without any worry about money. They would never let her handle the money and she had no idea how much there was, but it would be interesting to spend the king's money legitimately.

She still didn't remember if she had been to Wris. One dying city was much like another. It was built like many other cities, probably from about the same time period. The main keep was the center of the city, whether it was a palace, a manor home, or just a barracks. The next circle outward had temples to the east, security and guards to the west, farmlands for the keep to the south, and armories and tailors to the north. The next hub would be the shops for those who didn't live or work for the keep, often grouped by kind. The open market was usually in that ring. In a more disorganized manner came housing for the shopkeepers and skilled laborers, followed by housing and farmlands for the poor. Those poorer than that tended to congregate by the gates, where they drew less notice from the rich in the center but still had a chance of alms from those who could afford to travel. Like them. Kita still wasn't sure if she felt bad for signaling to the beggars that they were frauds that carried no money. It was both true and a lie. Kita didn't know how much they had, but she wouldn't be surprised if it wasn't enough for as far as they needed to go. It certainly wouldn't be if they started passing out money to everyone they saw who needed it. Who didn't need it?

Whisper was still in the area, though he was smart enough to wait outside the city proper and stick to the farmlands. Something was going on with that hawk. Kita hoped she'd be able to ask him about it soon. The last thing she needed or wanted was something going wrong with the closest thing she had to a friend.

Her nose found the market before her feet did. The

smells of baking bread, of meats and fish in various stages of freshness, of spices both local and foreign, and more. "What supplies are we buying? No, more important, how many days are we buying for?"

The knight gave her an odd look. What was he thinking? Did he find it odd that she would actually buy supplies? Or that she would care what was bought? "Have you been to Wris before?" Oh. Her indignation fizzled out like a spark under water to be replaced by confusion.

"I cannot recall. Why?"

"I was wondering how you knew the way to the market."

She managed to swallow the slightly hysterical giggles, but a laugh did emerge. "Can't you smell it?"

The knight stopped, closing his eyes briefly before inhaling with his nose and mouth. He had to take a few steps closer before he appeared to sense it. Then he opened his eyes and smiled at her. "Good nose. Very observant." He eyed her closely.

Kita shook her head. Of course, he had to keep a sharp watch on her. She was the dangerous thief who could run off at a second's notice. If she didn't kill them all in their sleep. Not that she planned to do that. The last part, anyway. "You still have not answered me."

"Very true." Sir Jors gave a tired sigh. "We need supplies for five to seven days. That's about how long it should take to get to Tediz, and I don't believe we should depend on there being any useful markets on the way."

"Then we should plan on eight or nine." He gave her a questioning look. "With our group?" He winced but nodded. "Besides, if something unexpected happens, we're prepared."

"Wise indeed. Though I do hope to teach a little bit about hunting, so we can feed ourselves if need be," Sir Jors said. "May

I presume you know a little?"

What was he implying with that? "I can catch the occasional rabbit, and a few other things." True, most of that was Whisper's doing, but she wasn't helpless.

"Oh, excellent. Different terrains will offer their own possibilities, of course. While in the grasslands, there are rabbits, quail, snakes, sheep, even the occasional deer."

He seemed to be expecting some kind of response, but for the life of her, Kita didn't know what he wanted. "Journey bread," she said instead, nodding to a stall near a bakery.

Sir Jors seemed startled but quickly recovered. "Ah, yes. I shall—"

"Might be best to let me get it," Kita interrupted. "They'll take one look at you and gouge the prices as high as they dare." If there was little love for the king's knights, that could be pretty high. One of the reasons she was wearing her old clothes instead of the travel robes.

He agreed with a sigh. "Six loaves. They won't last longer than that anyway."

Six loaves of journey bread would probably stretch about four days, maybe five if they were careful, and didn't eat it exclusively. "Two silver dous should do it."

Sir Jors handed her the coins with no sign of reluctance and even something close to resembling subtlety. Certainly more than the dirty bone mage or naïve scholar could manage. "I'll wait here. If there's trouble, call out. If you are not back in five minutes, I shall come after you."

With effort, Kita kept from snapping at him. That could have been as much for her safety as it was to warn her not to run off. "Fine. But try not to look like you are with me."

Kita waited until the knight had backed off before deftly weaving into the crowd. If there was one thing she knew about people, it was how to maneuver in a crowd. The man three people ahead of her had a pouch that would be easy to lift, but he also had a knife on his left side. The woman passing her wore a garb as poor as Kita's, but a bracelet that would easily fetch fifteen, maybe twenty gold dourats. The man in a green tunic was also a thief, but he had no idea what he was doing, stalking someone who pretended to have money, but obviously didn't. The man in a blue coat was a former soldier, best avoid him. The one in black robes was the most dangerous. Perhaps a bandit, or even an assassin. Either way, not someone Kita wanted noticing her. Fortunately, he didn't seem interested in anyone here.

Then she was at the baker's stall. The gray-haired man who ran the stall was probably the father of whoever was working in the bakery behind them. Perhaps it had been his bakery first. Maybe it still was. Unlike many bakers, he was wiry as a snake, and seemed about as friendly. "What will it be?"

Kita eyed the bread skeptically. It was fresh enough, probably about as good as they could get anywhere around here. But it never paid to be too complimentary of goods to be bought. "How much is your journey bread?"

The baker looked her up and down, clearly pegging her as not local, but not rich, either. "Two for a dou."

She scoffed. "Please, for this? I wouldn't trust it longer than a day. Two at most. Four for a dou."

As expected, the baker was not happy with her insult. "This is the finest journey bread in Wris. I sell it for a song as it is. Would you rob me like this?"

"A song? Does that mean that it is only worth throwing at one who sings? Remind me not to sing here. These are probably harder than stones." Kita moved to walk away.

He came from behind the stall, blocking her path. "You,

smell this. Can't you smell how fresh it is?"

She took a sniff, then shrugged. "I've smelled fresher." Also, much staler. But she had underestimated his desperation if he would follow her away from his stall instead of just calling after her. She might get a better price than she thought.

The baker snarled something that sounded suspiciously like 'Trovian scum' under his breath. "Three for a dou."

"First, you practically attack your customers, then you insult them? No wonder your business is failing." There was a flash of something in his eyes. She was right.

He opened his mouth to say something, before turning to one of the street children who had gotten too close. "You, Mud Girl! Get out of here! Before I call the guards."

The frightened child, who couldn't have been as old as seven, jumped, then dashed off to drool over the sweets from a safer distance. Kita swallowed hard. "Six loaves of bread and one meat pasty for two dou. Not a duc more. Don't think for one instant that I can't get as good a price or better in minutes from one of your neighbors." She held up the two coins to prove her point.

With an ugly snarl, the baker started wrapping up the loaves. "The pasty separate," Kita said, watching.

The loaves she put in her pack, the pasty she palmed. As Kita went to rejoin the knight, she searched out and made eye contact with the hungry child. Signaling with a slight jerk of her head brought the girl to her side at once. "Run an errand for you, Miss?"

"Hold out your hands." When the girl did so, Kita slipped her the pasty. "Don't let anyone see you eat that. Hide first."

The girl's eyes were as wide as the treat, but Kita just gave her a small smile and kept walking. Her smile grew slightly as she sensed the child dash off to some hiding place.

When Kita reached the knight, he was leaning against the side of a building. Had he seen her give the girl the pasty? If so, he would probably consider it a waste of their resources. Not that she regretted it, whatever the others may say.

Perhaps he hadn't seen. His eyes seemed mostly closed and he was relaxed. Almost as if he were resting.

"I didn't take *that* long. And I have six loaves, just as agreed. It did take all the money though."

Sir Jors turned and looked at her, blinking twice, as if to get the sun out of his eyes. "Ah, any trouble?"

"Not to speak of. The baker was more desperate than I anticipated. I might have been able to talk him down further if I had more time." And if she hadn't gotten so angry.

The knight frowned. "We don't wish to take advantage of honest citizens who are in times of trouble."

"We also don't want to run out of funds before our journey is finished. Besides, who isn't in times of trouble?"

That clearly didn't please the knight, but he dropped the subject. "Journey bread alone will not sustain us long. I think perhaps the butcher should be our next stop."

Like she had for the baker, Kita was the one to go forward to buy cuts of salt pork, smoked cod, preserved beef, and roast mutton. While the mutton would only be good for a day or so, it would be a nice treat and allow them to save the meats that would last longer.

Neither fruits nor vegetables were likely to travel well, but there were still a few bargains to be found. One dou got them some apples, two ducs bought some potatoes. Kita was also able to use a little of her own money to bargain for some spices. Salt, pepper, garlic, rosemary, bluetill, and slatrow. The last two only grew in Salardis, so they were especially expensive. She would keep the spices with her. Expensive as they could be, they added much to a dish. Besides, they were good to barter with.

"Any other food we need?" Kita asked.

"Food? No. But I would like to at least price travel robes. And Lakara will definitely need a pair of boots."

Kita smirked at that. Whatever the scholar's shoes were designed for; travel wasn't on the list. "She will indeed. Well, let's see what the market has to offer."

Chapter Four

Companions on the Road

Or

A journey of a thousand miles begins with dreams of homicide

Davorin shivered in the night air, still not used to this camping business. They were two days out of Wris, by a different road that didn't pass by Corvis. Only the thief didn't seem even slightly upset that they were avoiding the capital. But as nice as it would be to stop home, perhaps pick up more supplies that were bound to be of better quality, no one wanted to risk the king's ire by returning so soon with nothing to show for it. At least last night they had been able to stay in a Traveler's Hut.

The hut was a pathetic sod building that boasted only some protection from the elements and the fact that it was built to accommodate up to ten people at a time. Some supplies were available, but travelers were expected to replace or pay for what they took. Still, it meant no one had to keep watch and they were safe from the rain that began in the early evening until mid-afternoon the next day. Of course, waiting until the rain ended meant that it would take longer to get to Tediz. While Davorin didn't plan to mention it to anyone, the further they got from Wris, the more pleased he would be.

It would be another four to six days before they reached the grand temple of Vicaw in Tediz. After that should be Tratow, god of air. But that would be after they left the Endless

Grasslands for the Ocean of Sand. Perhaps fourteen days? At best? Rain, snakes, wildcats, unicorns, quagmires, bandits, pits, swordgrass, insects, mud, and more. Then the journey would really get difficult. Glee.

Keeping watch was exhausting, and he had only done it a couple of times. On one hand, it didn't seem fair that the thief could skip out on taking a turn. On the other hand, she'd probably skip out on them altogether if given even half a chance. So, it was the three of them, night after night, losing a third of their possible sleep. Wonderful.

The lizards were still awake, eyeing him as if he might be possible food. Davorin wrapped himself in his cloak, trying to glare them down. The lizards didn't look overly impressed. It was just his imagination or a trick of the firelight that the lizards looked like they were laughing at him. Probably.

Speaking of his imagination, Davorin fancied he had caught a glimpse of the hawk again during the day. It was unlikely. After all, why would the bird follow them and then wait around for the two days they had spent in Wris? Sure, he had fed the bird, but the raptor appeared to be well-fed and in good health. No need for him to follow around bedraggled necromancers and motley groups to get food.

Though if he did come back… well, his previous owner had probably taught him to hunt. While not a big hawk, he could probably take down rabbits, maybe quail, certainly ground squirrels. No, that was a foolish idea. They had neither time nor supplies to train the bird to work with them. And the lizards might think him a tasty snack.

Anyway, this was a bunch of rubbish thoughts. The bird wouldn't return. Davorin stirred up the fire to burn a little brighter before he fell off his stony perch in fright and shock. Large eyes were watching him, and they didn't belong to a lizard.

The necromancer fumbled for a lit stick, hands shaking enough that he was failing badly. He had to call out. Warn the others. Get help! But not a sound would leave his throat.

A sharp but quiet cry had Davorin flinching on the ground, arm raised to fend off some vicious monster. Then he saw the eyes' owner, and almost fainted in relief. It was no monster after all.

"You scared me, friend," Davorin said to the bird. "I didn't think you would come back." He should get off the ground, out of the ... wet ground, back on the rock. But his body simply wouldn't move. "Do you want more food?"

The hawk seemed to straighten, all attention on him. Davorin cast a quick glance at the lizards. One was asleep and the other nearly so. Neither seemed interested in a feathered meal. Good.

It took a moment to get his watery arm to work properly enough to rummage through his pack, picking at the smoked cod. His personal store, not the group food store. "Here we are. Perhaps you'll like this." He tossed it to the side, away from the fire and lizards. Once again, the hawk caught the morsel in the air, before flying to another rock to tear at it.

"Why are you back, Hawk? Surely there is enough food in the region for you without following us. Not that you aren't welcome." Did he really expect an answer? Lack of sleep must be getting to him.

The raptor looked at him, as if wondering if he was crazy, before calling out.

"Hush, hush. Yes, I have some more. Not that it is good for you to be getting food from me. You should be hunting on your own." Davorin tossed another piece of fish, again snatched out of the air.

The bird had ignored his comments about hunting,

not that the necromancer had truly expected the bird to understand him. "Perhaps I should give you a name if you are going to keep coming around."

He had never actually been good at naming animals. Previous attempts included three pigeons named 'Feathers', five named 'Beaky', and two named 'Bird'. Some had more original names, but usually only when he had a book for reference.

Davorin did have three of his magic books with him, but it was too dark to look at them now. Even with the fire, he probably wouldn't be able to make out the words. Besides, he was supposed to be keeping watch. Not reading, not even talking to hawks. Of course, if there was something to be alarmed at, the hawk would probably realize it before he did.

Almost as if reading his mind, the bird turned his head sharply to peer into the distance, then called out with a loud shriek. Before Davorin could say or do anything to hush the hawk, the lizards roused, turned in the same direction, and started growling.

Davorin barely noticed as the hawk flew off. "Wake up! Wake up!" Even before the words died on his tongue, Sir Jors was up, sword in hand. The thief was barely a second behind him. The scholar took a couple seconds more before she stumbled out asking who screamed.

"What's wrong?" The knight asked, eyes trying to pierce the darkness.

"I don't know, but the lizards are upset, and a bird flew off, screeching," Davorin said. He thought he saw the thief pivot towards him, but he wasn't concerned by that right now.

"Could be nothing?" The scholar suggested, not sounding very hopeful, even as she tried to move closer to the fire.

"Not a muddy chance. When animals panic, you need to be alert." The thief picked up a heavy stick. "There!" She pointed.

Sir Jors let out a string of swears creative enough to impress even the thief before apologizing. "Unicorns."

***

It was inevitable that they would have at least one encounter with unicorns, Sir Jors knew that. But he had hoped that their 'encounter' would be more of a distance sighting, that kept them far away from the aggressive herds. "We can't fight off a stampede. Our best chance is to convince them to avoid us. More fire! Build it up!"

Kita had found a stick, one of the few good ones around. "Kita, your stick, light the end." She gave him an incredulous look. "A torch. You'll do better with a torch than a stick. The rest of you, find something that you can use as a torch."

Sir Jors took one of the woven grass logs they had set aside for the fire and carefully lit the end. Lakara did the same, while Davorin had found another branch, much thinner. Soon Kita was the only one without a torch. "Light it!" Sir Jors shouted at her. Darting eyes in an ashy face met his. "Just light it." She dashed forward, shoving her stick partway into the fire.

"Now, wave them around! We need to convince the unicorns not to come this way." With little time, too. The pounding was getting louder, and he could feel the vibrations of the ground. "When your torch gets too low, throw it in the fire and pick up another!" He had his sword in hand, but it wouldn't do much good against a herd of unicorns. Might not even succeed against a single one.

His torch was the first to burn down, so he wasted precious seconds tossing it into the flames and lighting another. The pounding was so hard he could feel it in his bones. "Shout! Make lots of noise! We have to scare them away."

Shouts, screams, howls, and yelps rang out, filling the air with noise. Someone, Sir Jors didn't dare turn to see who, had come up with the idea of banging two metal objects together. One was probably the cooking pot, likely the other was a spoon. Was it working? Were the unicorns turning away?

He sensed, more than heard, someone fall at his side. Turning he spotted Kita on the ground. She had the cooking pot and a metal spoon in addition to her torch. The torch had burned almost to her hands. Sir Jors snagged it from her and tossed it into the fire before hauling the woman to her feet. "Keep banging that, we have enough torches!"

She nodded as she resumed her cacophony. Sir Jors took a second to check on the other members of the party. Both were upright and making plenty of noise, so he had to hope they were alright.

The unicorns were almost on top of them, but they were panicking. Would they panic and run through them, or panic and run away from them? Were they...? They were. They were turning away to avoid the fire and the noise.

Still, the group shouted and waved torches about until they could no longer feel the pounding hoof beats. "Enough. They're gone. We're safe," Sir Jors called, tossing his spent 'torch' into the fire.

Lakara and Davorin did the same. Davorin slumped to the ground so quickly one might think his legs were cut out from under him. Lakara paced about four steps back and forth, hands making quick darting gestures. Kita found a rock and sat down, putting aside the cooking pot and spoon before examining her ankle.

"Is anyone hurt?" Sir Jors asked. No one answered. No one *looked* seriously injured. "Burns? Kita, you fell, are you hurt?"

She didn't look up. "Nothing serious." He might have

believed her if he hadn't caught sight of a rivulet of blood running down her foot.

"Why are you bleeding?"

That caught everyone's attention. Both the scholar and necromancer leaned in to see as if they didn't believe him. Davorin saw the blood and leaned back. Lakara frowned and leaned in. "I have a kit."

"It's nothing," Kita said. "Just caught on a bit of swordgrass. It startled me enough to step back into a dip. I imagine we'll all have a run-in or two before we leave."

"You are likely right, but that's not an excuse to neglect it," Sir Jors answered, before turning to Lakara. "Do you have any tincture of yarrow?"

"Of course." A moment later, she handed him a damp cloth, suitably treated. Sir Jors rubbed it carefully over the cut. He knew it stung, but Kita didn't make a sound or change her expression, even as her foot twitched in his gentle grip. He also took a moment to check her ankle for swelling, but none was evident. Good. "This will help prevent infection and allow for faster healing."

"I know. It's not my first injury." By the time he was done with the tincture, she had some cloth for a bandage. "I can wrap it."

"I am certain you can, but it is easier from my angle." She didn't argue and he did his best to wrap her injury securely, without being too tight, by firelight. He might have to double-check that in the morning.

What time was it? Probably about one. "Those who can sleep should try now. I'll start my watch here."

"Sleep? You expect us to sleep after this?" Davorin asked. Lakara looked like she agreed.

"We have to be rested for whatever we deal with

tomorrow," Kita said, slowly standing. She turned to Sir Jors. "Thank you. Is your hand hurt?"

"My hand?"

"Did you burn yourself when you took my torch?"

He hadn't felt any pain, but it was possible that pain hadn't penetrated his fog of focus yet. A quick glance of his hands showed nothing to alarm him. Nor did rubbing his hands together hurt. "No, my hands are fine."

Kita nodded and entered her tent. After a minute or so of silence, Lakara followed her in. Davorin stood looking around for another few minutes, even looking to the sky for possible danger, before retreating himself.

Sir Jors, now alone, adjusted the height of the fire so it would return to its previous low. All considering, for their first time having to directly face danger, the bandits didn't count since they never confronted them, things had gone very well indeed.

"Move over to your side of the tent," one of the women said. Sounded like Lakara.

"I *am* on my side. You're the one taking up too much room."

"No, I'm not. I'm barely taking up anything."

"Will you both be quiet and go to sleep?" The necromancer called from the other tent.

Sir Jors sighed. It was going to be a long night. The necromancer tried hitting the side of the tent, presumably to urge the women to stop bickering. All it really accomplished was to bring the tent down on his head. He shrieked in surprise, causing the women to move and bring down their own tent.

Sir Jors buried his head in his hand. A very long night

indeed.

***

No one was in a good mood the next morning. Not enough sleep, having to put up the tents twice, a bad case of nerves from the night before; it all equaled up to a grumpy crew.

Kita supposed she had less reason to complain than most, but it didn't feel that way. True, she hadn't had to take watch, but that meant she hadn't had a decent moment or two on her own to check on Whisper. Had Whisper been the bird startled off by the unicorns? Had he been close enough that the diseased bone mage spotted him? Would he be able to tell that Whisper was hers? Was Whisper safe?

He'd be fine. She had to believe that. Which was more than might be said for her. The slash from the swordgrass burned, her ankle had swollen a little in the night, and her foot in general was letting her know that today was a terrible day for walking. If she had been on her own, she would turn the day into a rest day. There was even a stream not far away. She could catch enough to eat for the day, especially with Whisper's help. And if she didn't quite get enough to fill her belly, well, it certainly wouldn't be the first time, or likely the last.

But she wasn't on her own. She was with a group. A group that had a goal and didn't care about the discomfort of one lone thief.

Perhaps that wasn't quite fair. They had given her yarrow and bandaged her up. And the knight and scholar looked back at her as she trudged along, possibly in suspicion, but it might be in concern also.

It felt like hours before their first rest. Kita quickly excused herself from the group. Closing her eyes, she called silently for her winged friend.

Words were paltry for the amount of relief she felt. Whisper was both fine and nearby. He seemed to be up to something too, but she didn't have time to check. Maybe at night, once the scholar fell asleep.

The rest wasn't long, not long enough for her ankle, but she would not complain. Kita wasn't muddy stupid. King Zikkar hadn't sent her on this journey as a *mercy*, and probably not even to find this dirty jewel. She knew exactly why she was here. No one would shed so much as a tear if or when she died on this filthy suicide journey.

Did the others realize that? That they had all been sent to die? They didn't seem to. Perhaps she could use that to her advantage. Wait until they realized it, then when they were despondent, she could make her escape. People wracked with sorrow and grief were not very observant and generally cared little about those around them.

All she had to do was bide her time. Hopefully, it would be before they left the Endless Grasslands. She didn't know Salardis very well and had few if any connections there.

At the next break, both the bone mage and the scholar took the time to study their tomes. Kita watched with veiled interest, particularly the necromancer. Magic books could be worth a lot if you could find the right fence. Of course, finding the right fence, one who would be willing to risk the wrath of the original magic user and find another who was willing to buy... not dirty easy.

Kita really hadn't seen much in the way of books. Most people in her circles couldn't read any more than she could. Why bother? Books were rare and expensive, and there was little else that needed to be read. It might come in handy to be able to read signs, but most signs were made to accommodate those who couldn't read.

Still, sometimes she wondered. Those who had books

seemed to value them very highly. The scholar was so careful with books and scrolls, one might almost think they were precious treasures.

The day was long, spent mostly in traveling, and unless Kita was sorely mistaken, they had covered maybe six or seven miles today. She had days she considered a failure because she had only covered twelve or so miles. Getting to Tediz was going to take forever.

Sir Jors seemed to agree with her as he checked their food supply. "I had hoped we'd be further along by now. Tomorrow we will need to do some hunting to augment our food stores."

They weren't in desperate need, but Kita wouldn't blame the man for being cautious. Considering this group, it might well be a day or two before they managed to catch anything.

One of the lizards yawned, her mouth stretching open like a cave, with teeth. The scholar jumped back with a shriek, fell over a rock, and took the necromancer down with her. Sir Jors let out an exasperated breath and held out a hand to help them up.

The two flailed in the mud and only succeeded in knocking the knight on top of them. Kita shook her head and walked away. "I'm going to make the fire." Make that a week or two.

She had the base set up and was trying for a spark when the knight came up to her. "I can do that. If you like," he said, softly.

Kita blinked up at him. She had made most of the fires since they started, why was he offering this time? "I've got it."

He frowned and moved a little closer. "Any time you would rather not, I can do it." There was something in his eyes. "I don't have a problem with it."

Kita felt herself flushing. He couldn't know, could he? "Why?"

"Because I saw you last night." His words were almost too quiet for her to hear. "Fire frightens you, doesn't it?"

"I can light a fire just fine."

"Indeed, you can," he said placatingly. "But you also jump back from it and try to avoid getting too close. Lighting a torch actually scared you, didn't it?"

"Being cautious around fire is—"

"Is wise, I know. But I can at least keep you from having to deal with building it every day, if it bothers you."

Kita looked at the base she had built. Was he sincere? Or was he just waiting for her to show weakness? It wasn't that she *couldn't* light a fire, she did so nearly daily. She just didn't like getting too close. "I'm fine."

He nodded, clearly reading her tone. "Fine. But if you ever do want help, just ask me. I won't say anything to the others."

She didn't say a word as he walked away.

***

Lakara was privately convinced that even her blisters had blisters. When she got back to the palace, she would never leave again!

It had been five days since they left Wris, and it would be another three or four days before they arrived at Tediz if Sir Jors was correct. Of course, he always seemed a little surprised at how long it was taking them to travel, so it could take even longer.

Leading the expedition was exhausting. Though, if Lakara was completely honest, she wasn't sure she was really leading. Sir Jors knew a lot more about what he was doing, how they should travel, which way they should go, how long it would take. He deferred to her, but she, at least, knew that he knew what was going on more than she did.

For that matter, Kita probably knew about as much as Sir Jors, maybe more on some parts. But Kita didn't seem to care about leadership, either trying to take over it, or to follow it much. Master Davorin knew a little less than Lakara because his knowledge was far more specialized than hers, but it was pretty clear that he was only following her because everyone else was.

Still, like it or not, she *was* the official leader. Which meant that she shouldn't slump to the ground every time they took a break. She ought to be helping out. Building the fire, fetching water, checking on the pack lizards. Something. But she wasn't. She was sitting there while Kita built the fire, Sir Jors fetched water, even Master Davorin was making dinner.

Once the fire was built, Kita turned her attention to one of the pack lizards. She kept frowning as she checked the animal over. "Is there a problem?" Lakara asked. If there was, she should know about it. Even if she didn't like the pack lizards, she knew they needed them.

"I think something's wrong with Stripes. She's slower, warmer, and more aggressive."

More aggressive? How could she tell?

Sir Jors took her more seriously, coming closer to examine the lizard in question. "You named them?" He asked absently as he studied the animal.

"Yes, Stripes and Longtail."

Well, it was accurate enough. One always had a white stripe down her back, and the other had a much longer tail. "I think I brought something about lizards." She rummaged through her bag. "Here we go." It only took her a few minutes to find her section. "Are the eyes clear?"

"Yes." Kita scratched an eye ridge.

"How about the nose?"

That answer took a second longer, but the nose was also clear. As were the ears. The mouth was free of sores, though it took both Kita and Sir Jors to check as Stripes tried to bite.

"Is she still eating?"

"I think so. I know she's drinking water." Kita eyed the piles of fur and feathers the lizards always left behind.

No open sores. The feet were fine. The... other extremities seemed to be fine, though no one was happy about checking.

"We'll have to keep an eye on her," Sir Jors said once the examination was finished, revealing no answers. "Make sure she keeps eating and drinking. Perhaps it's a slight upset stomach or similar."

Kita was about to say something when Master Davorin stormed up. "Alright, She-Whelp, where is it? What have you done with it?" He loomed over the still-kneeling woman.

Sir Jors pulled himself to his feet at once. Lakara tried to stand too. Kita didn't bother. "What are you going muddy on about?"

"You know exactly what!" He looked like he wanted to stomp his foot and possibly throw a tantrum.

"*I* don't know what's going on. Perhaps you could explain it to me." Sir Jors stepped smoothly between the two. Now that she didn't have a necromancer towering over her, Kita stood up.

"She took my magic book!" He glared over the knight's shoulder, trying to fry the thief with his glare.

"I never touched your filthy book," Kita said, sounding disgusted at the thought.

"You're the only thief here." Master Davorin folded his arms, smug superiority at his logic radiating off of him.

"What would I *do* with it? I can't read it, there's no one to sell it to, and I can't use it for anything but kindling." Kita tossed her hair back before leaping backwards over Stripes.

"If you burned my book..." Master Davorin pushed past the knight only to stop shy of the belligerent lizard.

"I didn't! If I had, you would have seen it."

The logic of that seemed to pierce his angry haze. "I want her belongings searched! Starting with her bag."

Kita's hands flew to protect her pack. "It isn't glowing. Your filthy, diseased book isn't in there."

Glowing? Sir Jors and Master Davorin looked equally confused. "Glowing? What do you mean by that, Kita?" Sir Jors again stepped between the two.

"Glowing! Like when magic..." She stopped talking, apparently realizing the others had no idea what she was talking about.

"I've heard, well, there are legends of some who can actually see magic." Lakara went rooting through her scrolls. "Here we are." It was getting too dark to read, but she did her best. "There isn't much information, and it does seem to be quite rare, but there are a few who can see magic in an object. How they see it varies, but a glow is one of the more common manifestations."

When she stopped, everyone was looking at her. "Yes?"

"How many books did you bring?" Kita asked.

Lakara put the scroll back in her bag. "Just a few that I thought would be useful."

"Well," Sir Jors spoke up, breaking the awkward silence. "If Kita can see magic as a glow, that should help us find the book."

"Not if she stole it!" Master Davorin snapped.

"Enough!" Sir Jors stopped everyone in their tracks. "Everyone, take a bag. We'll go through everything until we find it." Soon everyone had a bag in hand. "Good. One at a time. I'll go first." He opened the bag in his hand and started going through it. It was a foodstuff bag. They had to keep the lizards away, but he went through the bag without any sign of a book. He packed it up, then looked to Kita.

The thief looked like she really wanted to be going through a different bag, but carefully removed the contents of her pack. A change of clothes, a leather pouch and a wooden box, both too small to hold a book, her dark glasses, cloths that Lakara wasn't sure she wanted to know the use for, a money bag, and something metal wrapped in leather. "What is that?" Master Davorin asked.

"Not a book." Kita grabbed it to put it back in her bag. Before she could, Master Davorin tried to snatch it from her. "Hey!"

In the struggle, the leather moved to reveal a dirk. "You stole this. She's hiding it to murder us in our sleep!"

Kita yanked it away from him. "It's *mine*. It was my grandmother's, and you can keep your filthy hands off!"

"Your grand*mother's*?" The necromancer scoffed.

Sir Jors, once again, stepped between the two of them, before drawing his sword. Everyone backed up. "This sword is Bloodwolf. It was forged for my great-grandfather and has been used by every generation since. Do you understand what that means?"

"It's a generational weapon." Kita eyed it with interest

and respect, though she didn't get any closer. "Magic infuses it, aiding in the protection of the wielder and his family. It is more powerful the more generations that use it. The power ends if the generational connection is lost." She nodded. "I knew it glowed, but I wasn't sure why."

It meant more than that, Lakara thought. But perhaps Kita didn't know some of the finer details. Like it being more powerful against the Queya or against opposing magic. If the dirk *did* belong to Kita's grandmother, then it could possibly be a generational weapon too, though not as powerful as Bloodwolf. It probably wasn't though.

"Correct. Now, I will let you hold *this*," Sir Jors pulled his scabbard free and sheathed the sword, holding it out, "while I examine your dirk."

Kita reluctantly made the trade. Sir Jors didn't seem any happier but handing over a generational weapon was not something done lightly. There was complete silence as the knight thoroughly examined the blade, the handle, and the sheath. Finally, he sheathed the blade and looked at Kita. "Your mother's mother or your father's?"

"Father's," Kita answered shortly.

Sir Jors nodded. "It is a well-made blade, and an early generational weapon. Wield it well." He solemnly traded it back for his sword.

"You're giving it *back* to her?" Master Davorin asked incredulously.

"I will not take a generational weapon from another unless absolutely necessary."

"But she's lying! Her grandmother?"

"It was forged for a woman. It has the feel of a generational blade. I believe her story." Sir Jors closed the argument. "Lakara, would you check your bag now?"

Lakara had taken the bag with the tents. The first one snagged as she pulled it out, and the second was even harder. Finally, she had both on the ground, and tried to smooth them down.

"There! It's glowing." Kita pointed to the second tent. Lakara and Master Davorin rummaged through the canvas, finding the book after a few minutes.

"How convenient," Master Davorin sneered at Kita.

"I think it's quite likely that you forgot the book in your tent. It probably got wrapped in your bedroll. Fortunately, Kita could see enough of a glow to tell it was there, or we wouldn't have found it until setting up the tents," Sir Jors said.

"Which we should probably do now." Lakara picked up the other tent. Maybe it would be enough to end the argument.

Kita didn't say a word as she helped Lakara set up their tent. The men moved to the side, setting up the other. The necromancer was muttering under his breath, but Lakara couldn't make out what he was saying and if anyone else could, they were ignoring him.

It wasn't until they had finished with the tent and were airing out their bedrolls that Kita spoke. A quiet murmur that Lakara wasn't sure she was supposed to hear. "What's so muddy great about books, anyway?"

Lakara blinked at that. What was so great about books? Everything! She couldn't remember a time she had been without books. Of course, she was one of the king's scholars. Books were not common everywhere, she knew that. But, surely! "Haven't you read any..." Lakara faltered under the thief's half-defiant, half-embarrassed glare.

"Can't read. At all." She shrugged as if it was no big deal before entering the tent.

It shouldn't be a surprise. Not really. Most people

couldn't. Lakara knew the statistics. But somehow, it hadn't occurred to her that Kita, coarse and lowborn as she might be, fit into the eighty percent illiteracy rate.

It wasn't like Kita would need to read. She had no books, little chance of getting any, and likely no desire for them. Most people couldn't read, so it wasn't like she was missing out on much. No reason for her to care. Lakara went into the tent and found Kita settling herself for sleep. "Um, I could teach you." There was just enough light to see her amber eyes focused, staring, gauging intent. "If you want, anyway."

"I... Yes, if you would. Please." Kita rolled over, looking to the roof of the tent. "After all, a proper lady should know how to read."

Lakara's breath caught in her throat as she remembered. Kita had demanded to become a lady if they succeeded. She didn't know that King Zikkar planned to refuse, and Lakara was forbidden to tell her. How had she forgotten that?

Because she hadn't cared. She hadn't cared about Kita, that she'd probably get nothing, even if they succeeded in accomplishing what was long considered impossible.

She bit her lip, trying to figure out what to do, before realizing from the change in breathing that Kita had fallen asleep. Sleep was a long time coming to Lakara.

Chapter Five

Journey to the Temple of Victory

Or

If this is victory, what's defeat?

Sir Jors was surprised to wake up the next morning to the strange sight of the scholar sharing one of her books with Kita. Particularly since, if asked, he probably would have put money on her not being able to read. As he got closer, he realized Lakara was explaining the different letters and sounds. Ah, so Kita *couldn't* read and Lakara decided to fix that.

He kept quiet about the whole thing. Being literate probably wouldn't change anything in Kita's life. He couldn't imagine that she would start collecting books or even have anywhere to store more than one. More importantly, if they were bonding, even a little, well, that would make traveling easier. Of all of them, Kita definitely had the least reason to want to be here. Sir Jors doubted she had any true loyalty to the group, and he couldn't exactly blame her. Some ties, some connections with the rest of them, some reason to continue, could only be beneficial.

So, he said nothing about the fact the women were mostly neglecting breakfast to pore over a tome. Pretended not to hear Kita stumble over words as she tried to sound them out with Lakara's help. Gave the necromancer a warning look when he opened his mouth, a disdainful look on his face. As long as they were ready to go when it was time to break camp, it didn't hurt anyone.

It was soon time to move out anyway. Lakara put the book away and, reluctantly, took the harness of one of the pack lizards, Longtail. Sir Jors took Stripes. If there was something wrong with the lizard, then he wanted to keep an eye on her.

Kita took point, as she often did, and Davorin fell behind, as he often did, so Sir Jors walked beside the scholar. It hadn't escaped his notice that she, and the necromancer for that matter, seemed apprehensive of the pack lizards. They relied on the pack lizards and everyone needed to take turns with them, but he could try to make it easier.

"You are a good teacher."

Lakara looked at him with a start, then shrugged. "Thank you. I've never tried to teach someone before. She seems eager to learn, though. That helps, I'm sure." She bit her lip. "Do you think it's a good idea?"

"To teach her to read? I don't see what harm it could do. In fact, it might be an exceptionally good thing. We have to take this journey together, and it will take a long time. We might as well try for friendship."

Lakara smiled at that. Sir Jors decided not to mention that it might play a factor in Kita deciding whether or not to abandon them at a particularly dangerous spot. There had to be at least *some* trust in the group to succeed.

Kita did seem to be keen to learn reading, as she either brought it up or quickly went along with the suggestion on almost every break. He tried to give them some privacy. No one liked looking foolish, and some element of that was inevitable when learning something new. That said, he didn't want to leave the group, so he overheard a fair bit anyway.

Lakara *was* a good teacher, seeming to know the right balance between when to help and when to step back and let Kita figure it out for herself. Occasionally she smiled at a mistake but never laughed or sneered. This was the third time he had seen them working together, and Kita seemed to be coming along nicely.

She was trying to read aloud from a book Lakara had chosen, one of the history of the kingdom. "The city of Cor... Corvis was found?"

"Founded. Built or established," Lakara corrected quietly.

"I know what 'founded' means," Kita murmured. "Founded in the regin?"

Davorin scoffed. "Reign. As in the rule of a king."

Kita glared. "Reign of King..."

"King Restos," Lakara said. "He was the first of the Grazin dynasty, which extends all the way to King Zikkar, who is currently the last of the Grazin dynasty."

Kita muttered something that was probably rude at best and possibly treasonous at worst, but she was ignored. "King Restos the Fist."

"First, She-Whelp! Honestly, if you are going to get ideas above your station and try to read, you could at least do it properly."

Sir Jors glared at the man and was only slightly surprised when Lakara stood up and glared him down too. "She's doing quite well, thank you. I'm sure you made plenty of mistakes when you were learning."

Kita hung her head and tried to hand the book back to Lakara. "This was a bad idea. Take your book back before I muddy it up."

"You won't," Lakara said, voice taut. "Keep trying."

"Look, the dirty—"

"Ladies do not swear." Lakara continued to glare down the necromancer.

"And I'm a dirty street thief!"

Lakara spun around. "Did you or did you not tell King Zikkar that if we found the Jewel of Ishni and brought it back, you wanted to become a lady? Remember, I was there. I heard you. You want to be a lady? Ladies do not swear, and they can read."

"But I can't."

"By the time I'm done, you'll be able to." Kita didn't look convinced. Lakara sighed. "Look, I'm a scholar, you know that. An adept. That puts me above the apprentices, the journeymen, and the scribes. The only ones above me are the masters and the Head Archivist. When someone in the palace needs information, they come to us. The king *himself* comes to us for information. We study, we learn, we preserve knowledge. Do you know how long it took me to learn how to read?" Kita shook her head. "Ages. Months, maybe a couple of years. You are doing so much better than I did when I started. By the time we get back to the palace, you'll be able to convince people *you're* a scholar." Lakara nodded firmly, as if ordaining her statement as prophecy.

Davorin opened his mouth to say something, but Sir Jors shook his head. When he seemed like he would say something anyway, Sir Jors made a show of fingering the hilt of his sword. The necromancer turned white and looked away.

"She's right. I don't know how long it took her to read, but I know it took me a few years to become good. Then again, I had little interest in my studies at the time." Sir Jors gave a fond smile as he thought of his childhood, where playing with the pack lizards, climbing trees, and stealing apples were more important than lessons, wars and battles were marvelous adventures that happened to other people, and nothing really bad could touch him and his.

It took a little more persuading, and a warning that he wanted to spend the next break working on sling techniques, but they got Kita back to reading. Good, he wanted time to think about the 'lady' revelation. So, Kita wanted to be a lady? Or at least told the king that she did. He had trouble believing the king would accept that. Then again, Sir Jors had been promised he'd be made a paladin. He didn't know what the others had been promised.

She seemed sincere in her desire. He was a little surprised that she had even thought of it and then had the audacity to demand it of the king. Probably, to a small child on the streets, nobility would seem like a dream. The epitome of all desires at one.

Sir Jors just wished he didn't have such a bad feeling about this.

**

Davorin was most certainly not sulking. Just because the rest of the party had forgotten their manners and sense of rank as far as to take the side of scum didn't mean he couldn't be the better man and ignore it. After all, if the thief were very smart, she wouldn't be here. Probably would not been a thief and almost certainly not have been caught and pressed into this quest. So, he should make allowances for her lack of intelligence.

Or he could ignore the whole thing. That might be best. But honestly, whatever could have possessed a street thief to demand to be made a lady? King Zikkar would never allow it. Even if he did, what good would it do? She had no money, no property, no manners, and no prospects. She would simply be a lady living as a street thief. But of course, she would never think of that. It would almost serve her right if the king threw her back into whatever dungeon he dragged her from. Almost.

No, he wasn't going to think about it now. They had months to journey together, and who knew how long to get back. It made him sick just to think about it. Better to focus on the more immediate. Tediz. They were due to arrive there in a day or two. He could only hope that Tediz was in better shape than Wris. He had known that Wris was but a shadow of its former glory, but nothing had prepared him for the dirt-hole the town had been. Even the formerly grand temple was in disarray. Why had King Zikkar allowed that? Perhaps he was unaware.

"Has anyone here actually been to Tediz?" Davorin asked at the next break before the females could start that ridiculous exercise of 'reading'. Honestly, it was like stones against his teeth to listen. The only thing worse was the sling practice the knight insisted upon.

"I was, once, for my acceptance of my vocation. That was over ten years ago, though," The knight spoke up.

"I've been a couple times. I think my last time was two years ago," The thief said.

The scholar shook her head, but he hadn't expected much from her. "What's the city like?" she asked. Good, then he didn't have to.

"I didn't see much of the city. We were there for two days, and most of that was spent at or near the temple and barracks." The knight seemed apologetic about it. "Kita?"

The thief shrugged. "It's a city. Not a huge one, but they get by. Or did. Trade's been hit hard lately. Everything has."

Davorin frowned. He hadn't noticed any decline in standards. "What do you mean?" He refrained from insulting her, mostly to avoid another fight.

She looked at him a moment before laughing bitterly. "Are you that muddy stupid? Think!"

"Listen, you guttersnipe—"

Sir Jors sighed deeply and waved an arm between them. "Could we please *try* to remain civilized? I'm certain that as far different as we all are, we all have different opinions and perceptions." He turned to the thief. "Kita, the rest of us live in Corvis, the capital. Even I've been there mostly exclusively for a few years. I'm sure some things are different there from the rest of the country. You may have seen or noticed things we haven't. Could you please explain?"

The thief frowned but spoke in a calmer voice. "Prices have gone up, on most everything. More and more people are finding it hard or muddy impossible to live life the legal way. More thieves, more bandits, which makes things even harder for those who try to stay on the side of the law. Tax collectors take more and more. People lose their homes and lands, end up in the cities with nothing, and no skills the city needs because someone else will do it cheaper. It's been like this for about ten years or so. Further you get from the capital, the worse it gets."

"But, why?" The scholar gasped out.

"You know why." The thief took to drawing on the ground with a stick. Or perhaps she was practicing her letters. If so, her handwriting was atrocious.

"No, no I don't," the scholar protested.

"You saw it. We were there."

Davorin frowned, trying to figure out what the shadows the thief was talking about. Sir Jors seemed confused too, while the scholar hunched over, apparently no more enlightened than the rest of them.

"Silk. Gold. Jewels. Think that comes cheap?" She stabbed the ground with her stick, breaking it.

The scholar gasped. "The throne room! Taxes have been doubled for ten years to pay for it."

"Exactly."

"But, but the throne room is a marvel of engineering! A wonder of the country," she said, almost desperately.

The thief shrugged. "So? Does it put food in anyone's belly? Does it stop anyone from being sick? It's not even warm. That room was cold. And that golden chair looks muddy hard to sit in. Does it make him more of a king?"

"I think we should stop this discussion now," Sir Jors cut in. "You have your opinions, Lakara has hers. There is no point in arguing over them."

Not to mention, the thief had been edging uncomfortably close to treason. Worst of all, Davorin wasn't sure she cared. He couldn't get her words out of his head, though.

To make matters worse, if Tediz was anything to go by, she might be partially right. Tediz was barely any better than Wris. The city was unclean, the people disheartened, and the very air crackled with Shadow Master's touch. He had felt the same at Wris, but that was to be expected in a necromancer's domain. Here, he should be the only necromancer. He hadn't been here long enough to affect the city, especially without using his powers. Besides, this didn't feel like magic, it felt more natural. Like a plague or a famine. Hopefully not a plague, they couldn't afford to get sick.

Davorin wasn't the only one to notice a problem. Almost as soon as they got close to the city, their motley group formed a tight knot. The knight was in the lead, breaking a path through the crowd, with the thief in the rear, leading both pack lizards, eyes constantly scanning the area. He assumed so, anyway. She was wearing those dark glasses again, but he could semi-see her head moving minutely in each direction. The scholar seemed more stunned than anything. This part of the city might not be as bad as Wris, or at least the part they saw, but it was far from hospitable.

"Do you have friends here?" The thief asked the knight. "Connections of any sort?" Left unsaid was that she was more likely to have connections, but not ones they could use.

"The main temple of Vicaw is here, so this is where my order is based. They may be willing to house us for a couple of nights."

"Even the bone mage?"

Davorin stiffened as the scholar sighed, "Kita..."

"To be fair, she actually has a point. We are not supposed to work with necromancers." Sir Jors frowned. "Nor would this be a normal traveling group. Especially if we are supposed to be inconspicuous."

That would be a problem. One look at his eyes and it would be obvious he was a necromancer. It had been one of many, many reasons he hadn't volunteered to help with the shopping at Wris, and the reason that the traveling group of three priestesses and their guard they had run into yesterday, had quickly decided that no, they didn't want to lunch with them. Fortunately, without his ceremonial robe, his eyes were the only immediate evidence. An enchanter could hide their silver fingernails with gloves, and a healer could hide their red arm rings with long sleeves. Not that either of them would want to hide often. But a necromancer had to find a way to hide their eyes.

"Alright, does anyone have any ideas?" Lakara asked. "Wait, Kita? How much do you need those glasses?"

The thief scowled, but slowly took them off and handed them to Davorin. "Be careful with these. They belonged to my father. I have very little of his, and I don't know where to get another pair."

Davorin nobly repressed the grimace at the idea of

wearing anything the she-whelp wore on her face on his but took the glasses. After gingerly wiping any uncleanliness from them, he put the glasses on. To his surprised pleasure, they did not impede his vision, though the bright day looked more like it was approaching dusk.

"So, Sir Jors, how often are knights commissioned to provide safety for travelers on the road?" The thief asked, after a moment of squinting and wiping at her eyes.

"We aren't supposed to use our abilities and training for personal gain but providing safety for travelers is commended." Sir Jors nodded approvingly. "So..."

"So, a merchant and his... wife Lakara, along with their servant, have somehow impressed upon Sir Jors for his protection on their way north." The thief nodded to herself.

There were a few complaints and grimaces, but everyone agreed they weren't going to come up with a better idea on short notice. Next time they would have to come up with a story before they got to other people.

It worked, too. While the Order of Vicaw was not willing to let outsiders camp in their barracks, they were able to tell Sir Jors where they could stay cheaply.

The recommended inn gave them a good rate because of the knight. Though Davorin did notice that Sir Jors seemed unhappy or suspicious about the place. They only had one room this time. Partially because of their story, and partially because Sir Jors said they shouldn't separate.

"We stay in tonight. No one goes out alone. No one." Sir Jors barred the door before moving to shutter the windows.

The scholar looked as puzzled by this as Davorin felt, but the thief just nodded. "The city is... wrong. Dying."

"Yes," Sir Jors agreed. "It feels like before an ambush is sprung. Let's get some sleep. I think we should try for an early start tomorrow." In other words, the sooner they left, the better.

The room had a double bed, a single, and a floor pallet. After some shuffling and bickering, it was decided that the women would share the double, Davorin got the single, and Sir Jors would take the floor pallet.

Neither man felt it would be appropriate to share a bed with either of the women, and while the thief had offered to take the pallet, Sir Jors argued against a woman, even a low-born one, sleeping on the floor while he had a bed. Davorin didn't care much as long as he had a bed. Lakara was almost half-asleep and very complacent.

It was the first time they had all shared a room, and sleep didn't come easily to anyone. Just as he started to drift off, Davorin's eyes snapped open as he heard someone outside the door. The handle rattled. In the dark, he could see the knight sit up, then stand.

One of the women, probably the thief, was on her feet almost as quickly. The other sat up but stayed in the bed. Davorin waited, trying hard to resist the childish urge to hide under his blankets. It would do nothing if someone did come. Not that he could do anything anyway. He had no weapon and none of his magic would do him the slightest bit of good.

The knight called out, "Is someone there?"

A foolish question. Or perhaps not so foolish, as Davorin heard quiet footsteps retreat. A minute passed. Two. Both the knight and the thief relaxed. "I doubt they'll come back. Not tonight." Sir Jors backed his statement by returning to the pallet. "Try to sleep. We all need it."

The thief was already back in bed, and slowly the scholar lay back down. Davorin just lay there in the dark, wishing he were back in his nice safe tower with his pigeons and his books. Or even back on the trail and wasn't that the first time he had ever wished that? Who would have ever thought he might feel safer in the middle of nowhere than in a city?

***

Kita eyed the temple warily and tried not to shy away from the guards. She had as much right to be here as anyone and hadn't stolen a thing since she left on this suicide trip. They had no reason to stop or delay her unless they could tell she was nervous about something. But she didn't like soldiers or guards. Didn't trust them and didn't want to be in their sights.

But there was no way around it. She couldn't stay at the inn and wasn't sure she really wanted to stay there alone if they would let her. There had been some discussion about someone staying at the inn, but they decided against it. Sir Jors knew the temple best and could get them in parts they might not otherwise be allowed to go. Lakara and the necromancer could read the language the muddy clues were written in and they didn't trust her on her own. Sir Jors said it might be unsafe for her, which may be true, but she was pretty sure that wasn't the main reason even for him.

Vicaw's temple was in both better and worse shape than Pirette's temple. There were signs of a shrinking level of devotion. Repairs lagged behind. Not too many people came while they were there. It hadn't been ravaged as badly, probably partly because of the knights and partly because there wasn't as much to steal. The goddess of victory didn't inspire as much art and finery as the goddess of craft. Which didn't surprise Kita in the slightest. Finery may be pretty and all, but it was filthy useless when it came to a fight.

The temple had its own beauty, but it was harsher and heavier than Pirette's. Kita thought she might appreciate it a bit more. She didn't feel like she was drowning in spider webs of silk. No, the beauty of this temple was in carved rock and wood. There was less gold and more steel, but Kita could appreciate the beauty of the statues. Particularly the two iron knights who stood, swords crossed, over the endless flame.

Lakara pointed to the words under the large bowl that held the endless fire, distracting Kita from her thoughts that one of the pack lizards could probably fit in the bowl if there was no fire. "Can you read that?"

She edged closer, trying to sound out the words in her head. "Fight?" Lakara nodded. "Fight for right, not for might?"

Sir Jors nodded. "Correct. That is the motto of our order."

"What's that supposed to mean?"

"It means that when we join the order, we take an oath to fight for whatever is right, not for our own glory and power."

Kita held back her scoff. Pretty words, but empty from what she had seen. She knew of plenty of knights who only wanted money, glory, or power.

Sir Jors approached the bowl, hand over his heart and head bowed. Kita bit her tongue. Maybe, just maybe, he still held to those words. Or maybe she just hadn't seen him in a position to betray them yet.

"I think I found the symbol," the bone mage said from another corner. As she followed the others, Kita spotted the faint glow before getting close enough to see quite what was causing it. The glow was one of the reasons she had been able to spot the clue in Pirette's temple. Of course, in a temple, there were other sources of magic. This clue was engraved in the base of one of the statues.

The scholar and the necromancer immediately started copying down the clue. Kita frowned when she realized these letters weren't the ones she had been taught, and Lakara promised she had learned all the letters of Graldish. Yes, she knew this was a different language, but didn't they use the same letters? Maybe she would ask Lakara later.

"Hm. There's something about ice and fire in this one." Lakara checked her copy against the words on the wall again. "Bearing them? Bearding them? Braving them? Something like that."

"They can all be interpreted similarly. Wherever we are supposed to go, we will face ice and fire, I suppose," Sir Jors said. "As far north as we are heading, I wouldn't be surprised by the ice, but fire?"

"A fire mountain, perhaps? Though I rather hope not. I think I brought a book that mentions them. I'll check later."

Kita wasn't the only one who gave the scholar a look. "How many books did you bring?" asked the necromancer.

"A few."

"We should make a sacrifice to Vicaw," Sir Jors cut in before anything else could be said. "I'll get the incense and... well, wait here."

Vicaw wasn't a goddess Kita had reason to worry too much about, but everyone learned at least the basics to avoid offending any of the gods. It was tradition to sacrifice either a token of the spoils of a previous victory or some blood to show devotion to the fight. Some of the especially devout did both. So, she wasn't surprised to spot the knight offering something small and gold in color to the flames before using a sacrificial knife to make a small cut on the back of his arm. The blood was caught in a small wax bowl that was also thrown into the fire.

She looked to see the other's reactions. The necromancer was pale and looking away, while the scholar was biting her lip thoughtfully. When Sir Jors returned with the incense, Lakara spoke first. "Should we make a sacrifice too? Like that? I mean, we all want victory. I mean, a successful quest."

"I... I do not know. Vicaw is my patron goddess. I would be remiss *not* to offer to her. You do have a point. But know that the goddess's pleasure cannot be bought."

"But her displeasure is something we wish to avoid," the necromancer said reluctantly. "We have no victories to celebrate. Is there an alternative?"

"Well, there is blood, of course. But some, especially a soldier before his first fight or a knight just initiated, will offer a token from their life before. Something of meaning to the individual." He frowned. "I would suggest choosing a token. Strongly suggest choosing a token."

Kita said nothing and thought about her belongings. She had very little 'of meaning' and even less that she wouldn't likely need on the journey.

"Does it matter what the token is?" Lakara asked.

"No, not as long as it has meaning to you and can be burned by fire."

Lakara came up with a token first. "I have a pen knife. It was given to me when I was made adept." She held up a small knife, suitable only for sharpening a quill, with the crest of the kingdom carved in the handle, traced in gold. Kita would estimate that it might be worth a gold dourat, maybe two. But it meant something to Lakara, clearly.

Sir Jors nodded gravely. "That will be excellent."

The necromancer scoffed. "You think I would bring something 'of meaning' on this journey that I don't need? The only thing I could possibly sacrifice would be my ceremonial robe."

"That would work. If you care about it," Sir Jors said. When the bone mage's eyes bulged out, he continued. "It wouldn't even have to be the whole thing. Just a part, preferably big enough to be noticeable. It is a *sacrifice*, after all."

Well, if cloth would work... "I have some pieces of my mother's last dress. What if I gave one of those?"

Sir Jors nodded. "Perfect."

"Fine." The necromancer dug out his ceremonial robe. "If *everyone* will, I will too."

Kita grabbed the first rag she came across in her bag. It was the one that had been used to bandage her ankle when the swordgrass cut her. So, blood and a token in one. Sort of.

Lakara went first, head bowed, tossing her knife into the fire, then stepping back slowly. Likely at prayer. The fire caught the knife quickly, a sign the sacrifice was accepted. The wooden handle burned faster than the metal blade and for an instant, Kita thought she saw the outline of the crest light up, before falling to the flames.

Kita went next, tossing her rag to the fire. The flame swallowed it greedily, sparking slightly. *There. Could we succeed? Please? Or at least, not die?*

The necromancer was still trying to rip off a sleeve. Since it was high-quality cloth, he wasn't succeeding. Finally, with a sound of frustration, he tossed the whole thing in. Perhaps because it was so big, the fire didn't devour it as quickly as it had her rag. Or maybe her rag had absorbed oil. Wouldn't surprise her at all.

They left the temple without speaking. It wasn't until they had left the grounds that Lakara asked if he had another necromancer's robe.

"Of course. Three of them. But they're all back in the castle. So, it's traveler's robes until then."

Kita fought a snicker at his disgruntlement. "Why did you not want us to offer blood?"

"Vicaw is the goddess of victory. No victory can be achieved without sacrifice. Offering blood means a willingness to suffer wounds or even death in the pursuit of your goal," Lakara answered.

Kita choked. "Just fresh blood, right?"

"Um, I think so?" Lakara gave her a questioning look.

Sir Jors winced. "Old blood?"

"Yes. Will..."

"Vicaw is a goddess. I'm sure she knows your heart and that you didn't intend it that way. Don't worry about it." She would have felt more reassured if he didn't seem so uncertain.

"Not much of a victory if you die, is it?" asked the bone mage.

"Victory is not always a personal thing. It is victory for your side, for your companions, for your kingdom. As a knight, we are called upon to be willing to die for our cause," Sir Jors said gravely.

"You sacrificed blood," Lakara pointed out.

"I am in charge of the safety of this mission. It is my duty to protect you all, even at the cost of my own life." No one had anything to add to that.

***

Lakara was relieved to leave Tediz. The whole city was unclean, unhealthy, and disturbing. Unfortunately, the next temple on their list was the great temple of Tratow in Seduk. They would have to cross the border of Salardis first.

While the temples were neutral territory, and cities known for their temples were often freer than most, some of the surrounding areas were known to be dangerous to pilgrims and travelers. Not to mention, they would have to cross another kingdom, without saying what their goals were. At least they spoke the same language. Most places, anyway.

But they were over a week from the border. As unfriendly as Tediz was, they still needed to resupply. They went as a whole to the marketplace, though usually Kita went to the stalls and shops alone to do the actual bargaining.

Even to Lakara, it was obvious that the supplies they were getting wouldn't last a week. Partially because there wasn't enough worth buying at a fair price. Well, there should be other cities on their way, or if they went slightly out of it. Still, judging by the displeasure of Kita and Sir Jors, it would probably be best to ration supplies carefully. And practice a bit more with her sling. She still couldn't hit a large target more often than one try in ten. Master Davorin wasn't any better. Sir Jors could hit rabbits most of the time, and Kita could get squirrels with ease.

The supplies were divvied up, making certain not to overburden Stripes. Kita's names for the lizards stuck, much to some people's disgust. So far, there were no other noted symptoms, but she did seem less well. At least they could verify that she was actually eating. A lot.

They weren't twenty minutes on the road out of the city when a man stumbled onto the path in front of them. He was naked, branded with the outline of a wolf on each side of his face. Lakara gasped. A Never-Was. The worst punishment in the land, possibly barring execution. The criminal was declared not to exist. Forbidden to own or buy any form of property, including food. No rights or protections under the law. Any friendly interaction towards them was forbidden, including talking to them. Worst of all, the punishment stretched to others touched by their life. Any children of a Never-Was were considered illegitimate, students were considered untaught. The one time a priest of AKAF was declared a Never-Was, the marriages he had performed were considered undone, the blessings ungiven, and the deaths he presided over were unconsecrated.

"Food, please! I've not eaten in days!" The Never-Was stretched out a hand to them.

No one said a word.

"Food! Before I die." He was so unclean, Lakara wasn't sure what was skin and what was uncleanliness. There were open sores that she could smell from where she was standing, fifteen feet away. His skin seemed to shrink around him, reminding her of the time she copied an anatomy text of the skeleton. She could name every bone.

Sir Jors stepped to the front of the party, making a show of grabbing the hilt of his sword. "I would rather not use this sword, but I will if that is what it takes to guarantee our safety." He angled his head so that his words were supposedly to them but were loud enough to be heard by the man in the road.

Kita frowned and stared into the overgrowth. "He's not alone," she muttered in a low voice. Taking a deep breath, she closed her eyes, listening. "Three others, I think."

More Never-Was? Those who survived longer than a day or two survived from crime. Theft at the very least, robbery and murder were more likely as that was how most of them ended up a Never-Was in the first place. If this was an ambush…

"Unmuzzle the lizards," Sir Jors ordered quickly. Kita was doing it before Lakara registered what he had said. Master Davorin was still as a statue. Hopefully, he was concentrating on using his powers to frighten them off.

Sir Jors stepped back long enough to reach into one pack, coming up with two pieces of wood that were clearly set up to be screwed together. He pressed that into her hands. "Put that together, as quick as you can." Then he moved back to the front.

Shaky, clumsy fingers put the staff together on her third try. When she tried to hand it to him, he shook his head. "It's for you. Anyone but us comes near you, swing hard."

Kita moved a couple steps to the side, probably so they wouldn't get in each other's way if they did have to fight. She had her dirk in hand, facing resolutely into some innocent-seeming spot of grasslands.

Nothing happened, no one moved. A minute, another, and a third passed. Then the Never-Was in front of them snarled and leaped right at them.

Lakara shrieked and flailed out with the staff. She narrowly missed Master Davorin, who still hadn't moved, but was nowhere near the Never-Was. Sir Jors stepped forward; sword extended. The Never-Was screamed as he ended up impaled on the blade, but Sir Jors didn't react other than to angle his sword down to let the man slide off, before stepping back, sword raised to meet more attacks.

As if the man's movements were a signal, three others, all with the outline of a wolf branded upon their faces, jumped out from a hollow in the grass. They wore clothes and had several weapons between them. Meaning they had to have robbed or murdered at least three people.

"No one else has to die today," Kita said, not seeming to care that she was breaking the law. "Let us pass and all will be fine." They ignored her, lumbering closer, more like beasts than men. "Are you in a hurry to meet Shadow Master?"

"Beats starving to death." The biggest one, who might have been blond once, spat on the ground.

"Does it?" Kita laughed, madness in her voice. "Are you sure? We have a necromancer with us. He can give you a personal introduction."

They paused, doubt and disbelief visible. Kita tore her dark glasses back from Master Davorin, revealing his solid black eyes. The biggest one stepped back.

Sir Jors spoke next, "She's right. *We* can kill you. *He*," he jerked his head in the necromancer's direction, "can have you..." He paused.

"Swallowed into Shadow Master's realm, leech the power from your souls for his own use, or summoned back from death whenever he chooses," Kita finished. That didn't seem *quite* in keeping with the known powers of necromancers, but maybe Kita didn't know much about what necromancers could and couldn't do.

Besides, whatever Kita did or didn't know, it would seem the outlaw band believed her. They ran, abandoning their comrade.

Gripping the pole firmly, Lakara forced herself to look closely at the man and his injury. The sword had pierced a lung, all the way through the body. Blood speckled his lips, and his breathing was wet. Medicine was not her specialty, but Lakara didn't feel the need to pull out a medical text to confirm the man was dying.

Master Davorin shook his head. "Shadow Master will take him before evening."

The Never-Was let out a hoarse choked laugh. "Finish it. Please."

No one said anything for a moment. Sir Jors hadn't sheathed his sword, but neither did he move.

Kita stepped up and looked between the two. "If you don't, I will."

Lakara blanched. Yes, she could understand killing in the heat of battle, she could even understand The Final Mercy, but the only women to perform it were healers or close relatives of the dying.

Sir Jors looked at her calmly. "Have you?"

She didn't answer.

Sir Jors stepped forward, sword pointing downward. Lakara looked away. There was a solid thunking sound and an exhale of air. She couldn't make herself look. She would have to look. They would have to walk past the... Her mind skittered away from admitting what had happened. There was a snort by her side, and she knew, just knew, it was Kita. A small hand touched her arm, making her jump. But she still didn't open her eyes.

"It's me. Only me." The words were quiet, and the hand gently urged her forward. "I won't let you step on him. He deserves that much respect."

Lakara was silent even as she felt herself walking off the path. After what felt like forever, Kita spoke. "You can open your eyes now."

Slowly, reluctantly, she did so. The road was clear. Master Davorin was with them, but Sir Jors wasn't. Neither were the lizards. "Where is Sir Jors?"

"Moving the body off the road and setting a marking stone. The lizards are with him to keep a watch out. He'll be back soon."

Lakara relaxed at Kita's words. Yes, that was... fitting. A Never-Was could not be consecrated for death, but a marking stone would surely be permitted. At very least, it wasn't forbidden. They certainly couldn't leave the body to rot in the road.

"You spoke to them. You and Sir Jors." Lakara hadn't meant to say that, but it came out of her mouth before she thought.

Kita shrugged, not seeming terribly disturbed by the fact she had just broken the law in front of witnesses. "It worked. If we hadn't scared them away, we would have had to fight them. Considering you almost took out your own teammate and the bone mage was standing around being muddy useless, I don't think we would have come out so well."

"I was not being useless, you ignorant She-Whelp."

"Well, I admit you made a great bluff. Thank you for not opening your mouth and ruining it."

Master Davorin sputtered. Lakara looked curiously at Kita, "So, you don't believe he could do all that?"

Another unladylike snort. "Please! I'm hardly convinced he's a necromancer at all. I've never seen him so much as converse with a ghost."

"I am standing right here. And I am more than capable of conversing with ghosts and doing many other things that you cannot even imagine. What you said may have been a bluff, but that doesn't mean you were entirely wrong. I could tell you horrors that would prevent you from sleeping soundly ever again. Remember that, *Child*."

Kita glared back. "I haven't been a child since I was five. You want to know horrors? In your clean, warm tower? Honored by the king, respected and feared by the people? You think you know horror? They," she waved her arm back to where the fight presumably happened. "*They* know horrors. *I* know horrors. *You* know *nothing*."

"I know *death*. That death is but a door. Do you know what lies on the other side?"

Before they could continue, Sir Jors walked up, leading the now muzzled lizards. "Are you two fighting again?" He shook his head. "Come. We go on."

Chapter Six

Crossing Boundaries

Or

"You want to do what?"

Kita stayed quiet as they put more distance between themselves and Tediz. Judging from the pace they walked, she wasn't the only one glad to be leaving the city behind. It was even worse than it had been on her last visit. For one thing, she hadn't been ambushed by outlaws last time.

On her own, she was rarely bothered by bandits or thieves. Any bandit worth his boots could tell at a glance that she had nothing worth stealing. With Whisper helping her keep an eye out, like he did today, she considered herself pretty safe.

Fortunately, no one had asked her how she knew how many bandits were hiding. Even without his help, she knew there were at least two, but she wouldn't have gotten the third one without Whisper letting her Borrow his eyes.

It was risky to do even a light Borrowing in front of them, but it worked. That's what mattered. It worked, they were all alive, and no one realized what she had done. Borrowing would get her into far more trouble than talking to a Never-Was. She had been caught doing that before and taken the whipping for it; she could do it again if she had to. Getting caught Borrowing meant they would kill Whisper. Kita wasn't sure she even wanted to know what they would do to her.

Lakara wouldn't report her for talking to the Never-Was, Kita suspected. Not unless she was asked directly about that or maybe crimes committed on the road. Even if she did tell the king or some official, she would probably mention that Kita only spoke to convince them not to attack. Completely different from offering comfort or help.

The knight wouldn't report her, he was equally guilty. Unless he wanted the same punishment, he'd keep his mouth shut. Or was he the type to do that? Admit the failings he had gotten away with and take punishment for them? Maybe. There weren't many that would do that for real, but there were a few. Anyway, he probably wasn't high-risk.

That left the bone mage. He hated her and he hadn't spoken to them. Would he report her? It was possible.

Well, so what? They needed her right now. Until they had their filthy jewel, they couldn't risk doing anything to her. Besides, until they got back to the palace, their word wasn't any better than hers. If she stuck around that long. Not that she couldn't take a whipping if she had to, she would just rather not, especially for doing what was necessary.

If King Zikkar came through with his promise to make her a lady, she wouldn't have to worry. A lady could not be whipped. Fined, imprisoned, even executed if necessary, but not whipped or maimed. No one was ever executed for talking to a Never-Was. Of course, Stripes or Longtail were about as likely to grow wings and fly as King Zikkar was to make her a lady.

"Perhaps we should take a rest here," Lakara said. It was a good two hours since their brush with the outlaws, but no one had suggested a break earlier. Kita knew she could go another hour or two easily, and it looked like Sir Jors could too, but Lakara and the necromancer were slumping and limping along. Mind, this was still far progress from the beginning.

Sir Jors scanned the area. "Yes, we can stop for a bit."

No fire this time. They passed around bread and cheese. When Kita finished, she examined Stripes again. "She's definitely warmer." She moved her hand as the lizard snapped at her. "And meaner. Still eating, though. In fact, I think she's put on a little weight."

"Perhaps we should see if the next town has an expert on lizards. Or if we pass a lizard village," Sir Jors said.

"What is the next town?"

Lakara pulled out her map. "Well, our next goal seems to be the temple of Tratow in Surduk. We'll need to make a stop or two for supplies before we get there, but only cities are marked on the map. Cities and major towns. Not small towns and villages. There are a few places, but I don't know how many. Hopefully, these places will be… safer than Tediz."

They wouldn't be. Probably not until they reached Salardis and that would cause its own problems. Still, Kita kept her mouth shut. The more disheartened everyone got, the less they would be watching her.

"Do you want to practice reading?" Lakara asked. The necromancer groaned but he was ignored.

"Alright." Especially if it annoyed the bone mage. Besides, being able to read might prove useful in the future, especially since people would assume she couldn't. Lakara pulled out the history book she was using to teach Kita. She knew there were several more books in the bag and vaguely wondered what else might be in them. She would probably never find out.

Kita gave the briefest thought of trying to steal some of the books when she made her escape but rejected the idea. Too heavy, too hard to fence, and Lakara would be devastated. Mostly the first two.

They finished the chapter, which seemed like a good place to stop, especially as they had been sitting for a while. "Are we moving on now?" Kita asked. There was no response. Lakara was packing up her book. The necromancer was scowling at the road. Sir Jors simply sat there, eyes partially open, looking at nothing. Kita frowned. "Are you asleep?"

He startled, looking at her strangely. "What did you say?"

"I asked if you were asleep."

Sir Jors stood immediately. "No, no. Not asleep. Just thinking. We should move on."

If she didn't know better, she would think he might have been Borrowing. But that wasn't possible. Was it?

***

They were going to be crossing into Salardis soon. Davorin refused to admit to being nervous about crossing the borders of Graldish. He had never done it before, the furthest he had been was the Great temple of Shadow Master in Chiswat, which was still well within Graldish's boundaries. He had also been three at the time and remembered only that it had been a terrifying experience for a young child. But that was as a child, he was an adult now. A fully trained necromancer, even, who had no reason to—

He stopped still as there was an audible rustle in the grass beside the road. The lizards halted and looked to the side. The other party members nervously looked around.

Something ran over his foot and Davorin jumped back with a manly yelp. The lizards lunged and the thief practically shrieked with laughter as a gray furry blur pivoted and darted back into the grass.

"What's wrong, Master Bone Mage? Did the evil ground squirrel attack you?" She pulled the harness of the lizard closest to her, Longtail, to get her back on the path. The scholar struggled a bit more with Stripes.

Ground squirrel. Yes, the gray blur had been a ground squirrel. One that nearly ended up as lizard lunch. Deciding that the most dignified response would be to ignore the cackling of the thief and muffled giggles and chuckles of the others, Davorin stomped ahead without a word.

"Oh, good idea. You've never taken point. We should spread the risk around," the thief said, laughter still echoing in her voice.

It was a jest. A joke. She was trying to scare him. Still, "Risk?"

"Certainly. The one who walks first is usually the first person attacked or the one who walks into the trap."

Davorin froze.

"Kita," the knight said, a disapproving note in his voice.

"Is that true?" Davorin asked.

The knight sighed. "To an extent. That is why the one who goes in front has to be observant. To spot traps and ambushes."

Hence why it was almost always the knight or the thief. Both were trained and knowledgeable travelers. Sir Jors was the one best able to defend himself and the group at large, and even Davorin had to admit the thief was sharp-eyed, sharp-eared, and good at noticing possible ambush spots. Whether that would translate to traps or not, they had not yet been in a position to check.

"So, can you keep an eye out for threats?" The thief asked, mocking in her tone.

Pride warred with fear. She was trying to scare him, but that didn't mean she was wrong. There *were* dangers. Though, to be fair, *not* walking first didn't necessarily mean that he would be safe, it just meant he probably wouldn't be the first target. But he probably wouldn't be the first target anyway. Any decent strategist would consider the knight a bigger threat than him. Correctly.

"I think I can manage." Davorin turned back to the path, eyes scanning the grasslands. Within a day or so, the grasslands would start dispersing as they reached the hills of Tradst. The hills not only marked the border between the Endless Grasslands and the Ocean of Sand, but also the boundary line between Graldish and Salardis.

For three days, the hills had been visible in the distance. If word was true, the hills were pitted with caves, many already inhabited. Wild cats, wild lizards, imps, and human bandits. It was a dangerous, desperate road, only surpassed by ocean travel.

Travel by boat could be faster, if one managed to avoid pirates, and if one could actually afford a boat in the first place. Graldish had never had an abundance of lumbar. When ocean routes were available, they could buy ships and boats from some of the nearby islands, some of which had once been part of Graldish. Not since fighting broke out with the Trovians. Some fishing boats remained, mostly in lakes and bays, avoiding the open waters. Some risked life and limb to farm on the closest islands. Many didn't come back.

No, as dangerous as land travel was, water travel was still worse, and that was without considering the forces of nature. But right now, everything seemed safe enough. For the moment. Walking slowly, eyes searching in every direction, Davorin led the party. Nothing would escape his attention.

"Hey, look!" The thief called out. Davorin didn't jump and anyone who said he did was lying. Quickly, he turned his attention to where she was pointing.

Off in the distance were unicorns. Three of them. Two fighting, horn banging against horn. The third, smaller, with less of a horn, watched. None of the unicorns were paying any attention to them.

"Mating fight," the thief nodded. "The one to the side is female. She's waiting to see who wins."

"Better not get close. Unicorns are aggressive enough under normal circumstances," Sir Jors added.

"Aw, I wanted to see if our necromancer could tame them." The thief didn't seem inclined to move, though. "We should be far enough away that they'll ignore us unless we do something that makes them feel provoked or threatened."

Vaguely, Davorin recalled her saying something about him trying to tame unicorns forever ago when their journey began. Apparently, she hadn't forgotten. But she didn't seem to believe that he could do it any more than she seemed to believe he could do any of the things she threatened the outlaws with. He didn't think he could do any of that either. For all that the legends said that a battle between necromancers had created the Dead Lands, Davorin was well aware that his power was weak.

He had animated three skeletons at the same time to prove his power before the king, but, in the thief's terms, he hadn't so much as summoned a shade since. He hated talking to shades. And yet, he was considered the strongest necromancer in the kingdom.

The scholar looked to be fighting back a blush. "Perhaps we should take a rest here, just in case. We can move on when they're gone."

"Fair enough. We'll build a fire this time. As you say, in case." The knight started clearing a section of grass, so they had room to build a fire without setting a wild blaze to devour the countryside.

With all of them helping, the fire was soon up. Sir Jors looked at the party, looked at the fire, and sighed. It was quiet, perhaps unintended, but they all heard him. Lakara was, predictably, the only one who bothered to ask him what was wrong. "It's nothing."

"Then you wouldn't have sighed," the thief said.

"Nothing important." He considered them, then continued. "The best part of campaigning is the campfires. Stories are told, songs are sung. In the army, they say you don't know a person until you've shared a hundred fires with them. We've shared several fires, but we don't know each other."

Davorin was fine with that. He didn't need to know these people, he just had to travel with them. The thief didn't seem interested either.

The scholar did. "That's a wonderful idea. What kind of stories?"

"Any you like. Some tell personal stories, some tell myths and legends, parts of history, anything that interests them."

"Fine, you can start." The thief leaned back into the side of one of the lizards, currently black.

Sir Jors thought for a moment. "Alright. Who wants to hear...? No, not that one. How about the time my brother and I decided we were going to tame a pack lizard?"

"You have a brother? Younger?" The scholar asked.

The knight smiled sadly and shook his head. "Older."

Knighthood was generally hereditary, going to the oldest son, rarely the oldest daughter if no sons lived. If Sir Jors was a knight, which he clearly was, either he had done something extraordinary enough to be granted a knighthood, something Davorin would have heard of; or his brother was dead, leaving him the title. Judging from the fact that Davorin had never heard of him before this expedition and the look on his face, it was the second. The women must have come to the same conclusion, as they both dropped the subject.

"So, taming a pack lizard? I'm imagining that didn't work out so well for you," the thief said, pulling her hair away from Longtail's mouth.

Sir Jors laughed. "No, no it did not. Anor was twelve and I would have been about eight. One of the other families in the village had recently purchased a young pack lizard, and their son, about Anor's age, was constantly bragging about how he was going to train the lizard which would be his specifically. Now, our family had pack lizards, but they were family lizards, not my brother's or mine. Anor had always had a rivalry with this boy. Otari was his name, I believe. I tended to follow Anor around like a shadow, so sometimes I got drawn in as well. Anyway, Anor knew our parents wouldn't give him, or even us, a pack lizard. Father had been injured by one when he was a young child, and a couple of years before I was born, there were claims in a nearby village that a small girl was killed by a lizard. I don't know if it was true or not, but my parents seemed to believe it. We were forbidden to go near the lizards without supervision."

"And you always listened?" The thief smirked.

"Not in the slightest." The knight admitted with a smile. "After all, we were young, convinced we were invincible. We were also quite lucky. Knowing what I know now, I wouldn't have let us near them, either. Though, I don't believe all the horror stories I've heard. Pack lizards can be aggressive, yes, but if they were as dangerous as some claim, there wouldn't be a single tame one in the kingdom. Anyway, Anor decided that to beat Otari in this matter, we would have to catch and tame our own lizard."

"Pack lizards are native to Salardis. I don't know where you grew up, but wouldn't that have been too difficult a trip for young children?" Lakara asked.

"It would indeed. We lived in Skartow."

"Medium-sized village about eight days southwest of Wris?" the thief asked. "Been there. Nice enough place, but not a good spot for pack lizards."

"That's the one. Perhaps fortunate for our plan, neither Anor nor myself had paid much attention to geography. Or biology. We were both of the impression that only a day or two out of the village would be lizards galore. We'd be able to take our pick of the herd, tame it, and bring it home, being hailed as heroes. Otari would be so jealous."

Lakara was trying to hide her laughter. "You made it to Alegna, didn't you?"

Pack lizards might be native to Salardis, but that didn't mean they couldn't be bred in Graldish. Dotting the country were small communities, usually called lizard villages, whose livelihood depended on the lizards. Breeding them, training them, selling the byproducts, etc. Alegna was one of those, famous for pack lizards trained for the army, especially the pack lizards that were used to fight, not just transport goods. Unlike most breeders, they didn't train the aggressiveness out of the lizards the way those who sold pack lizards for travel, food, or leather did. The lizards were also bigger and stronger. And Alegna was only twenty miles from Skartow.

"We did. We did indeed. It took us three, almost four days to do it. Our supplies had already run out, but at that moment, we didn't care. We had found our quarry. Now we just had to pick a lizard and tame him. We saw the village and figured they would be grateful for one less lizard to cause trouble. So, we picked the largest one we could find. He was sunning himself on a rock, a ways apart from the others. Anor had a rope, and we tied a loop into it, and tried to throw it to catch the lizard around the head."

That couldn't have gone well at all. The women looked to be trying not to laugh. Sir Jors seemed amused, too. "Did you succeed?" asked the scholar.

"Unfortunately, yes." That was enough to spark laughter throughout the whole party. Sir Jors wasn't able to continue his story for a few minutes. "It took countless tries, but Anor finally roped the lizard. Who noticed and was not pleased. At all. Anor and I started pulling, trying to herd the lizard towards us; while the lizard pulled, trying to drag us towards him. He was winning when the rope broke. That's when he charged us. Are you aware of how fast an angry pack lizard can move? A lot faster than two foolish boys, I can tell you. That was when we realized we were in trouble."

"You could have been killed," The scholar said with a wince.

"We could have been," the knight agreed. "We were fortunate. You see, we weren't quiet in our attempt to capture the lizard and attracted the attention of the herdsmen. Just when it looked like the lizard might indeed eat us, they came and commanded him back. With difficulty. Apparently, in our utter folly, we had chosen the most stubborn, aggressive lizard they had. They kept him for… stock because they couldn't train him enough to be useful for the military."

"Then you had to deal with angry herdsmen, whose livelihood you had just threatened," the thief predicted.

"We considered that better than dealing with the lizard. Initially." Sir Jors chuckled in memory. "They questioned us about who we were and what we thought we were doing and got the whole story from us. A runner was sent to inform our father of our whereabouts, then they gave us food and water, before putting us to work, cleaning the lizards' sleeping quarters. Father was only a day behind us, having figured out our plan, and arrived early in the morning. He paid them for their trouble and supplies and agreed that we would work another day at whatever tasks assigned to compensate them. Once home, both our parents promised to whip us both soundly if we ever did anything that stupid again."

"Did the other boy mock you?" The thief asked.

"Anor more than me, but yes. At least until they moved on to the next point of competition." He stood. "The unicorns are gone. We should probably move on. If we get another few miles in, we can probably shelter the night in a Traveler's Hut."

Since the sky was promising to rain at any moment, that was a worthy consideration.

***

As they approached the hills, Sir Jors insisted they make the most of the water sources they could find. The Endless Grasslands existed in part because of rains that didn't go past the hills, but even more because of the countless streams, creeks, and brooks that filled the area. The Ocean of Sand had neither the rain nor the boundless springs of groundwater. It wasn't devoid of water, or no one could survive there for long, but water was valuable and harder to find, even for the natives, let alone a group of Graldian visitors. Not being able to count on finding water on a daily basis, they would have to ration it carefully.

Fortunately, the lizards would be well suited to the drier climate. However, Stripes was still drinking more than Longtail. Well, perhaps the lizards would be able to help them find water.

Sir Jors was surprised and pleased that he had set an example when he told a story around the fire. Lakara had gone next, but had not been able to think of anything of her time as a scholar that she thought would be of interest to the rest of them. When he reminded her that sometimes the storyteller would recount myths and legends, histories or tales of the gods, she perked up.

"Oh, I could tell the story of how Vicaw and Tratow invented the javelin?"

"Certainly," Sir Jors agreed. "It's a favorite of mine."

"Right. Long ago when the land was young, Vicaw, goddess of victory, and her brother, Tratow, god of air, decided to visit a village in disguise. They wanted to see which of them the mortals honored more. As it happened, the village was in the midst of a famine. And so, instead of calling on Vicaw or Tratow, the mortals were entreating the mercy of Skoses, god of earth, begging for a rich crop. Annoyed by this, Vicaw and Tratow separated to try to persuade the mortals to call on them instead. Tratow brought a large flock of birds. For two days, the village had enough to eat and praised Tratow. Then the birds were gone, and the village was as hungry as before and went back to entreating Skoses. Vicaw led a team of hunters to success in hunting. For two days, the village had enough to eat and praised Vicaw. Then the meat was gone, and the village was as hungry as before and went back to entreating Skoses."

Sir Jors stiffened. How could he have forgotten? There was a reason he had decided against sharing about his first hunt. But it was too late to stop her now.

"Vicaw and Tratow, unable to win their competition, were angry and bitter. They left the village and entered the forest. A tree blocked their way and in a fit of anger, Vicaw picked up the tree and threw it. Tratow caught it with his winds, blowing it even further before letting it fall, frightening a herd of deer."

Sir Jors eyed the audience. No negative reactions. Interesting.

"As the herd ran away, the gods stood, considering. Now, there were many deer in the area, but no man could run as fast as a deer, and the deer were so nimble that they avoided any trap. No mortal could throw as far as a deity, nor could they control the winds. But a mortal could throw. Experimenting, they found that a thrown shaft could travel far and fast. A sharpened wooden shaft could be thrown, even by a mortal, allowing them to hunt prey they could not race or win against a distant enemy. Going back to the village, not in disguise, Vicaw and Tratow presented their invention, telling the mortals that this would allow them to hunt enough to keep them fed until the crops grew. As neither could agree on a name for their weapon, they named it after the town, Javel. And thus, we have the javelin."

Davorin was clearly familiar with the story and Kita might or might not have known it before. But neither acted like it was a strange story to tell. He would drop a small warning to Lakara at some point in private. Perhaps. As long as there was some degree of peace, it might be best not to stir up conflicts.

"Thank you for your story. Kita, would you like to go next?"

That surprised the girl. "Me? I don't have nice stories to tell. You know the histories, the tales of the gods much better than I ever will. And you don't want to know about my life."

"You could tell why you said you haven't been a child since you were five. That's an extremely specific number," Davorin said.

"That *is* specific," Lakara agreed.

Sir Jors hid a wince. He hadn't heard Kita say anything like that but could only guess that meant something horrible had happened when she was five. Didn't the other two realize that?

Lakara was the next to make the connection. "But you don't have to tell us if you don't want to. It doesn't matter."

Kita stared into the fire. "It was the first time I stole something. That's all."

"What could you have possibly done at *five*?" Davorin asked. "*Why* would you do that?"

Since Sir Jors vividly remembered stealing fruits from trees and vines that didn't belong to his family at that age and a little older, he doubted Kita could be blamed for that. He opened his mouth to say so, but she was speaking already.

"My mother was sick. Too sick to get out of bed. I had found a dou in the road. I figured if I could buy food, she would get better. Wasn't like I knew how to get medicine."

"But if you bought it, that's not theft," Lakara said.

Kita shrugged. "The baker didn't believe a filthy street girl could have a dou without stealing it. He took it from me, hit me hard enough to knock me flat, and told me to run away before he turned me over to the soldiers."

It was a sad, but not surprising tale. Well, not surprising to him. Davorin winced and Lakara looked aghast. "He did *what*? How could he...? What did you do?"

"I ran, of course. But he had taken my treasure and I still had no food. So, I went back, going in the store with a mother and her young children. He never noticed me taking a loaf of round bread and a meat pasty." She gave a wry smile. "I took those home, then went off to the butcher, stole a piece of soup stock beef, and disappeared into the crowd."

"Did your mother recover?" Sir Jors asked, being careful not to make any moral implications on her actions. She wouldn't want to hear them, and he didn't think he was in a position to judge.

"She did. That time. A few years later, we weren't so lucky."

"What about your father? Couldn't he help?" Lakara

asked.

Even Davorin winced at the scholar's naivete that time. There was likely a reason Kita had made few mentions of her father and none at all in this story.

"He Never-Was."

Like that one. Admittedly, it wasn't a reason he had thought of, but it was a definite reason. If her father had already been declared a Never-Was before Kita was five; that would explain several things. Such as her protectiveness of the items she had of his. And her seeming ignorance. It might be true ignorance, instead of pretense.

"I'm sorry. I didn't..."

Kita waved a hand. "It was long ago. It doesn't matter now."

Lakara bit her bottom lip. "My parents are attendants at the palace. If I hadn't been born during the Festival of Learning and shown skill as a scholar, I would be an attendant there too."

Now that surprised Sir Jors. Lakara had never once mentioned her parents. But then, she had always seemed a little class-conscious. Perhaps she didn't want to admit that her parents were barely better than servants.

"I was left as an infant at Shadow Master's temple in Corvis. Clearly, my parents, whoever they were, were devout, but not willing to raise a necromancer," Davorin admitted.

That was even more unexpected. Sir Jors would have bet money against the necromancer being willing to share something that personal. Davorin was lucky. Necromancers, powerful as they might be, were considered extremely unlucky. Only three were known to exist on the entire continent. Considering that hundreds of years ago, there were so many that a fight between them permanently destroyed a large swath of land, Sir Jors suspected that most necromancers didn't survive infancy, and probably not for natural reasons.

No one said anything of consequence after that until there was a general consensus to retire for the night. Sir Jors tried to sleep as Davorin took the first watch, but sleep was elusive. Vaguely, he thought he heard the necromancer talking to someone, but who? Not one of the women, and there was no one else around. Maybe he talked to the lizards when he thought no one else could hear.

Time passed. And passed. And passed. Eventually, he gave up and relieved Davorin early. It was a quiet night, what was to be their last night in Graldish for months. At least.

When Lakara woke to take her shift, he debated offering to finish the night. He doubted he would be able to sleep at all. But perhaps he was wrong. Even a little sleep would be better than none.

Sir Jors decided that might have been a mistake when the snatches of sleep he did catch were full of sharp teeth and black claws. Still, he was up and moving before his tentmate, and the women were having another reading lesson, so neither noticed any signs of sleeplessness. By the time they decamped, he felt he had successfully hidden any hints of fatigue.

The hills were just dangerous enough that they risked injury, without being dangerous enough for him to push his exhaustion aside. They let the lizards pick the path, following the agile climbers. Some had more difficulty than others, but by the time they stood in Salardis, none of them had acquired more than a few scrapes.

Sand spread before them in an endless sea. Bright enough to sting the eyes, monotonous enough that it was hard to tell where one dune ended, and another began. Light enough that their feet sank into it, and hot enough to burn. For a minute or two, they just stood there, trying to get used to the sand.

"We need to find a road. Walking will be easier on that," Davorin said, wiping his eyes.

"There's also more chances of bandits and patrols. People who will want to know what we're doing here. Staying off the road is safer," Kita argued. Thanks to her dark glasses, she was the only one who wasn't constantly wiping or guarding her eyes.

"We can make up our mind when we find a road. Let's move on," Sir Jors said.

Walking was more difficult. With every step, his feet sunk into the shifting sands. After a while, he noticed he was actually having the most difficulty with that, probably because his armor made him heavier than the others.

They had made ridiculously little progress, but Sir Jors was still about to take a break when Kita stiffened. "What's that?"

He looked in the direction she was staring but didn't see anything except sand swirling in the wind. No, not the wind. Something was moving in the sand. A moment later, he heard it too. A whistling chatter. Sir Jors drew his sword. Sure enough, small, black, scaly hands were becoming visible. Imps. "To arms, now!"

By the time he could get the words out, hundreds had appeared. A swarm. Sir Jors stepped in front of the party, sword steady, when he felt it. Sleep was overtaking him. *No. Not now! Vicaw, please! We'll die if I fall now.* But it was too late. The last thing he saw was the front line of imps closing in on them.

***

Lakara gripped her staff in bloodless fingers as she saw the creatures approach. She racked her brain for everything she knew about imps. Small creatures, about the size of a rabbit, bipedal, intelligent but not sentient, aggressive, especially when they came in swarms. The Queya, in particular, hated them, making Queya generational weapons uniquely skilled against imps. A large enough swarm of imps could render a human to a skeleton in minutes. Possible hive mind, so the only way to drive off a swarm was to kill enough that they decided it wasn't worth it and broke off the attack.

To her side, Davorin was cowering behind the lizards, whimpering like a kitten. Kita was snapping at him, as she unmuzzled the lizards. "Hey, Bone Mage! If you are a real necromancer, or even a real man, then stand and fight!" He moaned and flinched into himself. "Muddy useless!"

"Sir Jors, what do we do?" Lakara asked. They needed him to take charge. Maybe they could still pull this around. Pack lizards ate imps, that would help. Kita had her dirk, Sir Jors his sword, and Lakara was far enough away that she wouldn't hit anyone with her staff. "Sir Jors?" He wasn't moving.

Kita looked at the knight and frowned. She waved a hand in front of his face. "He's asleep!"

"What? He can't be asleep!" They were going to die. They were all going to die, torn apart by imps.

Kita scowled, first at the knight, then the necromancer, then the lizards, before looking to the hills. "We have a chance if we run to the caves. Run!" She pushed at Lakara's arm to urge her back to the hills.

"But what about them? They'll die!"

"We can't save them. We can't even lift the knight, and we'll never make it if we try to drag the necromancer. Just run!" Again, Kita tried to shove Lakara to the hills.

Lakara swung the staff at her, causing the thief to back up. "We can't leave them to die. We fight."

"Then we all die!" She looked from the oncoming imps to the hills. "Last chance!"

"You run and I'll kill you myself. Now stand and fight." Lakara glared her down.

With a snarl and several curses, the thief backed away, turning to face the imps. "We're all going to die. And it's your fault."

The first wave came. Lakara swung out and knocked a few back, but one of the imps grabbed her staff and wouldn't let go until she stabbed her staff into the ground. Kita danced among them, her blade dripping blue blood. The lizards seemed to be enjoying themselves, going after the imps with wild abandon. But it wouldn't be enough. None of it would. Kita was right, they would all die.

She swung again as the imps crowded in. Then a sword cleaved the air. Sir Jors waded into the fray, blade singing in the wind. "He woke up," Lakara gasped as she took out another two imps.

Kita spared a second to look, not missing a step of her deadly dance. "No, he's still asleep. Stay by the lizards, so you don't get surrounded."

Lakara followed her advice, bashing another imp. It did give her a little room to maneuver and watch the others. Davorin was still whimpering and moaning, but the imps hadn't come near him yet. Kita kept from being overwhelmed mostly by constant movement, jumping from one spot to another, and kicking any imp that got too close that her blade couldn't reach. Sir Jors was making repetitive, blocky movements, but between his armor and the size of his stroke, the imps weren't causing any damage.

The next wave wasn't as enthusiastic and the wave behind that was even more reluctant. But Lakara could barely swing her staff anymore and Kita was definitely slowing. Sir

Jors hadn't slowed down, but there was red in his wake, so he must be injured. Davorin was still lost in his fog of fear. Even the lizards were slower, not bothering to eat any more imps, just bite and scratch.

Just when Lakara thought they would be overcome, the imps turned and ran. Kita stopped, slumping over and breathing hard. Sir Jors kept moving, sword swinging. The blood seemed to be coming from his leg, but Lakara wasn't willing to check on him until he woke up. Or at least stopped swinging his sword around.

Kita trudged back to the lizards, drank a little water, and sat down, leaning on Longtail. "How long do you think until he comes out of it?"

Lakara ignored her. How could Kita have even suggested they leave the others to die? How could she trust her after that?

Being ignored didn't seem to bother her. Instead, she turned to Davorin. "Hey, Bone Mage! They're gone. You can quit your muddy flailing now."

Davorin gave no sign of having heard her. Kita gave a scoff of exasperation and leaned into the lizard. "Wake me when they're back to normal. Or if we face more imps."

Lakara stared at her in disbelief for a moment, before going back to ignoring her. Sir Jors was still moving. Hopefully, he would wake up soon.

Davorin came to himself first. The whimpering stopped, and he slowly sat up, shaking as he looked around. "We... We're still alive?"

She was tempted to say something stinging in rebuke, even if he did outrank her, but said nothing. Kita wasn't so circumspect. "Oh, yes. Thank you for the massive help."

Sir Jors seemed to be coming back to himself, so Lakara abandoned the other two to their argument to check on him.

He came to a stop about two hundred yards from their 'camp', and stood there, looking around.

Making sure she was far enough back that he couldn't hit her, Lakara called out to him, "Are you alright?"

He spun and looked at her. "You're alive?" He looked at the lizards and the others fighting. "We all survived? How?"

"I honestly don't know. You were fighting in your sleep."

He paled. "I see."

"How long have you been able to do that?"

"I didn't know I could. When I fell, I feared we would all be killed. Kita? Davorin?"

"Neither are hurt. Davorin panicked. He's only been up and about a minute more than you."

"Are you injured?"

"I'm not, but you're bleeding. We need to check that out." Lakara looked back. They were still fighting. She turned back to Sir Jors. "We have a problem. When the imps came, Kita tried to abandon us all."

Chapter Seven

Aftermath

Or

Trust and lack thereof

Kita ignored the uncomfortable silence as they continued walking. Silence had weight, something she had known since she was young, just as she knew that some silences were heavier than others. Their group was quiet half the time because they had little to say to each other. It wasn't quite a comfortable silence, but it wasn't bad either. There was the tired silence of the end of the day when no one really wanted to talk. That was a little less awkward. The silence they had mostly kept when they began their journey was very heavy, almost affecting the air itself, it felt like. But it had eased as time went by. Slowly, so slowly that she hadn't realized how much it eased until now, with a silence so much heavier.

The necromancer was quiet, as if he didn't want to be noticed. Even when they were arguing, he wasn't as sharp. Probably ashamed of his panic. As far as Kita was concerned, he was right to be ashamed. Things would have been a lot different if he hadn't been such a filthy coward.

The knight wasn't talking either, avoiding direct eye contact with all of them, but she was sure she felt him watching her. The scholar was angry. Mostly with her, for some reason, but also the necromancer, and she didn't seem pleased with the knight either.

Since she had no more desire to speak to them than any of them seemed to wish to talk to her, the silence was left unbroken for the rest of the day, except for comments on when to take a break and when to move on. It wasn't until they made camp for the night that things changed.

"I'm not sharing a tent with her," Lakara said, even before they had a fire built up, while they were still stacking the grass logs they had made in Graldish.

Kita startled, but didn't look up, trying to hide her hurt. She was angry at Lakara too, but not so angry to deny her somewhere to sleep. She lit the fire, watching from the corner of her eye.

Sir Jors looked between them. "We only have two tents, and we cannot fit three in a tent. Nor would it be appropriate, considering the circumstances."

"I don't care. I will not have her where I sleep. Not after she tried to betray us all."

"I did nothing of the sort!" How *dare* she try to twist the story?

"You said to leave them. You were willing to leave half our party to die!" Lakara snarled. "That's *betrayal*."

"I said to leave them because we couldn't save them. I did my best to save you, if you remember." Her argument wasn't getting through. "Think reasonably. Could the two of us, even working together, lift and move the knight more than a couple feet?"

"Probably not. My armor is heavy, and I outweigh you both," Sir Jors said, sounding mostly calm.

"Thank you! And the bone mage would have been only slightly easier to move." She ignored his sputtering. "We never would have made it! I haven't lived as long as I have without knowing when to walk away from the impossible."

129

"But you tried to save Lakara? How?" Sir Jors was the only calm one in the circle. Lakara still glared, face hard, and the necromancer was red in the face and mumbling.

"I tried to get her to run to the caves with me. It was the only chance I could see."

"So, you *would* just leave us to die," The necromancer sneered.

He backed down at her glare. "And if *you* hadn't cowered behind the lizards, whimpering like a baby, the *three* of us could have strapped the knight to one of the lizards and dashed for the caves together. With the lizards at the mouth, we would just have to take any imps that got over or around them. Between slings and close-range weapons, we would be at little risk. We would *all* have been safe."

There was silence for a few minutes. "A sound strategy," Sir Jors agreed. "That might well have worked."

"So, you're just fine with this?" Lakara asked, sounding outraged.

"I can see why she made the decision she did, even if it wasn't the decision I would have made in her place. But one more question. Kita, you said you tried to convince Lakara to run. Clearly, she refused." Kita nodded. "Why didn't you run and leave her there?"

"I threatened to kill her if she ran, that's why," Lakara mumbled.

"You had a staff?" Lakara agreed. Sir Jors went back to Kita. "I would bet my second-best suit of armor that you could outrun her with a staff. If you chose to run, right then, you would have almost certainly gotten away. Why did you stay?"

Kita had been asking herself the same thing ever since the attack. She had her pack, and she could have escaped to Graldish. As long as she avoided Corvis, the muddy king probably wouldn't be able to track her down. If he even remembered her. If everyone else was dead, there would be no one to tell him of her escape.

It wasn't that she wanted the others to die, but why had she risked her life to stay? Especially when she had been certain there wasn't a way out.

When she didn't answer after several minutes, the knight nodded. "I see. Lakara, why did you say she betrayed *all* of us?"

"Isn't it obvious? I told you what happened."

"You said that in a dire situation where it looked like we would all die, she wrote off the two of us who weren't moving as unable to be saved and tried to persuade you to do the same. Tell me, if I had lost a leg in the imp attack, would you leave me behind to continue the journey?"

"What? No!"

"Why not? I could no longer fulfill my duty, the protection of the party. To take me anywhere, you would have to sacrifice supplies, decreasing the survival chances of the party as a whole. In addition, there would be a large chance I wouldn't survive more than a couple days after the injury anyway."

"But we couldn't leave you to die in the desert," Lakara said, horrified.

"Even if I told you to?"

"I..."

"We could probably get you at least as far as the next town. You could receive medical care and either wait there to see if we came back or make your way back home when you recovered," Kita suggested.

"Alright, suppose I had lost my leg and we were low on

water. The only way to survive would be to find water quickly. I wouldn't be able to move quickly enough to keep up. You would literally have to choose between my life and the lives of the rest of the party."

Lakara wrapped her arms around herself looking white and shaky. "That's not going to happen."

"You can't promise that. You are the leader and may be called to make a decision like that at some point. And I would be the first to tell you to abandon me to save the party as a whole. As I said, Kita's decision might not have been mine, but I've known military leaders who would have done similar. Not because of hate or betrayal or cowardice, but because they saw that as the way to save those who could be saved. Do not mistake me, I am grateful that you were willing to face the fight with me, but I would have told you to run."

"But you said you wouldn't. Isn't that hypocritical?" Lakara asked.

"My mission is our safety. If I have to sacrifice my life to accomplish that, I will."

At least someone understood. It was enough that Kita changed her mind about asking what happened to him. It didn't matter, anyway. Lakara asked.

***

Sir Jors carefully didn't wince. He had known this would happen since they left Corvis. He hadn't anticipated having a spell at such a catastrophic time, but he had known it would be impossible to keep his secret forever. In fact, he had nearly been caught a few times now.

"I have been touched with Aloses's sleep curse. Sleep is elusive at night but may come on suddenly without warning at any time."

"I've never heard of that," Kita said.

"I have," Lakara said. "It's rare, isn't it? Very, very rare."

"It is. You said I fought in my sleep? Some with this sleep curse have been observed performing simple, repetitive motions. I presume my fighting was not very skilled?"

"Skilled, no. But your swing was large," Kita said. "I certainly didn't want to get close."

"And you were right not to. To my knowledge, I've never done that before. But considering the circumstances, knowing we were about to be attacked, I'm not completely surprised it happened." Perhaps it was a gift from Vicaw.

"I've caught you sleeping, haven't I? At least twice now."

No point lying now. "Yes."

"Wonderful. Just wonderful! We've got a necromancer who cowers when things get dangerous, a knight that could fall asleep at any moment, and a thief who's willing to abandon the rest of us as soon as a threat appears." Lakara huffed.

"And we're led by a scholar who doesn't understand anything that isn't in a book and is willing to kill the entire party rather than leave someone who's doomed," Kita snapped back. "I don't even care if you *are* willing to share a tent with me. Tonight, I'm not willing to share a tent with *you*."

Sir Jors rubbed his temples. "Fine. Just, fine. Let's go to bed before we strain things beyond repair."

Everyone gave him a look as if to say it was too late. Still, no one spoke. Kita took her bedroll and spread it out close enough to the fire to catch the warmth but not so close as to be in danger of sparks, using her pack as a pillow. She completely ignored Lakara fumbling with one of the tents by herself, or Davorin and Sir Jors setting up the other. As they finished, Davorin sneered at her, but didn't say anything as he sat to take his watch. Sir Jors retreated to the tent to take his rest.

He was pleasantly surprised to fall asleep quickly and

deeply enough that he actually had to be woken to take his watch. The desert was cold after dark, colder than the grasslands had been. Shivering, he tossed another grass log on the fire.

From the sounds of it, Davorin had already fallen asleep. Kita opened an eye when the bundle sparked, searched him out, then closed both eyes again. He would have left her alone to sleep, but unless he was mistaking things, there was a reflection of firelight caught on her face.

"Are you awake?" He asked, quietly enough that she could ignore him, pretending to be asleep if she didn't want to talk.

"No." She hunched into her bed roll.

He smiled lightly. "Do you want to talk?"

"Definitely no."

"That's fine. But I'm awake if you change your mind." Once he made the offer, he fell silent. It was his duty to stay awake, not hers. If she could manage to sleep, she should be left alone to do so.

Instead, he studied the stars. The Spear was nearly out of the sky and the Unicorn's Foal was starting to appear to the east. Winter was coming and fast. And they were headed north. It would have been wiser to send out the expedition in early spring. But King Zikkar ordered them to leave right away. How long had it been since they had left? A month? Not quite. Not yet. Soon though.

A little less than a month and it would be winter. Perhaps it would be wise to winter in Salardis rather than face the Mountains of Death at their most dangerous. It wasn't like they had been given a time limit.

"I wasn't betraying the party. I was saving who I could."

Sir Jors blinked in surprise. So, she did decide to talk. "I can understand that."

"She doesn't."

Ah, that's where the problem lay. Kita felt she was doing her part by trying to save Lakara. Lakara felt it was a betrayal to leave the others, Kita felt betrayed by Lakara's lack of understanding. To be fair, it was probably Lakara's opinion that mattered the most to her of anyone's. She definitely didn't seem to care what Davorin thought, and Sir Jors wasn't sure how much she cared about his own opinion. "Lakara is a scholar. She is trained to work with the other scholars as a group. One person doesn't succeed or fail, the group does."

Kita shifted to look at him. "That's ridiculous. How can anyone work that way?"

"That's what she was taught. Similar to what I was taught. To her, what you were suggesting was treachery."

"Alright, how about this? I was trying to make sure some of us survived to meet our goal."

"You've expressed doubt that the Jewel of Ishni even exists."

"But we're still going after it, aren't we? Besides, if it really does exist, it would probably be worth something."

Sir Jors shook his head. "It might at that. Not that you're going to be allowed to just take it."

Kita simply smiled.

"If Lakara couldn't move and I could, would you suggest we leave her?" Sir Jors asked, testing a hypothesis.

"You could carry her."

"That's not an answer."

"You wouldn't leave anyone who wasn't actively dying unless we would all die if you didn't."

"Also true, but still not an answer."

Kita frowned. "Why are you asking?"

"You and Lakara developed a friendship. She's been teaching you reading. You don't argue with her or insult her the way you do Davorin, who does the same to you. And she's never thrown your past in your face, that I've heard."

"Neither have you."

"Thank you. But it's different with Lakara. You spend the most time together, talk to each other the most, and share a tent. I'm wondering if you wanted to save Lakara, less because she was the only one still moving, and more because she is your friend, and you didn't want her to die."

Kita was silent for a long time, watching the fire. Just when he thought that she would never answer, she spoke again. "I don't want any of you to die. Not even the useless bone mage. But that doesn't mean I'm willing to die in your place. Or with you in a useless stand."

"Fair enough. But you and Lakara are friends."

"Were."

"Are. If you want to be. You're mad, she's mad, you'll both get over it. We've covered less than half our journey to find the jewel, and then we have to return. Even if it takes a few days, or even weeks, sooner or later, you two will forgive each other, simply because you have no choice but to put up with each other."

Kita humphed.

"Fine, I'll let you sleep, but do remember something. Anger is a burden, a heavy one, and hatred is an even heavier one. We don't have room for extra weight on this trip."

She didn't say anything to that. Still, Sir Jors was sure that the women would be able to salvage at least some of their friendship. They would just have to learn to trust each other again. It would probably happen faster than anyone in the party trusting him again.

***

It was two days after the imp attack that they reached Surduk. A long two days. The thief still slept outside a tent, which may or may not have been why Davorin hadn't seen his hawk friend recently. No stories were told. No one talked more than they had to. The women hadn't tried any more of those ridiculous reading lessons. In fact, he wasn't sure those two were talking to each other at all. Not that Davorin planned to get involved.

He was trying to avoid all mention of the imp attack, especially his actions and inactions during it. As much as he hated to admit it, all the others had some justification for their actions. The knight had been cursed. The thief wanted to do what he probably would have done if his brain and legs had worked for him instead of against him. The scholar was naïve enough to believe she was doing the right thing. Despite everything, all of them fought. He had fallen apart.

Davorin supposed he should be relieved that they made it to Surduk at all, especially with the enmity and awkwardness of the previous two days. But he wasn't. Surduk should have been a relief. It was in much better shape than Tediz or Klat, the last town they visited in Graldish. Klat had been in such bad shape that they didn't stay longer than the hour needed to buy more supplies.

Surduk was clearly much more prosperous than any of the places they visited recently. More like Corvis, in fact. Odd, considering that Surduk wasn't anywhere near the capital of Salardis. It wasn't even a major city if he understood correctly.

But it wasn't a relief to be here. The city crackled with distrust and paranoia. Considering how much the group had

137

been feeling the same, it was amazing they even noticed it in the city. But Davorin was quite sure that he wasn't the only one picking up the unwelcome feeling and wanting to leave.

No one talked loudly. No one offered hospitality and everyone watched everyone else carefully. As newcomers to the city, they were particularly under suspicion. For the first time in two days, their party closed ranks together, simply out of necessity.

"We need to get out of here. Quickly. Something's wrong with this city," the thief said.

"But what?" The scholar asked.

"I don't know, and I don't care to stick around long enough to find out. Let's pay our respects and move on." The thief's eyes darted around. "Same story as Tediz."

It would have to do if they were questioned. Not that what they were doing was illegal, but it was better to be discreet. Hence the code, 'pay their respects' instead of 'find the clue' which could only intrigue someone who heard it. Davorin couldn't remember who came up with that, but it was something they had all agreed upon where they could be overheard.

He was again wearing the thief's dark glasses, which, unfortunately, attracted a few strange looks themselves. However, he had seen at least one or two others who had something similar. It helped not to be completely unique, even if it was still very unusual. And it didn't cause the stir that revealing he was a necromancer would.

When they got to the temple, the knight offered to stay with the lizards while the rest searched. It seemed a better option than having the lizards stabled, being both cheaper and allowing them to leave faster, so the others agreed.

Tratow's temple was primarily open-air, mostly an

ornate courtyard surrounded by elaborate pillars. As Tratow was the god of air, birds were sacred to him. Hence why it was required to give thanks to Tratow before eating any sort of bird. Birds of all kinds thrived at Tratow's temple, where it was, of course, forbidden to harm them and they were often fed by the devout.

How would they find the clue? Earlier clues were scattered in various places, but often on or near the walls. There were no walls, and it could take hours to check every column. Even longer if they had to maneuver around the flocks of birds that filled the area. Taking that long would be an annoyance at the best of times, it would be much worse with everyone suspicious for unknown reasons.

"Where do we even begin?" He asked, not really expecting a solution.

"Buying some incense and food for the birds?" The thief suggested.

"Couldn't hurt. Perhaps Tratow would be more inclined to help us if we honored him in his temple." The scholar led the way to the priest and priestess who kept charge of the incense and bird food. It wasn't the most direct path as birds seldom moved much for mortals in the temple, and it necessitated some going around.

The incense was lit in the central altar, smoke wafting through the air, spreading a perfumed scent throughout. He and the scholar stayed until the incense was entirely consumed, as was traditional. The thief stayed for a moment or two, before taking some of the breadcrumbs and walking away.

Davorin ignored her, even if he was certain she was eating the breadcrumbs herself instead of offering them to the birds. He hadn't forgotten how she ate the sacrificial pomegranate at AKAF's temple.

But to his astonishment, when he turned to survey the temple, not only was the thief feeding the birds, but she also actually had two sparrows eating out of her hands, balanced on her fingers, and a crow on her head. She was smiling as she held absolutely still.

Lakara gasped, recognizing the significance as well as he did. Only one who had the blessing of Tratow would have such fortune with his birds. How could a street thief who did so little to honor or please the gods, who didn't even seem to care for their approval, have such a blessing? Yet it was unmistakable and might well be the first bit of luck they had gotten in weeks.

Davorin took a share of the breadcrumbs and knelt, offering it to the birds. None responded to the food in his hand until he dropped some in front of them. By the third try, the birds would peck at the food in his hands, but none actually came to rest on him.

The scholar didn't even try. She gently scattered the crumbs around her and left to start looking around the temple. When his share of crumbs was gone, Davorin joined her. The thief took the longest. When she joined them, she was playing with a black feather left behind.

Lakara was the one who spotted the symbol. It was part of the mosaic on the floor, which became evident when some pigeons moved out of their way. For the second time in ten minutes, Davorin found himself kneeling on the floor, as he copied it down, while the thief did the gods only knew what behind them.

"I recognize 'eye', and I think 'through'," Davorin admitted.

"Yes, I think it says, 'through the eye of the needle'; either that or 'the needle through the eye'."

"I'm going to hope for the first," the thief said from

behind them. Davorin turned to scold her, stopping when he saw her leaning against a pillar, stroking a pigeon that had landed on her hand. She had no more food with her, so the bird was staying simply because he wanted to. There was a small smile on her face as she lightly rubbed the chest feathers of the temple bird, and she seemed more relaxed than he had ever seen her.

"I think we all are. But I don't know what it means." The scholar turned around, freezing when she clearly noticed what he had.

"Time to go?" the thief asked.

Lakara nodded.

"Right. Go on, little bird." She removed her stroking hand and extended the other. The pigeon flew off, leaving a white downy feather floating behind him. The thief caught it before it hit the ground. She didn't look at them as she tucked the feather in her pouch and turned to leave the temple.

***

Lakara had barely been willing to look at Kita since the imp attack. She was still furious at her willingness to let the others die. Then the thief had the nerve to be angry at her for being angry. Lakara had been so upset that she hadn't slept at all that night. If she had, she would have missed an illuminating conversation Kita had had with Sir Jors.

In her fury, Lakara had pushed thoughts of that conversation away and focused on other things. Like the fact that no one was talking to each other or seemed to care enough to change that. No one trusted anyone else. She didn't trust the others to keep watch and only didn't put a stop to it because she couldn't afford to stay up all night every night herself. Unless she was mistaken, the other two felt the same way.

When they first left Corvis, she had felt safe, knowing

she was traveling with a brave knight and the most powerful necromancer in the land. She hadn't expected the knight to be cursed to drop off to sleep at random times or the necromancer to be a sniveling coward. It was the thief who worried her, and the thief had actually put her in the least danger. Even when Kita tried to flee, she wanted Lakara to go with her. When Lakara refused, Kita hadn't called her bluff and even gave her good advice that kept her alive.

But Lakara hadn't been forgiving. They had been traveling together for a month, but somehow it wasn't until today that Lakara realized Kita might have been her first friend. The other scholars at the palace weren't friends. Colleagues, yes, but she had never tried to cross over to friendly terms with any of them. And if any of them had made overtures of friendship to her, she had overlooked it completely. She doubted any of them would count her as a friend on any but the shallowest terms. Kita called her a friend, but even she had used past tense.

The longer things went like this, the worse the chances of reconciliation, but Lakara kept telling herself that she didn't care. She didn't want reconciliation. Kita certainly didn't seem to care. She barely looked at Lakara, slept every night by the fire without even a glance to the tent, and had spoken to her more since entering the city than she had the previous two days put together.

Lakara told herself that it wasn't a loss. Who would want to be friends with someone who would commit such base treachery? Bad enough she was foul-mouthed and uncouth. That could be justified by her upbringing. Bad enough she was a thief, according to Kita, that was mostly desperation. But that treachery...

But Kita didn't consider it treachery. She had an explanation. Not one Lakara could agree with, but one she could almost understand. At first, Lakara thought it was an excuse, but Kita seemed to be genuine. The last straw had been at the temple.

When Kita wandered away from the incense before it was extinguished, Lakara had brushed it off as another sign of her disrespect of the gods. But if Kita had such disrespect for the gods, why would Tratow bless her in such an obvious way? Not only had multiple birds actually landed on her, at least two left feathers behind, a clear sign of blessing. Why?

Davorin was able to entice the birds to eat from his hand, which was a good sign for him, as well. Lakara had never had the slightest luck with birds. Then again, she didn't particularly like animals of any kind. They tended to spread uncleanliness.

So, she hadn't been surprised by her failure to achieve any sign of blessing from the god, only by her companions' successes. But if the gods saw something worthwhile in them, perhaps it would be wise to keep an eye out herself.

Once they met up at the lizards, it was decided to split up again. "We're the wrong size for a traveling group. Too small for most, and too big for a single traveler or family. Two people attract less attention than four," Kita pointed out. "Sir Jors and I should go to the markets and meet up with you outside the city. You'll need to take the lizards."

"I agree," Sir Jors said, before anyone could protest. "The faster we are away from unfriendly eyes, the better."

She didn't like the idea, but she liked staying here even less. "Fine. Be quick." She took Longtail's harness, leaving Stripes, who they still hadn't managed to get looked at, for Davorin.

From the corner of her eye, she saw him grimace, but he took the harness and followed her. Carefully, they made their way through the wary crowd until they got to the gates of the city. No one stopped them, though Lakara was certain she felt the eyes of the guards upon them a few times.

Once out of the city, they walked about half a mile, before stopping to rest and wait. Kita and Sir Jors joined them quickly enough that they must have rushed through their shopping. Everyone looked relieved to be away from Surduk.

"I don't know what was wrong with that city. It should have been fine, seemed perfectly healthy. And well off. But it was so... oppressive," Lakara found herself babbling.

"I couldn't hear much, but there were whispers of spies," Kita said. "That would explain the fear and hostility."

"Spies? From where? Graldish and Salardis have been at peace for almost a hundred years, and I think they actually get along a little better with the Trovians than we do." There hadn't been any major conflict in the area since the Wars where Graldish and Salardis banded together against the Queya and the fear of a Trovian invasion. But the Queya almost never leave their woods now, and the Trovians almost exclusively remained on the sea.

Kita shook her head. "That's what I heard. No details."

"Well, we aren't spies, so we shouldn't have any trouble," Davorin said.

Kita snorted. "Unless 'spies' is noble's code for 'I don't like you so I'm accusing you.' Then we could well be stuck."

"Also, our reason for travel is not one we can give, and any story we may give means that we are actually lying. That could well make us seem suspicious." Sir Jors relieved her of Longtail's harness. "It might not be a bad idea to split up the group when we reach towns and cities or join with a larger expedition to defray suspicion."

"I don't know, each has a few problems. Splitting up is dangerous because we're weaker in smaller groups or alone. Joining another party? Then we're outnumbered and we need to provide reasons for doing so," Lakara mused aloud.

"Simply something to consider. It should be at least five days before we come across another town, and even longer before we reach one we absolutely must enter," Sir Jors said. "The next temple we need to visit is Shadow Master's in Juztoc, correct?"

Lakara nodded. Kita took Stripe's harness and simply started walking. It was late enough in the day that had the city been any more welcoming, they would have stayed the night at a local inn. Instead, they managed to put about five miles between themselves and the city before camping for the night.

As Kita built the fire, Lakara pulled out one of the tents and started setting it up. It was harder to do by herself, but she had gotten a lot of practice over the last few days. Kita hadn't been interested in helping to set up or tear down a tent she wouldn't be using, which Lakara had to admit was fair enough. No one said anything about her getting ready so early, but she did get a strange look or two.

Dinner was quiet just like the previous two days, and soon Davorin was preparing to take his watch. Lakara waited, watching for her moment. Just as Kita grabbed her bedroll, Lakara spoke, "Are you coming? It's easier for you to settle in the tent first, so I don't have to climb over you to take my watch in the morning."

Kita stared at her for a moment. It wasn't the most eloquent way to solve the problem, but it was the best she could think of. Lakara wasn't quite ready to apologize. She still thought she was right, even if she was willing to admit Kita might not have been completely wrong. But she was ready to move past it.

Fortunately, Kita seemed to discern what she really meant. "Sure. Can't deprive you of your beauty sleep, can I now?" Without another word, she unrolled her bedroll in her side of the tent and settled down to sleep.

Lakara took her place, gingerly, trying to read her mood. Well, they weren't necessarily friends again yet, but it was a start. Hopefully. But what if Kita was still angry and just didn't want to sleep outside anymore? What if she was even more angry at Lakara now? What if...

"Goodnight, Lakara," Kita said in a quiet mutter.

Lakara felt the edges of her lips start to rise. "Goodnight, Kita."

Chapter Eight

Unexpected Meetings

Or

"You know him?"

Davorin greeted the morning with mixed feelings. First, there was the very fact that it was morning. Early morning. Salardis, despite being further north than Graldish, tended to be hotter during the day and colder at night. Or at least, that was the case in the Ocean of Sand. After a day or two, they adapted by waking and breaking camp earlier in the day, resting when the day was at its hottest, then continuing until almost dark. It was still being debated if they were traveling more or less this way than they had in Graldish and how much other factors played. It helped them avoid the worst of sun poisoning and heat stroke, but it did mean getting up early.

On the other hand, waking up meant they had survived the night; something Davorin was no longer willing to take for granted. Not since the first night after Surduk when they had another imp raid in the middle of the night. Fortunately, it was a much smaller imp swarm, Sir Jors, who had been on watch, hadn't gone into a sleep, and the imps were afraid of the fire. He hadn't gone practically catatonic, that time, but it would be an exaggeration to say he was much help.

Davorin put those thoughts from his head and exited his tent for breakfast. It was gruel, as it had been for much of the journey. He supposed Lakara made it since she was the one keeping watch first thing in the morning. Well, after the first day, when the thief had taught her how to make it. Surprising no one, the scholar had not been taught how to cook when she lived in the palace. Which was probably why she always made some variant of porridge. She didn't know how to make anything else.

Davorin could have been in similar straits, as he could easily have ordered all his meals directly from the kitchen. But during his apprenticeship, his mentor had insisted he learn some cooking as well. According to her, knife techniques would serve him in good stead for rituals, and it was important to know how to feed oneself.

He helped himself to some of the gruel, noting with surprise that evidently the reading lessons had begun again. It had been almost a week without. The thief was getting better, he had to admit.

"King Restos the First established the Kingdom Tax in the third year of the Great Wars to pay for the cost of the army. Standard tax was three dou a year for every acre of land owned and two dou for the cost of a room. This led directly to the pop...oo...larity, popularity of the one-room cabin and the establishment of great halls that served multiple purposes. This tax was resended?"

"Rescinded. Removed from the law," Lakara corrected gently.

"Rescinded ninety years later, when the Great Wars were won, by King Virtus the Second. No kingdom-wide taxes have been placed on Graldish since." The thief paused. "That's not true. What about the King's Tax?"

"The King's Tax was established almost twenty years ago. This book was written before that. I think this book was written about thirty years ago," Lakara said.

The thief frowned. "But it's wrong. It should be fixed."

"It was true at the time. Anyone writing a history now would include the King's Tax. But this book is left as it is because it is representative of the time it was written. In a hundred years, anyone reading this book will know what was considered important at the time the book was written. Then they will read later books to see what changed." The thief still didn't seem satisfied, but Lakara encouraged her to keep reading.

"Actually, we should probably move on. Perhaps you can read more later." Sir Jors stood and started breaking down the camp.

The thief jumped to her feet. "Good idea. There's water nearby. If we're lucky, we can rest there at noon."

Lakara looked puzzled. "How do you know there's water nearby?"

The thief went still. Before Davorin could ask, Sir Jors spoke up. "Look at the horizon. Do you see how it's a muzzy gray-green over there? That's a good indication of plant life."

"And where there are plants," Lakara smiled. "There's probably water."

Which turned out to be the case. The closer they came, the more obvious it was that there was an oasis there. Unfortunately, it wasn't as close as it had seemed. Settling down for a break during the hottest part of the day when they could see trees in the distance seemed almost a cruel joke. But it was still hours away. Instead, they hoped to be able to camp there at night.

While they didn't attempt to set up tents for the midday rest, they did set some poles and drape cloth into a rough lean-to to give themselves some shade. Davorin tried to make himself as comfortable as possible in what shade they could get. Maybe he could doze a little. If he didn't melt in his robe. And if his companions would settle down and be quiet.

The thief was jittery and getting more so as the day went on. She kept watching the sky, too. Actually, looking back on it, she often watched the sky. But it was more obvious today. Still, she denied there was a problem when Lakara and Sir Jors asked. Every time they asked.

Well, if she wasn't going to admit to a problem, then what business was it of his? He had other things to worry about. Like how they would probably be racing the dark to get to the oasis and set up camp before it was too dark to see. Or that the next temple to visit was Shadow Master's and Davorin was trying not to think about how much that frightened him.

Suddenly a cry split the air. Davorin jumped, poking his head out of the lean-to in order to spot the source. Then he saw it. The hawk. His hawk friend. The hawk gave another cry and fell towards the earth. Davorin jumped to his feet and ran forward to catch it, exhaustion forgotten.

The thief outstripped him, catching the bird. "Whisper!"

For a moment, he was angry at the thief for daring to touch the bird he was almost considering his, and then shouting about whispering. Then he stopped as realization hit. *Oh, of course.* The bird was *hers*. That's why Davorin kept seeing him. His hawk friend had been following because of *her*.

"Kita, is that your bird?" Sir Jors asked, sounding confused as he moved closer for a good look.

"Yes, I've had him for three years. His wing is torn, he must have been attacked." The words came out in a breathless rush.

"Oh, I have a book of birds! I'll get it."

Of course, the scholar had a book about birds. Davorin shook his head. "I raise pigeons. I've seen torn wings before. Let me see."

The thief looked at him skeptically. "He doesn't like most

150

people."

He restrained a bitter laugh. "He seems to like *me* well enough. If you call bothering me for food while I'm on watch, liking me."

"He did?" The thief stroked the bird. "Come on, let us see the wing, please, Whisper?"

The hawk cried out but didn't attack either of them as she gently stretched out his injured wing. "Looks like he got in a fight with another raptor. The injury isn't deep. If we can prevent infection and wrap the wing so he doesn't use it until it heals, he should be fine."

"Can we use the yarrow tincture on him?" The thief asked, worrying her bottom lip.

"The book doesn't say," Lakara said.

"Yes. I use it on my pigeons." He looked between the bird and his concerned owner. "I need you to hold him very still. We don't want to make his injuries worse while trying to heal him."

She nodded, and carefully wrapped her arms around the bird, holding the wing extended. Whisper must have been well-trained. He shrieked as they treated him, but no one was scratched or pecked. Considering the damage a hawk could cause, Davorin was quite pleased that they avoided that.

Once his wing was wrapped, the thief set Whisper on her shoulder. "We should hurry so we get to the oasis tonight. Did he really bother you while you were on watch?"

Now that the emergency was over, Davorin found himself feeling betrayed. He had been thinking of the hawk as his. To find that the hawk already had an owner, and for it to be the thief of all people, rankled. Still, 'bother' wasn't quite the right word. Even now, he couldn't find himself wishing he hadn't met the bird. So, he was perhaps a little stiffer than needed when he answered. "I saw him several times. He was quite adept at conning food off of me." He was about to make a scathing comment about the bird's reflection of his owner, but never got the chance.

"I never saw him," said Lakara. "Not once."

"Nor I. Has he really been following us since Corvis?" What, neither of them? He had been the only one to know?

The thief gave a small smile. "He has." Then she took a deep breath. "Thank you for helping me with Whisper. He is very dear to me. I don't know what I would do if I lost him."

It was sincere, even if it lacked the usual forms. Whisper looked at him and called. Davorin forced himself to look, actually look, at the thief. She had streaks on her face where tears had been. "You are welcome... Kita."

***

Sir Jors warily eyed the hawk that seemed to be watching him from a rocky perch. He had nothing against birds in general, and even appreciated the use of hawks and falcons in particular. But there was something about this bird. It wasn't that it belonged to Kita. It wasn't even that the bird had somehow managed to follow them for weeks without his being aware of it, though that did leave a sour taste in his mouth. Well, maybe that was part of it.

But his biggest problem was just how intelligent the bird seemed. While he had never practiced falconry himself, he knew others who had. He had watched enough to get, what he thought, was a good impression of the birds. In his experience, the hawks and falcons used in falconry were a little smarter than a pack lizard and a little easier to train. Not by much, though. The falconers he knew would frequently keep their birds hooded when not confined or in use. They kept the birds on a tight rein. While he wouldn't expect Kita to have the knowledge or training of the proper way to train and care for a hawk, it would only make sense for her attempts to lead to a half-trained bird, wild and reckless.

Instead, the bird had followed them for weeks, leaving only the barest traces of his presence, even without Kita being able to give instructions. He had never heard of a bird that could be trusted to follow orders for longer than an hour or so. Never, even in the wildest tales he had heard of falconry, had he heard of a bird following vague orders for weeks at a time without reinforcement.

Whisper would have had to eat, drink, and sleep, without losing the party or being seen. Well, for the most part. Kita probably caught glances of him, and the bird apparently sought out Davorin for reasons even Kita was unaware of. As curious as he was why the hawk had chosen Davorin as a kindred spirit, that question was both unlikely to ever be answered and the least of his concerns.

Nor did he particularly need to know how Kita managed to acquire, raise, and train a hawk given her nomadic lifestyle. He was a little more curious as to why she put so much effort into hiding his existence, but he had a few guesses about that, too.

Falconry was the sport of the rich. While it was not illegal for someone outside nobility to practice it, if Kita had been caught with a trained bird, it was likely she would have been punished for her presumption and Whisper would have been confiscated. Possibly killed if he wouldn't respond to someone else's orders. The same would happen if someone suspected or claimed that she had trained the bird to help her steal, whether it was true or not. So, for both of their protection, Sir Jors could understand her determination to hide him.

And if there was even a single whisper of Borrowing... well, the less said about that, the better. However, it might explain the hawk's extraordinary intelligence, and that Kita could give or reinforce orders while not being physically there. If she was, like he suspected...

No. Unless and until he had reason to believe otherwise, he wasn't going to so much as think about that possibility. Let alone mention it to anyone else.

"Whisper? What are you doing?" Kita walked over, sweeping the bird up to her shoulder. "Watching the fire won't get you your food any faster." She stroked his chest feathers. "Don't worry, your wing will be fine in no time. Then you can catch your own dinner and not worry about making do with ours." She looked from the bird to Sir Jors, and for a second, he was struck by how close their eyes were in color. "Was he bothering you?"

Not wanting to confess his unease, or cause trouble when the group was *finally* beginning to get along again, possibly better than before, Sir Jors immediately denied any problem. "No, he's fine. Hungry, is he?"

Kita smiled. "Probably. He often is. And most of his usual prey is missing, even if he could hunt on his own." She pulled a bit of jerky out of her bag and offered it to the hawk, who took it with great enthusiasm. "Still, I'm sure he'll manage once his wing is fine."

"I'm sure. Mind you, keep him away from the pack lizards. Just to be safe." Neither lizard had made an aggressive move towards the bird yet, but Sir Jors had seen them eye him in an interested manner. Pack lizards could move deceptively quickly and were far from picky eaters. While a bird as smart as Whisper seemed to be would surely be fine if he could fly, he would, of necessity, be at a disadvantage while grounded.

She shot a suspicious look at the pack lizards, as one hand flew up as if to ward any harm away from the bird. "Don't even think about it." One of the lizards gave an unimpressed yawn. "Yes, you. I will turn you into boots if you try."

"That would make traveling very difficult," Sir Jors said, stroking his beard to hide his smile. "True, we would have boots to trade, probably several pairs, but we'd have no way to transport them. I'm afraid we need the lizards."

Lakara, probably having missed most of the previous conversation as she approached, seemed horrified. "Of course we need the lizards! We'd probably die before we reached the next town without them."

Kita shrugged the shoulder that didn't have a hawk on it. "You just like to travel the easy way. You'd be amazed how far you can get without a pack lizard." She picked up their cooking pot. "Come on, Whisper. You can help me find water."

Lakara watched in disbelief before turning to Sir Jors, "She wasn't serious about… the lizards, was she?"

Honestly, Sir Jors wasn't going to kid himself about having any idea of what Kita would do if she felt pushed too far. "I doubt it. Besides, it matters little. She threatened the lizards about what she would do if they tried to eat her hawk. I have great faith that she will not be careless enough to risk Whisper like that, especially before his wing is healed."

She thought about that for a moment before nodding. "You're right. So, it doesn't matter." Then she cocked her head. "How far *can* one travel without a pack lizard?"

"Since a pack lizard only makes it possible to take more things with you as you travel, I would have to say, indefinitely. It would clearly be harder and less comfortable. More dangerous as well, since you cannot take as much food and water with you. But theoretically, any distance that could be traveled with a pack lizard, could be traveled without one."

The scholar shook her head. "Remind me never to travel without a pack lizard. Actually, you won't need to. When we get back to the palace, I doubt I'll ever want to travel again."

Sir Jors hid a smile. Yes, of the party, Lakara was the least traveled of any of them. He had traveled in the army, Davorin admitted to vague memories of his confirmation in Shadow Master's temple in a different city, and Kita couldn't remember spending more than a season in the same place since she was about ten. But Lakara had never left Corvis, had barely left the palace, her entire life before the quest. "You may find you miss it, eventually."

She looked at him as if he was trying to convince her that the lizards spoke to him when no one was around. "What could I possibly miss about this? My feet are in constant pain. My blisters are just starting to heal. I have never been so unclean in my life. I am separated from the library, my favorite place to be. Food and water have to be rationed, and there are a million dangers on the way."

"Is that all that bothers you?"

"Isn't that enough? What else?"

Sir Jors didn't look at her, choosing to watch the horizon where Kita, evidently having found water, had somehow pulled Davorin into helping her fetch it. Even from a distance, he could tell they were bickering, but neither were getting worked up about it, so he felt no need to intervene. "You said nothing about your travel companions."

"My..." Lakara was silent for a moment. From the corner of his eye, he could see her turn and smile as Davorin took the cooking pot from Kita and marched forward, Kita radiating smugness behind him. "Well, maybe."

"Maybe what?"

"Maybe the companionship I would miss. Eventually." She winced as they got close enough that their argument was audible. "Some people I might miss sooner than others."

"Indeed. Suppose we help them before our water

becomes a casualty of their latest squabble?"

"Good idea."

***

Kita cooed nonsense words to the bird as she checked the bandages. Thanks to the daily treatment of yarrow, no infection had occurred, and the damage seemed to be healing quickly. To her surprise and relief, no one had said a word about her using their limited supplies on a bird. Whisper didn't like it, that was obvious, but Kita was grateful to have it and that no one complained. She probably wouldn't stop just because someone complained, but no one so much as questioned it. In fact, everyone seemed interested, in varying amounts, in his recovery.

Lakara seemed to ask to be polite since she didn't seem to actually like Whisper much more than she did the lizards. But she didn't say anything about Whisper sleeping in the tent and even talked to him sometimes. In fact, Kita was fairly sure she had seen the scholar slip him some food on at least one occasion.

Sir Jors watched Whisper a lot. Which seemed to be mutual. Kita hadn't found a good time to do a deep enough Borrowing to find out what that was about. She was going to have to be a lot more careful about Borrowing now, especially since they knew about Whisper. Sir Jors asked about the bird at least daily. Possibly to be polite, or possibly to know when he would be flying again. Maybe he wanted Whisper to help with the hunting.

Her biggest surprise was Davorin. She would have expected him to kick up a fuss about wasting supplies, both food and medicine, on a bird. *Her* bird, moreover. Or at best, ignore Whisper entirely. But apparently, his claim that Whisper had visited him before was true, and Davorin cared. Half the time he was there when she changed bandages or applied yarrow to the wound. He talked to Whisper without any signs of feeling self-conscious and didn't hesitate to share food with him.

For Whisper's part, he seemed to judge Davorin a favorite. If he wasn't on her shoulder or watching Sir Jors, Whisper was usually near the necromancer. Yesterday, Davorin had even walked next to her for over an hour, telling Whisper about the pigeons that he kept at home. Kita did her best not to react to anything he said, afraid that if she drew attention to herself, he would stop talking, realizing the awkwardness of talking to a bird perched on the shoulder of someone he despised.

Or did he still? He called her by name now. Something he hadn't before Whisper came, and that Kita had privately suspected he never would. So, she started calling him by name too. The first time she called him by name, testing his reaction, the necromancer looked at her in surprise, but said nothing about it. No rants about how a filthy mud girl had no right to use his name, particularly without 'Master' in front of it. Nothing about she-whelp. Maybe he was just glad she stopped calling him 'bone mage'. They still argued, a lot, but not as harshly as before.

Three days since Whisper's injury, and if his wing continued healing at this rate, he might be flying again in another couple days. Good. She'd feel a lot better knowing he could get away from the pack lizards if need be. Though the lizards seemed to have taken the addition of the hawk well. They watched him, yes, but neither seemed to realize that Whisper was edible, basically a larger version of a common prey. Even when he was close to the ground, neither lizard made any aggressive moves. Whisper, on his part, was smart enough to stay away from the lizards.

Once the bandages were in place, Kita exited the tent to rejoin the others, helping Whisper to her shoulder as she walked. Lakara was putting the final touches on breakfast, while Davorin finished packing up his tent. Sir Jors wasn't visible, but she had heard him say something about restocking their water supplies, so she wasn't alarmed by his absence.

Dawn was barely painting the skies, and they would have to be on their way soon. Both the season and the hour were conspiring against them, it was cold still. Kita dislodged Whisper long enough to throw on a second traveling robe. She'd end up discarding it within an hour or two of walking, and probably want something lighter than a single traveling robe a couple hours after that. Still, for the moment, she was grateful for the extra warmth.

Once done, she looked back at Whisper, who was now on Davorin's shoulder. The necromancer looked pleased by this outcome, judging by the way he absently stroked Whisper's chest feathers. Davorin sat, making sure to be a sufficient distance from the pack lizards. "Morning check-up done already? How heals the wing?"

Lakara looked up at her for an answer, even if she didn't pause in spooning porridge into wooden bowls. "He's healing well. The yarrow is helping. I'm hoping he'll be good to fly again soon." Kita decided to take advantage of Whisper's being safely somewhere else to break down the tent.

"Good. Have you fed him yet?" Davorin asked, pausing in rooting through his bag. A bird owner himself, he recognized the danger of overfeeding, particularly when Whisper couldn't fly.

"Not yet. I was about to. Apparently, he decided he wanted his breakfast to come from you this morning."

"He may want to wait," Sir Jors said, marching up, two dead sand rabbits in hand. Unless Kita missed her guess, they were imp killed. "I scared a small pack of imps from a fresh kill. We could all use some fresh meat, and you can give Whisper some of the organs. Probably healthier for him than cooked or dried meat."

"How fresh?" Lakara asked. "If you're wrong about the time..."

"I witnessed the kill. Do you know how to prepare rabbit?"

"I do," Kita volunteered.

It made for a later start, but the fresh meat was a welcome treat for all of them. Whisper seemed especially pleased, almost like he had caught them himself. Kita saved the furs, knowing they could come in handy. Possibly as something to trade, or to line something to make it warmer. The fact that it would be muddy hot in a few hours didn't change the fact that winter was less than a month away.

Sir Jors mentioned the possibility of wintering somewhere before trying to climb the Mountains of Death. Proving that everyone had at least a little self-preservation instinct, it was unanimously agreed, even if no one could agree on where. Kita didn't care. Spending weeks, even months, in one place would dull their watchfulness. Some day she could just wander off and not return. If there wasn't a better opportunity beforehand.

Actually, as sad as she was that Whisper was hurt, if it had to happen, it was a good thing she was still with the party when it did. They had medicine, Lakara had a book on birds, and everyone had helped her with him.

The next reading session after Whisper's injury, Kita asked why they were reading a history book if Lakara had a book on birds with her. Seeing no reason not to change books if that was what Kita was interested in, Lakara agreed. Since Kita had little concern for things that happened centuries ago, but great interest in anything that might help her take care of Whisper, the change in books made her even more determined to learn.

At first, she thought she had made a mistake. There were so many new words that Kita had never heard before. Why invent 'pinions' when 'wing feathers' did fine? Lakara was no help with this, as the only things she knew of birds were what the books told her. Davorin was better at helping her transition from the terms she always used to the 'proper' terms.

Then there were times that what the book said didn't match up with what she knew. Lakara seemed scandalized that she could suggest that the book might be wrong, but Davorin backed her up. He said his own experiences with pigeons contradicted the book's claims. Finally, Lakara let it drop, saying, "Always remember how little you know. It's the scholar's code."

"Maybe you can write a new book," Kita suggested.

Lakara laughed. "When we're done, you'll be able to write the book."

"I can't write."

"You can read now. Well enough, anyway. Learning how to write should be simple enough."

"And a fitting occupation for a lady," Sir Jors added.

Kita shot him a look, searching for any sign of mocking. But he seemed sincere enough, even if Lakara looked like she had just swallowed a stone. "Perhaps." Not a filthy chance. She wasn't sticking around that long, and even if she did, even if they succeeded, the dirty king would likely have her executed for her pains.

But there was something appealing about the idea of her, Kita the street thief, writing a book about hawks, and other people reading it and thinking about how truly knowledgeable she must be.

***

Lakara still wouldn't describe herself as good with animals, but she was starting to warm up to them. A little, anyway. While she wasn't willing to sit leaning against the pack lizards like Kita did, when she didn't have Whisper with her, Lakara was proud of the fact that she no longer hesitated to take the harness and could even help check the lizards over. Yes, something was definitely off about Stripes, and they had to check her over daily to monitor her.

Nor could Lakara, not that she wanted to, tempt Whisper to perch on her shoulder or arm. He did decide to rest on her head once, but Lakara didn't consider that a pleasant situation, and was glad Kita quickly ushered the bird away. Since Kita claimed Whisper didn't like most people, Lakara was not disappointed by his behavior. Besides, Sir Jors had even less luck with the bird than she did, judging by the way they were always watching each other.

But Kita was her friend, which Lakara would even admit to if asked, and Kita cared about Whisper. Which was why they were all standing, breath-baited, to see if the bird had recovered enough to fly.

"Don't push it. Don't strain your wing. We can carry you, no problem. Just fly as far as you are comfortable with," Kita said, stroking the bird, seeming almost physically ill. Lakara forced herself not to remind Kita that Whisper was a bird and couldn't understand her.

The hawk balanced on Kita's arm and stretched his wings before, with a cry, leaping up, wings flapping. He circled higher and higher until he was almost out of sight. Kita shaded her eyes above her glasses and whistled a three-note scale. The bird shrieked in reply.

Kita laughed in relief, wiping a tear from her cheek. "He's fine. He's going to be just fine."

"Will he be able to keep up?" Sir Jors asked in a solemn

voice.

"Keep up? Mud, he'll be ahead of us. Especially if we don't start moving."

"You can call him back?" Davorin asked, as they started walking.

"Absolutely. Besides, I'm sure he'll come back when he needs to rest."

Her prediction proved true. Whisper joined them whenever they took a break, and at least twice when they didn't. Clearly, the hawk wasn't pushing himself.

Unfortunately, Lakara wasn't sure the same could be said for them. Since they left Wris, there hadn't been a single day that they hadn't spent traveling. Tediz was the last time they spent the night indoors. Traveler's huts had gotten scarce close to the borders, and none of the cities or towns on their way seemed safe enough to linger in.

Maybe they needed time to rest. While things weren't as bad as they were directly after the imp attack, neither were things good. Traveling through desert was a lot different from traveling through grasslands. Walking was hard when the ground crumpled around your foot at every step, burning as it snuck in any gap. Nor was it possible to travel far when hours had to be spent resting or the sun would make you ill.

So, perhaps a day of rest would be good. For all of them. She brought it up during their next break.

"A rest day?" Sir Jors asked, pausing in handing her a dried piece of beef. "Yes, you may be right."

"I certainly wouldn't complain," Davorin said. "Tomorrow?"

"No, I think we should wait," Kita objected. Lakara fought down her hurt when she continued. "We should be near another oasis. Once we get there, we can camp out for a day, maybe two."

"Having fresh water would certainly be ideal. But how do you know there's an oasis?" Sir Jors asked.

"Whisper. Remember, he brought back a flower today. It's fresh, so it must have been near water. Close enough that Whisper could fly there and back before it wilted, far enough that we can't see it yet."

Whisper *had* brought Kita a flower, dropping it on her head, to everyone's general amusement. Lakara had wondered about that but hadn't gone as far as to question where the flower came from. "So, he brought you the flower so you knew there would be water? He must be very smart."

"He's trained to help me find things I might need."

"Very useful trick, that," Sir Jors said.

Kita shrugged. "Anyway, I don't know where the oasis is, but he flew in the direction we're going, so we should be able to spot it tomorrow."

With that hope in mind, the next day's trip was easier. The promised oasis was evident even before the afternoon rest, but it was far enough away that they would probably have to spend part of the night traveling to get there.

Still, having an end in sight helped more than Lakara would have believed. It was probably midnight or later when they all but crashed into the oasis. A fire was built, and the bedrolls were unrolled, but no one bothered to set up a tent.

Lakara regretted that somewhat in the morning, waking up with the sun in her eyes and sand in places it was never meant to be. But that was nothing new. She and Kita set up their tent after breakfast. Afterwards, Lakara washed up to the best of her ability and looked forward to a day of not traveling anywhere.

She first celebrated by getting more sleep. While

spending part of the night on watch didn't seem to be draining her as quickly as it was Davorin or Sir Jors, the latter of whom always looked exhausted, between keeping watch and constant travel, she was usually tired. Lakara wasn't the only one who tried to catch up on sleep either. Even Kita dozed for a while, and she didn't have a watch shift.

After a refreshing nap, Lakara read. She had missed reading. Helping Kita learn to read was rewarding and exciting on its own, but it wasn't the same as actually reading herself. For pleasure, instead of to research or double-check a fact.

Lakara was so into her reading that she missed Kita and Davorin getting into their latest fight until Davorin took off running with Kita chasing him. She blinked, feeling lost as the two sprinted around the dunes. Then she turned to Sir Jors who was shaking his head in resigned exasperation. "What did I miss?"

"Not much. Just another argument."

"I've never seen them run because of an argument."

"That's probably because they don't usually have the energy. Though, to be fair, Davorin shouldn't have said..." Sir Jors trailed off. "What he said. I don't blame Kita for being irate."

"What did he *say*?"

"Nothing suitable for the ears of a lady."

Chivalrous of him, but Lakara didn't count as a Lady. On the other hand, she wasn't sure she wanted to know. Except, she really, really did. "May I have a hint? Simply so I know not to mention it?"

"You wouldn't anyway." Sir Jors eyed the fighters as Davorin nearly ran headfirst into a stunted tree, dodging at the last moment. Kita took the swerve much easier. When he saw Lakara turn from watching them run to stare at him, he seemed to blush. Maybe it was from sun. "He referred to some of the alternate life paths Kita might have taken."

Perhaps she was missing something, but that didn't seem so wrong. "You mean like learning a trade? Granted, she might have had trouble finding an apprenticeship, but it would have been ideal."

Now she was sure he was turning red, and it didn't seem to be the sun. "Some have called it a trade. Not that it would be any more legal than her current path."

It actually took a few minutes for Lakara to realize what he was implying, and then she probably blushed harder than him. "Yes, well. Um, should we stop them from fighting? We don't want either to injure the other."

"I don't think they will. Kita would have caught Davorin by now if she were actually trying. And I don't see Davorin suddenly deciding to stand his ground and fight her."

Lakara took another look, watching Davorin run around the lizards and Kita leap over them. Yes, he had a point. Kita was definitely faster and more sure-footed, even on sand. "Well, then I suppose we should let them have their fun. I'm certain he'll think to apologize sooner or later."

"True." Sir Jors winced slightly as Davorin fell as a dune gave out under him. Kita didn't hesitate to follow. "At least she left her bag here. She doesn't have her dirk."

She smiled at that. Her smile died as Sir Jors jumped to his feet and drew his sword. Lakara scrambled up, heart racing as she tried to figure out what was wrong.

"Oh, that won't do you any muddy good. Put it down and you might get out of this alive," a strange voice said. Lakara turned to see a band of fifteen or twenty men approaching. All armed. Bandits.

Their leader was a big man, broad-shouldered, with

unclean dark hair that he wore long, and a frightening collection of scars. "I said, put it down. Before I kill you and take what I want anyway."

They couldn't fight this many. Not even if all four of them were there, let alone missing two people. Even if all of them were fully trained knights, they would still be slaughtered.

Lakara tried to hide her shaking legs and shallow breaths as the leader came closer, looking her up and down, a hungry gleam in his eyes. What would they do? What *could* they do?

Suddenly, Kita's voice rang out from behind her. "Jalen? Jalen, you filth pot. What are you doing here?" She walked forward, passing Lakara who wanted to scream at her. How did she know this man? What was she doing insulting him like that? And why was she getting closer?

To Lakara's shock, Jalen seemed surprised and pleased. "Kita! You old mudlicker, you! I could ask you the same." They embraced like old friends.

Slowly, Lakara started to breathe again. They might survive this after all. Then Jalen looked from Kita to the rest of their group. "Who are these?"

Chapter Nine

Finding Inner Strength

Or

When all else fails, fake it.

Sir Jors was certain his fingers were white as he gripped the hilt of his sword. As soon as he had seen the bandit crew, he had known there was no chance to fight them off. If they were lucky, the bandits would take what they wanted and leave. If they weren't, the bandits would kill them, take what they wanted, and leave. So, when the leader ordered him to put down the sword, Sir Jors actually considered it. But that would leave them all defenseless. The women were especially vulnerable, and Sir Jors would rather die than stand back and let something like that happen, even if it did mean they all lived through the encounter.

So, with a prayer to Vicaw, Sir Jors kept hold of his sword, trying to figure out if he could possibly hold the bandits off long enough for *anyone* to escape. Lakara, much to his dismay, was probably doomed. She was between him and the bandits and hadn't even thought to start running yet. Nor was she likely fast enough to avoid being hunted down. Besides, if the imp attack was any indication, she might not run even if ordered.

Davorin and Kita were beyond him and out of immediate sight. If they were very clever, very lucky, and very fast; one or both of them might get away. Perhaps, if he shouted as loud as he could for Lakara to run, the other two would hear and know there was danger.

Then Kita appeared out of nowhere. Appeared and called the bandit chief by name. If they both knew the other's names and were comfortable insulting each other that thoroughly, then they must know each other well.

Lakara started to relax. He didn't. This situation could very well have just gotten even more deadly than it had a few minutes ago.

"Who are these?"

If Kita told the truth, this could well be their deaths. Kita had no reason to lie. *Vicaw, give me the bravery to face this fight. If my death should come, so be it. But if possible, please let the others escape.*

Kita didn't even look back. "They're my crew."

Jalen looked between them and her. "You don't work with a crew."

She shrugged. "Sometimes the reward is worth it."

"A job then."

"I'm not in the Ocean of Sand for my health. Are you?"

Jalen smirked. "What do you think?"

"I see." Both Kita and Jalen held their right fists over their left flat palms. They hit their palms three times and then pointed at the same time. Kita pointed to the north, while Jalen pointed to the southeast.

"A pity. I would love to know what job *you* considered worth enough to work with a crew. You've been turning me down for years."

"Please, I wouldn't join *your* crew if it led to the treasures of Reznik."

Jalen laughed and slapped her back, knocking her forward a few steps. Considering Jalen was two heads taller and much heavier than Kita; Sir Jors was surprised it didn't knock her down. "Not even a hint on what tempts you?"

Kita restored her balance, rotated her head and shoulders, and smirked at him. "Now, now. You know the rules. Let's just say that if I pull this off, you'll hear about it in time."

"Fine. How long will we have the pleasure of your company?"

"We leave at first light."

Jalen nodded. "Then we share the oasis tonight, feast and drink. That won't be a problem, will it?" Clearly, he meant to do it whether she had a problem with it or not.

"So long as you have better alcohol than you did last time. Lizard blood would have been better than that."

"And yet, you still drank more than anyone."

"Not my fault you keep challenging me to drink you into a coma." Kita stepped back. "Set up your camp. I have things to do. Call me when you have your grog ready."

Kita walked back, snagging Lakara as she made her way to Sir Jors. Davorin had come up while they were bantering. As soon as they were all together, Kita spoke in a low voice. "I need you to play along. Pretend I'm in charge. But be *careful*. Jalen has a few shreds of honor, and I've proven myself to his men, mostly, but you are unknowns. Stay together. Particularly you," she said to Lakara. "Don't go anywhere alone or let yourself be caught alone with one or more of his men."

Davorin looked ready to argue. Sir Jors cut in before he could. "Do you trust him?" It hadn't escaped his notice that, once away from Jalen, Kita looked almost as uneasy as he felt.

"I trust him not to murder me in my sleep, especially as long as he thinks I can be useful or can hurt him if he tries.

He even follows the thieves' code, meaning we don't steal from each other. I trust that he has enough control over his men that they won't kill us either, at least, without a reason. That's it." Kita shot a glance back to where the bandits were setting up camp. "Put up with it tonight, and we'll leave as soon as possible in the morning. There'll be a drinking contest. I've drunk his whole party under the table before, but he has a few new men. Just keep in mind that in an hour or so, most will be filthy drunk and foolish. Hopefully, if they are drunk enough to do something foolish, they'll be drunk enough to be bad at it."

"Isn't getting drunk a bad idea? Especially around..." Lakara trailed off, trying to find a polite way to describe their current companions.

Kita gave a humorless smile. "I don't get drunk. I have to go. Remember what I said. Don't go *anywhere* alone." With that last comment, she dashed off, back to Jalen's side.

Sir Jors took what felt to be his first unimpeded breath. They could make it through the night. As long as no one did something foolish.

"What do we do?" Lakara asked.

"Exactly what she said. We play along, pretend she is in charge, and keep care for the night," Sir Jors said. "Don't let your guard down, and don't go anywhere alone."

"Why so much caution? I mean, aren't they Kita's... friends?" Lakara asked, even as she looked askance about using the word 'friend'.

"Think for a moment," Davorin whispered. "*Kita's* friends. Or associates may be more accurate. She doesn't seem to like them either."

"Maybe, but still..."

"Kita, who was forced into this journey against her will.

Kita, who doesn't want to be here," Davorin murmured. Sir Jors immediately nodded. He had certainly had plenty of time to think the same thing.

Lakara paled. "She wouldn't..."

"I think if she planned to tell them, she would have by now. But I, for one, will not rest easy until we are away." Sir Jors eyed the tents. "Why don't we eat dinner, and retire early? Don't worry about keeping watch. No one is going to attack a bandit camp this big. I'll stay awake, in case of internal problems. I doubt I could sleep tonight, even if I wanted to."

Jalen's crew, as Kita predicted, were quick to start a noisy revel. As the alcohol was opened, the group got even louder. Fortunately, none of them seemed to notice or care that the three of them all but huddled together quietly on the outskirts of the celebration, not joining in. One by one, the bandits gave way to the effects of alcohol, passing out or becoming lost in their own worlds.

Kita was as loud as any of them, and as time passed, seemed a little shaky as well. Sir Jors strongly suspected it was faked though. Especially since she snapped alert whenever some drunken idiot wandered too close to her or them.

"How is she not unconscious?" Lakara asked in horrified disbelief.

"Probably long experience," Davorin said dismissively.

Sir Jors had planned to keep his mouth shut, but that changed his mind. "No, that isn't it. Haven't you figured it out yet?"

Lakara and Davorin looked at him questioningly. "Think about it. Beyond human alcohol tolerance. Sharp ears, best sense of smell, remember how she could always locate the market first. Her eyes are more sensitive to light than any of ours. Her talent with animals, including a bird that seems to understand everything she says. The ability to see magic. Even the style of her dirk. Neither Graldish nor Salardis made dirks for women."

Lakara got it first. "But the Queya did. And because they live in deep forests and caves, they depend more on hearing and smell than sight. Famous for their skill with animals, and Queyan magic is different from human magic, which might be why she can see it. But they also fear fire and loud noises. Kita always makes the fire."

"And draws back immediately. Plus, if her hearing is better, of course she wouldn't like loud noises," Davorin said. He eyed the celebration before them. "She does not seem to be enjoying herself."

"No, she doesn't," Sir Jors agreed. "I haven't actually asked her if she is, but I strongly suspect it. Probably only half or a quarter Queyan. I'm not sure even she knows about it. She doesn't respond at all to references to the Queya or hunting deer." The Queya believed they were related to the deer, and therefore, any hunting of deer was strongly forbidden regardless of reason.

"How could she *not* know?" Davorin asked.

"She said herself that the dirk came from her father's mother. She also said the dark glasses were his. Since he was… gone, by the time she was five, it is unlikely he could have done much to instruct her in their way." Sir Jors shrugged. "If he wasn't full Queyan himself, it's possible even he didn't know much. But whatever the case, I doubt we will find out. Besides, regardless of her background, Kita is the same person she was this morning." He wasn't sure he convinced them. Perhaps having the night to think it over would help.

***

Kita would never go so far as to call Jalen a friend in any but the loosest fashion. A possible ally, certainly. An occasional

173

source of safety even. She had once spent three weeks in his company while recovering from a job gone wrong. Jalen had never even suggested that she owed him more than a few good stories, and a night or two of drinking for the incident. The fact that she had 'lost' a good bit of her gold and a very shiny ruby to him in various games of chance probably helped with that.

Jalen respected her skills, respected her blade, and had enough honor to declare to his men that she was not to be targeted by them. Kita appreciated it, but never depended on that grace. Partially because she couldn't remember an instance where they met when some muddy idiot *didn't* force her to prove she wasn't a weak target. And Jalen wondered why she didn't want to join his crew.

Though, in all fairness, three months ago, if someone had asked Kita to name the people, Whisper didn't count, she trusted most in the whole filthy world, Jalen would probably be one of them. She trusted he wouldn't murder her in her sleep or leave her to die if he found her injured, provided it wouldn't endanger him or get in the way of a big payday. He might, and Kita wouldn't stake anything on this, hesitate to turn her over to the law for money. At least if the money wasn't really high amounts.

Kita hadn't really trusted anyone after Mother died. Part of it was her nomadic lifestyle. She didn't stay in one place long enough to make true connections or come back to the same place very often. The fact that she was clearly part Trovian, the bandits of the sea, certainly didn't help. Besides, she was a thief. She didn't want *friends* because friends were people you couldn't steal from. People you had to rely on, and people who relied on you in turn.

So, it was almost a surprise to her to realize as she drank her seventh or eighth tumbler of whatever truly wretched liquor Jalen had acquired, that the three people who she was currently trying to defend from her ally, were friends. For all the bitter circumstances that forced her to be here, Kita hadn't hesitated to side with them when faced with Jalen. If, the gods forbid, things actually did come to a true fight, instead of one of the many mock fights she had seen, even participated in, on nights like this; she would be with them. Even if it meant Jalen killed her.

But it wasn't going to come to that. Jalen might or might not be suspicious about her claims, but he wasn't going to push the point. Whatever his men thought, they would follow Jalen's lead.

Better, her 'crew', regardless of their own opinions on this matter, and she had little doubt they would let her know those opinions in the next few days, were smart enough to know to follow her lead for now. While a few of Jalen's men might wonder why they watched instead of joining in, no one cared enough to ask.

Still, Kita felt relieved when she saw them retreat to their tents. Less chance of something going wrong and making Jalen suspicious. Less possibility of someone, on either side, doing something stupid. Less of them seeing her act like drunken street trash.

It was necessary. She would never have gotten the respect she had from Jalen and some of his men if she hadn't been able to drink them all into a stupor or prove her blade was worse than her bite. But she hated it. Hated the cheap filth she was drinking, hated acting like a drunk, hated acting like the gutter trash everyone always assumed she would end up. The gutter trash that she had probably become.

Not that there had been much choice. She could have ended up as a thief, someone's bed warmer, or dead. Some self-righteous merchant had said that when she was four and Mother was offering to sweep the floor in exchange for a loaf of bread, pointing out that she had a child to support. Kita hadn't understood what he meant then, but it didn't take long.

Prostitutes were common enough if you knew where to look. And it didn't take a scholar to notice how quickly they aged and died. But from the point of view of a young child, what really struck Kita was how dependent they were on others. A prostitute only ate if someone else found them appealing. A thief ate if they succeeded in stealing something.

Orphaned at eight, with no one interested in wasting resources on a bastard part-Trovian street rat, Kita decided early on that there was no one she could rely on, and she wasn't interested in depending on it. She had done many things she wasn't proud of to survive, but she had decided early on that becoming a bed warmer wouldn't be one of them. Theft might not be legal, and she might well have deserved the execution King Zikkar had threatened, but at least she could say she had survived on her own. Not that she was opposed to working with others, but she didn't want to be dependent on them.

Kita was pulled from her musings as a dagger landed near her foot. Plastering on a smirk she didn't feel, Kita stood, drawing her own dirk. She was being challenged.

Her opponent was one of Jalen's new men, one she hadn't seen fight yet. He was also big. Not as big as Jalen, but still big enough that she would pause to get on his bad side if it could be helped. From the looks of it, he was drunk enough that his ability to feel pain was reduced, but his coordination was still somewhat decent. Muddy wonderful.

Kita rolled her shoulders, trying to look drunk while sizing up her options. She couldn't lose. Losing meant she wasn't worthy of respect, worthy of protection. Losing a fight was never safe, but especially not tonight. Not when the rest of the group's safety depended on Jalen's willingness to consider her a valuable ally.

She couldn't refuse. Refusing was worse than a loss. A close loss meant she still had ability, potential. Refusal meant that she knew she was outmatched.

"First blood?" Kita asked. It was typical terms, especially when fighting an unknown.

"Third."

Kita arched her eyebrows. No one called third blood with someone they had never fought. Third blood was only when fighting someone you knew was near your equal. She had fought Jalen to third blood once, but that was the only time. "Unusual."

There was a murmur from those sober enough to understand what was happening. Her opponent, who Kita mentally dubbed Rash, leered at her. "Third blood," he repeated, "with stakes to the winner."

No prizes for guessing what he wanted. She pretended ignorance anyway. "What stakes?"

"I win, you're mine tonight. You and the other girl."

Kita fought back a snarl. It wasn't the first time she had been part of the stakes, but she had never had someone else depending on her before. "And if you lose?"

He blinked at her as if the thought of losing was something that had never occurred to him. "If I lose?"

"Yes, lose. Someone always loses in a contest. If you lose…"

He gaped at her, allowing her a not-so-lovely look at rotting teeth by firelight. Just as she was about to declare his idea void, he thought of something. "If I lose, you get this." He pulled out something from a pouch. A rock of some sort. Rash tossed it to her, letting her examine it.

A green stone, cut and polished. Probably an emerald, and as far as she could tell from a brief examination, it was real. Must have come from someone's jewelry. Take it to the right fence, and it could be worth somewhere between three and five hundred dourats.

All Kita could think was *Filthy, muddy rot!* The best chance of refusing the challenge, or at least the stakes, would be if he couldn't provide something equal or greater than the stakes demanded. But not a single one of Jalen's men would consider her justified in refusing those stakes.

So, she smirked and handed the gem to Jalen for safekeeping. "Then, I accept." Kita moved to the cleared area around the fire. "On one condition."

Rash looked at her, stupidly. "What condition?"

"One stone? One person. You win tonight, you get me. Not her." It was useless to even try. Losing this fight could well deprive them all of their protection anyway, but Kita found that even theoretically she couldn't agree to putting Lakara in danger. "I don't wager my crew." Then she gave a humorless laugh. "Besides, I doubt you could handle *me* for a night. Let alone two of us."

Rash clearly didn't like that, perhaps especially considering the value of the stone he was wagering. It wasn't like Kita was worth much herself. But Jalen had some sympathy. He probably understood not risking those under his command. "Fine. I declare the challenge open. Kita versus Lavos, stakes are Kita or this emerald. Are the fighters ready?" Bets were already being made.

She not only had to win this fight, but she had to do so quickly enough and decisively enough that no one else wanted to challenge her tonight. So far, no one had come up with the strategy of having enough people challenge her in a night that she had no chance to win. Nor was she going to suggest it. "I'm ready."

Rash, or Lavos, she supposed his name was, nodded with a grunt. "Begin!"

Lavos ran at her, charging like a unicorn. Kita waited until he was committed to his charge before sweeping to his left side, slicing at his arm with her dirk. Not the most effective use of her knife, which was designed as a stabbing weapon, but she wasn't actually trying to kill him.

"First Blood, Kita!" Jalen announced. There were cheers and jeers from the crowd. Kita ignored them, as Lavos turned on her. For a large man, he could move quickly.

The shining blade danced towards her, parried by her own knife. She needed more room to maneuver. Lavos was too big, too strong, for her to want to be in close quarters with him. But she also had to be close enough to draw blood. Some creativity was allowed in how that blood was drawn, but it had to be close. She could stab, slice, scratch, bite, hit, even kick him. But throwing things didn't count. That was poor form and the actions of a coward.

Kita stepped down on his foot as hard as she could, her blade scraping his leg when he drew it back instinctively. But she couldn't quite evade his blade that was flying towards her head. Turning, the dagger missed her eye, but she did catch a scratch high on the temple.

"Kita, two. Lavos, one."

One more. She just needed one more. As her infuriated opponent reached for her, she had an idea how she would get it.

Lavos roared and, ignoring the knife, grabbed her by the throat. She gripped his arm with both hands and used every scrap of leverage she could get to swing her legs up, hitting his groin with all the force she could muster. With a strangled shriek, he dropped her, falling to the ground. Kita wasn't even sure he felt her stab him in the shoulder. "Third blood," she declared.

Kita ignored her downed opponent and walked back to her place, diverting just long enough to collect her winnings from a startled Jalen. The crowd watched with a mix of amusement and horror. Jalen recovered his shock first and started laughing. "He won't make the mistake of challenging you again."

That was the point. With the precedent set, the aftermath was the same as any other challenge. Money changed hands, with taunts and cheers. The chances of someone else wanting to go up against her tonight were slim. They were safe.

Another challenge was made to someone else. Kita ignored it. She didn't care if half of them killed the other half, as long as they left her and hers alone. Now that people weren't focusing on her, she could take a moment to examine her own scratch. It didn't feel like much, about half a finger's length long, high enough on the temple that it could be hidden by her hair. Perhaps it wouldn't even be noticed. Even if it was, there were plenty of possible explanations.

Kita cast a quick look at the tents her group was in, something she had done at various times over the night. Then her eyes narrowed. Was that Lakara? What was she doing?

**

Lakara didn't think she could possibly sleep while such crude, lawless men were carousing nearby. Even disregarding the noise, it was nerve-wracking. If she didn't know Sir Jors was awake and watchful, she would probably fall apart. Kita, provided she didn't pass out, would probably stay awake the whole night too.

Part Queya. Lakara had never even considered the option. But looking back, it did explain several things. No wonder she took out more imps than Lakara and Sir Jors combined. Queyan generational weapons were especially effective against them. Queya also tended to become ill if confined indoors for too long, which might explain why Kita always traveled. They were generally skilled at working with animals, which might explain why Kita was the only one in the party who could just sit on the ground and lean into one of the pack lizards. Even Stripes, who still tried to bite almost anyone who got close.

Lakara's eyes snapped open as she remembered something else. The Queya were infamous for the ability to Borrow. To befriend an animal so closely they could temporarily share a mind with them. The animal frequently became more intelligent, and some suggested longer-lived, as a result. Either suffered if their companion died. If the animal died while being Borrowed, the Borrower never recovered their mind. But when it worked, Queya and animal working in tandem, they were able to accomplish more than either could separately. It was a tactic the Queya had used during the Wars, with such devastating effect that both Graldish and Salardis put a blanket death sentence on anyone caught Borrowing for any reason. If Kita could do that…

No, that was silly. Despite both countries' haste to condemn the act, there was no proof it could be done by anyone other than a full-blooded Queya. It certainly wasn't possible for humans. If Kita was only half or a quarter, or less, then she probably wouldn't be able to Borrow even if she wanted to. Not that she would want to. Not with those laws in place. It would be far too dangerous to even attempt. And for what purpose?

Whisper seemed to understand her perfectly as is, and she was the only one who could get away with inspecting Stripes without someone else holding the lizard's mouth shut. It was just her natural skill. Kita certainly wasn't Borrowing, and Lakara would never, ever bring up the topic.

In fact, she was going to go right to sleep. Lakara closed her eyes and tried to relax all her muscles. Only to discover her body was suddenly telling her that she needed to relieve herself. And no, it absolutely would not wait until morning.

With a frustrated sigh, Lakara extricated herself from her bedroll. Yes, Kita had told them not to go anywhere alone, but it couldn't be helped. Besides, as far as Lakara could tell, the promised drinking contest had led to the unsurprising result of everyone being either unconscious or too drunk to move.

Lakara was quiet as she crept by the men's tent, not wanting to worry Sir Jors, and cautious as she made her way to the spot they had designated as the latrine. She encountered no one on her way, relieved herself quickly, and was heading back when she discerned a darkened figure moving towards her.

She stiffened, heart seizing, then calming as she realized the figure had the same build as Sir Jors. He must have heard her leave and wanted to make sure she was alright. Lakara was about to apologize and explain when she noticed the person coming towards her was walking wobbly, as if drunk. As he neared, it was obvious that he was actually a little bigger than Sir Jors and reeked of cheap alcohol.

Lakara froze. It was dark, and he had been near the fires. Maybe he couldn't see her. Perhaps he would walk past her, and she could hurry back to the tent while he was distracted. The man kept walking, or perhaps stumbling was more accurate. Lakara held her breath, leery of making any noise that might draw attention to her. Also because he stank to the heavens.

For a moment, she thought it worked. For a minute, he seemed ready to walk past her. Then it all fell apart.

With a laugh, the drunk reached out and grabbed Lakara's arm in a bruising grip. "What's the matter, Cutie? Don't want to join the party? That's okay, we can have a party right here. Just you and me."

Lakara tried to pull away but couldn't get his hand to budge. She inhaled deeply, ready to scream, when a very unclean, very large hand roughly covered her mouth. "Uh-uh.

No screaming. Then they'll all want to join in. I want you to myself, first."

She tried to kick out, but he only chuckled and said something about being 'feisty'. The hand that had been on her arm was moving up to her shoulder, but she still couldn't get enough leverage to get free. How could he be this strong when drunk? What could she do?

Panic was appealing more and more, when her attacker suddenly screamed and fell back, letting her go. Lakara stumbled back a couple steps in surprise. Someone else was there. Someone smaller, who held something that glinted in the moonlight. "Foolish move. Very foolish." Kita!

Kita pushed the man back and moved so she was standing between Lakara and her attacker. "She's mine. You don't touch."

The man rallied. "You filthy trash! You'll—" He froze, Kita's dirk at his throat.

"Watch your tongue, watch your hands. Or I'll remove them."

"What's going on here?" Jalen and three of his men came up, torches in hand. Jalen was drunk enough to slur his words, but his walking was steady. As they got closer, Lakara could see the man who attacked her was bleeding, stabbed in the side.

Lakara tried not to shake. Why hadn't she listened? They had only slightly better chances of surviving a fight than they had when the bandits first showed up. This was sure to provoke them, and it was all her fault.

Her attacker snarled and was about to talk, but Kita cut in first. "Your dog overstepped his bounds. I expected you to have better control of your…" She paused, eyeing the bleeding man, "*crew*. He should know better than to insult an ally and attempt to take what doesn't belong to him."

Jalen scowled. "Risto! What did you do?"

Hands pressed against his bleeding side, Risto grimaced. "Nothing! And if she cares so much, what was the girl doing by herself?"

Jalen looked between Kita and Risto, frowning. "I see. Are you done?"

"As long as you keep him under control, I'm done." Kita took Lakara's arm, much more gently than Risto had, but no less insistently. "Come on. Back to bed with you."

They made it about halfway to the tent when Jalen called after them. "Is that why you would never join my crew? You required another woman?"

It actually took Lakara almost a minute to realize exactly what he was asking. Kita had figured it out much faster, and again Lakara had a hand covering her mouth. "My crew, my choices, my business. Not yours."

"Fine, fine. Another cup?"

"Not tonight. Next time I'll drink you into a coma." Then she whispered to Lakara, "Keep walking, do not say a *word*."

The hand slipped from her mouth and Lakara hurried to the tent, Kita's grip almost painful on her arm. Sir Jors was standing outside his tent when they got back. He looked at them in concern, but Kita shook her head. "Tomorrow. Go back to sleep. We have to move on in the morning."

Then Kita all but pushed her into the tent, climbed in after her, and fastened it shut. Lakara was trying not to shake, and Kita slumped to the ground, letting out all the air in her lungs with a whoosh. After a moment, she sat up straight and glared at Lakara.

Only part of her was aware of that. Lakara couldn't stop shaking and she felt like her head was wrapped in silks. Her mind kept running through what nearly happened. If

Kita hadn't followed them... If she hadn't somehow persuaded Jalen not to kill them... She was almost... They could have all been killed! And it was all her fault.

"Lakara? Lakara!

Lakara snapped up, staring at Kita in wide-eyed fright. Once again, Kita slumped. "I can't even yell at you right now. You can't pay attention, can you?"

"I... I... You... He..."

"Right. Just, breathe. Deep breaths. In and out." Lakara followed her instructions. When she was in slightly less danger of hyperventilating, Kita made her drink some water. Then she handed Lakara one of Whisper's feathers and told her to hold it steady in her palm, not letting it move. Confused as she was, she did her best, but was far from successful. After some time, Kita told her she could stop.

"What was that for?" Lakara asked when Kita took the feather back.

"It gave you something to focus on and let me know how badly your hands were shaking. Feeling any better now?"

Lakara swallowed hard. "I think so."

"Good. Get some sleep. We have to leave in a few hours. I want to be far away when these people are ready to move."

Well, that was something she could definitely agree with. But, "I can't sleep. He was going to —"

"But he didn't. It didn't happen." Kita paused. "He didn't hurt you, did he?"

"I... Probably a bruise or two."

Kita nodded. "You'll be fine." She stretched out her bedroll, taking the part nearest the tent entrance, normally Lakara's space. "Everything will be fine. He won't come near you again. Jalen will make sure of it, and I'll make doubly sure."

Lakara just sat there, until Kita rolled over to one side, head supported on one hand. "Seriously, if you aren't going to sleep, at least lie down and rest. We are going to need a rest day to recover from our rest day."

Still being just shocky enough to not want to argue, Lakara lay down and stared at the roof of the tent. Nothing was going to happen. Sir Jors was keeping watch, and Kita had put herself between Lakara and the entrance. Besides, Kita had just proven willing to stab someone to save her.

That was frightening on its own merits. Kita had stabbed an ally to save Lakara from her own folly. Folly that Kita had explicitly and repeatedly warned her against to begin with. "Kita?" Lakara whispered before she realized it.

"What?"

"How did you know what he was going to do?"

Kita gave a quiet, bitter laugh. "This isn't my first encounter with Jalen and his crew. More than one of them thought I might be an easy lay. It's not the first time I had to convince them otherwise with my blade. So far, I've been lucky. I hoped they wouldn't try touching you, but I wasn't willing to bet on it. So, when you left, and Risto followed you, I followed him."

"Oh. Thank you."

"Don't bother. No one deserves that." Kita moved slightly. "Probably earned a little more respect tonight. Always seem to when I prove I can hold my own." There was a pause. "Would have been better if you could have done it, though. Then they'd know not to touch you even if I wasn't around. They might consider me weak for acting on your behalf."

"Did he really think that we were... That you were... um."

"Jalen keeps his mind in the gutter. His men are worse.

186

Truthfully, I don't care what any of them think as long as they leave us alone. My reputation has taken far worse hits than this."

"So, that's why you didn't correct him?"

"If it means I don't have to deal with him and his crew offering to bed me next time we run into each other, he can believe the four of us throw orgies every night. *I do not care.* You shouldn't either. Scholars don't hold with bandits, and you don't have to tell anyone when you get back to Corvis."

"That's true. Do you think *you'll* associate with him again?" Lakara tried to fight off the embarrassment that flamed in her at Kita's blunt suggestion of impropriety.

"This is the fifth time we've run into each other. A sixth wouldn't surprise me." She was quiet for a minute. "Thieves aren't bandits, but that doesn't mean we don't *associate* with them. From time to time. It's not like I'm a lady."

Lakara swallowed hard. Kita didn't know. And she was forbidden to tell her. But Kita could have left her tonight. Could have left her to suffer from her own folly. "Kita?"

"Yes?"

"King Zikkar, he... He doesn't..." She couldn't betray the king! But she couldn't betray Kita.

There was a quiet whisper from the other side of the tent. "I know."

***

Davorin usually hated mornings. Hated waking up early, and especially hated that every morning meant that they were traveling further and further away from home. But he couldn't wait to move on this morning. The faster they got away from this group, the better.

So, he didn't grumble, complain, or try to get out of

chores as they packed up the tents and their belongings. Lakara hadn't made her normal variation on porridge, but Sir Jors passed out bread and smoked lizard meat to eat on the way.

No one spoke, and unless Davorin was imagining things, his companions seemed even more troubled than he did. Perhaps he'd find out why later.

The bandits were mostly asleep or lounging about suffering the aftereffects of the liquor they drank the night before, but no one wanted to risk sparking any tempers. Jalen, the leader, was at least semi-sensate, watching them. Which was why everyone tried to pretend to defer to Kita.

For her part, Kita did less to break camp than her wont, adopting a more supervisory role. When everything was packed up and they were ready to move out, Kita nodded to Jalen and started to lead the way.

Bile rose in Davorin's throat as Jalen stood in a slow, half-stumbling manner and approached them. His sweaty palms grasped Longtail's harness as he wondered if they stood any chance if a fight broke out. Probably not.

Kita was still as a statue, watching Jalen's approach with an emotionless mask carved out of stone. Like her hawk watching movement, try to decide if it was food or threat. She hadn't decided yet.

Lakara shifted so she was more behind Kita, and Sir Jors had a hand tight on the hilt of his sword but didn't draw.

Jalen ignored them all, focused on Kita. "Well, Mudlicker, it's good to see you again. Sure you won't join my crew? You could bring your woman with you. There *won't* be another... incident."

A smile, colder than the desert at night, flit over Kita's face. "Tempting as your offer may be, no. Perhaps next time we meet, we'll have a tale to tell. 'Til then, —"

They spoke in unison, "Gold be plentiful, and shadows be your friend."

Jalen clapped her on the back, leaving Kita to stumble and smile through her wince. "Next time, I want to know what was so tempting that *you* worked with a crew."

"Perhaps I'll tell you. But I must leave in order to find it." Kita started walking, leaving the rest to follow her.

Davorin was certain he didn't take an unimpeded breath for the first hour. They even postponed taking a break until they had been traveling nearly two hours instead of resting after an hour as their usual habit.

When they did take a break, Davorin was quick to slump to the ground. "We're safe?"

"From them. They didn't follow us," Kita said, slipping to the ground herself.

Lakara all but collapsed on the ground, next to Sir Jors who also looked weary. "Good. I never want to see them again," the scholar said.

"What happened last night?" Sir Jors asked.

Lakara looked gray. "I did something very foolish."

Kita leaned against Stripes, absently batting the lizard's mouth away from her hair. "She walked away from the camp and was followed. I stabbed one of Jalen's men to prevent him from raping her, and now Jalen thinks I protected her because I'm having sex with her. His men probably think so too." Kita shrugged. "And yes, that *was* foolish. But it was still his fault, not yours."

"Kita!" Lakara looked scandalized.

"What? That wasn't a secret, was it?"

"You don't talk about things that way. It's crude." Lakara covered her face.

"I don't see why not. Even if you wanted it a secret, they would have found out eventually. Why hint around when it's quicker just to say it? I didn't even swear!"

"Are you unharmed?" Sir Jors asked, looking to Lakara.

"I... yes. I will be fine. Kita stopped him very quickly. He only had time to grab my arm."

"Good. I'm sorry I didn't hear you leave."

Davorin stayed quiet. How many times had Kita been forced to defend herself from Jalen and his men or those like them? Had she ever accepted their advances for her own safety? He found that he couldn't really blame her if she had. But he strongly suspected that the Davorin of a month or two ago, the one who lived in the Necromancer's tower and never left, would have. Even the Davorin of yesterday hadn't actually understood or wanted to.

Those were thoughts he didn't want to think about, so he changed the subject. "You stabbed one of Jalen's men? How did we leave this morning? Doesn't he know?"

"He knows. I threw it back on him, saying I expected him to have better control of his crew. So, he saw it as his job to make sure no one touched us." Kita scratched Stripe's eye ridge, causing the lizard to curl in towards her in pleasure. "We probably wouldn't have been so fortunate if I had caused more damage. Then again, it could be argued that his man violated the code. We might have been fine."

"I think I am just as glad not to test that theory," Sir Jors said. "Still, I'm glad it worked. We should move on. Perhaps we'll camp early tonight."

No one had any objections to that. Davorin had probably had the most sleep, and he doubted he had four hours of it. Besides, they were approaching the temple of Shadow Master, and that was something he was in no hurry to encounter.

As they stood, Lakara turned to Kita. "What was that thing you did, with the pointing?"

"When Jalen and I met? Part of the code. See, with thieves, we tend to be a little free with other people's belongings. If one thief knows of a treasure, if they tell someone else, they risk that person trying to get the treasure, either first, or from the first thief. But you also want to make sure that you aren't after the same thing as someone else, because then you both are more likely to be caught, or one might decide to knock off the competition. So, part of the code is that when two known thieves or bandits meet, they point to which direction they are going, at the same time. If they are going different directions, then they don't share what they are after, unless they're trying to get the other on the job. If they are going in the same direction, they try to narrow things down without revealing their target."

"Oh, so because we're heading north and he was heading south, you don't tell him where we're going?" Lakara asked.

"Right. And I don't know what he's after, either." Kita took Stripes' harness. "Can't say I care, either."

He was going to regret this; he knew he was. But he had to ask. "Why did you lie to Jalen?"

Kita stared straight ahead, not looking at any of them. "I didn't. Not really. We're heading towards the same goal. We're crew. I might have implied that I was the one in charge, but I didn't actually lie." She shrugged. "Besides, Jalen would never have let me hear the end of it if he 'rescued' me. And I will *not* be in his debt like that. Not if I can help it."

That, he could understand. No one said anything else about the encounter. As Sir Jors suggested, when they set up camp to avoid the afternoon heat they didn't bother moving on when the heat broke.

Davorin was grateful. They were less than three days

from Juztoc, barring misfortune. Unless Juztoc was a lot friendlier than Surduk, they probably wouldn't stay there long. Maybe they wouldn't even all enter the city if they tried splitting up. Unfortunately, even if that were the case, it was unlikely he would be able to avoid the temple. As the group's only necromancer, he would be expected to be there.

Since focusing on that would accomplish nothing but make him nervous, he decided to focus on something else. Like Kita, performing the now daily examination on Stripes. "Any change?"

Kita held a hand to Stripes' side. "She's pregnant! I'm sure of it."

"That's impossible. She's unmated. They both are." Sir Jors came closer.

"Are you certain? Because I can feel movement."

Sir Jors had to be much more careful around the aggressive lizard, but he was eventually able to hold a hand to her side. "You're right. And she's close. Probably within a few days. But I swear, she's unmated."

"Um," Lakara looked up from a scroll she had pulled out when the conversation started. "While it hasn't been well documented, there are stories, rare ones, of an unmated female pack lizard giving birth. Always to a male lizard. It's considered a good omen by the breeders." She skimmed her scroll. "It's possible."

Davorin shook her head. "How many scrolls did you bring?"

"Just what might be useful."

"Does the scroll say what to do when the lizard gives birth?" Kita asked. "Because I don't know that she'll get as far as the next town. I've worked with pack lizards before, but not when they were giving birth. All I know is that they don't lay eggs like most lizards."

That was more experience than either he or the scholar had, so they turned to Sir Jors. "No, I don't have any experience either."

A very white Lakara answered, "Well, the scroll does give some advice. I'm sure we'll be fine."

Famous last words. Stripes refused to move when they got about five miles outside Juztoc. Deciding that she was probably going to give birth within hours, the group somehow, and Davorin wasn't quite sure how, decided that he and Sir Jors would travel ahead to Juztoc and find the clue, plus buy more supplies, while Kita and Lakara stayed with the lizards. They would meet back afterwards and continue from there.

Davorin's first impression of Juztoc was that it was definitely *not* friendlier than Surduk. Shadow Master's power touched every corner of the city, leaving shadows that Davorin was positive no one else could see. The whispers of the dead and dying, something he could usually only hear when other noises didn't drown them out, were loud with occasional audible words.

There was no need to ask for directions or look for the temple. It was obvious where the magic originated from. Almost every city had a temple devoted to Shadow Master, but Shadow Master didn't treat every temple the same. This was an important temple, and a seat of Shadow Master's presence. And it showed. The temple was so enveloped by Shadow Master's power that Davorin could barely see it through the shadows. Maybe he should ask Sir Jors what it looked like to him.

To Davorin, the temple was black stone, shrouded in shadows. Very few made pilgrimages to Shadow Master's temple and many went out of their way to avoid the place. As if avoiding the temple allowed them to avoid the deity.

The closer they got, the louder the voices of the dead and dying rang in his ears. A quick glance showed no sign that Sir Jors noticed anything. Lucky man.

Pressure surrounded Davorin, like a pack lizard was lying on him. His mouth was dry as sand and his bones felt like water.

The entrance of the temple was proudly inscribed with Shadow Master's words of wisdom, "Death is but a door." Unlike other temples, the doorway was deliberately made narrow enough that only one person could enter at a time, and not even that if they carried much with them. Just as death came to each individual in their time, and nothing went with them.

He wanted to run until his legs gave out under him. He wanted to scream until his voice drowned out the voices of the dead. Scream until his throat bled, proving that he was *alive*, not pulled bodily into Shadow Master's realm. He wanted to throw away the dark glasses Kita had once again lent him, and stare at the sun, until it was so fixed in his eyes that he would never see dark again.

Sir Jors started to climb the steps of the temple. To Davorin's horror, the shadows of death began to surround him. This wasn't a trick, not an illusion. If Sir Jors went inside, he would die.

"Why don't you get the supplies? I can check the temple myself," A voice broke the silence. It was a calm, confident voice, so it was to Davorin's huge surprise to realize it was his own.

Sir Jors looked back at him. "Are you certain?"

"Of course. You won't be able to read it or copy it anyway. And if you get the supplies at the same time, we can be back and meet up with the women quicker. If something goes wrong with the lizards, they'll probably want our help."

For one heart-stopping moment, the knight seemed about to refuse. Then he nodded. "You make some excellent points. We'll meet in the square." As he walked away from the temple, the shadows relinquished their prey. By the time he crossed the street, no shadow touched him.

Davorin looked himself over. No sign of shadows on him. What posed such a threat to Sir Jors, but not to him? Perhaps it was Shadow Master proving a point. Shadow Master was harder to understand than any of the gods but AKAF.

While the shadows did not cover him, they did wave him in. He was expected. Invited in, even. "Will I be allowed to leave?"

No answer was given. Not that he truly expected one. With a deep breath, Davorin forced himself to enter the temple.

Chapter Ten

Matters of Life and Death

Or

A state of mess, pain, and confusion

Lakara read through her information on pack lizard reproduction for the fifth time. Pack lizards, unlike many of their smaller cousins who laid eggs, gave birth to live young; usually one or two at a time. Signs of a pregnant lizard were scarce until they reached the point where movement was visible, though running hot and eating more were symptoms.

Fortunately, according to her sources, pack lizards seldom needed assistance in delivering. On Kita's suggestion, they staked Longtail's harness some distance away. Pack lizards were opportunistic eaters that were not above occasional straying into cannibalism. Stripes, as the mother, would be less of a risk as long as she was not too stressed or underfed.

"What are we going to do with a baby pack lizard anyway?" Kita asked, staying near Stripes' head, stroking to calm the lizard. "We never discussed it. He'll be too young to carry anything for months. Not able to travel quickly or for long distances for a while. Certainly we weren't planning on having him."

"Well, no, but what can we do? Surely you aren't suggesting we let the lizards eat him?" Lakara asked, horrified.

"Of course not. But we could sell him. After the first

few weeks, anyway. Or we could keep him and eventually have another pack lizard to carry things. Or even a spare food source for ourselves in case of emergency. Do not look at me that way, I know you've had lizard."

"Of course, I have. But not…"

"Not a lizard you know personally. You would make a muddy lousy farmer." Kita smirked. "But in all honesty, I wouldn't want to do that either. That's why I said, in an emergency."

Kita was right on all points. "Well, as you said, even if we were going to sell him, we would have to wait a few weeks. We're planning on wintering somewhere before the Mountains of Death, which gives us plenty of time to decide. If we even can. I'm not sure we can claim ownership of these two, let alone any offspring they have. I'll ask Sir Jors when he comes back."

"What?" Stripes let out a strange growling sound. Kita went back to calming her. "I think it's time."

"Right." Lakara positioned herself behind the pack lizard, out of reach of the tail. While she would have preferred not to have this part of the job, they both knew that Kita would do better calming Stripes than Lakara ever could. "The lizardling should be born headfirst."

Kita nodded, her focus on muttering soft nonsense words to the agitated lizard. "How long is this supposed to take?"

"Not long. A few minutes once the lizardling starts to emerge." Stripes was black right now. Not a good sign. Probably pain or agitation. But this would be Stripes' first time giving birth. It probably confused her. "I think I see something."

She did see something. But it wasn't a lizard head, it was a tip of a tail. "He's backwards!"

"Anything about that?"

"No!" There wasn't a single mention of that or what to do.

Stripes tried to pull her head away, causing Kita to readjust her grip with a muttered curse. "It's okay, Precious. Everything will be fine." In the same tone, she started talking to Lakara. "Your hands are clean?"

"Of course. I was studying a scroll. I wouldn't do that with unclean hands. Why?"

"Because if Lizardling gets stuck, you're going to have to adjust him."

"What?" Lakara almost shouted.

"That or hold Stripes still so I can do it." Stripes pulled again, almost bodily lifting Kita. "If so, say something now."

Lakara swallowed hard. "No, I can do it." Hopefully, it wouldn't be necessary. Most of the tail was visible. One blink later, and a pair of legs were out. "Halfway."

It was the second set of legs that caused a problem. One leg emerged cleanly, but only half of the other. Stripes growled again and pulled. Nothing changed. "He's stuck!"

"You'll have to help. Carefully."

"I..."

"Lakara!"

"Right." She moved forward, bracing the tail as far as it would go so Stripes couldn't use it to hit her. Lakara tried to ignore the slime, mucus, or whatever it was that covered the lizard, and gingerly tugged at the stuck leg. Nothing seemed to happen. "Come on, little Lizardling." She tugged harder.

Stripes growled and snapped, but Lakara couldn't take the time to look. Suddenly, the leg slipped free. A blink later and the lizardling was completely out; on the ground and trying to look around.

Both women immediately retreated, leaving Stripes to care for her baby in whatever way her instincts told her to. Stripes turned from black to blue almost as soon as she spotted the small lizard and promptly started licking him clean.

"Good job," Kita said, lightly smacking Lakara's shoulder.

Lakara eyed her slime covered hands and tried not to gag. "Thank you. I think."

Kita laughed, but she did help pour some water so Lakara could clean her hands.

***

Davorin couldn't see anything. Black surrounded him; before, behind, and to every side. To his surprise, he couldn't hear anything either. Even the calls of the dead were silent, for possibly the first time in his life.

Slowly, he stretched his foot forward, not putting any weight on it until he found floor. Then he repeated the process with his other foot.

Davorin.

He knew that voice. Shadow Master. The one who had no gender, no birth, and no death. "Yes, Master of Shadows?"

You have come at last. But not by choice.

As lying to the deity of death was more foolish than Davorin wanted to think of himself as, he was honest. "Not entirely. No."

Few do. And yet you are here. Partially by choice, if not completely.

Davorin doubted he would ever willingly come to Shadow Master.

You will. In time.

"Master of Shadows?"

The time will come when you come to me of your own free will. I have seen it. I know not when or why, but you will.

He wanted to run, far, far away. But if this was to happen at a later date, then he must be alive for it.

I have not brought you here to kill you.

"But you would have taken Sir Jors if he came in?"

Yes.

"Why?"

Do you know why you are weak?

That wasn't an answer to his question. On the other hand, he had questioned a god and not been smote down. Perhaps he should count himself lucky. "No."

You are my most powerful champion alive today. Yet my power withers in you. You are afraid. Of me, of yourself, of your powers. I am disappointed.

The smart response would be to apologize. Disappointing a god was frequently fatal. The honest response would be more along the lines of admitting he didn't want those powers to begin with.

Few want them. Particularly not those that have them. But I gave you them for a reason. You must learn to master your fear and master the power I gave you. If you do not, your quest will fail, and you and your companions will be in my realm shortly.

His throat was dry as sweat beaded on his back and hands. "It depends on me?"

It depends on all of you. It always did. You will all have trials to master. Failure by one means failure for all.

"I see." They were doomed.

Not yet. I cannot foresee if you will succeed or fail, but your progress is being watched with interest.

Wonderful. Even the gods were intrigued. "I'm supposed to find a clue in your temple."

Past the dead that you may live.

"What does *that* mean?"

I know not, nor would I be permitted to say if I did.

Of course not. That would be too easy. After all, the whole point was that even the gods didn't know where it was. "Thank you. Um, I should probably be going now?"

Almost. There is something I wish to show you.

Before Davorin could respond, a glowing sphere appeared in front of him. Images spun by in a dizzying fury. His servant, Trois, was caring for his pigeons while taking care not to touch his books. King Zikkar was talking to his general about something as they watched soldiers drill in front of them. Lard Sartik, the king's personal advisor, was lying on a sick bed that the shadows declared he would never leave. Someone he didn't recognize but looked rich and important was talking to a group of other rich, important people, all of whom looked troubled. The nobility of Salardis, perhaps? Then the images ended.

Yes, the last was the king of Salardis talking to his nobles. All images are the present. I showed you what you need to know. Now, continue your journey. Master your fear and my power will grow in you.

There was nothing to say to that, so Davorin settled for a deep bow. When he turned around, he was outside the temple.

***

Sir Jors made his purchases as quickly as he possibly could. It meant they were probably paying a little bit more than if they had more time or if Kita was the one haggling with the merchants. But right now, he felt speed was a decent trade-off for a little extra money spent.

Something was wrong with Davorin. He was acting odd. While no one had called him on it, it was obvious to everyone that he didn't want to come here. Any more reluctance on his part and he probably would have made himself sick.

When they decided to split up the group, it was clear that Davorin would have loved to volunteer to be in the group that stayed with the lizards. To his credit, he outright admitted he should probably be one of the ones to go to the temple.

So, when Davorin offered to handle the temple himself, sounding as if it would be no more difficult than taking down the tents, a task Davorin had become quite adept at, Sir Jors thought he could be forgiven for being confused. Part of him suspected that Davorin was trying to cover up his fear with bravado. He had seen that plenty of times among soldiers. That didn't seem quite right, though. To his shame, Sir Jors even wondered if Davorin would skip the temple entirely. But there was no other way to get the information they needed.

He was going to refuse, offer to explore the temple with him; but something stopped him. Davorin had a point. They could finish faster if they separated. Besides, clearly something was going on that he didn't know about. Maybe it was a necromancer thing. Paladins were not permitted to work with necromancers, perhaps Shadow Master had rules about knights in his temple.

Even as he walked away, Sir Jors watched from the corner of his eye. Davorin hesitated at the doorway, but did enter, head high. When Sir Jors finished collecting supplies, Davorin wasn't waiting for him in the square. Sir Jors positioned himself where he could see the entrance of the temple and tried to look inconspicuous.

Not the most beautiful he had ever seen; Shadow Master's temple was stark. All sharp angles and narrow entrances, almost no windows. Black as onyx, the building seemed to leach out the sunlight surrounding it.

Davorin appeared suddenly at the doorway. Sir Jors navigated the crowd to reach him just as the necromancer reached the street. "Davorin?" He didn't respond.

Sir Jors touched his shoulder. Davorin jumped back, gasping, before staring at him with eyes so wide that Sir Jors could see them beyond the dark glasses. "Easy. Peace." Sir Jors stepped back; hands raised.

Recognition came slowly, with relief lapping at its heels. "You have the... supplies, that's right. You have them?"

"I do. You... paid your respects?"

"Yes. I have it. Let's get out of here."

Sir Jors waited until they were out of the city before asking, "What happened? You look awful."

"Shadow Master wanted to talk. Apparently, our progress is being watched with some interest."

The air in his lungs turned to lead. A personal audience with the gods? That rarely went well. Though, if the legends were true and the stone had been coveted by the gods, it only stood to reason that they would be interested in the result of their quest. "I see. Are you...?"

"I am unharmed. But confused."

That was probably the best that could be hoped for. "Perhaps when we regroup, you can share your story. Whatever portions you wish to share, at any rate." Likely parts would be private.

Davorin nodded but didn't say anything. The remaining walk was silent. Since they had been separated for half a day,

Sir Jors was unsurprised that there was a baby lizard addition to the party. As he had never seen pack lizards this young, he was a little surprised at how small he was. A full-grown pack lizard was between nine and eleven feet long and close to three feet tall at the shoulders. This baby lizard was maybe two, two and a half feet long and less than a foot tall. Of course, they grew fast. He'd be three-quarters of his full size within a year.

"All went well, I hope?" Sir Jors asked, eyeing the new addition.

"There was a slight complication, but we took care of it," Lakara said. "The lizardling was born tail first and got a little stuck."

"I'm calling him Trouble," Kita said calmly. "Only an hour or two old and he's already gotten into a fight with a scorpion, nearly fought with Whisper, and tried to eat Longtail's harness."

Lakara nodded. "He really has tried to get into everything."

That explained the makeshift harness from a spare tent cord. Sir Jors chuckled at that. Since it was almost sunset, they would camp here for the night, moving on tomorrow.

"Did you get the clue?' Lakara asked.

"Yes. It's 'past the dead that you may live.'"

Kita scowled. "What does *that* mean?"

Davorin gave a bitter, hysterical laugh. "That's exactly what I said."

"Um, not that I doubt your translation, but may I see your copy?" Lakara asked.

"I don't have one. Shadow Master told me directly." Davorin slumped near the fire and rubbed at his face. "Apparently Shadow Master wished to talk to me. I was told the clue and shown a few things. I do not know why."

"What were you shown?" Kita asked.

"My servant caring for my pigeons. King Zikkar talking to his general. Lord Sartik is dying. And the king of Salardis was meeting with several of his nobles. I was told that all images were the present, but I heard nothing."

No one seemed to have any idea why Shadow Master would choose to share those particular images. Or why Shadow Master would wish to talk to Davorin at all.

"Is that all that was said?" Lakara asked.

"No. My power was also discussed. But that is personal."

Sir Jors nodded and dropped the subject. Lakara did as well. Kita did not. "Power? You've never shown any signs of power."

Davorin's jaw went sharp. "Yes. That was the point reached."

"So, do you have it, or don't you?"

"I do." The necromancer's face could have been carved from rock.

"Have you used that power at all since we left?"

"No." There was pain in that voice.

Even Kita seemed a little regretful, but she didn't stop no matter how much Sir Jors was silently urging her to. "Why not?"

"Because I'm afraid!" Davorin exploded, standing up to pace. "I'm afraid of my own powers and refuse to use them. I'm losing them through atrophy and if Shadow Master is right, we'll all die if I don't learn to take control of them. But I'm afraid. Happy now?"

Lakara stared at him, aghast. Sir Jors tried to think of

something, anything to recover the situation. Kita, who had looked just as surprised at the beginning of his outburst, was now as calm as still water. "Yes. Because that's something that can be fixed."

"What?" Davorin stared at her.

"We're all afraid. Lakara, were you afraid to leave Corvis? To fight the imps? To help with Trouble's birth?"

"Well, yes..."

"But you did it anyway. Sir Jors, you've been in battle and no one is doubting your courage. But you were still afraid, weren't you?"

So that's where she was heading. Sir Jors nodded gravely. "I was. Only a fool would be otherwise."

"And me. I was afraid when we met up with Jalen. I was afraid when one of his men challenged me to a fight. I'm afraid now, on this journey."

"But I'm not like you! I... I'm a coward."

"You were afraid to enter the temple," Sir Jors said. "But you did it anyway."

Kita stood up and walked over to the sputtering necromancer. "You have power, do you? And you're losing it because of lack of use? So, use it. Now."

"But..."

"We're here. All of us. We might be afraid, but we stand with you. Just as you stand with us. Show us what you can do."

***

When the ground started shaking, Kita began regretting her decision to push the necromancer on this. Actually, she had started regretting it before that, but if there was one thing she had learned; it was that the longer one was a prisoner of fear, the harder it was to get free. If their lives depended on Davorin learning control of his abilities, then the sooner that happened, the better.

Which sounded a lot better in her head before the sand parted, revealing skeletons. A lot of skeletons. Skeletons of men, lizards, and imps were the most obvious, but there were other, mostly smaller skeletons that she didn't even try to identify. It seemed like anything that had died within twenty feet of them was coming to the surface. That was creepy enough. Then they started moving.

Three man-shaped skeletons started marching in unison, while four complete pack lizard skeletons and one partial crawled out as if scouting. The imp skeletons started digging through the sand.

The live pack lizards were becoming increasingly agitated, and she could feel Whisper's fury and fear at the bizarre circumstances. Lakara and Sir Jors stood, watching in horrified amazement. Kita managed to control herself until a skeleton bird raked past her face. Even then, she was proud that she didn't scream; only gasped and stepped back.

Davorin was even whiter than his usual pasty skin, gazing at his work in horror. Then it all stopped. The skeletons lost their animation and fell to the ground but were not reburied. Davorin started to crash to his knees, but Kita grabbed him as he fell. Lakara and Sir Jors were only a moment behind her.

He was shaking and almost in shock. Like she had with Lakara, Kita made him drink some water. When he seemed to have recovered enough that she thought he could hear her, she spoke, "Well done. I am truly impressed."

He glared at her.

"I mean it. I honestly didn't think you could do that. Clearly, the talk of you being the best necromancer in the land has merit."

"Did you think otherwise?"

Yes, yes, she had. "Would you blame me? Since I've known you, the only thing that told me you were a necromancer were your eyes."

Sir Jors stepped in then. "You did well. Were you afraid?"

"Of course, I was! Didn't you see that?"

Kita cut back in. "Yes, and I was afraid too. I'm sure Sir Jors and Lakara were, too. But we're all still here. Besides, you did that, right?"

"Clearly."

"Then you can do it again. Not tonight," she added quickly. "And preferably not without warning. But it didn't hurt you or us."

"Enough! No more for now." Davorin looked drained.

"Fair enough. Actually, I think there is something else we can do." A thought had been percolating since Risto tried to attack Lakara. She hadn't mentioned it yet because Lakara was still jumpy about the whole night. But perhaps now was the time. "Lakara, how did you fight off Risto?"

Lakara went white. "Back then? I couldn't fight him. You saved me. Thank you for that."

"You're welcome. But you did something. I heard him call you feisty."

"Do we have to discuss this?" Lakara asked.

Sir Jors agreed, frowning. "I am not certain this is proper."

"I have a plan. Now, what did you do?"

"Well, I *tried* to kick him, but I didn't do a very good job."

Kita smiled. "Then you need to learn. That way, next time, you might not need someone to come to your assistance."

She expected trouble from the others over this. Sir Jors might be on her side or might not. Lakara would probably be the hardest to convince. To her surprise, Sir Jors had the most trouble with the idea of a woman fighting like a brawler. Lakara was quiet, thinking.

"I'm not planning on taking her into a bar fight, I just want her to know how to defend herself."

"But—"

"Is it more proper for a woman to give up and die?" Kita asked.

"No, of course not." Sir Jors seemed horrified. "But—"

"I want to learn," Lakara spoke up. "I never want to be in a situation like that again. But if I am, I need to know how I can defend myself. Not panic and hope someone comes by in time to save me."

Sir Jors fell silent.

Kita nodded. "I don't know fancy fighting. I don't know any 'rules of combat'. I do, however, know the quickest ways of turning a fight to your advantage. It isn't pretty or easy. It definitely isn't muddy *fair*. But if someone tries to hurt you like that, you can change their minds, quick like."

Lakara nodded. "You said something about being challenged to fight?"

Filthy mess, she had, hadn't she? "One of the forms of entertainment. Drunken idiots challenge each other to see who can draw the other's blood first. I get challenged once a visit." She smirked. "*Only* once a visit. Because I make sure that when I win, no one else wants to challenge me."

Sir Jors seemed either impressed or skeptical. "You are undefeated?"

"They *are* drunk. Besides, do you think Jalen respects me because I'm a woman? Because of my charm? Even because of my thieving skills? He respects me, he let us live, partly because I make sure not to lose. I can't afford to."

Lakara was pale but determined. "Teach me."

They started small that night. Little tricks, like where to hit that really hurt, or how to hit someone so you didn't injure yourself as well. Perhaps in time, they would include some weapons training, but right now it was about how to hurt someone without one. When to kick and how. How to stand. How not to leave yourself vulnerable.

Since Davorin seemed interested, Kita got him up and practicing too. When Sir Jors realized there was no way to naysay them, he helped by giving the advice he had been taught in the army.

"The whole point is to take down your opponent enough that they can't hurt you, and you can get away. They can be alive; they can even be conscious. But they shouldn't be willing or able to chase you." That was Kita's philosophy of fighting.

Unsurprisingly, Sir Jors had a different philosophy, but he admitted that his philosophy was better suited to fighting as a unit against other soldiers. "In the occasion you might actually need any of this, Kita's way of thinking will do fine."

Once Kita was satisfied that both Lakara and Davorin knew how to throw a punch without hurting themselves, could kick without losing their balance, and knew three good areas to target, they stopped for the night. It was almost too dark to see, anyway. Besides, they had time.

The next temple they had to visit would be the temple of Cryswayr, goddess of fire, in Yarel. In order to get there, they would have to cross the Mountains of Death. Since the plan was to winter somewhere before they attempted to cross them, it would be months before they got there.

Now all they had to do was find somewhere to stay the winter. Since the towns they had been in so far were unfriendly, a winter village might be their best plan. Winter villages dotted Salardis, especially near the mountains, for travelers to safely spend the season. Most who took advantage of the winter villages were poorer travelers. Those on pilgrimages, poorer merchants who couldn't afford a storefront in a real town, retired soldiers who had not found a place to settle, and the like.

All they had to do was reach one. Unfortunately, they were too small to be marked on the maps they had. Whisper would be able to find one, but Kita wasn't sure how she could direct the group without admitting to Borrowing. Perhaps they would find another group of travelers who could tell them.

Well, it was nothing to worry about tonight. They would find something in time. Winter shouldn't set in for a couple weeks yet. Even traveling slowly because of Trouble, they should be able to find *somewhere* by then. They would be fine.

Chapter Eleven

Winter sets in

Or

"Is it spring yet?"

Pack lizards were terrible with cold. Davorin hadn't known that. Nor had he cared before being forced to travel with them. Every morning it was harder to get the lizards moving. They crowded by the fire at night. Trouble cuddled whenever he could. With Stripes or Longtail, with Kita, even with the rest of them if need be.

Not that Davorin blamed them. He hated the cold, too. Fortunately, someone had the foresight to buy heavier travel robes. They weren't enchanted, but they were decent quality. Usually, he would put on a normal travel robe and a heavier one over it, removing the heavier one as the day passed and warmed up. But these past two days, he hadn't needed to remove the second one. They needed to find one of those winter villages soon.

He made the mistake of saying so out loud at breakfast. Lakara agreed with him. But Kita and Sir Jors shared a troubled look. Wonderful. "What?"

Kita looked at him calmly. "What?"

"Don't try. You two know something or are thinking something. What?"

While she could, and probably still did sometimes, lie to

his face, she didn't this time. "You're right. We do need to find someplace and soon. It's going to snow. A few days at most."

Snow. Davorin swallowed hard. Why couldn't she have lied this time? He had never seen snow before. But he had heard stories.

Everyone knew that the first snow of winter made the mountains impassable, locking the northern part of Salardis in the grip of winter until spring came and thawed them out. He had heard of snow so fierce that no one could see more than a foot in any direction. Snow that buried houses. Pack lizards can't move in snow. It freezes them immobile. "How many days?"

"Two or three." Kita stared at the sky. "I've asked Whisper to scout ahead. Hopefully, he'll find something."

Right, so they were depending on a hawk being able to understand what she meant well enough to find someplace they could stay and then lead them to it. Lovely. But if it worked... Well, as long as they didn't freeze, Davorin wasn't sure he cared how they did it.

Even if Whisper did find a village and was able to show them, they would still have to get there before the snow swooped in. They had to keep moving.

They still needed to take breaks several times during the day, both for their sake and the lizards. Trouble may be a bundle of energy, but that energy ran out quickly. But if everyone took some more of the supplies, and Longtail carried the bulk of the rest, then there was room for Trouble to ride on Stripes' back for a while.

The heat of the day was far cooler than it used to be, which was both good and bad. Good in that it was cool enough that they could walk through it. Bad in that it proved that winter was indeed breathing down their necks.

About two hours before sundown, Whisper rejoined them, much to Kita's obvious relief. The tired bird perched on her outstretched arm. Davorin convinced Lakara to pour water into his cupped hands so Whisper could drink. Kita nodded to him in thanks, as she dug out a bit of salted beef. "Good Whisper. Excellent job. You found somewhere?"

Whisper shrieked.

"Excellent. Excellent. Good, I need you to lead us. Show us which way to go. Just for a bit, then you can rest with me."

With another cry, the hawk took wing, flying to the northwest instead of the northeast. Kita didn't hesitate to change bearings to follow, leading Trouble and Stripes behind her.

Davorin was more hesitant about the idea. He liked Whisper, and Kita had an almost unnatural way with animals, probably the result of her Queyan ancestry. But was she good enough to communicate on that level? He trained pigeons and was well aware that his birds understood almost nothing he said to them. Hawks might be smarter, and Whisper certainly *seemed* to understand her well, but to this extent? If they were led astray, if they didn't find the village before the snow hit, then they would all die.

Sir Jors and Lakara also hesitated to follow, eyes meeting. Whatever silent conversation they had; he was not part of it. When they broke eye contact, they walked after Kita.

Davorin stayed in place until Sir Jors looked back at him. "Are you coming?"

"Are you sure about this? What if...?" What if Kita and Whisper were wrong? What if there was no village? What if there was one, but they couldn't get there in time?

"Do you have a better idea?" Sir Jors asked.

A fair question. Going in the direction they had been

going might or might not lead to shelter. Following Kita might or might not lead to shelter. But staying where he was would definitely lead to his death. Besides, the rest of the party, and therefore the supplies, were heading northwest.

So, he followed. Sundown came and went. By unspoken agreement, they kept walking. It was dangerous to travel at night, but not as dangerous as facing snow without a shelter.

It was almost midnight when they agreed to stop for the night. They would have to set out early in the morning, but if they made the village then there would be time to catch up on sleep there. If they didn't, then it wouldn't matter.

No one bothered with tents. It was just one more thing that they would have to deal with in the morning. A large, improvised lean-to accomplished much the same, without taking as much time to set up or dismantle. Morning came much too quickly. Quick and cold.

"Up. Everyone up! We have to move on." Kita dropped Trouble on him and Sir Jors to rouse them.

Davorin sat up with a yelp as Trouble investigated the edible properties of his hair. "No, bad lizard. Kita!"

"Up! We need to get moving."

Sir Jors fumbled upright. "What's wrong?"

"I was wrong about the snow. Or the storm is moving faster. It's coming tonight. I can smell it in the air." Kita had her bedroll packed away and Lakara was rolling hers up. "We can eat while walking. I'm not sure the storm will wait until after sundown."

Sir Jors moved to look at the sky. "I believe you may be right." Quickly, he started rolling up his bedroll as the women started taking down the lean-to.

Davorin didn't smell anything unusual, but he could see the clouds that were starting to fill the air. There was a white-gray quality to them that he had never seen. So, those were snow clouds. A shiver that had nothing to do with the cold ran through him.

"How far is this village?" Davorin gathered his belongings with haste, before helping with the communal supplies.

"I have no idea. Have you ever tried to ask a bird about distances? Not close. We can't see it yet."

Meaning it was a race to see which came first. Did they find the village before the storm found them? It took about ten minutes for them to go from waking up to walking, and that included rousing the lizards.

Whisper flew ahead of them, close enough that they could see him and use him to keep their bearings. Kita was the only one who didn't seem to have any doubts about Whisper's ability to lead them to shelter, but no one said anything. As Sir Jors pointed out, there wasn't a better option.

Breaks were taken only when they had to be and kept short. Davorin tried not to be ashamed that he was one of the reasons those breaks were necessary. Kita and Sir Jors certainly didn't seem to need half of them. Lakara and he did.

Shortly before noon, Whisper shrieked, flew in a wide circle, then flew back to them. "He's seen it. We're getting close." Kita wiped sweat from her forehead. Then she stared at the sky before closing her eyes and inhaling deeply, tasting the air. "It'll be close, but I think we can beat the snow. Or at least, the worst of it."

Amazing how much hope of an end could add strength to tired muscles. Even the pain in his feet, his knees, his back, and his hips faded to something manageable as Davorin kept putting one foot in front of the other. The slight sweat that they all broke into despite the cold receded to a minor irritant. Even the ground seemed surer. Which actually was the case, as it changed from sand to a sandy soil.

Instead of a prolonged break for lunch, they had a short break, passed around food, and kept walking. It was about an hour before Kita claimed she spotted the village in the distance. Another half hour of walking, and Davorin could tell there was definitely something there, but not what. Still, something was better than nothing. By the next break, everyone agreed that it was indeed a village or town.

Kita was silently smug, but no one seemed bothered by it. Davorin thought that Whisper deserved a reward for possibly saving their lives. If they could just reach the place in time.

Two more hours passed, and the walls were rising large in their view. "Do winter villages have walls?" Davorin asked. He really didn't care what this place might be; winter village, city, town, or private fort; provided they could stay.

"Yes. It's to keep anyone from wandering off and getting lost in a storm. Also, it keeps the place a little warmer," Kita said. "I stayed in one once."

Judging from her reaction, it wasn't a pleasant experience. "Was something wrong with it?" Lakara asked.

"What? No. Not really. I just don't like staying too long in one place. And some people didn't believe that, how did they put it, 'the whelp of some Trovian dog' should be staying there." Kita shrugged. "There's no fighting allowed, though, and no one wanted to risk being expelled so it wasn't anything serious. Nothing I haven't heard a thousand times before. Most of the time I'm far enough south not to worry about it."

Davorin tried not to wince. He had said almost the same exact thing to her. Well, he called her 'She-whelp' a few times. Maybe more than a few. And she had called him bone mage several times. Kita didn't seem to care, and he wasn't sure if he could or how to apologize.

The day grew dark, and the clouds deepened in color. But it wasn't until Davorin saw slow white flakes falling that he became truly worried. "Is that snow?"

"Yes." Kita scowled. "We're about an hour, maybe two, out. We have to keep moving."

"But—" Snow meant death. Everyone knew that.

"We know where we're going. It's not snowing hard yet, and if we're lucky, it won't for a while. Besides, it's that or we lie down and die here. You can if you want, but I'm going to that village." Kita started walking faster.

No one wasted the breath to argue with her. There was no point. Having no desire to freeze to death, Davorin kept walking.

***

The occasional snowflake gave way to light but steady snow. Each melted upon touching the ground, but it was taking longer. Sir Jors was relieved it was not interfering with visibility yet. They were a mile, maybe two, out from the village. The lizards were dragging, even as the people tried to move faster. Kita was actually carrying Trouble, who was repaying her kindness and impatience by trying to eat her hair and robe.

Perhaps the only thing they had going for them was that the sand had given way to grassy land, probably because this area actually got rain and snow. All of them had more experience walking on grasslands than sand.

The snow intensified and began to stick to the ground. But the village was close. If they didn't have the lizards, they might have been able to run to it. But the pack lizards were slow, trudging, and resistant to any encouragement. They were too heavy to be dragged and pulling at the harnesses did very little to budge five hundred pounds of lizard.

Just when Sir Jors feared they might not make it, they arrived at the gate. He pounded at the door. A window opened and the watchman looked out. "Who goes there?"

"Travelers. Travelers seeking shelter for the winter," Sir Jors answered.

"One hundred gold dourats per person, and fifty for the lizards."

He hadn't expected it to be free but that was far more money than they had to spend. "We haven't that much."

"That's the price. No money, no admittance."

"You'd let us die? Over money?" Lakara asked, sounding horrified.

"Those are the rules," The watchman said, showing no concern.

"We are poor travelers. We have," Sir Jors made some mental calculations. "One hundred dourats."

"That will let one in." There was no reasoning with him.

Before Sir Jors could get angry, Kita stepped up. "But you've forgotten! Your reward for saving that merchant." She reached a hand into his pouch and pulled out an emerald half the size of a chicken's egg. An emerald he knew had not been in his pouch that morning. "Surely this would be enough to let us winter?"

He could see the gleam of greed in the watchman's eye. "Let me see."

Kita ignored the outstretched arm and held it up to the watchman's face, angling the stone around. "Do we have a deal?"

"The stone, plus a hundred gold."

"Fifty." Kita didn't seem to realize they had absolutely no

bargaining power.

The watchman's window slammed shut. Lakara sucked in a noisy breath, and Davorin held his arms. As Sir Jors feared they had been left to freeze, the doors creaked open. "The stone and fifty gold." Kita handed him the emerald while Sir Jors hastily counted out fifty dourats. "You stay at cabin five. It has an attached barn. Communal meals are in the long house. Everyone works to support the community. Your jobs will be determined tomorrow." He pointed to a small house with a barn, not far from the gatehouse.

They hurried to the cabin as the snow thickened. Once inside, the lizards were much faster. The barn might not be large, but it was warm and had an earthen pit big enough for them.

Sir Jors and Kita got the lizards settled before joining Lakara and Davorin in the house. The downstairs had a firepit, a table with six chairs, a chest of blankets, and a large bed. There was a good-sized cooking pot over the firepit, and a wooden tub, the kind used for bathing, to the side in front of a stack of firewood. Steps led to a loft, which, according to Lakara, had a smaller bed, a smaller table, and two chairs. One door led to a privy, while another led to a pantry. Whisper made himself at home on one of the ceiling beams.

"Not bad," said Kita after she finished looking around. "Last time I stayed in the communal dorm. I had a bed and a chest that I didn't dare leave anything in. I shared the room with about ten other women."

"It's certainly better than freezing to death," Davorin said, even as he eyed the place warily.

"I'm sure it will be better when it's clean," Lakara said. Then she turned to Sir Jors, "Where did you get the emerald?"

"I didn't." He looked to Kita. "I know you didn't have that at the beginning of the journey. How did you get it?" He tried his best not to sound accusatory even though he couldn't think of a way she could have legally acquired it as they traveled.

Kita rummaged through the chest of blankets, paying him little attention. "I won it. Off of one of Jalen's men. He wagered it over something."

"What did you wager?" Sir Jors asked.

"Nothing worth a third of that."

"So, the emerald is stolen," Davorin said.

"Probably. Though I doubt that thief of a watchman cares. When I was in a village, about five, six years ago, I only had to pay fifteen dourats. True, I didn't get a cabin, but still..." She looked them over. "Is someone going to build a fire?"

"I will," Sir Jors volunteered. Trafficking in stolen goods was illegal and could well get all involved in trouble with the law. On the other hand, Kita had gotten it semi-legitimately and passed it on the same way. She could, and likely would, claim that she had no idea it was stolen. And if she was right about the watchman gouging up the prices, he might be careful how he sold it, especially if he suspected it was stolen.

"What did he mean by jobs?" Lakara asked.

"The work done to support the community. Hauling water, cooking, hunting when possible, gathering food, planting, etc. Spinning, weaving, leather work, anything you can do?" Kita asked as she lit a candle or two. "I usually did the basic chores. Hauling water, cooking, cleaning. Also candle or soap making."

"I know how to spin flax," Lakara said. "I haven't done it in years, but I can do it."

"I'm pretty used to hunting and would be willing to help wherever strength without training is needed," Sir Jors said as he got the fire to spark.

Davorin sighed. "I don't know any of those."

"Then they'll assign you general chores. You can cook. You may wish to volunteer for that." Kita passed around blankets. "We should warm up. And close the shutters. It will make it warmer in here."

The two windows had glass barriers, but Sir Jors agreed. Covering them would make the small cabin warmer. Once the fire was in place and a couple candles lit, it was enough light not to miss the windows. Besides, the snow had picked up enough that there was little light coming through outside.

From the sounds of it, there might be mice, but between the hawk and the lizards, Sir Jors doubted they would be there long. "I think it would be best if the women were to take the loft. If you believe you will be warm enough."

"Heat rises. And there are several blankets." Lakara wrapped one of them around her. "We made it, didn't we?"

"Just in time, too." Kita peered through a crack in the shutters before closing it. "There may actually be a day or two's delay before they assign us tasks. We have food for a few days, right?"

"At least four. Possibly more," Sir Jors agreed. "We pushed ourselves hard. We should eat and then rest."

As Davorin cooked up a stew, Kita pulled out the wooden tub and dragged it outside. She came back a moment later, brushing snow from her hair and clothes, but without the tub. Sir Jors nodded in approval.

Dinner was quiet, though the chance to eat something warm was appreciated. They hadn't taken the time to do that yet today. Kita checked on the lizards and came back to report all was well. "They're warm, they have food and water. What more do they need?"

"What more indeed?" Davorin said. A yawn cut him off.

"I think sleep might be in order."

"The tub should be full of snow by now. I may need help getting it back," Kita said.

"I'll bring it in," Sir Jors said. Opening the door, Sir Jors found himself briefly wondering if he had gone blind. There was nothing but white before him. But he found the tub, now indeed full of snow, and managed to drag it inside and next to the fire. It would melt overnight, giving them water in the morning.

The women retired first, with Lakara carefully taking a candle up to their loft. Davorin pulled the cooking pot away from the fire so the leftover stew didn't burn, while Sir Jors damped the fire so it would burn low all night. The last candle was blown out, and they were left in their small, dark sanctuary from the howling wind and cold.

***

It was almost amazing how quickly they fell into a pattern at Winterwatch, as Lakara learned the town was called. Kita had been right about the snow causing a delay. It had continued to snow for at least a full day, leaving piles that went beyond Lakara's waist. They had been completely housebound for most of two days, and the first task they had participated in was working with everyone else to move the snow to the middle of the village for easy water collection.

Since then, Lakara spent most of her days spinning flax. Davorin worked in the kitchens. Sir Jors helped with hunting and building. Kita kept the most varied roles, filling in almost anywhere that was needed. Hauling water, gathering food and fire fuel, and hunting small game when the weather was nice enough. Cleaning, candle making, and soap making when it wasn't. She seemed to prefer the outside tasks.

It had been two weeks since they had arrived, with it snowing more days than not, but no more blizzards so far. In some ways, it felt like they had only been there a day or two. In others, it felt like they had been there for months.

The pattern was comfortable, to Lakara at least. They woke in the morning and broke bread together, before heading to the longhouse where tasks were assigned based on skills, necessity, and volunteering. They generally did not see each other for lunch which might vary in time depending on the jobs they were assigned; but made a point of seeking each other out for dinner, both of which were served in the longhouse. After dinner, they would head back to the cabin. At least one, sometimes more, person would check on the lizards, who were happy with their current state, so far. Then they would sit around the table or fire to talk before going to sleep.

They shared interesting tales of the day. Lakara still helped Kita with reading and had progressed to writing. Kita taught Lakara and Davorin some tricks for fighting. Sir Jors promised to teach some weapons training when they were ready. Davorin was practicing and refining his necromancy skills on a much subtler level than the time in the Ocean of Sand, much to their relief.

Lakara thought she was probably happier than she had been since they had set out on their journey. Possibly longer than that. Yes, she missed the library, and dearly wished there was one in Winterwatch; but that was the only thing she missed. She had no real personal connections in the palace, having not seen her parents in years, even though they lived in the palace, and had made no friends among the other scholars. Her quarters in the palace were nicer, and definitely cleaner, but the cabin was suitable. The mice were gone, and they kept the place neat.

Most importantly, it was a warm, secure place to be during the winter, and when she left in the morning, she knew she would be back in the evening. It was quite possible that by the time spring came, no one would want to move on.

Well, Kita would probably be ready to leave. And Sir Jors took their responsibility seriously and would want to leave as soon as they safely could. Davorin and Lakara would be the reluctant ones. Just as they had been in Corvis.

A bell chimed, signifying the end of the workday and the dismissal to dinner. Lakara stayed seated as the forewoman looked over everyone's output, handing out chits according to their work. Today, Lakara was given three chits for her work. Once she had managed to retrain herself on how to spin, she averaged two or three chits a day, though she had managed four once or twice. The first day, she barely managed one.

One chit was worth one meal or a portion of food for the lizards. Davorin's work in the kitchen allowed him to take some of the extras or food that hadn't turned out well, which they ate for breakfast. Kita and Sir Jors were normally able to earn enough to cover themselves and the lizards. Back at the cabin, they kept a stockpile of extra chits. There were five so far, in a wooden bowl hidden in a cabinet. Five wasn't much, but they had only been there two weeks so far, there should be plenty come spring. Then they could trade the chits for supplies when they needed to move on. Privately, Lakara suspected that Kita, and possibly Davorin, had personal stashes of chits, but she wasn't going to confront them about it.

Lakara took the metal chits and followed the other spinners to the hall. A girl, maybe about twelve, with a withered leg, sat to the side of the door, collecting a chit from everyone as they went in. Lakara handed over her chit and looked around.

She spotted Kita first. Kita must have gotten out at least five minutes before she did because the other woman had her food and was seated near the end of one of the long tables. No one was sitting near her, so if Lakara was quick, she would be able to join her. Kita met her eyes and nodded.

Dinner was neither new nor exciting, but it was food, and it was hot. Stew and bread, with small meat pies. By the time Lakara had gone through the line and had her food, Davorin was heading towards Kita and Sir Jors was part of the line.

Soon they were all seated and eating. "I made the meat pies today. Well, some of them."

For the first several meals, Kita made a point of asking what Davorin had made, claiming it was to avoid eating that. Then she would promptly try it, claim it was good, so clearly someone else had made that particular one. Davorin would pretend to be insulted. Now he just volunteered what he made.

Kita, true to form, immediately tried a bite of meat pie. "Rabbit?"

"Yes. Mostly."

Lakara firmed up her lips and promised herself not to ask. Neither did anyone else.

"Not bad. Slatrow? They actually let you use that?"

Slatrow was not a cheap spice. Not as expensive as some, but not something for cheap, bulk food. Though it was native to Salardis, so it was cheaper here than in Graldish.

"A little. Not much. I'm surprised you can taste it," Davorin admitted. He took a bite. "I made it and I can't taste the slatrow."

Kita shrugged. "I buy spices when I can. They really add to a dish and are good to bargain with." She frowned. "Speaking of bargaining, do we have enough to feed the lizards without my chits tonight?"

A quick tally indicated yes, with an extra to put aside. "Why?' Lakara asked. "Did you have trouble today? Do you need to borrow a chit?"

"No, I'm fine. But I've been invited to join in a game."

Davorin groaned. Sir Jors frowned. It took Lakara a moment to understand what she meant. "Gambling?" She squeaked in a whisper. "Are you sure?" While discouraged, games of chance were not forbidden, and many people whiled away a few dark, cold hours winning and losing their chits.

"I would recommend against it," Sir Jors said in a calmer voice. "While it is your decision, I do not believe it to be a good plan. You could lose your hard-earned chits, through either luck or a cheating opponent. Or if you do succeed, you risk someone trying to take your winnings by force, leaving you poorer than when you started. And for what? Do you enjoy these games?"

Kita had been looking irritated and was about to respond, only to stop at his last question. She paused and seemed a little more contemplative. "To an extent, but to be honest, it's more of a way to fit in. I'm not blind nor deaf. When one of you claims a seat, you have to spread out so there is room for everyone to join you. When I do it, no one comes close. Well, there was one muddy idiot who tried to challenge me to move because dogs weren't welcome at 'his' table. I pretended I couldn't hear him, and he went away. Today, he 'invited' me to join their card game. I'm not stupid. I figure he plans to take me for everything I've got. But if I'm careful, I can let him win the first few games, then win modestly. I've made 'friends' that way before. I might come out of the night a little poorer, but with one less enemy."

Lakara gaped at her. She had never realized Kita was being harassed. Kita wasn't the only one who looked to be part Trovian in Winterwatch. However, Kita was the only woman. The other two were men who were big and strong enough that Lakara could imagine bullies leaving them alone.

"Who?" Sir Jors asked.

"No fighting," Lakara whispered.

"I shall not fight him."

"Not even go and talk to him?" Kita asked.

"I shall do nothing, provided he leaves you alone."

Kita sighed. "He's not going to leave me alone, and I can't go everywhere with one of you. Besides, he can't hurt me, or he'll be expelled from Winterwatch."

Davorin cut in. "The man who invited you. Is he about Sir Jors' height, big and broad-shouldered, with a ratty-looking beard?"

"Yes, why?"

"He works in the kitchens and was absolutely smug about something he was planning tonight. He said something about teaching someone a lesson she'd never forget. I think he was after more than money. Don't go. It's not worth the risk."

Kita eyed him strangely, taking a few minutes to think before speaking. "I don't know that you're right. And I can handle myself, especially when he has to be restrained. But I'll stay home tonight."

It was a bit of an odd night. Kita was restless like she was some nights when she had been indoors all day, but she channeled it well, cajoling Sir Jors into helping her demonstrate basic knife fighting. Davorin tried to summon a shade, but none came. Lakara was even able to read for a while, before deciding it was best to save the candles.

Before blowing out the last candle, Lakara went to stash away the extra chit. She smiled when she realized that this new chit made nine.

***

Kita was not pacing. Some might think she was, including her housemates who were watching her with varying amounts of irritation, but she was not pacing. Simply stretching her legs. The snow had kept them trapped in the house for almost three days now. Fortunately, there had been enough warning about the storm that they were able to stock up ahead of time.

The storm was likely to blow itself out tonight, but it would probably be at least one more day before leaving was possible. Two months of winter so far. Probably another two months to go before they could travel on. Maybe more.

She reached the door and turned, heading back to the other wall. Lakara sighed and Davorin muttered something, but Kita ignored them both. How could they stand to just sit there?

"Would you like to borrow a book?" Lakara asked. "You've progressed enough that I doubt you would need more than the occasional word explained."

It was an idea, but Kita didn't think she could sit still long enough. "I finished the bird book and I'm not interested in the history of kings." Though she had liked the bit about the responsibility of the royal family to the people. Kita had always assumed that most leaders were more interested in their own power. She hadn't known that the king had to swear an oath to protect the people and rule for their benefit.

"I have a scroll on lizards," Lakara offered.

"Lizards. I think I'll check on the pack lizards." Kita changed direction to snag a lantern before opening the door to the attached barn. Stripes and Longtail looked up, only to relax when they saw her there. Trouble was more active, climbing over a haystack, looking for either food or a warm spot.

"Hello, how are you enjoying the storm?" The barn was warmer than the house, being smaller with thicker walls and no windows.

The water trough looked low, so Kita refilled it. One good thing about the snow was that water was rarely in short supply, so long as one was patient enough for it to melt. Trouble snuggled up to her side to lick at the water. Kita smiled as she stroked his neck and back. He was getting big. He was almost as long as she was tall now.

Stripes and Longtail eyed the water with interest but didn't move towards it. Well, they would when they were thirsty.

"So, do you miss traveling, or are you enjoying staying in a nice, warm barn all winter?"

Longtail put her head down, eyes closed, and relaxed in the lizard posture of sleep. Kita laughed. "Lazy lizard. I get it. You're perfectly happy here as long as it's warm and you're fed and watered."

Trouble scrambled around her. "At least you have energy." Kita stood up.

The lizards seemed fine, but she wanted to double-check. If there was an injury, it would be easy to miss it. It took weeks to realize Stripes was pregnant and they were with her constantly at the time. Now she saw them for less than an hour a day, and some days she saw them not at all. A missed injury, even a minor one, could lead to a major problem. And with their claws, minor injuries were not hard to come by. Kita tried to check them over at least every few days.

Longtail did not appreciate being woken for a brief examination, but Kita avoided being bitten or scratched, and there were no injuries or signs of anything wrong. Stripes was a little more docile. "Good. You're both fine. Trouble? Where did you go?"

Not expecting an answer, she wasn't disappointed. After a moment, she realized she was hearing something. Someone chewing. "Trouble, what have you gotten into?" She picked up the lantern and headed in the direction of the sound. Trouble had found the harnesses and was gnawing on them. "No, bad Trouble! Stop that!" She batted him away from the harnesses and scooped them up. Where could she put them that the lizards couldn't get at them? She had thought they were secure where they were. Perhaps inside the cabin would be better.

The brindles she could hang from a peg, especially if she looped it a few times. But there was the mat that was harnessed to the lizards so they could be loaded with packs. That was bigger and apparently it was being stored somewhere in Trouble's reach. Yes, she probably should move it to the cabin.

Kita readjusted her bundle, stopping when she heard the distinctive rustle of paper. That was a sound she hadn't known well before this quest and doubted she'd hear much afterwards. Paper was expensive and rarely used except for books, which were even more expensive and rare. What would paper be doing in a lizard mat?

Chapter Twelve

Truth and Lies in the Dark

Or

"Who are you loyal to?"

When Kita stormed back into the cabin looking even more agitated than when she left, Sir Jors was not ashamed to admit he jumped. So did Lakara, and possibly Davorin, but Sir Jors couldn't see the necromancer at the moment.

"Kita, what—" Lakara tried to ask.

Kita ignored her, stalked up to the table, and thrust some papers down with enough force to echo in the small cabin. It had to have hurt her hand, but she didn't seem to notice. "What. Is. This?" The words escaped through gritted teeth as Kita trembled with suppressed emotion. Sir Jors had always known she was a thief, but he had never considered her violent. Right now, she seemed more dangerous than a feral pack lizard or a crazed unicorn.

Davorin left the pantry to join the others at the table, while Lakara studied the papers, confusion on her face. Carefully, Sir Jors picked one up and held it to a candle. There was writing on it, writing he didn't recognize.

Surduk:

Five battalions of guards

Three grain store houses

Gates close at sunset, unguarded during the day

One armory

Turnuy:

Three battalions of guards

Two grain store houses

Gates manned

Armory and barracks

Noble House

Juztoc:

Four battalions of guards

Two grain store houses

Gates unmanned

"What *is* this?" Sir Jors asked. The other papers seemed to have similar writing.

"It's... information. Not even accurate information. Surduk had at least two armories and there were watchmen on the gates," Lakara said. "And we didn't even enter some of these places."

"Where did this come from?" Davorin asked, leafing through the papers.

"It was in one of the lizard's mats. Trouble got into them and chewed one open. I heard paper..." Kita looked slightly calmer with the realization that no one else knew about this either, but she was still vibrating.

"Why would anyone put something like this in a lizard's mat?" Lakara asked, baffled. "Even if we knew about it, it doesn't seem to be accurate. But we didn't know about it, and honestly, we don't need this information. What do we care about grain stores or battalions of guards?"

The answer hit Sir Jors with the force of a pack lizard's tail. "A spy would gather this kind of information. To prepare for war."

Kita had figured it out already, and it looked like Davorin wasn't far behind. Lakara, naïve, honest Lakara, hadn't seen it yet. "But we aren't spies. We're on a quest. We don't need to know this."

"A quest we aren't supposed to admit to, and honestly sounds unbelievable anyway," Kita snarled. "While every city we've been in since entering Salardis has been on the lookout for spies. One guard finds this..." She pounded the table with her fist. "Probably has a description of us too. We've been set up!"

"But..." Lakara stuttered. "That doesn't even make sense. Why would anyone make it look like we were spying? No one gains from that."

"Not true." Davorin sat down heavily. "My vision from Shadow Master. I saw King Zikkar talking to his general while soldiers trained. If he is expecting, or planning for war, that sets him up to advantage. If Salardis is pushed into attacking or declaring war before their army is ready, then King Zikkar is more likely to win quickly."

"But we've been at peace for a hundred years!" Lakara said. "Why would he even want a war?"

"Money. He's torn through most of Graldish's resources over the past ten years to build that filthy throne room of his, possibly to raise his army too. Even the outskirt cities of Salardis were in better shape than most of the cities in Graldish we saw. If he can win against the Salardin army, even if he doesn't gain new territory, he can demand tribute." Kita was pacing again.

Lakara looked like she wanted to argue but couldn't find a decent rebuttal.

"It fits." Sir Jors felt actual pain admitting that. Admitting that the king he had sworn fealty to might well have set them up to die in order to facilitate a war for personal gain. "But we can't know for sure."

Davorin sat up suddenly. "Yes, we can." He stood. "Stoke up the fire. I need to fetch a few things."

***

In the few moments it took Davorin to gather the implements he needed; a bronze bowl, a censor, herbs, and Shadow Master's incense; Kita had managed to coax the fire into a blaze. Everyone looked at him as he brought his tools. "If the king has indeed set us up to die in order to start a war, who would know about it?"

"The king," Kita said. "Maybe his general?"

"Lord Sartik," Lakara said. "He was in the throne room when we were sent off and he is the king's closest advisor."

"Was." Davorin began preparing. "Lord Sartik was dying months ago. It is very unlikely he is not in Shadow Master's realm by now. If I can summon him, we can question him. Ghosts cannot lie to a necromancer. Not on anything they knew in life."

During the time it took him to prepare, they decided on what questions they wanted answered. If he did successfully call Lord Sartik over, he probably wouldn't be able to keep him here for long, and it was difficult and dangerous to call up the same shade too many times. There were ways to keep a shade longer, like Virn had done. But the acts required to do that were beyond anything he was willing to do. Even if he were willing to cross those lines, the rest of the party would have stopped him.

Davorin took a moment to center himself, gazing into the fire for a focus. Slowly he found the shadows only he could see, the whispers only he could hear. Tracing them, he focused on looking for Lord Sartik. The flame began to dance before him, blown by an unseen wind.

Then, just as he thought it would fail, he felt it. Lord Sartik's shade. "Lord Sartik, I, Davorin, Master Necromancer, bid you come." There was resistance. Davorin mentally tugged harder. He was the necromancer, Sartik was a shade. He *would* win this.

The fire changed, revealing Lord Sartik's shade. "Why have you summoned me?"

"I, Davorin, Master Necromancer, order you to answer truthfully and completely all questions we ask." He would be asking the questions unless someone came up with one at the last minute, but he didn't want to take the chance that Sartik would be able to lie to one of them.

The shade grimaced and tried to pull away. Davorin tightened his magical hold. "Ask your questions. I shall answer them. Truthfully and completely."

"Why did King Zikkar send us on this quest? Does he even believe in the Jewel of Ishni?"

Sartik hissed but was compelled to answer. "King Zikkar wishes a war. He believes he can defeat Salardis. You were sent to be captured and executed as spies. Either Salardis would declare war, or King Zikkar would claim Salardis was in the wrong, executing prominent citizens on a pilgrimage on false charges. We expected you to be caught by now. Your descriptions have been given and proof of your spying manufactured. Neither of us believed in the jewel or expected you to get this far."

"If we did bring him the jewel, what would he do?"

"Probably execute you all and use the jewel to take over Salardis and the Queya if possible. That was another part of the plan. If you did survive Salardis, you would be killed by the Queya who would hopefully assume Salardis was declaring war. If those two fought, then King Zikkar could sweep through and take over whatever was left."

"Who else knows of his plans?"

"General Lysaz knew to prepare for war, but not why. No one else knows anything much. Even the one who planted the evidence of spying was killed to make sure she didn't talk."

"Why us?"

"Why not you? The thief insulted the king by first stealing from him then refusing him. The knight was a liability with his sleep curse. The king never wanted or needed a necromancer, and a scholar was picked at random to ensure you actually got to Salardis."

He was losing control of the shade. "What was his plan if that failed? If we weren't caught as spies and didn't bring him back the jewel?"

Sartik snarled, fighting him. But no shade could compete with a necromancer. "Then he'll find another pretext. He had several contingency plans when I became ill."

"Such as?"

"Claim they are aiding the Trovians in raiding Graldish. Fake an assassination attempt. Send assassins after King Hertayz of Salardis. Claim to have caught spies from Salardis. Just—" The connection was lost, and Lord Sartik disappeared.

Davorin was silent a minute, trying to absorb what he had been told before gathering his tools. Only after his things were put away did he look at his companions.

Lakara was white, fingers folding, unfolding, and refolding a strip of her robe. Horror warred with disbelief. Sir Jors was grim-faced and quiet. Resigned. Kita was pacing again, her legs like knife blades cutting up the floor. If Lord

Sartik or King Zikkar were to suddenly appear in front of her, she probably would not hesitate to kill him. Davorin felt numb.

He hadn't suspected the truth, but somehow, he wasn't surprised either. Especially once Kita found the 'evidence' that they were spies. Thank the gods that she had found it, and not a guard somewhere.

"What do we do?" The question was on all their minds, but it was Lakara who asked. "We've been ordered to find the Jewel of Ishni, and even if we were set up to die, refusing the king's order is treason."

"So, we just go and die? Because of him? Oh, no! I've refused to lie down and die because he wanted me to, twice. I'm not dying for him now!" Kita snarled.

"What? When did he—" Lakara asked.

Sir Jors spoke at the same time. "What was the king's offer that you refused?"

Kita grabbed one of the chairs and pulled it away from the table, away from the group. She spoke to the floor, energy mostly gone. "Before all this, I broke into what I thought was someone's manor house. I had to use something personal to bribe a guard a day earlier and was hoping to get it back. Someone told me it would likely be there. Either he had the wrong information, or he was setting me up, because I got caught. Caught searching through a counting box that was apparently the King's Tax. On the day King Zikkar came by to collect it. Almost got away, too. I jumped out the window, but there were too many guards on the grounds. They snatched me up before I could disappear."

She gave a bitter laugh and kicked at the ground. "Apparently, I impressed the king, because he visited me in my cell with an offer. He'd drop my prison sentence if I became his bed slave. I don't know much about servants and slaves, but I know that bed slaves have no protections under the law. Not even life. Even concubines have some rights and protections. Don't know what you've heard, but the rumors I heard, if they're right; I wouldn't have survived long there. I spat in his face. So, I guess it wasn't much of a surprise that the next time I saw him, he threatened me with execution."

That... actually explained quite a bit. "I haven't heard rumors, but I live a very isolated life in the palace," Davorin said. "I don't imagine those are the types of rumors that would spread amongst any but the servants and attendants. No one of standing would dare say anything, even if it were true." Sir Jors and Lakara agreed after a moment of hesitation.

"I don't need pity. But I don't feel any loyalty to the king, and you can't expect me to," Kita said, looking up for the first time.

"He *is* your king. And what you are saying is treason." Sir Jors stood.

Kita jumped to her feet, sending her chair flying. "Are you going to execute me?" She was nose to neck with him, glaring him down. "Knight?"

Sir Jors took a step back, reducing the tension. "No. But he is still our king. You cannot expect us to throw aside our loyalties that easily."

Kita made a sound that Davorin hadn't known could escape a human, or even mostly human, throat before grabbing an extra robe and forcing the door open. Everyone shivered as wind and snow were driven in, but Kita didn't hesitate.

***

It took fifteen minutes, maybe ten, for Kita to decide that going out in the storm might well have been her most foolish idea since breaking into the king's manor house. True, she needed to leave before she said something that would have possibly led to violence, but she probably would have been better off with the lizards.

They would be stuck in Winterwatch until winter ended and it was safe to travel. Two months or so, most likely. She had to put up with the others until then. But no longer. Even if they were determined enough to fetch some shiny for a tyrant, Kita wasn't going to have any part of it. Maybe she could slip away before they left. With at least a night's head start and Whisper to help her keep watch, she should be able to evade them. If they even bothered to search.

But the first step was not freezing to death in Winterwatch. Kita made a careful turn and followed the path she had made back to the cabin. It was faster going back since she wasn't plowing a new trail, but she had lost enough ire to feel the cold.

Frozen fingers opened the door and she pulled herself inside before slamming the door to shut out the storm. The warmth was actually painful. But the most surprising thing was that instead of the tension she expected, the others seemed relieved to see her.

"You're back!" Lakara said. "You must be freezing. Here, sit by the fire." She fluttered off to get a couple more blankets.

Kita shrugged off her outer robe and took a seat. It was sit or be forced to sit. Lakara wrapped two blankets around her. Kita took them and focused on thawing out the ice in her bones.

"Are you well?" Sir Jors asked once she had stopped shivering and discarded one of the blankets.

"That depends. Do I need to sleep with one eye open?" She tried to hide the tension in her sinews as Sir Jors walked closer, taking a seat by the fire.

"No. Your opinions are your own, and I do not doubt you

feel justified in them. But I would consider it a personal favor if you would attempt to not malign the king in my hearing."

Kita thought about that for a moment. It seemed a fair request, for the time being anyway. "Agreed."

"Thank you. It would probably be best to table further discussion until later. When tempers have cooled, and the weather has warmed."

"On one condition," Kita said. "We burn those papers. No point keeping them."

"Good idea," Lakara said, scooping the papers up and tossing them into the fire before anyone could object. If anyone had plans to object.

The papers caught fire quickly, curling in, red then black. Kita thought she felt a little lighter just watching them turn to ash. They might still be questioned, charged as spies, but at least they didn't carry 'proof' of spying. Might be enough to prevent them from being executed.

If they questioned what's-his-name again, then they should ask what description of them had been given. Probably something about them claiming to be doing a pilgrimage and including a necromancer. That might be why they hadn't been stopped. With Davorin borrowing her glasses, and them claiming him to be a merchant most of the time, they wouldn't fit the description.

"Good thing you found that," Davorin said.

Kita nodded but didn't say anything. If Trouble hadn't started chewing on the harnesses, she wouldn't have found the papers. She wouldn't have known. None of them would have. Not until some guard somewhere searched them and found the papers.

"I need to do something," she said.

"What do you need to do?" Lakara asked.

Kita shook her head. "Not like that. I need to *do* something. I can't sit here thinking. I just keep getting angry."

A look around the cabin didn't reveal anything promising. Stew was cooking in the firepit and didn't need anything from her. They had already cleaned the dishes from lunch. She had checked on the lizards not even an hour ago. It was too cold and wet to gather fire fuel or snow for water, and they had plenty of both. Whisper was asleep and didn't need anything.

"Like I said earlier, I could let you borrow a book."

She shook her head. "Thank you, but I need to *do* something."

Sir Jors stood up, rummaged through his pack and came back with a hatchet. Kita stared at him. It was far too small to behead someone with, and he had pretty much promised he wasn't going to execute her. "You can chop some of the firewood into smaller portions. Not all of it. We do need the larger logs, but some of it."

With a shrug, Kita stood and took the hatchet. It was something. Busy work, but something. Besides, the mood she was in, attacking something with an axe might make her feel better.

She split wood until her hands hurt and sweat ran into her eyes. Even then, she only stopped because Sir Jors was very cautiously pointing out that they still needed some of those longer pieces intact.

Kita arched her back, feeling it crack in three places. "Thank you. That helped."

"Good." He took the hatchet from her, trading it for a wet cloth. Kita took the hint and wiped her face, hands and back, before laying the cloth aside.

The rest of the day was quiet. Kita volunteered to do the

laundry, getting most of the rest of her frustration out with scrubbing. No one spoke of anything important, and everyone retired early. The storm had finally blown itself out, but it was another day before they could get around. That day was quiet, too.

The day after that, everyone was back to work. Kita spent the day shoveling snow. Occasionally she saw Sir Jors in the distance, also shoveling snow, but they were seldom close enough to nod acknowledgement, certainly not close enough to talk. Which was just as well, as she didn't really want to talk to him right now.

Why did he have to have such loyalty? If he didn't, Kita thought she could probably persuade Lakara and Davorin to drop this muddy suicide run. Maybe. They claimed loyalty to the king too, but they didn't have the same 'I am called to die in the service of the king if need be' that he had.

Davorin would be easier to persuade, she thought. He was cynical and a little more practical, wanting to know where he stood to gain in transactions. This wasn't a transaction where he stood to gain anything.

Lakara would probably be harder, the other person likely to bring up that this was technically treason. She was more indoctrinated. Probably because as a scholar, she would have been dependent on the king for everything, but she could be interchanged with any other scholar. As the only necromancer in Corvis, Davorin had leverage in a way most people couldn't dream of. Even if he only used a sliver of power, he was used to being compensated for it. He had independence. Lakara just did whatever she was told.

Could she persuade one or both of them to quit this journey? It would be risky. If they couldn't be persuaded, then they would be warned that she planned to flee. But if it worked…

If she could persuade one, either one, but not the other, then they could leave during their turn at watch. It would be hours until they were discovered, giving them the head start they needed. With Whisper's help, they could disappear. If she could convince both, then they could stand up to Sir Jors and outright refuse to continue. He wouldn't be able to force all three of them. He could either go on by himself or quit as well.

And then what? Kita could and had spent years traveling at will and whim. No place she called her own, but nowhere to hold her down either. She was fine with that, and managed on her own, eating what she hunted, bought, or stole. Making money through trade or theft. It was enough to support her. Usually. It certainly wouldn't support another person or two. And neither Lakara nor Davorin were travelers like her. They resented constant travel and really weren't good at it.

If they agreed to drop the whole quest thing and couldn't go back to Corvis, they would still want to settle down somewhere. But Kita couldn't really see either of them, or even both of them supporting themselves. Sooner or later, people would realize Davorin was a necromancer. It hadn't happened at Winterwatch, but that was because there was dim lighting inside, and people were often too busy to look at people's eyes. Davorin also made it a point to not spend long socializing with anyone outside the group. Necromancers were too scarce for rumors not to spread, and people were frightened of them. Winterwatch might not evict him if someone found out, but only because that would be a death sentence right now. Come spring, however...

Nor did he have other skills that would be enough to support him. Same with Lakara. Winterwatch was as forgiving as it could afford to be about people's abilities, because they had no choice but to stay. Lakara might be able to spin flax, but she was making between two and four chits a day for it. Anyone who could spin should be making at least that much.

And from what Kita could tell, most housewives spun their own flax. Not so much wool, especially for broadcloth, but Lakara didn't know how to do that.

According to Lakara there were only two major libraries in Graldish. One was the king's library, in Corvis and the other was the library of Chiswit, which was between Wris and Skartow. The libraries were close enough that they sent several delegations to each other every year. If Lakara tried to set up in Chiswit, King Zikkar would find her quickly. If he remembered her name.

So, if neither of them would be able to find work to support themselves, or a place to settle down, what would they do? She couldn't see either of them easily agreeing to resort to thievery like she had.

Well, so what if they couldn't? It wasn't her responsibility, was it? Except, if she tried to persuade them to drop the quest because it would kill them, didn't she have to offer something that wouldn't?

Clearly, her plan needed work. But there were still two months or so until it would be safe to leave. Surely, she would come up with something by then.

***

Spring had always been Lakara's favorite season. Even for someone who stayed inside for days at a time, the arrival of spring was unmistakable. From her quarters, Lakara could overlook the royal garden, watching the flowers come alive. She had never seen but there were stories of the Endless Grasslands becoming blanketed by wildflowers of all kinds and colors. Spring was when the first of the four annual delegations of scholars met, and information was exchanged with the library of Chiswit. The royal soaps were made, and for weeks certain areas of the palace were saturated with the smell of honey, of flowers, and of clean spring.

This year, she dreaded it. Lakara hated how the snow blew itself out, each storm weaker than the one before. She was almost ill the day she realized she didn't need her winter weight cloak to go outside. She was quietly furious as the ground was slowly plowed. At times, she found herself almost praying for another blizzard.

She *was* ill the day the first group left Winterwatch. Because that meant that spring had truly arrived. They would have to leave soon. Not immediately, the group was united on that. The first group had been heading south, where it would be warmer. But they would be heading north, into the mountains. Being caught by even a mild snowstorm in the mountains could well be their death. They would have to wait until the mountains were as safe as possible to travel.

But everyone knew it would be coming soon. A week, two at most. They had saved up seventy chits over the winter to buy supplies to travel with. No one discussed the invisible unicorn prancing around the room. To leave would mean to die.

Kita was adamant that they shouldn't even try to continue the quest. She didn't bother to hide it. Nor had she said what she would do if they continued anyway. Lakara had her suspicions though.

Sir Jors was equally adamant that their duty to the king kept them honor bound to obey his orders. The closest he had gotten to admitting something was wrong about those orders was when Kita sarcastically asked him if they should go to the nearest town and claim to be spies so they could be caught and executed as the king wished.

Sir Jors winced at that. "No. Our orders were to find the jewel, not be executed as spies."

"Ah, loopholes." Kita rolled her eyes.

There was something about the whole thing that

resonated with Lakara. Something that felt like if she could just remember the right thing, she might have an answer. But so far, she had nothing.

Spinning was useful for thinking. Repetitive movements kept her hands busy, but her mind could wander. Lakara had been thinking and thinking, trying to come up with a solution that wasn't treason and wouldn't start a war. For two months she had been thinking about it. Unfortunately, she was good at learning what other people had done, not coming up with original plans of her own.

The bell rang. The day was done. Lakara collected her five chits. She had definitely gotten better at spinning this winter. Saving one chit for her dinner, Lakara put the chits in her pouch and went to the longhouse. As soon as she got to the dining hall, she could tell something had happened. People were talking and there was an excited buzz in the air. But she couldn't tell what they were saying.

Lakara got her food and joined Kita and Sir Jors. Kita was stone-faced and barely touching her food. Sir Jors looked grave. "What's wrong?" Lakara asked.

Davorin sat down, across from Lakara, next to Kita. "Is it true? The Cryswayr Pass is open?"

Sir Jors nodded once, slowly. "That is what I heard. An expedition to the temple of Cryswayr is leaving in two days. It would probably be safest to travel with them."

The bread turned to ash in Lakara's mouth. Already? Now? She wasn't ready. There was no plan yet.

Davorin took a deep breath. "I see. Yes, if we are going to the temple of Cryswayr, then that is the safest way to travel."

Kita stabbed a piece of raw carrot with enough force to spear it through but said nothing.

"I think we should probably discuss things tonight," Sir

Jors said.

"What's to discuss? I thought it was decided?" Kita asked her plate angrily.

"I am not in charge of the expedition and there may be better options," Sir Jors said calmly.

The two had been awkward around each other since Kita found the papers. They hadn't come to blows, and were usually civil to each other, even friendly sometimes, but only when neither brought up the quest.

Lakara forced herself to eat, knowing she would need her strength. Everyone else seemed to have the same idea.

Dinner ended and they went back to the cabin. Kita built the fire while Lakara added the extra chits to the house funds. Davorin put their leftovers in the cupboard, and Sir Jors checked on the pack lizards. Kita and Lakara joined to help with the lizards, getting them to move around and be ready to travel. Trouble was getting big, almost half the size of his mother.

When everyone finished, they met back at the cabin. There was an awkward silence, finally broken by Sir Jors. "I believe it would be safest to travel with this group. I have asked, they are the only ones making a pilgrimage to Cryswayr. But I'm not the leader, so it isn't my decision."

"Why not?" Kita asked. "It doesn't actually make sense for you not to be."

"She's right," Lakara said. "You're a much better leader than I. You've taken charge several times when I had no idea what to do. I think you should take leadership."

"I'd actually forgotten you were the leader," Davorin said. "No offence to the scholar, but she's right. Putting Lakara, a scholar who had never left the city, in charge, it was probably one of the ways we were supposed to get caught."

Lakara nodded. "Probably. So, Sir Jors, will you take charge of this rag-tag band of misfits? We may still fail, but I think we'll get further with you in charge."

Davorin quickly agreed. Kita stayed silent. Sir Jors sighed. "That makes this easier and harder." He straightened. "The king has ordered us to find the Jewel of Ishni. Apparently, he never expected us to succeed, but he did order it. I am dutybound to obey my king. As such, I intend to continue attempting to retrieve the jewel." He looked them all over. "In light of our discoveries, I understand a reluctance to continue. So, this is my offer. I will continue. Those who choose to come with me are welcome. Those who choose not to are under no obligation. We will divide up supplies so you have your fair share, and you may leave."

Not surprisingly, Kita was the first to react. "So, if I say I'm out of here, you'll let me leave? With my pack, and food, and Whisper?"

"You can even take Trouble with you if you like. He's big enough to carry your supplies, and he likes you best anyway. As far as I can determine, since the lizards were gifted to us for our use on this quest, their offspring would be ours as well." When Kita kept staring at him, Sir Jors held up a hand. "I swear on my sword and oath, I am telling you the truth. Nor is this a one-time offer. You can continue with me and whoever else goes with me, and still choose to leave at any time." He smiled. "But you can't leave with the Jewel of Ishni. That is the only condition."

"We'll see about that," Kita said. But she was smiling too.

"The caravan is in two days. We have time. Everyone should think it over. But I meant it. Anyone can leave at any time." Sir Jors looked them each in the eyes.

"You can't even read the clues," Lakara pointed out.

"Shadow Master said it would take all of us," Davorin

said.

"I never said I would succeed. Only that I would try. Yes, I may fail, possibly even die on the way. This is what I agreed to when I became a knight. When I swore fealty to the king. But I cannot, will not, force any of you to join me." No one said anything. "Think on the matter carefully."

The next day was spent buying supplies and figuring out how it would be proportioned. Mentally, Lakara was dividing most of the supplies into fourths. While no one other than Sir Jors had said what they would be doing, Kita would almost certainly be leaving. Not that Lakara could truly blame her, but she did hope for the time to say goodbye at least.

Lakara planned to continue. She knew Vesrop the best of the group and had been the one to figure out what temples to visit. If she was wrong about one, then Sir Jors would need help finding the right temple.

Davorin hadn't said anything about his plans. Honestly, Lakara had no idea what he would do. Even if he left, he probably wouldn't go with Kita, not long term. Nor did she think he would survive long on his own. The only one less suited to traveling alone would be Lakara herself.

Finally, it was time to go. Everyone was packing up the last of the bags when Sir Jors brought up the heavy topic. "I need to know how many for the caravan."

Lakara spoke first. "I'm going. You'll need my help to translate the clues."

Sir Jors nodded to her. "I appreciate the help. Davorin? Kita?"

Kita spoke next, not looking up from her pack. "I've heard the Mountains of Death are lovely. Never seen them before. Or the great temple of Cryswayr. Might as well since we're here."

Davorin choked on a laugh. "She has a point. Besides, even if I don't plan to continue, this isn't the place to separate. A nice, safe town, maybe. But not here."

"So, four for the caravan. I'll let them know. I appreciate you all coming. However far you continue to go."

Soon they had the lizards loaded up and it was time to meet up with the caravan. "So," Kita huffed. "We go on."

Chapter Thirteen

The Temples of Cryswayr and Yestav

Or

Fire and Water

Mountains. Actual mountains. Topped with snow. Dangerous rocks that could slide on their heads at any time. Kita was beginning to suspect her teammates were crazy. She had crossed hills before in the past. But to her, mountains were those pretty parts of the landscape you sometimes saw in the distance. The far distance. Very far.

Stones shifted underfoot with almost every step, and Kita thanked the gods that whatever else they had given her in her life, she had always had almost inhumanely good balance and the ability to know where to step. So far, she was the only one of the crew, and one of the few in the caravan, who hadn't fallen or nearly turned an ankle or worse. The pack lizards were fine, they could climb a sheer cliff face.

Kita threw up a hand to catch Lakara as she stumbled when the rock she stepped on turned out to be looser than anticipated. Lakara fell into the hand and used it to rebalance herself. "Thank you."

"You're welcome. How much further?"

"Tomorrow, I think. How come you aren't falling?"

"Good balance. And I test the stones to see if they'll hold me before putting my weight on them. See?" Kita picked a stone she would bet a couple bronze ducats on being unable to hold her. She put one foot on it, holding herself on her other leg, allowing just enough weight to make the stone shake. "That one wouldn't work." She picked another rock that seemed safer, tested it, and it held. "That one will." It was slow progress, but no slower than the caravan was already traveling. Certainly faster than traveling injured.

Lakara's eyes narrowed in concentration as she tried imitating her. Unfortunately, she didn't have any skill in visually assessing what rocks and stones might be safe. Oh well, at least she'd be less likely to fall this way. If Kita knew how to explain how she knew this stone might be safe but that one probably wasn't, she would try. But she didn't. It was instinctive. Maybe she was part mountain deer.

The mountain deer flourished here. They hovered in the background, watching the foolish humans who tried to traipse through their mountains. They leapt from rock to rock, making mockery of the earthbound who could barely walk through the stony pass. Always far enough away to avoid becoming a meal for the hungry travelers, but close enough to watch in what felt like amusement.

The sun glinted bright on the leftover snow, making her wish for her glasses, even if she agreed Davorin needed them more. Pity she only had the one pair. But she had never seen them for sale anywhere, and she had looked.

It was weird, traveling with so many other people. Before the quest, she had traveled almost exclusively by herself for years. When she was conscripted, she had hated it. Kita despised being forced, being at the mercy of strangers. She loathed the lack of privacy. Every word, every look felt like condemnation rang through it. She lived in fear of them discovering Whisper, and mentally plotted escape routes and techniques as she fell asleep.

Slowly, things changed. She got used to other people

responding when she spoke. Her safety wasn't completely reliant on Whisper or herself. There wasn't as much disdain as she thought or it dried up quickly, for the most part. They discovered Whisper and nothing bad happened. Opportunities to escape were written off as 'unfavorable circumstances.' Kita had gotten used to them. Still wasn't interested in dying for this filthy 'quest', but she was still here, even when she didn't have to be.

But the rhythm they had found and lost and rebuilt stronger again and again; it only lasted between the four of them. Right now, they were surrounded by about thirty strangers that they knew nothing about and who knew nothing about them except that they were all headed through the Mountains of Death to get to the temple of Cryswayr. That made them safer. And less safe. They were safer from bandits and bears and wild cats. But there were a lot of people. People she had no reason to trust and had no reason to trust them.

If they found out Davorin was a necromancer, would they be driven from the group? Would they be attacked? Who was safe to be alone with? Who shouldn't be left alone? Group dynamics were never her specialty. She could evaluate targets and threats for herself, but not for a group. Even worse, she couldn't use her usual technique. Kita was used to fading into a crowd, becoming the next best thing to invisible, beneath notice.

But she couldn't do that here. There were too many people here who knew her. Even those outside of the quest group had gotten used to seeing her. Gotten used to talking to her. Which meant she wasn't just background. She was a known entity.

Still, it would be over soon. They would reach Cryswayr's temple, probably tomorrow, and the caravan would dissolve or leave, and they would go on by themselves.

Kita scanned the group by habit, making sure she knew

where her friends were. Then she frowned. Sir Jors wasn't moving. At all.

***

Sir Jors trudged his way through the mountain pass, carefully picking his way through the rocks. He would stand by his decision to join the caravan, but he couldn't say that he preferred it. He was constantly caught between an instinctive desire to try to shield the whole caravan, and his desire to make sure the three who were his responsibility were safe and sound, including from others in the caravan. No one in the caravan had presented as an active threat, so far; but right now, he felt paranoid around everyone but their small group.

Sleep had been elusive the night before, which was probably increasing his tension and definitely his tiredness level. There was the pressure and pain around the eyes, the slightly slower reaction time, and the faint wisps of a headache. Sir Jors ignored it until the outside edges of his vision started graying, clouding up. Sleep was pressing in.

There was no fighting it. All he could do was hope he didn't attack anyone in his sleep this time.

It started with the flap of bird wings. As the sound faded, a tower rose before him, stark and black across the sky. Red flashed. Fire, blood, the jewel. It was all and none. Someone screamed.

Sir Jors opened his eyes. He was back on the mountain pass and surrounded by his crew. His friends. Lakara was checking him over, a smile breaking out as she saw he was back to his senses. Davorin had his right arm in both hands, ensuring he didn't draw his sword while in the grips of a vision. Kita was a few feet ahead, with her back towards them, blocking the view of onlookers, loudly claiming everything was fine, it was just a touch of mountain sickness. He was fine. No need to worry.

"It's over," Lakara muttered in a low voice.

Kita stepped to the side, allowing them to look. "See, he's fine now. We can continue."

Sir Jors managed an embarrassed smile and a wave that seemed to reassure any holdouts. In another minute, it was just them. "Did I do anything?"

"Far as I can tell, you just stood there. Didn't move at all." Kita looked him over. "Didn't last long, either. Definitely shorter than with the imps."

"If you did reach for your sword, I was supposed to take it," Lakara admitted. "We were afraid you might try to fight someone."

"Fortunately, you didn't," Davorin said, stepping away.

"I am grateful for your attempts to minimize any damage I might cause," Sir Jors said stiffly. He was grateful, he really was. But he wished it weren't necessary.

Had Vicaw given him a vision? It wasn't the first time he had seen something when sleep took him captive. Sometimes he suspected he had seen a vision. Other times, he thought they were waking dreams. If they had enough privacy, he would share what he had seen with the others. But there was no privacy, and these generally didn't stay with him long.

For the rest of the day, he pondered what he had seen and heard, in between making sure he didn't fall and injure himself. He was so deep in his pondering that he was actually a little surprised when they stopped for the night. According to Davorin, they had made such good time that they should be at Cryswayr's temple in the morning.

Maybe it was the day of walking, maybe it was the sleep attack, or the vision, but Sir Jors felt weary down to his bones. Luckily, sleep was kind to him for a change. He slept quickly and deeply, without even having to take a watch shift.

They approached Cryswayr's temple at dawn, a sacred time for the goddess of fire. The temple gleamed red-gold in the rising sun. In front of the temple was an eternal flame, much like the one at Vicaw's temple.

The town that sprawled around the temple was small and possibly nameless. Unlike Wris, there was no sign that the town had ever flourished. It was big enough to support the temple, and provide supplies for pilgrims who crossed through, but not much bigger. This temple was significant for its age, but it had only briefly been the primary temple for Cryswayr. Several larger and grander temples of the fire goddess existed.

The pack lizards were harnessed and herded into a pen with the other lizards of the company, leaving the people free to explore the temple. Like the outside, the inside was red and gold wherever one chose to look. Another large fire formed the centerpiece of the temple, with smaller fires and torches in multiple places.

It lacked the elaborate touches of Pirette's temple or the harsh starkness of Vicaw's. He hadn't seen the inside of Tratow's or Shadow Master's temples. But Cryswayr's temple glinted and shone. Everything seemed to be metal; soft, malleable metal. Mostly gold, or at least gold colored. Maybe some amber.

The inside was hot, probably the result of the omnipresent metal picking up the heat many flames. At one wall, there was a row of little fires, with bowls of powder nearby. The supplicant paid the priest or priestess for a handful of powder to toss into the fire, asking Cryswayr for a blessing. A powder for wealth, a powder for health, a prayer for success, and a prayer for protection. Then there was the random one. A white powder that could result in anything. Most used it as a way to gauge their fate.

Sir Jors went first, paying a bronze duc for a handful

from the amber bowl. The fire turned green when the powder ignited. A prayer for success. *May we succeed in this quest.* Davorin went next, choosing the redstone bowl for protection, turning the fire blue. Lakara followed his lead. Kita hesitated over the powders. Part of him expected her to take from the jade bowl of wealth, turning the fire yellow. Likely not the crystal bowl of health, turning the fire pink. To his surprise, she chose from the clay bowl. The unknown. The fire turned purple.

"What does that mean?" Kita asked, body tense.

"Change. Great change. Great loss and greater gain," the priestess said, staring at it. "Ominous, but not the worst possibility. But your life is in upheaval or will be soon. Perhaps you wish a prayer of protection? Or the goddess's blessing?"

"Good idea." Kita quickly dug out two silver dou and handed them to the priestess. The priestess took the coins and prayed in a loud and solemn voice. Not that Sir Jors understood what she prayed. His knowledge of Restor was limited to about five phrases and maybe twelve other words, half of which were unsuitable for use in front of all but the crudest of company. Odds were high that Kita was similarly disadvantaged, but she didn't even blink at the strange words.

In fact, he might have concluded that Kita had a previously unsuspected education in the language if he hadn't caught her, once safely away from the priestess and any other interested audience, whispering to Lakara, "What did she say?"

Lakara answered in a low tone. "That Cryswayr would protect and refine you during your trials. That you would come through like gold, cleansed by a fire. That the blessing of the gods would rest upon you and strengthen you."

Kita frowned. "I was hoping for more of a prayer to avoid whatever trouble."

Lakara shrugged. "Sorry, you're still stuck with us for

now. I think that will give you troubles aplenty."

Kita huffed and turned aside to try to find the clue hidden in the temple, but Sir Jors heard her mutter, "I knew I should have gone with a different choice." He smiled but said nothing.

It was Davorin who found the clue they needed, carved into the altar that held the eternal flame. Both he and Lakara copied it down diligently, while Kita and Sir Jors stood around looking and feeling useless. Well, he did. Who knew what Kita thought?

"Why are the letters wrong?" Kita asked.

He hadn't expected that. "I beg your pardon?"

"Lakara said she taught me all the letters. I'm getting good at reading, but I don't know these."

"You are getting quite good at reading. But that's Graldian and this is Vesrop."

She gave him an exasperated look. "I know that. I'm not mu... I'm not stupid. But the letters are wrong."

"No, you aren't stupid. But Vesrop uses a different alphabet than Graldian does. Restor is in between. Most of the letters are the same as Graldian, but it has a few Vesrop letters too," Sir Jors explained, trying not to smile. There was no reason for someone who was illiterate a few months ago to know that other languages might have different letters. And Kita was obviously slightly touchy about it.

She shook her head. "Ridiculous idea. They should use the same."

"Perhaps. But it's too late to change it now."

Lakara stood up with a grimace before extending a hand to help Davorin up. Sir Jors immediately moved to assist the necromancer himself. Davorin had lost weight over this journey, as most of them had, but he was still a little heavier than Lakara could handle by herself.

"Did you figure it out?" Kita asked.

Davorin stood with assistance. "Perhaps. We are both agreed to the literal translation, but not what it means."

Lakara tidied her notes, without looking at anyone. "It seems to say, 'A single coal burns out quickly.' Why the need to mention that, I'm not certain."

"It means that one person can't find it on their own," Kita said without hesitation.

Sir Jors tried not to wince but had to admit that she was likely correct. Already, the dangers they faced would likely have killed any one of them if they were alone. It could only be more dangerous from here on out. But he had sworn and was determined to keep his promise that he would not force anyone to accompany him.

Lakara had agreed to stay with the journey at least until all the clues were gathered. He was grateful for that, as he couldn't read Vesrop at all. Davorin and Kita had agreed to come to this temple, probably because it was only a few days' travel. He had yet to hear any mention of either of them going beyond.

Nor was he quite sure how to ask what their intentions were now. But he needed to know. As they exited the temple, he turned to Lakara. "Where is our next destination?"

Lakara paused to double-check her notes. "The temple of Yestav in Cortna. We'll have to go past the Swamp of Despair and partway through the Sea of Tears first."

"Lovely names these places have." Kita shook her head. "Well, we'd better get started. The sooner begun, the sooner done."

She didn't look at anyone as she spoke, but Sir Jors

doubted anyone was blind to her tension. But as long as she was willing, he wasn't going to argue. Instead, he gave a side glimpse to Davorin.

The necromancer took a deep breath and let it out slowly. "She has a point. And this certainly isn't a place I would choose to settle. For now, we go on."

***

Lakara had two books and one scroll on the Swamp of Despair. They told her about the dangers of the bogs that could suck a person in, never to be seen again. She read about snakes, both venomous and benign, that abounded here. There was information about swamp lizards, a slightly smaller cousin to their pack lizards, that lived almost invisible in the water, and could kill by drowning, or by using their teeth, claws, or even tail. There were mentions of the various kinds of insects that lived in the Swamp of Despair. But they didn't tell everything.

They didn't mention just how painful those insect stings and bites could be, or the way they liked to congregate to the eyes. There was nothing about spotting bubbles only a few feet away and seeing the eye of a swamp lizard, knowing the lizard could drag her underwater faster than she could react. No mention of the split-second of terror when a step onto seemingly solid ground ended up with her foot sinking to her knee before she was pulled back by her teammates. Nothing in the books mentioned just how fast a snake could move when one lunged at her arm.

The snake was caught and decapitated by Kita before it got within striking distance. "Dinner," she said calmly, cleaning her dirk. Lakara didn't even blink, barely bothered by the incident. Which disturbed her more than the incident itself.

"Can you imagine," Kita said as she gave a hopping step over an exposed, twisting root, "if there wasn't a road at all?"

Despite the overcast day, she was wearing her dark glasses. Probably to keep the insects from her eyes.

"I don't want to," Davorin grumbled. "A bad road is better than none at all."

Lakara had to agree with him. While the road had not been properly maintained and was in pieces, there *was* a road. So, there were parts where they could be certain the ground was at least mostly solid.

She stepped down, not even wincing as her foot sank slightly in the wet earth, and took another step, the earth releasing her foot with a wet squelching sound. Her clothes would never be clean again, and she needed another pair of boots when they reached the next town. While she was the only one needing new boots, her companions were in similar states. Only the lizards were able to transverse easily, being closer to the ground with their weight spread out better.

Sir Jors stumbled slightly, only for Lakara and Kita to immediately grab his shoulders and pull him back a step. "Not a bog, just a tree root."

Every one of them had found bogs the hard way at least once. Which was why they each carried a long stick and had tied ropes between themselves. By walking in a tight cluster, they were able to make sure no one was lost to the mire. Thank the gods the party wasn't any smaller.

"We should probably camp for the night soon, the light won't last much longer," Sir Jors said. "Though I don't know where we can set up the tents."

Everyone looked at the wet unstable ground that stretched as far as the eye could see, that they would have to travel through for days. Travel in the dark would be impossible, but a camping site?

"I don't know. I think we might be better off in the trees."

Kita eyed the large tree nearest her. Widespread branches, with a few hanging low enough that it should be easy for any of them to climb.

"I think I heard of that, actually." Lakara racked her brain. "Yes, soldiers in the Wars. They ended up stringing tents and other cloths between the branches or sleeping in the branches themselves."

"Yes, I believe I've heard stories too." Sir Jors eyed the trees. "We'll need a fire. No one go far, we'll build here in the road. Maybe tomorrow we can figure out the best way to string up the tents, but for tonight, I think we should just sleep in the branches."

The fire was reluctant to catch. Nothing was dry enough to burn well. But they finally had one going. Just in time, the gloom of twilight was giving way fast to the dark of night.

Dinner was prepared quickly, since no one wanted to be on the ground when the swamp lizards emerged to hunt. Lakara stirred up the fire, trying to get a moss-covered stick to catch.

"So, which watch do I take?" Kita asked, not looking up from her pack. Not even when the rest of the party turned to stare at her.

Lakara hadn't even thought about it. They had gotten so used to their watches, even with the complaints. Not to mention, they hadn't needed to have someone on watch since they arrived at Winterwatch. But since Kita had freedom to leave any time she wanted, there was no reason not to give her a shift. Besides, this was definitely not a place to leave on one's own.

"Well, we can split the night into four watches, or we can keep it to three, and alternate it so each person has one night in four completely off." Sir Jors rubbed his beard. "I would recommend the second, personally." He looked around but no one objected. "Suppose you take first watch tonight, I'll still take second, and Lakara, if you'll take third? We can figure out tomorrow's schedule tomorrow."

There was a murmur of assent. "I'm taking watch in a tree," Kita warned.

"Yes, I think we all should. Just make sure the fire keeps burning and the pack lizards are safe."

They tied the supplies to branches off the ground, before making sure everyone could actually climb to a safe location in one of the nearby trees. Fortunately, no one had too much difficulty.

"No one goes off alone, no matter what," Sir Jors warned, as everyone made sure they were somewhat comfortable and wouldn't fall out in the middle of the night. Some actually tied themselves to the trunk or branches of their respective trees. "If you need to get up in the night, make sure someone is with you. We can barely see the bogs in daylight, we certainly can't at night." Everyone agreed. "Fine. Kita, wake me about two, please."

In the dim firelight, Lakara thought she saw Kita nod, before turning to tend to Whisper who was roosting in the same tree, a few branches further up. But she was too tired to think about it. It had been quite some time before she had traveled so far in one day. Not since before Winterwatch. The caravan had been forced to travel slowly, to accommodate for so many people and the terrain. Sadly, the months of inactivity had caused her to lose whatever stamina that she had gained up to that point. Hopefully, she would gain it back soon.

Davorin might have the same problem, he had worked in the kitchen. But at least he had been on his feet most of the same hours she had been sitting and spinning. But Kita and Sir Jors had much more active jobs. Perhaps even deliberately.

Swamp walking was much harder than crossing the

Endless Grasslands, and possibly more dangerous than the Ocean of Sand. At least the trees should provide them some protection, though not from the insects. More insects seemed to have come out at night, and all seemed to either bite or sting. Lakara ended up wrapping up completely in her cloak, trying to leave only enough space to breathe.

Despite how tired she was, sleep eluded her. She was in the drifty stage of almost asleep when a sound woke her. A thudding sound. Suddenly alert, Lakara moved her cloak so she could see.

Sir Jors was asleep in another tree, almost immediately opposite hers. He had tied himself to a branch, possibly to avoid a case of sleepwalking. Davorin was in a tree close to his, also asleep. Kita…

Kita was on the ground. What was she doing? Lakara watched, trying to look like she was asleep. Surely Kita wouldn't choose now to leave. Not here of all places.

Whisper was awake, watching her. When he gave a quiet trill, Kita shushed him. She reached for something that Lakara couldn't see. Oh, a stick. Kita used it to stoke up the fire, before checking on the lizards. Stripes gave her a sleepy look while Longtail didn't move at all. Trouble seemed to think it was a game, but he stilled when Kita took a moment to stroke him to calmness.

Then she climbed back into her tree. Whisper pulled a little at her hair, and she let the hawk groom her as she continued to watch. Lakara smiled and closed her eyes. They were in good hands. She didn't know anything else until Sir Jors woke her for her watch.

***

Davorin shifted, trying to find a position where he didn't have a branch poking him in the back. There wasn't one. True, he was on watch and wasn't supposed to be sleeping yet, but was a tiny bit of comfort too much to ask for? Probably.

Tonight should be their last night in the Swamp of Despair. Lakara's map and Sir Jors' and Kita's ingrained senses of navigation agreed, they were almost to the Sea of Tears. Even he could smell the increase of salt in the air as the swamp got even swampier. If that was a word.

In about an hour, he would be waking Sir Jors. They had unanimously decided to continue their old watch pattern with Kita rotating and taking everyone's shift in turn. This was her night to rest, which meant tomorrow would be his. His rest would likely be better out of this great dismal swamp.

According to Lakara, the temple of Yestav was on an island in the middle of the Sea of Tears. Davorin had never been on a boat before, and he would wager that his companions could say the same. At least they didn't have to enter the ocean, putting themselves at the mercy of the waves and at risk from pirates.

Not that the Sea of Tears was safe by any stretch of the imagination. But now wasn't the time to worry about the possibility of storms, or whirlpools, or sea monsters, or...

Davorin shook his head, refocusing himself. Even if they left the Swamp of Despair early in the morning, it would still take the better part of the day to reach the Sea of Tears, and they would probably spend at least one night in one of the fishing villages first. And even if they were to reach the Sea of Tears first thing in the morning, all the worry in the world did nothing to change the danger, either to increase or decrease it.

No, the best he could do was to stay alert for his watch, and then try to sleep when the watch ended. He didn't have much longer anyway. Davorin stoked up the fire as much to kill time as to make sure the fire burned all night.

As if realizing Davorin was thinking about him, Sir Jors stirred. Davorin made no noise, but the knight woke anyway.

"Is it my watch yet?" Sir Jors asked in a low voice.

"Almost. About fifteen minutes, I'd guess."

Sir Jors carefully pushed himself from his canopy of cloth onto the branch. "I'm awake. Get some sleep."

Davorin could have argued but didn't see the point. Besides, he wanted the rest. If only he could find a comfortable position. Turning slightly put the tree knob that was in the middle of his back under his right shoulder blade. Not exactly an improvement.

Several minutes of experimentation had Whisper and Sir Jors staring at him, one in curiosity and one in exasperated amusement, but achieved nothing as far as comfort. Finally, Davorin picked the pose least likely to make his back scream at him the next day and closed his eyes to try to sleep.

Only to open them again immediately at the sound of movement and metal sliding against metal. Davorin sat up. Kita had too, and Sir Jors was sitting still as a statue, sword half out of its sheath. The pack lizards were awake and troubled, looking to something he couldn't see. Whisper fluffed up and flew to a higher branch with a shriek, waking Lakara.

"What is it?" The scholar asked, resituating so she could see.

No one answered for a minute. Then, "Look! There." Kita pointed. "Swamp lizards."

Two of them, out of the water to hunt. "Well, we're safe, aren't we?" Lakara asked, voice shaking. "They can't climb trees."

"*We* are safe. And our supplies," Sir Jors answered, with a gravity that Davorin didn't like.

"The pack lizards. They can't climb either." Kita pulled her dirk. "Will the fire hold them back?"

Davorin looked at the approaching swamp lizards, who showed no fear of the fire yet. The pack lizards were slightly larger than the swamp lizards, with much the same claws and teeth. There was no way to predict how a fight between them would turn out, but it would probably be ugly. They couldn't afford to lose the lizards. But climbing down meant death. Death...

"Everyone, stay in your trees." Sir Jors pulled his sword and moved to leap down.

"That includes you!" Davorin yelled back. "I have an idea." He hesitated only long enough to make sure Sir Jors stayed. Probably more out of surprise than anything else, but he'd take it.

The Swamp of Despair wasn't named that because someone liked the name. It was named because of the dangers and deaths that occurred there. Finding the dead was easy. Too many had been swallowed by the bogs and mires, never to be seen again. Until now.

Sensing the closest deaths, Davorin pulled. The bogs fought back, unwilling to relinquish their treasures, but Davorin just yanked harder. In a minute, he had two swamp lizard skeletons and two more dead but well-preserved swamp lizard bodies waiting. Another pull and he had a soldier, still in armor, even if only his skeleton and his sword remained.

Animating was harder, but they all had the same job. Attack, drive off the swamp lizards. Vaguely aware that he was frightening their own lizards, and probably his teammates, Davorin tuned it out to focus on the task.

The skeletons went first. Teeth and claws still worked, drawing blood. The live ones fought back. There was no blood for them to draw, and the bones didn't react much to claws and teeth, but they fragmented and broke under blows from the tail. Soon, the skeletons were reduced to chips and powder. The live swamp lizards were bleeding but undaunted.

Next, Davorin sent in the preserved bodies of the bog swallowed swamp lizards. They may have had flesh and muscles that were vulnerable to teeth and claws, but they had no nerves to feel pain and no brain to run. They were nothing but puppets to follow his orders. He focused on the more injured swamp lizard, hoping that if the fight went poorly enough, the lizards would retreat. If he could kill one, he'd have another to control. Quickly. The strain was thrumming through him.

The dead swamp lizards didn't hesitate or back down, no matter how they were bitten, scratched, or torn apart. The live lizards seemed more apprehensive now. They had backed off after biting the dead swamp lizards, knowing something was off about them. But they weren't ready to run yet.

His skeletal soldier moved in, sword at the ready. Just as one of the live lizards tore a leg off one of the dead lizards, the soldier managed to impale his sword through the lizard's brain. It collapsed, dead.

Davorin took a breath and prepared to animate the newly dead lizard, but the remaining live one turned and ran. Good. He couldn't handle the strain much longer. Carefully, Davorin released his pull. Trying not to shiver as the dead fell silent and still.

No one moved. No one spoke.

Trouble, irrepressible lizard that he was, cautiously skittered over to the soldier and nudged the skeleton. Davorin didn't think he was the only one who winced as the no longer animated skeleton fell with a clatter, bones scattering with no ligaments or magic to hold them together. Trouble nosed around before satisfied there was neither food nor anything else interesting there and returned to his mother.

"Well, that was... impressive. I didn't know you could do

269

that," Kita said, before hopping down. She gave the dead a wide berth, shortening Trouble's lead so he couldn't go so far again. "You saved the pack lizards." She eyed the newly dead swamp lizard. "Is he safe to eat?"

Lakara gasped at her, but Davorin found himself laughing slightly hysterically. By the time he got his breath back, everyone was watching him. "No reason he shouldn't be. My magic doesn't leave a taint that way. I wouldn't try with the other two, or the parts where he was bitten, just in case, but that's still plenty of meat."

"And leather," Kita said, scrambling back up her tree. "No point in wasting resources."

"No, but we can't stay either. We'll see." Sir Jors sighed, before turning to Davorin. "That was a brilliant move on your part. You probably saved the pack lizards, and possibly me as well. Thank you."

He was shaking slightly and couldn't stop. "You're welcome."

"Those who can should try to sleep," Sir Jors reminded everyone. No one argued this time. Not even Davorin who was positive that he'd never manage it. As it was, the release of hysteria and the strain of using his powers had him asleep in minutes.

There was a delayed start the next morning, as they cut off and cooked some of the swamp lizard meat, not more than a day or two's worth of supplies. It would have taken more than a day to skin the newly killed swamp lizard and possibly the two preserved ones. Kita argued the delay would be worth it, but was overruled, so they took only what could be taken during the morning before breaking down camp.

"What about the man?" Lakara asked. "I know we can't bury him, but..."

"We may have no choice but to either leave him exposed or turn him back to the bog." Sir Jors didn't seem to like the options either.

"How about a marker? He's still wearing armor, and that looks like a family crest on his breastplate. Throw the body to the bog and tie the breastplate to the closest tree." Kita looked him over again. "Would it be wrong to take his sword? We could use it."

There was a debate about that, which Davorin stayed out of. Eventually, they did what Kita suggested, putting him to rest with his sword. The tipping point was when Sir Jors said it had the feel of a generational weapon. Kita agreed, saying there was a glow to it. He had forgotten Kita could see magic.

Sir Jors took care of the actual disposition of the body while Davorin and Kita used vines to tie the breastplate to the closest tree. Once it was in place, he studied the crest. "This is old. Very old."

Lakara was already checking a scroll. "The Crastlas House. That's the insignia they used up to three hundred years ago."

Kita shrugged. "Does it matter?"

Lakara gave a small smile. "Probably not. But it is interesting. The Crastlas House sti..." She lost her smile. "No, it doesn't exist anymore. Lord Sartik was the last heir to the house, and he had no children."

"Oh." Kita eyed the insignia again. "If he was from a Graldish noble house, what was he doing here?"

"I don't know. That's far too long to be part of the Wars. Perhaps a different battle. Or maybe he was on a pilgrimage himself." Lakara rolled up her scroll and put it away. "The insignia was used for a few hundred years, and just because he had the armor didn't mean he belonged to the family. He could have been one of their trained fighters. We'll never know. We don't even know his name."

The whispers of the dead, always on the edge of his hearing, got louder. "Lartis." He didn't realize he had spoken until everyone looked at him. "His name was Lartis. He was young. Not more than twenty. There was a war." Davorin closed his eyes and shook his head. "I don't have anymore."

"That's... enough," Kita said. Davorin didn't open his eyes until he heard wood being chipped. "How do you spell 'Lartis'?" Kita asked, trying to gouge a line in the wood beneath the armor.

"I'll do it. You don't want to ruin your dirk," Sir Jors offered, bringing out a common knife. "And I know how to spell it."

Kita stepped away. It was only a few minutes to carve the name into the tree before they were on their way. No one spoke for hours.

Because of their delay, it was almost dark before they reached one of the fishing villages that dotted the Sea of Tears. Fortunately, there were several inns. Without even discussing it, they fell back to their usual roles. Davorin claimed to be a merchant, with Lakara as his wife, Kita as their servant, and Sir Jors hired for their protection. After the first town, they adapted the story slightly. People had asked what he sold and why he didn't have his stock with him. They said he was a spice merchant, searching for new spices. This also explained why he needed the protection, as everyone knew that spice merchants could get very rich.

No matter how many times they claimed this role, it felt strange. Kita acting deferential, Lakara pretending to be happily married to him. It didn't feel right for either of them. Sir Jors didn't seem to like it either. But they didn't have a better plan.

Because of their story, the inn gave them two adjoining rooms. One room for the married couple, and one for their hired help that was notably smaller, darker, and colder. Davorin was unsurprised that Sir Jors proposed they take the smaller room leaving the women the better one.

At the beginning of their quest, Davorin knew that he would have objected. He was the king's necromancer. Sir Jors was a knight. If they were to split along gender lines, which he was fine with, then the women were clearly lower ranked and should take the smaller room.

Now he was happy enough to have somewhere safe to sleep that he would have taken the floor. Besides, Davorin thought he had learned enough about rank to realize there were more important things. His rank would not have protected him from a single one of the dangers they had faced so far and was unlikely to safeguard him in the future. And if the king had sent him out to die, then his rank was probably more in his mind than anywhere else. Was this what Virn was trying to warn him about?

Honestly, when he thought back to the Davorin that had left Corvis on this quest, he was amazed that the others put up with him this long. Arrogant, lazy, selfish, and a coward. No wonder Kita never had any respect for him, and the others lost it quickly. It had taken a long time to earn any back. Not that they respected him as Master Davorin, the greatest necromancer in the land. Only as Davorin, their fellow traveler, who was stuck in the same messy problem they were and could usually be counted on to be semi-useful. Somehow, he liked this better.

Sir Jors came back from making sure the lizards were settled. "There's a boat leaving for the temple at dawn. They have room for passengers but can't take the lizards and aren't going all the way across the Sea of Tears. We have to visit the temple, come back, retrieve the lizards, and either find a ship going across or travel around the sea. I've been looking into ships. It may take a day or two to find suitable transport."

"Not the worst place to be holed up for a few days." Kita bounced slightly on the bed. "We at least have beds to sleep in."

"Where's Whisper?" Davorin asked. He hadn't seen the bird since they approached the town.

"The docks. Plenty of fish to eat, and a bird around the docks is less memorable than a bird traveling with a group. He'll make his own way across when we leave."

"You have that bird incredibly well trained." Davorin shook his head. "I can't train my pigeons a tenth of that."

Her smile went brittle. "He's my friend."

"Of course." He dropped the subject and quickly looked for a replacement. "Dinner?"

While they were probably all hungry, Davorin suspected that wasn't the reason everyone leaped on the subject change. He was an idiot. Obviously, Sir Jors and Lakara either knew or suspected what he had just realized. Kita must, absolutely *must*, be Borrowing to have a bond like that with Whisper. It was the only explanation. No wonder she had been devastated when he was injured. He should have known as soon as he discovered she was part Queyan.

Borrowing meant a death sentence. Both for the practitioner and the animal Borrowed. Kita would never willingly admit to Borrowing, and they would never ask her. But he knew. They all had to know.

To be fair, they had been sent on this quest to die, what did it matter if they committed another capital offense? They talked to Never-Was, associated with bandits, and discussed treason openly. Confessing even half of what they had done would see them all in the dungeons. What difference would Borrowing make?

Still, some things may not need to be spoken. And what they did not *know*, they would be under no obligation to speak of. If any of them felt a sense of obligation now.

Forget it, and sleep. Dawn would come early, and they were all exhausted. Doors that locked meant no one had to keep watch. The sleep would do them all good.

Morning came too early, again. This particular morning brought new revelations to Davorin. Namely, that he did not like boats. At all. Less than ten minutes from the dock and his stomach was rebelling. Why had he ever climbed out of his semi-comfortable bed?

As had become second nature to them all, he cast a quick look around to his companions. Lakara stood a few feet away, hands wrapped firmly around the rail, sharing every fact she knew about the Sea of Tears. Why she thought that knowing things and sharing those facts would make her less apprehensive, Davorin never figured out. But he certainly recognized her tactic by now. Sir Jors did too, and he stood there, trying to reassure and distract her.

Kita was missing. She had been with them a couple minutes ago and couldn't have gotten off the boat. With a muffled groan, Davorin pushed himself away from the side of the rail and went looking for her.

She wasn't with the group of devoted singing songs to Yestav, which didn't surprise him. She wasn't either a participant or spectator in any of the games of chance that had broken out, which might have surprised him. He finally found her sitting behind the back cabins in a space so small he wasn't able to join her.

"Are you well?" Davorin asked, noticing her slightly gray complexion, labored breathing, and what might be tears, might be sea spray on her face.

"I'm fine. You can go," Kita snapped without looking at

him.

A sudden lurch made him gag and Kita push her head all the way back, breathing heavily and swallowing several times. Exactly the way one does when trying to avoid vomiting.

"*You* get *seasick*?" Davorin whispered in disbelief. It wasn't possible. Not only was she part Trovian, and everyone knew they were born seafarers, but she was *Kita*. Every environment they traversed, everywhere they had gone, she had adapted the easiest. Times when Sir Jors, with all his training and devotion to the mission, looked like he wanted to give up, or at least rest a few minutes, Kita seemed perfectly able to continue. If she had gone on her own, Kita might well have gotten the jewel and been back by now. So, he felt he was justified in being surprised. He hadn't meant anything insulting by it.

Judging from Kita's poisonous glare, she disagreed. "I'm *fine*. Go away." Davorin couldn't help but notice that she didn't try to move.

She didn't want his company. She didn't need his help. And she might well dive overboard before admitting it if she did. So Davorin started to leave. Until the boat rocked hard enough to throw him into the rail.

It could have been worse. The pain was manageable. He would probably be colorfully bruised but nothing broke. But it took him everything he could to swallow back the bile in his throat and force his meager breakfast to stay put. More than a minute passed before he settled enough to notice there was a strong grip on his ankle. Blinking past the water that welled in his eyes, he saw Kita's hand holding him like a lifeline. Her hand was shaking. Just a little, but more than the boat's movement could account for.

If she was sick enough to be shaking... Davorin scanned her again and stopped. Because he had been mistaken. Kita might actually be seasick, but this was less seasickness and more... fear.

"Kita?" She pulled her hand back as if she had been burned and turned away from him. "Kita? What's wrong?"

"Nothing. I'm fine. Be careful and no more going over the edge."

"Are you..." She wouldn't admit it. Or would she? She had admitted to fear in the past. "Are you afraid?"

Kita laughed bitterly. "Afraid? Of what?"

He couldn't join her in her spot, but Davorin slid down to sit as close as possible. "Of anything. Right now, is something scaring you?" Kita glared at him. "I'm afraid." She stopped glaring. "I can't swim. If something goes wrong... And we both know the Sea of Tears has many dangers. You know I'm a coward. Of course I'm afraid. Lakara is too. She's currently reciting every fact she knows about the Sea of Tears. Alphabetically." Kita snickered. "Pretty sure Sir Jors isn't comfortable, either. Besides all that, I *am* seasick. But I seem to recall someone telling me that fear can be fought."

Kita closed her eyes and leaned back. "Drowning is a horrible way to die. I was on a fishing boat once. Not a big one. I was supposed to travel with them for a week. They were going to pay me two dourats and a share of the fish. Claimed that since I was part Trovian, I'd be a natural. They thought it hysterical I was seasick for the first day. But I got over it. And I was good. I know how to read the weather. I have good balance. I'm strong and not squeamish. They talked about keeping me on longer. I considered it. Seriously considered it."

Davorin fought not to wince. He wasn't going to like this story. "But you didn't. What went wrong?"

"Storm came. We had about two hours' warning but were three hours from shore. Little, tiny fishing boat on a big lake. I don't know exactly what happened but the boat just," she held her hands together before separating them violently, "in minutes. I blacked out, woke up so far under water that I almost died before I broke surface. Managed to grab a piece of the boat that still had some rope attached, tied myself to it and just held on." She shook her head. "The storm raged most of the night. It was a day before another boat came by to pick up survivors and scavenge what they could. Crew of twenty. Seven of us survived. I never went on another boat since."

"Until today." Davorin sighed. He wanted to ask why she hadn't said anything, but he knew why.

"I didn't think I'd have a problem. It wasn't the first time I'd seen death, wasn't the last. Wasn't even the first or last time I nearly died."

Unfortunately, he believed her. "I'm sorry."

She shook her head. "I was lucky. *Filthy* lucky."

"So are we." Kita met his eyes again. "That you survived. We wouldn't have gotten this far without you."

"Me? I'm a street thief. There're thousands of us around. The king could have sent any one of them."

"Perhaps. But none of them are you. With your connections, your ability to bluff a group of renegades, your knowledge of how to convince a stubborn, cowardly necromancer to use a power he had feared and avoided his whole life, your trained hawk who is smart enough to find a winter village for us. Shadow Master was right. This quest requires every one of us. You included."

"Maybe. But I wish it didn't require boats."

"You and me both."

Chapter Fourteen

Sea of Tears and Forest of Gloom

Or

Cartographers are optimists

Sir Jors was heartily relieved when the boat made landfall. Personally, he had felt the chance to travel by boat to be an adventure. He had never done so before and was pleased to take the opportunity. The constant rocking of the floor beneath his feet had taken some getting used to, but he was not bothered by it much. He wasn't interested in giving up his knighthood to become a fisherman, but he had no serious issue with the travel.

His companions, on the other hand, seemed to feel otherwise. Lakara tried to hide her apprehension, but it was useless. They had shared a hundred fires together and then some. She could no more hide her fear from him than he could from her. So, he did what he could to distract her, ease her tension.

Unfortunately, an hour into the trip, he realized that in trying to help Lakara, he had lost track of where the others were. It was unsettling. Outside of Winterwatch, it had been rare to be separated by more than a wall, and even then, he had some idea of where they were and what they were doing.

It was not a large boat, so there was nowhere to go. He trusted them both, not to go looking for trouble. Nor was trouble likely to go looking for them on a pilgrimage boat.

If one or both of them wanted some sense of privacy, or to withdraw and be alone for a while, who was he to begrudge them?

So, he kept his ears open, but didn't go looking for them. Odds were, if something were to happen, either they would seek him out, or it would happen so quickly that his being there wouldn't make a difference.

The boat eventually met dock, allowing everyone to disembark. Lakara took a deep breath and smiled as she reached the gangplank. "We made it."

"Of course we did. Did you doubt it?" Kita asked, from just beyond Lakara's shoulder as if she had been there the whole time. Davorin stood next to her. Had they been together? Or had they simply returned together? Or had he been so focused, he simply missed when they returned?

Lakara smiled with good grace and didn't comment on their disappearing reappearing act. Perhaps she hadn't noticed. "Well, now I can say I've been on a boat. Hopefully, the voyage all the way across the Sea of Tears will be as calm."

"Agreed. Come, let's see the temple. The boat departs in two hours," Sir Jors said. Feeling solid ground under feet again felt strange, as his legs seemed to think he was still on a boat. He had been warned this was a side effect of water travel and would pass soon.

The temple of Yestav, goddess of water, was made of blue and white marble. It had a narrow entrance but inside, the building quickly widened to a circle. As befit the protector of the oceans, nautical themes predominated. The fountain in the middle was shaped like a silver fish, coral decorations and pearl accents abounded.

Fish swam in several pools, protected by the goddess. Like in Tratow's temples, penitents could buy some food for the fish, but it was not required. Still a wise precaution. They would need safe passage across the Sea of Tears more than once. If the goddess's blessing could be gained, they would be fools not to try.

So, they fed the sacred fish and took the sprinkling of blessed water. Unlike most of the other temples, no incense or candles were lit. Instead, mineral crystals were purchased and cast to the main fountain to dissolve in the water.

Then they spread out to find the clue. There wasn't much time. Of the two hours they had, an hour had almost passed already.

Twenty minutes more went by. Tension rising, Sir Jors was studying one of the pillars when Lakara walked by him. "Kita found it. Come on."

He followed without question. Davorin was there already, kneeling to read something carved onto a marble statue of a ship. No, it was on the wave.

"Good." Sir Jors nodded first to Kita who was watching avidly, then to Davorin. Neither paid him much heed. Not that it mattered.

"It's long." Kita eyed it.

"Some clues are longer than others, I suppose." Sir Jors stepped back, urging Kita to do the same. Davorin and Lakara might need room to work. "How did you find it?" This section was not well lit, and he probably wouldn't have noticed it if the clue hadn't been pointed out to him.

"I decided to check the glowing bits one at a time. Starting with the areas that didn't make sense."

"As logical a suggestion as any. Out of curiosity, what else glowed?" Kita's ability to see magic had come up a few times, including stopping them from purchasing supposedly enchanted items that she declared frauds. But he had never stopped to wonder how much it changed what she saw from what he could see.

"The fountain, of course. Some of the bowls. The fish pools. Two of the priests and one of the priestesses, plus three of the other pilgrims all either glowed or had something on them that glowed. That statue had a little at the base, and there is something glinting at the top of that pillar." She nodded at it discreetly, before squinting. "Looks like words."

He would have to trust her on that because he couldn't see anything but shadow there. Nor were they likely to persuade someone to light a chandelier in the time they had left. Sir Jors resigned himself to not knowing what was written there. Lakara did not.

"Can you see each letter clearly?"

Grumbling a bit about needing Whisper's eyes, Kita moved to get a better angle. "Maybe."

"Good. What does the first letter look like?"

"A sideways harp with no strings?"

Lakara bit her bottom lip and closed her eyes. "New plan." She pulled out a different scroll. "Do you see that letter on here?"

After examining the scroll for a minute, Kita pointed to a letter that Sir Jors had to admit did look a little like a sideways harp. Lakara copied it down. "Next letter?"

It took time, but Kita carefully pointed out each letter she saw. Twice she admitted she couldn't tell between two similar letters, and one she couldn't read at all. "That's fine. We'll manage. Now, let's get out of here before the boat leaves without us."

***

Translating the texts gave Lakara something to concentrate on during the voyage back to land, much to her relief. While she would have preferred having Davorin around to check her translation and her notes, he had disappeared somewhere. Probably to do his own translating. Sir Jors stayed with her, which meant she was able to work uninterrupted, even when a sailor made a few uncouth remarks to her. Sir Jors persuaded the man to apologize, and she was left alone after that.

Kita was gone somewhere too. Perhaps for the best. Maybe Lakara should try to teach Kita at least the letters of Vesrop. It would be impossible to teach her much more than that in the time they had, but if she had known what the letters were called, it would have made their transcribing a little faster. A sideways harp indeed. Still, she had come a long way from the illiterate street thief who had started the journey with them.

They had all come a long way. Lakara wasn't sure she would even recognize her past self if she were to bump into her. The scholar who had never left Corvis, who barely left the palace and thought she knew things because she read them in books and scrolls. For all she knew the scholar's code, she had forgotten it. *Always remember how little you know.* But she thought she knew. How little she had known. Even less had she understood.

But recollections did not get her work translated. The second fragment was easier to translate than the first. She had seen it before. But now she realized she hadn't translated it quite correctly before. The first part, the clue, took longer. By the time the boat docked, she was pretty confident she had translated both of them to the best of her ability.

When everyone was gathered in the larger room at the inn. Lakara took a moment to compare her translation to Davorin's. He didn't seem to have gotten as far as she had, but what he did have was close to her translation.

"So, what does it say?" asked Kita, as she picked at the

bread in her hand. She had the interesting habit of picking out the interior of her bread and eating it first, before eating the crust.

"The clue seems to say, 'By the light of the full moon is the black sea still.' I'm not sure what that means."

Davorin grimaced. "It means we'll probably need to take another boat."

"That… may be. Or it could be a metaphor."

Kita waved her explanation away. "We'll figure it out when we get there. What about the other one?"

"Ah, now that was interesting. We've come across this one before. In AKAF's temple. Though, I think I slightly mistranslated it then. At the time, I said it was, 'Those that go, do not return.' But I forgot some of the subtleties of the language. If I'm right, there isn't an exact translation into Graldish, but it's closer to saying that those that go, don't return the same."

"Of course not," Kita scoffed. "Anybody would change after a journey like this."

"She's right," Sir Jors agreed. "We have all changed as a result of our quest, and I consider that to be a good thing. Without changing, we might not have made it this far."

"True. I don't know why it was there. Or even if it relates to the jewel. But I am glad to have a better translation of that." Lakara sighed. "Two more temples and we still don't know where the jewel is."

"Aloses and Skoses?" Kita asked.

Lakara nodded. "Aloses's temple is deep in the Forest of Gloom. But we'll have to cross into the Dead Lands to reach Skoses's temple."

No one quite shivered at that. Traveling through the

Forest of Gloom almost guaranteed a meeting with the Queya who were notorious for their protectiveness of their land. Strangers were distrusted and allowed entry grudgingly, if at all. A small group like theirs, on a pilgrimage, had a chance to be allowed through unhindered. A small chance, but better than a group of soldiers.

Kita might be their best chance. Or perhaps not. She didn't look visibly Queyan, who were known for a gray cast to their skin. Would the Queyans know she was part Queyan by looking at her?

That is, if Kita decided to come. Davorin might stop too. This fishing village certainly wasn't the biggest town they had traveled through, but it wasn't the smallest either. It had a solid, though not wealthy, economy, and had been more welcoming to strangers than most places they had stopped at in Salardis. Strangers willing to work could find a home here.

Well, perhaps not this town. They had lied about who they were. But there were several similar villages dotting the border of the sea. But she hoped they would stay. Both for personal reasons, and because they needed them.

Sir Jors took a deep breath. "How many should I be looking for passage for?"

Kita and Davorin exchanged a long look. A very long look. Did they know something she didn't? Finally, Kita shrugged. "No point staying here. They'd probably imprison me for running away from my 'master'."

"And I have no spices to sell them." Davorin sighed. "How much time does a boat save us?"

Sir Jors arched his eyebrows. "Between two and four weeks. The Sea of Tears can be crossed in a day or two if we take a boat."

Another long look. "Passage for four," Kita said. "Unless

you plan on staying here?" She looked at Lakara.

"Me? No. Of course not." She had said that she would stay at least until they had all the clues.

"Thank you, all of you." Sir Jors smiled. "I will see what I can do for passage."

Kita shook her head. "Let me. I've worked with fisherfolk before." She slipped out the door before anyone could say anything.

"I'm going to go over the previous clues. Maybe something will stand out now that didn't before," Lakara said.

Davorin offered to help, so they pulled out the clues from the various temples. 'Heart of Earth', 'A solid shout to the sky', 'Brave the ice, brave the fire', 'Past the dead that you might live', 'Through the eye of the needle' or 'needle through the eye', 'A single coal burns out quickly', and now, 'By the light of the full moon is the black sea still'. At Sir Jors request, she read them out loud to him.

"I may be wrong, but the last temple on our list is the great temple of Skoses, the god of earth." Sir Jors scratched his beard. "I know we said that the 'heart of earth' probably related to going north, but could it be related to that?"

"Certainly possible. Vesrop was a language that delighted in puns and wordplay." Davorin said.

"Of course," Lakara gasped. "You're right. They did love wordplay. And the word for shout was almost identical to the word for tower."

"So 'a solid shout to the sky' could mean a tall and sturdy tower?" Sir Jors asked.

"Where better to hide a treasure?" Kita asked. Lakara jumped. She hadn't heard her come back. "Found one, but there's a couple conditions."

"Such as?" Sir Jors asked.

"It doesn't leave for five days, and we'll be acting as crew. It's a fishing boat. They'll take us and the lizards, but it will be three or four days across."

Sir Jors was quiet for a few minutes. "It is still faster than attempting to cross on foot. And if we are crew, it's probably cheaper than any deal I could manage."

"We get a share of the fish," Kita said. "No money, though. I told them that the rest of you have no experience. They're cheating us if we were actually looking for work; but for transport..."

Sir Jors nodded. "Good. You did well."

A little tension eased, but more of it remained than Lakara would have predicted. Gradually, over the next few days, that tension increased in small ways. Something about this leg of the journey was making Kita anxious.

Not that she was the only one, of course. Lakara was hardly looking forward to it either. Boats were not a safe method of transportation. Nor was she thrilled at the idea of working as a fisherwoman. The scholar from the palace had lost a lot of her squeamishness, but not all. Fish stank and were very... unclean. But she wasn't afraid of hard work and would do her part.

Davorin didn't like boats either, hardly mentioning the topic without a grimace or frown. Like her, he didn't complain verbally. It wouldn't do them any good.

Still, when the morning of their sea voyage dawned, Lakara didn't think she was the only one reluctant to leave their safe, mostly clean, inn. Even Kita seemed reluctant to leave, and she was always the first to want to move on.

Whatever reluctance she may have felt, Kita breezed onboard the boat with a large smile. A familiar looking smile.

It took Lakara a moment, but that smile was an almost exact match for the smile Kita had worn when meeting Jalen at the oasis.

Lakara bit her bottom lip. Should she say something? She looked at Sir Jors, walking next to her. Judging from his frown, he had noticed as well. It wasn't just her imagination. Pretending to adjust Stripes' harness, she looked at Davorin. He was watching Kita too. He knew.

Kita and Davorin had been talking a lot recently, without arguing, so perhaps he knew something. "Does Kita know this man?" she asked as quietly as possible.

"Met him for the first time five days ago," Kita answered. "Come on, they're going to show us where to bed the lizards."

The lizards were led, with difficulty, to a pen deep in the hold of the boat, not far from where the crew was to bunk. Five other lizards shared the pen with them. To Lakara's eye, none of them looked happy to be on a boat. Trouble had tried to run back down the gangplank when boarding. It took Kita and Davorin to get him in place. He was over half his full size now, which made him too big to control easily.

"I don't remember reading anything about pack lizards not liking boats," Lakara said, tying the harnesses to the post in one corner.

"Can you blame them? And don't mention reading," Kita murmured. "We're poor travelers who need to get work as we travel. Poor travelers can't read."

Lakara nodded. "Good point. Now what?"

"Now we get our assigned jobs." Kita eyed Lakara critically. "Volunteer to repair nets."

"That... might be for the best." She didn't have the strength to haul nets full of fish or the precision to gut a fish quickly and cleanly. But she did know how to tie knots.

Within an hour of being taught what to do she could repair a net without the Net Mistress, Selta, throwing up her hands and making her re-do it. That kept her busy enough that she didn't know what the others were doing. Not until Sir Jors came by with food.

For this leg of the journey, it had been decided that they would not be letting on that Sir Jors was a knight. Just like them, he wore his oldest traveling robes, foregoing his armor. He also decided to go by Anor. No one asked him why he wanted to go by his brother's name. It was a little strange to see him this way.

"What do they have you doing?" Lakara asked, before taking a bite of bread.

"I'm helping haul nets. Davorin is cleaning fish. Kita is..." he shaded his eyes and looked up at the rigging, "up there. Apparently, some of the ropes got tangled."

Sure enough, if Lakara looked up, she could see a few people climbing over the ropes. "I hope she's being careful."

"I'm sure she is. How are you doing?"

"I'm fine. Net Mistress Selta no longer glares at me like she wants to throw me overboard." Though she was glaring. Probably because Lakara wasn't working. Lakara took another bite, swallowed, and went back to the nets.

Sir Jors smiled. "I better get back as well."

A million or so nets later, Kita staggered by. The very fact that she was staggering had Lakara's attention. "Are you well?"

Kita swallowed. "Fine. It just takes me a day or so to find my sea legs."

"Oh. Um, I'm sorry?"

Kita shook her head, then inhaled sharply. "Nothing to be sorry... ooohh, for." She exhaled slowly. "I do not like seasickness."

"No, I imagine you don't. I, um, never thought you would... be susceptible."

"No one ever does. I denied it when Davorin asked."

Lakara looked her over. Ashen complexion, sweat beading on her face despite the cool breeze, and a refusal to open her eyes when she didn't have to. "I doubt he believed you."

"Oh, he didn't. Not by a long shot."

Lakara was on the verge of asking why Kita had even bothered trying to hide it, when a tall fisherman came up, laughing raucously. "Never thought I'd see the day. A seasick Trovian." He clapped Kita's back hard enough to bend her over, gagging twice. He backed off quickly, as Kita tried to regain her breathing pattern without vomiting. "Maybe you should work on repairing the nets for a while. Boat doesn't rock as much here."

Eyes closed, still trying to control her breathing, Kita nodded, gagged once, and slowly sat down. "I'll try not to mess up your clothes."

"Are you sure you'll be alright?" Lakara eyed her dubiously.

"I'll be fine. Tomorrow you won't know there was a problem."

Kita was right. The next day she moved about as freely as if she had been on boats all her life. Davorin, still seasick, made no secret of his jealousy.

Mending nets was difficult work and rough on the hands, but Lakara did appreciate that it kept her busy. Even more, she appreciated that she had not fallen victim to seasickness. While she had no interest in ever getting in a boat again, Lakara thought she was managing well. Until the storm came.

The last night before they were to reach shore, the wind picked up. Lakara had ignored it. But she was one of the few to do so. Just as she was one of the few to not realize the significance of the aches and pains several people onboard were feeling, like her own headache.

Sir Jors informed her. A storm, strong and soon. Kita insisted that they all stay together once it came. Preferably by the pack lizards. She didn't give any reason for this, but no one argued. Especially when Davorin backed her up.

Only the most experienced sailors would stay on deck to deal with anything that came up. Everyone else was to stay in the hold, out of the way. As none of them counted as the most experienced, they did as Kita suggested, congregating around the pack lizards.

When the water got choppier, Lakara decided that maybe Kita had a good idea. And maybe Kita was a little more scared than she wanted to admit to. Which deepened Lakara's fear.

"We're pretty far from land, aren't we?" Lakara asked.

"The boat's moored. To keep it in place. Safer than trying to make it to shore." Kita wrapped the harnesses around her hand, unwound them and wrapped them again. "Does anyone here know how to swim?"

"I do," Sir Jors said. "Anyone else?"

"Swimming wasn't considered an important skill for scholars."

Davorin shook his head.

"Not enough to keep from drowning." Kita gripped a hitching post as the boat rocked violently. "Especially in a storm." She eyed the lizards. "I don't know if they can swim or not."

"What about Whisper?" Davorin asked.

"We both knew this was brewing for hours. He's already on the shore, and smart enough to find a decent shelter."

The boat shuddered and everyone scrambled to take hold of something. The lizards were agitated. Kita would be the best to calm them, if she wasn't so agitated herself.

Wind howled and shrieked. The boat groaned and fell, Lakara was privately convinced her stomach had been left behind at the rise. She had avoided seasickness so far but if it was even a tenth of this, anyone who suffered from it had her complete sympathies.

Davorin was ghostly pale, eyes shut and breathing slowly through his mouth. One hand he kept braced on the boat's wall, and with the other he was gripping Kita's hand hard enough to cut off circulation. Or maybe it was Kita's grip, considering her other hand was wrapped equally tightly around the lizards' harnesses. Sir Jors had planted himself between Lakara and the boat wall, keeping his arm free and able to catch her if she stumbled. Or at least, she assumed that was why he was watching her like that.

Before she could contemplate on that, the boat rose again before falling swiftly. Bile flowed up her throat, but she swallowed it down, concentrating on finding her footing. Sure enough, Sir Jors caught her as she floundered. "Just hold on. We're going to be fine," He spoke in her ear to be heard over the wind.

Not sure she could talk without violently ejecting her stomach contents, Lakara nodded and held onto his arm. It couldn't last forever. The storm would pass. They would make landfall safely. Then she was never getting into another boat again!

Kita's head came up and she started looking around. The way she did when she sensed something no one else had yet.

"What's that sound?"

"It's the storm!" Davorin shouted back.

Kita shook her head. "No, it's different!"

For a moment, Lakara heard nothing but the wind's eerie screams and the boat's moaning dirge. Then another sound clarified. It was faint enough that Lakara wasn't certain she was hearing it at all. A deep chittering sound, like nothing she had heard before.

They weren't the only ones to hear it. Other people were mentioning it too. Someone called it 'Caloth', but the word had no meaning to her. If any of the others understood, they weren't volunteering.

The boat shook as it hit something solid. A rock? Surely not. They hadn't moved far enough to hit a rock. Not if the boat was moored like Kita said. Unless the ropes had broken. But they hadn't, had they?

Water was seeping in through the walls and the ceiling. It must be swamping over the sides. Another solid thump on the other side. What was happening? The chittering faded. More rocking about. Lakara closed her eyes and prayed that the storm would end.

***

Nothing lasts forever, not even storms. Something Kita was grateful for. The storm may have raged half the night, but it did pass eventually, leaving the boat intact, along with all inside it. And she was *never* going in another muddy, filthy boat again! To the dirt with them all.

Still, they were alive and able to make landfall by early afternoon. "Are we spending the night in town?" Kita asked, trying to make her legs work properly, while directing Trouble away from a young female lizard he wished to meet.

"Yes, I think that would be best," Sir Jors said. He had

Stripes' harness. "Usual story?"

"No, we clearly came on the fishing boat. We are pilgrims, looking for work as we travel." Kita tugged harder at Trouble's harness. "You, lizardling, are growing up too fast."

"They do that," said Davorin, leading Longtail. "My pigeons are the same way."

Kita nodded but didn't respond. She knew Whisper was nearby, but she hadn't spotted him yet. While there were no signs that he might be injured or anything wrong, it had been days since they had been able to truly connect, and she wanted to see him with her own eyes. Besides, the sooner they got away from the boat, the better.

There had been talk of a sea monster during the storm. One of the fishermen was telling anyone who would listen that he had seen the *Caloth* grab the boat with its tentacles. None of the others had traveled with fisherfolk before, so maybe none of them knew what he was saying. Well, she wasn't going to muddy tell them.

Lakara was saying something, but Kita tuned it out. She could see Whisper perched on the roof of a hut. He seemed unhurt. Just to make sure, Kita closed her eyes. Not a true Borrowing, just touching base. Yes, he was fine.

As much as she wanted to deepen the connection, she didn't dare. Not here, not now. Reluctant but determined, she pulled back to herself, opening her eyes. No one seemed to have noticed. No one was looking at her.

"Is that Whisper?" Davorin muttered in her ear.

She nodded slightly. "He's fine."

"Good."

They found an inn to take them, using the story about being pilgrims. It meant cheaper, lower quality rooms, but no one cared. Perhaps when they went to bed, she could take the time to Borrow Whisper and check with him more thoroughly.

Since no one could sleep during the storm, everyone was tired. After dinner, sleep wasn't so much discussed as assumed. Tired as she was, Kita feigned sleep to talk to Whisper.

He was ecstatic to sense her beckon. He had missed her as she had missed him. The fish were good here, but the other birds weren't friendly, and Whisper was ready to move on. The storm had been trouble, but he found a hollow in a chimney to hole up in. But he felt her fear and wanted her close. Tomorrow they could be close.

It almost made Kita smile as the rush of feelings and impressions washed over her. She sent reassurance and impatience for the next day. Then she released the connection and slipped back to her own body. The one without feathers or wings. The one that was being shaken.

Wait, shaken? Kita snapped back abruptly and immediately remembered *why* she didn't do that. Nausea and intense headache aside, someone was indeed shaking her.

Kita grabbed the wrist right above her shoulder with one hand, twisted and rolled so she half fell off the bed, scrambling for her dirk with her free hand. It wasn't on her. Why wasn't it on her?

Forcing back the pain and squinting through the darkness, Kita tried to make out who was there. It was easier when the figure gasped. "Lakara? What are you muddy doing?"

Lakara flinched slightly. Right, she was still squeezing her wrist. Kita let go, but there might well be a bruise or two. "Sorry about that. But you should never try to shake me awake. Call my name."

"I did. Three times." Oops. "We have to evacuate. Fire."

Kita had her shoes and robe on and was grabbing her bag

before Lakara could say anything else. "Let's get out of here!" She was *not* going to stay here and burn to death. She could ask Lakara what 'evacuate' meant later.

There was confusion as everyone was trying to leave the inn at once. Davorin and Sir Jors had lingered long enough to make sure both women left their room, but soon they were all outside in the courtyard.

By now, Kita could tell that the fire wasn't in the inn itself, but another building nearby. Close enough that there was a risk it would spread to the inn. Possibly the barn where the park lizards were. There was no way to remove the pack lizards from the barn, so they would have to make sure that the fire didn't spread that far. "There should be a bucket brigade. We need to join them." One advantage to living on the Sea of Tears was that water would be close.

As Kita predicted, there was a line already formed, transporting buckets of water. They were able to join the second line forming. Bucket after bucket she took from Lakara to give to Davorin. Her whole world focused down to the buckets in her hand, and occasionally the runners that took the empty buckets back to the start. The smoke continued to fill the air and the crackle of the fire was too loud, too strong. But she didn't let herself think about if their efforts were working. If the fire was dying. If the fire was spreading. If the lizards would be safe.

The sky was lightening before the cry went up that the fire was gone. A ragged cheer rose from the group before questions started being asked. How far had the fire spread, had anyone been injured or died?

Rather than depend on rumor, Kita caught Sir Jors eye and received a nod. Permission to check it out herself. She would meet them back either here or at the inn, provided the inn was safe.

It didn't take long to find the smoldering wreck where the fire had been. A building, no way to know what kind, had been devoured by fire, which had also scorched the buildings on either side. One seemed to have been a shop, the other, she suspected, was a house. The house might be able to be repaired. The shop, probably not. But it hadn't spread further. The inn was safe. Their supplies were safe. The pack lizards were safe. And, as a voice in her head reminded her, Whisper was safe.

Everyone was waiting for her at the inn. "We were lucky. One building destroyed, two more badly damaged. Could have been much worse. I haven't even heard anything about anyone hurt or killed."

"That is fortunate," Sir Jors said. He looked them all over as if to make sure for himself that none of them were hurt. "Why... Never mind. Another time. We should sleep. We need to move on today."

"After we've collected our share of fish." Kita shrugged at Sir Jors' questioning look. "That was the wages agreed to. It would look weird if we didn't try to collect."

"Besides, a share of fish means that we can save on buying other supplies," Lakara said.

"Both true. Now, everyone, to sleep." Sir Jors stood and left, Davorin following.

To Kita's relief, Lakara collapsed on the bed, forgetting to ask why Kita had been so hard to wake.

Leaving the town took longer than expected. First, everyone slept in, tired from both the storm and the time spent fighting a fire. Then they had to collect their share of fish. The head fisherman tried to refuse them, saying they were incompetent fisherfolks. Kita countered by saying she had warned him that, and they had learned quickly. Then he tried claiming the fish had been sold. Kita said that was fine, he could pay them instead. Final agreement was that each of them was given two pounds of smoked or salted fish and one fresh fish, plus one gold dourat.

Kita didn't mention that Whisper had stolen one of the fish while they were being preserved. Not that he was the only bird to try or even to succeed. Lakara noticed and gave Kita a reproachful look. Kita shrugged. What? They expected her to tell him not to?

After they had their fish, they had to buy the rest of their supplies. One of the fresh fish was traded for some smoked lizard meat. Some of the leather they collected from the swamp lizards was traded for spices. A little more was traded for two spare robes and another pair of boots. Lakara's had been damaged in the Swamp of Despair and completely fell apart on the boat.

They did delay long enough to eat lunch, but then they were off. At their current rate of speed, almost twice as fast as when they began, it should take about two days to reach the Forest of Gloom. Whisper swooped down to perch on her shoulder when they were about a mile out.

Kita smiled as she stroked his breast. "Good fish?" Whisper squawked and nibbled at her hair.

"You should let him steal fish like that," Lakara said. "They worked hard for that."

"I promise, Whisper wasn't the only one. I imagine the local sea birds are quite adept at stealing a quick meal. Besides, they underpaid us, even counting what Whisper took." Kita found herself reluctant to deny that she could stop him. That would be a lie, and she would rather not lie to them.

"You didn't say anything at the time," Sir Jors said.

Kita shrugged the shoulder that Whisper wasn't perched on. "I expected to be cheated. Not like we have room to carry a lot of fish. This was a little better than I expected.

We got across the Sea of Tears, that's what matters. But even for inexperienced fisherfolk, we should have been paid about a third more." And she actually did have experience, so she should have been paid another half as much again.

"Then why didn't you continue to press?" Davorin asked. "I'm certain you could have gained more."

"Probably. But it was more important to move on."

"Why did we have to move on right away? That's two nights in a row of bad sleep, why not wait another day?" Lakara asked.

"The fire," Sir Jors said, but didn't elaborate.

When it was clear the other two didn't understand, Kita filled them in. "When something bad happens, people look for someone to blame. Who better than wandering travelers that no one knows? Most of the fisherfolk probably come through sometimes, and they tend to be superstitious. Doesn't take much to decide that the storm and the fire are connected. The gods are angry at someone. We show up out of nowhere before everything goes muddy wrong..."

"That... That wouldn't happen!" Lakara was white and wide eyed.

"I've *seen* it happen. Been on the wrong side and seen it happen to others. Best case scenario, people get sullen and snarly. Some refuse to sell to us, and the ones that do double or triple the prices. We're encouraged to leave. Or driven away. Or worse."

"She's not wrong." Sir Jors picked up the pace a little. "All things considered, I thought it best to leave. And it might be wise to avoid that particular village on the... in the future."

On the return. Did he really believe there would be a return? Kita didn't ask. Neither did anyone else.

"I guess people really do fear the different," Lakara

mused. "I wonder if that's why there is a death penalty on Borrowing."

Kita choked on air. A *death* penalty? She had known it was illegal, even serious, but *death*? "Are you sure?"

Lakara looked at her oddly. "Well, no. That's why I just said, 'I wonder', but… Oh! Yes, I'm sure there's a death penalty on Borrowing. Didn't you know that?"

Kita shook her head; not sure she'd be able to speak. Death. If she had known that, would she have dared to latch on to Whisper like she had? Was Whisper worth the risk?

Picking up on her emotions if not the why, Whisper started to preen her hair to calm her down. She stroked him in thanks. Whether she would have considered it worth the risk three years ago or not, she couldn't imagine life without him now.

Pulling herself together, Kita mentally swore as she noticed everyone was looking at her. "What?"

"Are you… well?" Davorin asked, looking between the two of them.

"Fine. Just… fine."

Sir Jors frowned and stepped forward. Lakara and Davorin went quiet and took a step back. Kita resisted the urge to backstep herself and met the knight's eyes, head up and eyes straight. "We will not, any of us, ask you if you have or are capable of Borrowing. Nor will we report it if you should admit to using it either in the past or on this quest."

"And afterwards?"

"Then I suppose it would depend on what was done with it. But I have shared a hundred fires with you. I believe I know you well enough to know that while your actions may not always be legal, they are rarely malicious."

Sir Jors may have been the one speaking, but Lakara and Davorin were nodding agreement. They knew. They *knew*! But they wouldn't tell. Kita felt shaky as her body tried to decide if it should be relieved or afraid. "I see. Well, then I wouldn't report it if any of you did it either." Lakara stifled a chuckle and Davorin looked vaguely insulted for a second, but Sir Jors simply nodded gravely.

"As long as we have an understanding."

"I believe we do." Kita started walking a little faster. As much as she appreciated the support, she had no intention of confirming their suspicions. And she certainly didn't plan to mention that while she had never tried it, she suspected she could Borrow Trouble if she tried. She had to keep some secrets.

***

Davorin frowned at the green-gray haze they were heading towards. The Forest of Gloom. Some claimed the name came from the frequent fogs and mists that permeated the place. Some said that the thick tree canopy prevented most light from reaching the ground, causing the name. Others said it was because those that wandered the forest were likely to lose themselves and never return. Of course, the Sea of Tears, the Swamp of Despair, the Mountains of Death, the Ocean of Sand, and the Endless Grasslands weren't known to be safe either. None of them should be as dangerous as the Dead Lands.

But somehow, there was something about the Forest of Gloom that he dreaded. Davorin wasn't sure what or why he was so repelled, but it would be wise to be careful and pay attention.

Tomorrow they should reach the border. He considered saying something of his unease but decided against it. The entire party already knew he was a coward. Why prove it by jumping at shadows? He *was* jumping at shadows, wasn't he?

Whisper shrieked suddenly before landing on Kita's shoulder. Automatically, the party clustered together, checking every direction for a threat. Sir Jors' hand rested on his sword and Kita had already drawn her dirk. But as Davorin looked, he couldn't see anything that would cause such alarm.

"What's gotten into you, bird?" Kita asked, any harshness belied by the way she stroked his ruffled feathers. If the hawk told her anything, she didn't pass it on.

"Any signs of… anything?" Lakara asked.

"Nothing I can sense. Kita? Davorin?"

Nice of the knight to have some faith in his abilities, but it was misplaced. "I can't see or hear anything amiss."

Kita shrugged, eyes narrowed. "I'm not getting anything, but something has Whisper spooked." She paused. "Maybe I should take point for a bit."

"No, I'll do it," Sir Jors said. "I have armor."

"Only over parts of you," Kita muttered, but subsided.

With a care that rivaled their travel through the bog-filled Swamp of Despair, the party moved forward. Even the lizards seemed to pick up on their trepidation, moving slowly and darting their eyes around. Or maybe they were responding to whatever Whisper had sensed.

An explanation would be nice. Something that gave them some warning about what was ahead. What they were walking into. But no such warning came.

They walked for at least an hour, dealing with nothing worse than the uneven road. But every time Davorin wanted to relax, he'd see Whisper stare off in the distance, or the lizards would act weird, or he'd think he saw something out of the corner of his eye. Finally, with nothing else for it, they set up camp for the night.

Kita built up the fire, like usual. As she did so, she spoke in a low voice. "Can't prove it, but I think we're being watched."

Sir Jors was the only one to not look around at her pronouncement. "Are you sure?" Lakara whispered.

"No, I'm *not* sure. But I think we are. It... feels right."

"You could be correct," Sir Jors said, even as he sat on a rock. "We are close to Queya land. If it is the Queya watching us, it would behoove us to act as peaceful as possible."

"So, we aren't going to do anything?" Davorin asked, incredulous.

"Their land. Not ours." Kita didn't look up from the fire. "And I'm willing to bet they outnumber us by no small bit."

"It's not a fight we can hope to win," Sir Jors agreed. "Best try to avoid it completely. We'll be careful. Whoever is on guard will have to stay extra alert. But I think it's best to ignore it for now.

Davorin doubted it would be that easy for anyone. He had first watch tonight, and for once, he didn't regret it. He doubted he'd be getting any sleep tonight. Kita had Lakara's usual shift tonight, so if there was an attack, as long as it wasn't on his watch, they should be forewarned.

Despite his pessimism, the night was quiet. If they were being watched, their watchers chose not to show themselves. Kita refused to even speculate if they were still being watched, while Sir Jors counseled them to behave as if they were.

Lakara made porridge, as she commonly did, throwing in the last of the preserved fish. Davorin didn't say anything, even though he had hoped to use it for dinner. Hunting had been scarce lately, especially since only Sir Jors and Kita had any skill in hunting. He and Lakara depended more on luck than ability. Perhaps the Forest of Gloom would hold more opportunities. He asked.

"It's possible. But we must be careful what we hunt." Sir Jors lowered his voice. "Under no circumstances must we hunt deer or even mention the possibility."

Davorin and Lakara nodded at once. Kita paused in offering Whisper a piece of her fish. "Why not? I mean, you aren't particularly good with a javelin, I noticed, but why not even mention it?" Everyone stared at her. Kita forced her chin up and said nothing.

She truly didn't know? Sir Jors answered her when the others kept staring. "The Queya believe themselves linked to the deer. I do not quite understand if they believe they came from the deer, or believe their spirits become deer after they die. Maybe both. In either case, they call the deer brothers, and the killing of deer, or use of their skins or meat is strictly forbidden."

"Oh." Kita shrugged and went back to feeding Whisper. As if it didn't concern her at all. Perhaps it didn't. Maybe she truly didn't realize she was part Queya. Maybe she wasn't. Sir Jors had been certain, but what if he was wrong? No. The evidence was too strong to deny. Her preternatural relationship with her hawk, her dirk, her senses, even her ability to see magic was more in tune with the Queya than human ability. How had it taken Sir Jors to point it out?

So why didn't Kita know? Then again, who knew what she knew or had been told about the Queya? She didn't know about the deer, and that was one of the first things anyone learned. That and Borrowing, which she was also surprisingly ignorant about.

It was a few hours before midday when they entered the canopy of trees, but the sun didn't look it. The light was gray and dismal. Especially once they were surrounded by the forest. There was no road at all, and they had to make do with trail paths formed by deer and other animals.

Davorin prayed that his teammate's skill with environments didn't fail them now, because he could barely tell one tree from another. No wonder so many people got lost forever here. There wasn't enough room for Whisper to really fly without exiting the canopy, and if he flew above the trees, they would never see him.

When they stopped for lunch, Davorin wondered if they had even covered as much as two miles. The trail had narrowed to almost nothing in places, following no rhyme or rhythm they could decipher.

Sir Jors winced as he took a seat on a fallen tree. Attuned to each other as they had become, everyone noticed. "You're hobbling," Kita accused. "Blisters or a rock in your boot?"

"Rock. A sharp one, I'm afraid." He moved to fix the issue.

Having no interest in watching the process he had seen and done many times before, Davorin chose to look for the unseen birds he could hear calling to each other. Until Sir Jors called out in pain.

Lakara started and looked about wildly. Kita was kneeling by Sir Jors, dirk in hand. "What happened?" Davorin asked.

"Something struck me," Sir Jors said. "I believe I'm fine now. Maybe a tree branch."

"No. It was a snake. But it escaped before I could get a good look at it." Kita pushed herself to her feet. "Better put some yarrow on it. Just in case."

Lakara treated and bandaged his foot while Kita poked around the area with a long stick, hoping to get a glimpse of the snake for identification purposes. Sir Jors insisted his foot didn't hurt, and didn't seem to be lying, so after a longer than usual lunch break, they moved on.

Davorin didn't think anything more of it at first. They had all accrued minor injuries on their quest. He still had a burn mark on his hand from his time cooking in Winterwatch, though they all were fairly sure it wouldn't scar. This was neither the least nor the worst. But as evening came, he noticed that Sir Jors seemed to be slowing and walking more gingerly. The women noticed too, judging from the look they shared.

Sir Jors did not object to the idea of stopping early for the night, especially when they found a small clearing, almost big enough for them and the pack lizards to sit comfortably. They would probably have to sleep in the trees again.

As soon as the fire was built, Lakara insisted on checking on Sir Jors' foot. Davorin tried to ignore his apprehension as he noticed the knight had much more trouble removing the right boot than the left. To no one's surprise, the foot was swollen, and possibly redder than it should be. It was hard to tell in the dim light. Lakara treated it with yarrow again.

"In the morning, I'll check my books to see if I can find some more information," Lakara said as she packed up the yarrow. She hesitated, but no one asked her how many books she had.

"Hopefully some rest will give the yarrow time to work." Sir Jors smiled reassuringly.

Davorin would have been more hopeful if he didn't think he could see the shadows starting to form.

Morning proved him right. The foot was easily two, maybe three, times its normal size and deeply red. There was no question of him walking on it, and the shadows were forming. Still wispy, still possible to disperse, but only if they used the right remedy. But what was the right remedy for the venom of an unknown snake?

Lakara studied at least three sources while Kita went hunting for food. Davorin stoked up the fire. Food turned out to be three squirrels and some blue berries that looked somewhat familiar. "The animals were eating the berries, so I figured they were probably safe. I ate one almost ten minutes ago. No tingles or anything else."

"Just ate one? Like that?" Davorin asked, aghast. Didn't she know the dangers of poisonous plants?

"Not exactly. I tested it first."

"How?" Lakara asked.

Kita gave them a look like she didn't understand why they were interrogating her like this but answered the question. "Sniffed them first. Rubbed one. Waited a few minutes, then squished one. I sniffed at, then licked the juice. Waited. Nothing happened. So, I ate one. At least three different kinds of animals had been eating them. Should be fine." When they still watched her, she huffed. "I've been on my own, traveling, for a long time. I know what to do, how to find food. Food that isn't going to make me sick or kill me."

"They look a little like riverdew berries," Sir Jors said. "Perhaps a variety?"

Davorin hoped so. Riverdews were perfectly edible, even if they were better for dye than food.

"A little sweeter. But the leaves were similar," Kita said.

"Most blue berries are safe to eat," Lakara said. "It's the red and white ones you have to be especially careful of."

All the same, they were careful with the berries. No one ate more than a small handful. If they turned out to be completely safe, they could always get more later.

After breakfast, Lakara made a point of quizzing Sir Jors about his symptoms. "Are you having trouble swallowing?"

"I am not."

"Breathing?"

"No."

"Pain in the area of the bite?"

"I can still walk."

Kita scoffed. Davorin shook his head. Lakara got indignant. "No, you cannot walk! We aren't going anywhere today. And if I am going to have any luck identifying a cure, I need to know your symptoms. So, stop trying to be brave or noble and be honest!"

"Yes, there is some pain," Sir Jors answered slowly, still staring wide-eyed at the woman. Davorin felt like doing the same. Kita was silently shaking with laughter.

Lakara nodded, apparently unsurprised. "How about tingling?"

"Some."

With surprising frankness, the scholar took hold of the knight's wrist and held on for a moment. "Fast heartrate." She went back to her books. "Apparently the poison affects the blood, not the nerves. I suspected as much. Nerve poisons rarely swell."

"Can we drain it back out?" Kita asked. "Maybe a small cut to let the bad blood run out?"

Lakara frowned. "I don't think so. Maybe when it first happened, but none of the books suggest something like that, especially after all this time. They do recommend use of a snake stone, which we don't have, I checked; or a poultice of specific plants, which we also don't have. Best we can do is yarrow and hot, wet rags. Wrap the foot in it and keep it elevated. And no moving! We don't want the poison circulating more."

Sir Jors grumbled a little about the delay but was soundly ignored. The rags were switched out every few hours with yarrow administered in between.

Davorin said nothing about how the shadows continued to grow.

He didn't need to. The next morning, Sir Jors was clearly weaker than the day before. His foot was more swollen and almost purple in color. Extremely painful to the touch, too, if the way Sir Jors could barely keep from swearing every time something jostled it was any indication.

No one made any attempt to break camp or even mentioned doing so. Not even Sir Jors, possibly because he kept slipping into restless sleeps. During one of those, Kita quietly suggested to Lakara that she read up on amputation. The possibilities and risks.

Lakara went white but didn't object. Davorin admired the woman for her grit, because he knew he wouldn't be able to so much as research it, let alone perform the task.

Which left the question of who could? Davorin couldn't. He didn't have the strength; mental or physical to do so. Lakara, while an able enough researcher, and a surprisingly good medic when pressed, probably couldn't either, physically or mentally. Sir Jors probably could, if he weren't the patient in question.

It would have to be Kita. She was pragmatic enough to see the possible necessity faster than either of her two uninjured companions, and despite her smaller size, stronger than either of them as well. But was it strong enough?

Even if she was, with what? The hatchet they used for firewood wasn't strong enough to cut bone, not easily or cleanly at any rate. Sir Jors' sword might be a better choice, but that might not be enough either. Besides, it was a generational weapon, and it was hard to use those against their owners and would almost certainly break the magic if they did.

Then there was the risk of infection or worse. But it might be Sir Jors' only option. Which was why Davorin found himself badly shaken when an ashen Lakara quietly informed the two of them that she didn't believe amputation would be possible or useful.

"I don't think it would help. His leg is too warm, all the way up to the thigh." The scholar blushed but continued. "I don't think we could remove enough to save him without him succumbing to blood loss or wound fever. And if it isn't going to help, I don't think we should cause him that kind of pain." She was hesitant, reluctant to make her point. As if begging someone to disagree.

Davorin looked at the shadows gathering over his friend but couldn't argue with her. Kita looked like she wanted to but relaxed with a sigh. "No, we won't put him through that unless we have reason to believe it could work. But we will do everything else in our power. I'm not giving up on him."

"Of course." Davorin nodded. "None of us will."

Lakara smiled shyly. "Absolutely."

Sir Jors started to stir. Lakara took immediately to his side, offering him water as soon as he was awake. The knight took it gratefully. Then he looked at his leg and shuddered, before leaning back again, eyes closed. Davorin thought he had drifted back to unconsciousness, but Sir Jors soon turned and looked them all over. With a gravelly voice, he spoke. "You should move on in the morning."

How he thought he'd be up to travel the next morning was beyond Davorin. Lakara was the one who said it. "You won't be ready by then. We can take a few days." Kita just glared.

Sir Jors shook his head. "No. *You* should go on. I... I

don't think there is any continuing for me. Lakara, it is time to take back leadership. For the good of the party, leave me and continue. Search out the Jewel of Ishni, or do not. Whatever your conscience demands. I have done my part."

Lakara and Davorin cried out in wordless denials. Kita, who had probably understood from the start, moved in front of him. "You aren't getting out of this that easily. You have a job to do, remember? Protect the party, find the jewel, and keep me from stealing it for my own selfish purposes. If anyone's abandoning this filthy quest, it's going to be me. I promise you, if you die, I'm stealing that jewel. The king will never see it. Not ever."

Sir Jors gave a shaky laugh. "I doubt you could do worse with it."

"That's what you think. I'd demand magical powers. I could turn people I don't like into pack lizards. I could turn invisible, able to open any lock. I could steal anything I wanted." Kita tossed her head. "It would all be your fault, you know. King Zikkar would live out the rest of his days as a pigeon in Davorin's tower. *Lakara* would be left in charge of the kingdom. And she'd probably drive everyone insane, insisting on neatness and reading and—"

"I don't *want* to be in charge of the kingdom!" Lakara shrieked, half in laughter, half in dismay.

"Well, *I* certainly can't do it," Davorin said. "I have to take care of a pigeon king. And with Kita becoming a legendary thief, I don't think she'd be a good choice either."

"I'll steal your books until you agree. Your libraries will be empty of books and full of birds and no one will know why. Birds everywhere. Messy, dirty birds."

"See, you can't leave us. The kingdom would collapse," Lakara said. "You have to recover."

Sir Jors gave a sad smile. "I will do my best. I can promise no more."

"That's all we can ask," Kita said.

"I can make up a tea for pain, if you think it would help," Lakara offered.

Sir Jors appeared as if he would refuse, but accepted. "That would be most kind."

They had kept the fire going non-stop but controlled. Davorin hoped the tea worked because the strain didn't seem to let up.

Kita disappeared for a while, coming back with more berries from yesterday and some kindling. "We're being watched," she breathed on the wind, quiet enough that Sir Jors couldn't hear. In a louder voice, "How about a story? Lakara?"

The young woman jumped several inches at the call of her name. "A story? But…" Kita glared at her until she got the message. "Oh, me? Well, I could. If everyone wants?"

"That would be lovely," Sir Jors said, easing to a more comfortable position.

That killed the last of her resistance. "Very well. Let me think." She looked at her audience. "What kind of a story? Tales of the gods? Tales of heroes and kings? A romance? A story of revenge? All of the above?"

"Wouldn't that be hard? To combine all those in one story?" Kita asked.

"Oh, not at all. There are dozens of them. Like Sala and the golden veil. Or Torchiv, King of the Sunlit Kingdom. Vali, the thi…, no, not that one. Um, oh! Corton the Valiant!"

Kita chuckled as Lakara cut herself off from mentioning Vali the thief king. Not surprising. While not commonly told stories among the aristocracy, they were supposedly very popular among the poor.

For a moment, Davorin thought that Kita would ask for one of Vali's stories, but she sobered and turned to Sir Jors. "What would you like to hear?"

Sir Jors gave a small smile that failed to hide his pain. "How about Torchiv of the Sunlit Kingdom?"

Lakara nodded and immediately began. Davorin had heard the story a good dozen times before and it wasn't one of his favorites anyway. So, he mostly tuned her out in favor of trying to keep watch. He couldn't see anything, but he didn't doubt Kita's word.

Kita seemed confident in her claim. She was quiet, but always in motion. Stoking up the fire, checking on the pack lizards, making sure the entire party was staying close, double checking her weapons, etc.

Even Sir Jors seemed to be aware that there was more going on than a story. Davorin could read the anger and helplessness on his face that he was unable to protect them.

About the time Tratow had sent the giant eagle to spirit Torchiv and his bride, Clisa, away to the Sunlit Kingdom, even Davorin could see the shifts in the shadows revealing their watchers.

Lakara continued with her story. Sir Jors was stoic, even as he fingered the pommel of his sword. Undoubtedly, he was aware that his sword might well have been a broken twig for as much use as it would be in his condition. Davorin suspected the man was praying. He would be doing the same if he could think of anything to say other than to beg Shadow Master not to take them just yet.

He couldn't read Kita. She could fight but might not consider this a fight worth having. Maybe she'd run this time. Like she almost did the first time the imps attacked. Davorin wouldn't blame her if she did. But he didn't think she would. No, one way or another, he thought the party would stick together. Come what may. Now if only he wasn't so sure that 'come what may' was likely to be a javelin in the chest.

There were between ten and fifteen watchers visible. Slowly, three came closer, approaching the party. The man in the middle appeared to be in his fifties, dressed in breeches of tan and a half tunic of mossy green. Around his neck was a dark stone suspended by a leather strap. A gold bangle was around his upper arm with a stylized picture of a deer. He had a javelin strapped to his back and a short sword, without a sheath, suspended from his thigh. In his hand, he held a thick stick. It could be a walking stick. It could also be a handy club. A small lizard, about the size of Davorin's hand, perched on the man's head.

To his right was a woman, slightly younger. Her tunic was oak bark brown, with small blue beads embedded in it. Her javelin was in hand, and she had a dirk like Kita's at her belt. Her hair was long, braided in an elaborate pattern. Possibly one of special significance.

On the left, was another man, younger than his companions. This one wore tan breeches, but no shirt. Two javelins were on his back, and a sword strapped to his waist. No jewelry. His stick seemed like a simple walking staff. Davorin wasn't fooled. This one was the bodyguard. The other two were important. Ceremonially, if nothing else.

Lakara stood, as did Davorin. Sir Jors tried to, before falling back with a grunt of pain. Kita, who had had her back to them as she methodically peeled the bark from a branch with her dirk, put the branch down, rolled her back and turned, dirk in hand.

Davorin winced as Kita, oh so casually, came forward in a position that put her in front of Sir Jors, and to a lesser extent, blocked off Davorin and Lakara. Then she opened her mouth.

Whatever she was going to say was forgotten as the Queyan woman caught sight of her dirk. *"Tisalla!"* She screamed.

Everyone froze. Did that mean attack? Before anyone could react, the strange woman was in front of Kita, comparing the dirks side by side. Kita didn't move but he could see the tension vibrating through her spine. With more calmness than Davorin thought he could dredge up, Kita quietly but clearly asked, "I'm sorry. I don't understand. What does 'tisalla' mean?"

The older man came forward. "It means 'sister'. Welcome, daughter of the forest." Without hesitation or another word, he literally picked Kita up, embracing her and kissing her on each cheek and the forehead.

"WHAT?"

Chapter Fifteen

The People of the Forest

Or

What makes a family?

Sir Jors thought he could be forgiven for not having a clear understanding or memory of the next few days. He had, after all, been dying of a snake bite. Then the Queya showed up. Granted, that didn't *necessarily* mean they intended to kill them all, but it didn't mean they didn't either.

The best Sir Jors had been hoping for was for the Queya to impose conditions on their journey, but to allow them to continue. Moderate was for the Queya to order them off their land as trespassers. Worst, well, Sir Jors was already praying for dignity to face his death, in whatever form it came. Even if the Queya came in peace, there was still the poison that swam throughout his body. One way or another, Sir Jors was certain he had seen his last sunrise.

He had seen the party that approached them and considered it a good sign. If they wanted to talk first, then perhaps the others would be allowed to leave safely. Even now, he wasn't quite sure how they so quickly latched on to Kita being part Queya. Not that he cared. Well, a little bit. Mostly he was grateful that they immediately took her in as a long-lost family member and expanded that to include the rest of the party.

And he was more grateful than he could say that the

Queya knew how to cure his snake bite and didn't hesitate to help him. It was two, maybe three days since the Queya had all but kidnapped them to their caverns, and according to the healer, if Sir Jors understood properly, he would be able to start walking around tomorrow.

He wasn't sure about the time, as he still spent most of his time in and out of sleep. Rousing from a light doze, he turned to see Kita there. It surprised him as he hadn't seen much of her since the Queya took them in. Lakara or Davorin, sometimes both, were frequently around, but Kita he had seen only once or twice. Apparently, the Queya were quite serious in their adoption of the young woman and monopolized the majority of her time. Or perhaps the girl who had been so long without a family was unwilling to give up the time she had.

"I hear you are recovering well," Kita said.

"So they tell me. Thank you."

She gave a huff. "I had nothing to do with it."

They both knew that wasn't quite true, but he didn't argue. "It's a shock, isn't it?"

"What?"

"Finding family again."

Kita rubbed her hands on her face. "I never... never expected anything like this. They know *exactly* who I am! It's an identity that I never thought I had. I never cared either, but now..."

"How? I think I missed part of what was going on."

Another huffed laugh. "Hardly surprising. My dirk, actually. They recognized it. About a century ago, the Queya *Kafila*, it means 'leader', commissioned matching dirks for his two daughters, Kalina and Tivna. Tivna married the next *Kafila*, while Kalina left with a hunting party. She never returned. According to others of the party, she fell in love with a Trovian by the name of Haldor. She was considered lost to them."

"Yet they welcomed you, presumably her granddaughter." If Kalina was rejected for the mixed marriage, wouldn't Kita fall under the same stigma?

"I wondered the same thing. Apparently, she wasn't lost because of the marriage, but because she never came back to the forest." She shrugged. "They didn't seem to care about the rest."

"I see. Are you related to the *kaf-lia*?"

"*Kaf-fil-a*. Yes, apparently so. Not as closely as some, but yes. They say I could probably, with a little training, become a *lisnow*, which is a combination of a priestess and a, well, ranger, I guess. Not exclusive to the *kafila*'s family, but many of them are. They also said that if I chose to stay, I would be considered part of the *kafila's* household and under his protection.

"Stay?" Now he knew he was getting slow. The thought hadn't even occurred to him.

Kita bit her lip. A nervous habit he had seen on Lakara more than once, but never from Kita. "They said I could stay if I wanted. Permanently. Actually, they said we could all stay."

Sir Jors let out a slow breath as he cautiously moved to a seated position. "I see. That was very generous of them. What did you tell them?"

"That we would have to talk about it once you were fully well."

"Do Davorin and Lakara know yet?"

"Not yet. I meant to tell you all together, but…"

Sir Jors nodded slowly. "Do you need to give your answer at any particular time?"

She shook her head. "They seem pretty relaxed on time here. Also, according to Malni, what is meant to happen, will happen, whatever we will. She also said something about my ties to the forest, but I didn't understand that part."

"Who's Malni?"

"Malni is Tivna's heir. The woman who had the matching dirk. She is the primary *lisnow* right now. She offered to make me her apprentice."

Sir Jors swallowed hard and forced a smile. This would be where they lost Kita, then. Why would she choose to leave? And he couldn't ask her to. At least she would be safe. "You would be good at that."

Kita stared at her hands. "Perhaps. I have to go. Malni said she was going to teach me more about my grandmother." As she rose, Sir Jors noticed her clothes. Instead of the traveling robes she had been wearing during most of their journey, she wore a tunic, in the Queyan style.

He watched her leave, wondering if this was the end of their quest.

***

For a change, Davorin was the first to notice when the hunting party came back. Not because he heard or saw something before the Queya did, but because he sensed Shadow Master. Someone was dying. Kita was a member of the hunting party.

Davorin dropped the leather they had been teaching him to braid and hurried over to where he sensed the call of death. Before he could get close enough to see what was happening, voices were calling people to stay back. One of the voices was Kita.

Using a tree to support himself, Davorin stepped up onto a stump where he was out of the way and had a slightly better view. A young man, one Davorin recognized visually, but could not remember by name, was being carried by a makeshift sheet of vines. There was so much blood. If he wasn't able to see that the shadows were still growing, he would have thought the boy already dead.

The young man was taken and laid out on a flat table just inside a cave they had been told was sacred. Malni came quickly, wearing what was clearly a ceremonial robe, and started calling orders to two other women who seemed to know what they were supposed to do. Davorin's knowledge of the Queyan language was still poor, but he recognized a magic rite when he saw it.

Kita came up beside him, silently, ashen and shaky. She probably witnessed the initial injury. Lakara came, helping a still unsteady Sir Jors, so Davorin relinquished the stump, allowing him to sit.

"What happened?" Sir Jors asked.

"It happened so fast. Apparently, there were some snares, traps to catch animals. Tovor lost his balance and set one off. I wasn't sure we'd get him back here in time."

"In time for what? What are they doing?" Lakara asked. A question Davorin shared.

"I didn't understand all the explanation, but Malni told me that the Queya's souls are more... flexible than some. That's why we can Borrow. We share our souls briefly with another. She's trying to bind his soul to his body to keep him from moving on until he can heal. Failing that, the soul will move to the land, perhaps to the deer, or the next Queya to be born."

"I don't see how that would work," Lakara said slowly.

"But it is. The shadows are starting to recede." Davorin rubbed at his eyes, hardly able to believe them. "I believe he may yet live."

Kita let out a slow breath and relaxed. "They said he might. They couldn't promise, but they said if we got him to the sacred cave, he had a chance."

"But it had to be here? In the sacred cave?" Davorin asked.

"If I understood correctly. It glows, some. Maybe that's part of it."

"Perhaps." Davorin watched as the shadows continued to abate. They weren't gone, but the boy had a chance now. More of a chance than Davorin would have expected for anyone with that kind of injury.

Eventually, Malni had apparently decided she had done what she could for now. Two others came to care for him, and people started to disperse. It was a waiting game now.

A waiting game that they won, surprisingly enough. Two days after his injury, the boy's appetite picked up, and a couple days after that, he was slowly shuffling around with help. Davorin doubted he would ever regain complete mobility, but the boy, Tovor, could live a full and complete life. The shadows retreated daily until they were dispersed completely. Even infection declined to cause problems.

A day after Tovor was pronounced healed enough to return to his own dwellings and his mother's care; Kita asked the *kafila* for permission for their group to take a trip a day's journey away. According to Malni, it was tradition for anyone planning to leave the group to ask permission. Also according to Malni, permission was always granted.

Good knowledge to have, but he still wondered why Kita felt the need to make this trip, especially without talking to any of them about it. Or did she? Lakara seemed as puzzled as he was, but Sir Jors seemed less surprised.

"Are you... up to a day's journey?" Lakara asked quietly

as everyone dispersed from the evening meal.

"I do not believe she actually plans to go that far. But if this is what I believe it is, I can understand why Kita wishes some privacy," Sir Jors muttered back, as he walked between Davorin and Lakara. Not leaning on either of them, he had passed that days ago, even if he still used a walking stick most of the time.

Lakara tried to question more, but Davorin shook his head at her. If Kita wanted to make sure their hosts were out of earshot, then there was probably a good reason. Probably, hopefully, not a dangerous reason. But if anyone would know, it would be Kita. She had traveled more, learned more of the language, met more of the people than any of them. While she had clearly reveled in the adoption and inclusion, she would also be smart enough and paranoid enough to spot a trap.

Perhaps he should be ashamed of himself for suspecting a trap. The Queya had certainly saved Sir Jors' life, and possibly the rest of them as well. They had offered hospitality freely and without having asked anything in return, so far. But Davorin, like everyone in Graldish, had been raised on stories of the evils and treacheries of the Queya. Not quite human, with abilities no mortal should have.

Not that he had met any of them before this. Besides, Davorin was a necromancer! What right did he have to chastise anyone else's innate abilities?

Morning dawned gray and cold. At least, Davorin thought morning dawned. He hadn't been able to tell since they entered the forest. Throwing an extra travel robe on, Davorin left the half-wooden half-cave shelter he had been sleeping in since the Queya took them in. Kita, of course, was already up, talking to Malni in Queyan, too fast for Davorin to catch more than the occasional word. Something about 'river' and 'clearing'. Probably their destination, then. Malni nodded a lot, with the occasional course correction.

Lakara, yawning, shuffled up to Davorin, and passed him a warm roll. "Here, breakfast. It's berry."

"Thank you." Davorin took a bite, not surprised at the blue filling inside. The Queya called them *valitna*, but Lakara had been adamant that they were related to riverdew. Consensus was that they tasted a lot better than riverdew berries in Graldish, and only Lakara cared what they were.

Sir Jors came up a moment later, looking more awake than either Davorin or Lakara, even if not quite as steady on his feet. Lakara handed him her remaining roll. "Thank you. Are we taking the pack lizards? They aren't harnessed."

Davorin hadn't even noticed that. "No, we don't need them," Kita said as she joined them, nibbling on her own roll. "We're not going far and can carry our own supplies."

As she finished speaking, some of the older children came running up, bringing the types of packs the hunting groups used when they went on day trips. Davorin took his, stumbling over the Queyan word for 'Thank you', making the children giggle. Judging by the weight, the packs had been filled with enough provisions to last them for at least two or three days.

"How long will we be gone?" Lakara asked, sounding nervous as she jiggled her pack.

"I plan to be back by evening. But it's important to be prepared. They call it, enough extra to get lost." Kita gave a smile that suggested she might not be completely confident either. "Anyway, I know where we're going. Shouldn't take two hours at an easy pace."

"Well then, we go on," Davorin said.

***

Lakara felt curiosity and nervous anticipation flow through her like ants in her veins. She had been enjoying her time with the Queya. While the vast majority spoke little to no Graldian, there were enough who spoke it fluently or at least enough to get by. *Everyone* was willing to teach her Queyan. Lakara wouldn't try to claim fluency by any stretch of the imagination, or even that she had gotten as good as Kita, who had blossomed like a flower in the spring, but Lakara had managed to understand common questions and answers, counting, colors and common foods, and was working on a dictionary. Her work would have been faster if the Queya had a written alphabet, but they didn't. Their oral tradition spanned centuries, but nothing was written down anywhere.

As a side project, Lakara was working to develop an alphabet, one that included sounds that Graldian didn't. In addition to the language, she had tutors in how to track, how to make baskets and pots, how to identify edible plants, and even a little bit of weather prediction. Sometimes one or more of her travel companions was with her, sometimes she was by herself as the others learned other lessons. So, she found herself a little put out that she had to leave all that.

It was maybe about ten when Kita led them to a clearing that was actually open enough to see some sky. Lakara wanted some answers, but Kita suggested they have some of their provisions first, and the others agreed.

With a sigh, Lakara wiped down a boulder and settled down. Rooting through her pack, she withdrew a canteen and two meat pastries wrapped in a broad leaf. Rabbit, at best guess.

While she ate, Lakara looked over the group. Davorin looked as puzzled as she was. He had taken off his second traveling robe, using it to cushion himself. Like her, he seemed to be analyzing. Sir Jors looked almost completely recovered from his injuries, though he wore Queyan forest slippers instead of his usual boots. His foot still tended to swell if he walked too much. He seemed serious, perhaps a little sad.

Kita, as she had since their second day with the Queya, wore a Queyan tunic, staring stubbornly at her pastry. Whisper flew overhead, seeming to enjoy the chance to stretch his wings.

Just as Lakara felt ready to scream and shout to demand answers, Kita finished her last bite and looked around. Everyone was done eating. With a deep sigh, Kita leaned back, stared at the sky and said, "How is everyone enjoying their time with the Queya?"

That wasn't where Lakara had expected things to go. "It's... good. I'm learning a lot. They're very hospitable."

"I agree. They have been extremely kind," Davorin said.

Sir Jors didn't speak until everyone looked in his direction. "I owe them my life. But that doesn't mean I can stay."

"Wait. Stay?" Lakara asked. Stay? Her mind went in two directions at once. One shrank at the idea of leaving, the other wondered who had said anything about staying. Surely, they would continue on. Eventually.

"Yes." Kita rubbed the seam of her tunic between her fingers. "The Queya have said that we are welcome to stay. All of us. For... well, forever, if we want."

Stay. She would have all the time she needed to finish her alphabet and dictionary. Time to learn the oceans of lore that was unique to the Queya. It wouldn't quite be the end of traveling, as the Queya traveled the forest; settling in one place for a few months before moving to another. But that would be traveling a much shorter distance with a large group.

"But, what about the quest?" It wasn't until the words rang out in the clearing that Lakara realized she had been the one to say them.

"The quest we were assigned to by a king who doesn't even believe it exists? The one that we were meant to fail at and *die*? In an attempt to start a war? That quest?" Kita asked, knuckles white. "He can choke waiting, for all I care."

"That's treason." The harshness of the knight's words was belied by the softness of his tone.

"Doesn't matter. You know I'm right," Kita said.

"Which is part of the problem," Davorin cut in. "Remember what Lord Sartik said. He had other plans. Sooner or later, he's going to give up on this one bearing fruit and try another. Then what? It may have already started."

That sobered everyone. "We can't let that happen." Lakara snapped a few blades of grass in half. "All those people."

"Any ideas how to stop it? If a war has already started, and you could well be right, then isn't it an even better idea to stay here, away from all that?" Kita raised her hands at Lakara's glare. "I don't like the idea of a filthy war either! People like me are the first to die! But what can we do?"

Davorin sat up with a jolt. "We can use the jewel ourselves." Everyone stared at him. "We use the jewel and... I'm not sure yet; but once we know what's going on, we'll have some idea. Something one of the gods would agree to in exchange for the pretty bauble."

Silence rang in the glade as everyone pondered the implications. "That... that might work," Kita muttered.

"But we were *ordered* to give King Zikkar the jewel," Sir Jors pointed out. "Failure to do so is *treason*."

Lakara gasped. "No, no we weren't." She barely noticed the stares. "I was there, in the throne room as everyone else was... commissioned. We were ordered to *find it*. He even mentioned bringing it back a couple times. Not once did he say anything about *giving* it to him." She laughed, madness in it. "We could find it, bring it back to Corvis, and use it for ourselves, without breaking a single order." She shook with mirth and tears. "Loopholes. The answer was there all along."

Sir Jors let out a shaky breath. "While that would follow the letter of our orders, we all know that is in violation of what the king wants."

"May I please point out, once again, that the king wants us *dead*?" Kita asked, biting back a snarl. "I don't know what he promised you, but I know for a fact that he planned to betray me."

Lakara winced. "That's true. He even admitted it. He didn't say anything about the rest of us, but I... Well, if he expected us to die, I don't think he planned to give any of us what he promised.

"Odds are he'd have us all executed even if we gave him the jewel," Davorin said, eyes watching Whisper's path. "He'd almost have to. We would have accomplished the impossible." He gave a sad half-smirk. "Can't have people like that around." Sighing, he sat back. "Maybe staying with the Queya isn't such a bad idea after all."

Sir Jors started to say something about loyalty. Kita cut him off. "Didn't you tell me yourself that the king owes his loyalty to the people? Protect the people and rule for their benefit. Please tell me, when was the last time the king made a decision that benefited the people instead of his coffers? Was it when he doubled taxes for the past ten years? How about when he decided to start a war, one where you know he'll be safe and sound in his palace of silk and gold, while thousands of others die? Or how about when he sent the four of us on a suicide mission?"

"Enough," Lakara said. "We all need a little time to think."

"It's like at Winterwatch," Sir Jors said. "No one can compel another to go against their conscience, and now there is actually a safe alternative."

Wordlessly, Kita got up, stretched, and walked off into the trees. Her pack remained on the ground, so she planned to return. After a moment, Davorin stood and wandered off in a different direction.

Lakara leaned back on her boulder until she could see the sky, watching clouds drift overhead. From the corner of her eye, she saw Sir Jors study the river, but she tuned him out. He couldn't make this decision for her. No one could.

Her thoughts whirled around with snippets popping up here and there. *Can't betray the king*, was one. *Can't let that many people die for no reason*, was another. *What could we use the jewel for*, came through a few times. *Does the king deserve loyalty? Who am I to ask that question? How can I not?*

Lakara didn't realize she had drifted off until a hand touched her shoulder. Wincing, she sat up, rubbing at her back and neck. Boulders do not make comfortable mattresses.

The sky was starting to dim, and it would be getting dark within a few hours. "Unless we want to camp here tonight, I would recommend we start heading back. We can eat on the way," Kita said.

Sir Jors adjusted his walking stick. Davorin offered her a hand up. Lakara took it and swayed on her feet. With a sigh, she spoke first. "I think we should try to get the jewel. Once we have it, we can figure out what our options are. Besides, I promised to go along at least far enough to translate the clues."

Sir Jors winced a little. "Agreed. No point making plans before we know if the jewel even exists or if we can get a hold of it."

Kita spun on her heel and started to lead the way, not speaking a word. Davorin followed, not giving any indication of his thoughts.

Lakara closed her eyes and shook her head. She would

miss them. Sir Jors offered an arm, and she took it, more for his balance than her own. "When do you want to leave? Not until your foot stops swelling."

"I've been assured that should stop within a few more days."

Kita's voice trailed back, no expression in the tone, "There's a feast in five days, before moving to the summer houses." The Queya never stayed in one place more than a few months, to not burden the land or the hunting.

"That could work," Lakara said. "We can leave at the same time as everyone else. Might not be in the same direction, but it would be a good transition time."

Privately, Lakara hoped that they would be traveling in the same direction for at least a little while. Maybe a day or two. If she dared daydream, maybe far enough to get to the temple of Aloses. She was doomed to disappointment. As soon as they started discussing plans with the *Kafila*, it was obvious they were going in different directions.

He seemed disappointed that they didn't all want to stay, but philosophical. "The forest may yet welcome you again. When it does, you will find us welcoming you too. What is meant to be, shall be."

Lakara had only the vaguest memories of the feast as she woke up with a throbbing headache and the sworn vow to never *ever* drink Queyan wine again. Not a promising start to the next leg of their journey. Sir Jors looked only barely better than she did. They exchanged a rueful nod that had Lakara, at least, wincing and clutching her head. Eyes squeezed shut, she tried to feel her way to the lizards. Most of their supplies had been packed last night, but they would still have to harness and load up the lizards.

Unsurprisingly, she walked into something. No, the slight grunt suggested a person. Peeling one eye open, swallowing back the nausea that rose in her throat, Lakara saw a pale Davorin. "Sorry," She rasped.

"It's fine," he groaned. "Never, ever again."

She smiled weakly. "What will you do next time?"

His eyes opened, looking shocked. "I'm going with you."

"You... you are?"

"Yes? I mean, don't you want... You'll probably need me." He shrugged, wincing as his body regretted the sudden movement. "Or at least, the best I can do."

"You are certainly welcome," Sir Jors said, coming up. "But I thought you wanted to stay. You and Kita, both."

"What about me?" asked Kita, leading the pack lizards, already harnessed and loaded up. She wore her traveling robes.

"You're coming?" Lakara gaped. "But your family... your people. I thought you wanted to stay."

Kita gave a wan smile and a shrug as she passed over a harness. "We'll be back on the return. I've come this far. I want to see it through." She laughed, a little spirit returning. "At least I'll have a chance at seeing this treasure of the ages."

"They welcomed you quite heartily," Davorin said. "No one minds you leaving?"

Malni walked up then. "Kita is a daughter of the forest and shall always have a home here. Currently, her path takes her elsewhere, with you. May your paths lead you all back to us again."

Holding up her hands, Malni sang in the Queyan language. A blessing. Lakara caught parts about safe journey, cooperative weather, and predators avoiding them. Sir Jors bowed, thanking her on behalf of the group.

"So," Davorin took Longtail's harness, as they edged

away from the migrating Queyans, "Where is Aloses's temple anyway?"

***

Kita resolutely ignored any attempt on anyone's part to question when she had decided that she would be going with them instead of migrating with the Queya or why. Changed the subject, pretended not to hear, tripped on a tree root that she could have avoided easily. Perhaps almost twisting her ankle wasn't the best of solutions, but they did get the hint and stopped asking, much to her relief.

Because she didn't have an answer. Or she had several, she wasn't sure. No one, no one at all, had asked her what she had decided. Kita knew that her travel companions figured she would choose to stay with the Queya. The Queya hadn't said anything one way or another.

Kita hadn't known her own mind. The more she tried to think about her options, the more her thoughts whirled around until it was like trying to grab the fog. On one hand, she thought part of her planned to stay with the Queya until she got dressed in traveling robes that morning, instead of a Queyan tunic. Another part of her thought she knew she would be going with them as soon as she knew they'd be leaving.

"Two more days for the temple, you said?" Kita asked, as they settled for the evening. It had taken three days to find what used to be a broad road for the use of pilgrims. Now mostly overtaken and swallowed by the forest, it still let them know they were going in the right direction. "Is there going to *be* anyone there? Or has the temple been abandoned?"

Lakara rooted through her pack to find a scroll, pausing as everyone exclaimed, "How many books did you *bring*?"

"Not that many. Anyway, while the temples in Cratys and Vesni are certainly the most famous today, and of

331

course, *any* city would have a temple to the god of healing, this particular temple is one of the oldest. According to my research, which, granted, is older than I am, a small group remains to care for the temple and any pilgrims who come. Not that there have been many in recent decades. Not since the water ways closed and the temple in Vesni was completed."

"I probably should have asked before, and you have clearly been correct on all counts so far, but how did you determine which temple the clues were in?" Sir Jors asked. "While some were in the primary temple, not all of them were."

"Age, primarily. The temple had to be ancient. The clue was hidden in a temple that either existed when the jewel was supposedly hidden, or shortly after. That rules out anything newer than four or five hundred years. Primary temples can change over the centuries." Lakara sighed. "I wish I could say there was a list given and we're following it. But I can't. Oh, lists of guesses have been made. We aren't the first to attempt to find it, by any means. I studied the lists, looked at the age of the temples, how important they were at the time, and ruled out those that don't exist anymore." She grimaced. "I'll be honest, this is one of the ones I'm least sure of."

"And, if it *isn't* this one?" Davorin asked, sounding considerably more nervous.

Lakara winced. "Second choice is far, far south. At least three weeks past Wris. And third choice got destroyed in the Wars."

Kita couldn't help but laugh, more in hysteria than mirth. "Then let's hope your record continues. Or that we can somehow find the jewel without it."

"If it helps, I'm *positive* about the temple of Skoses. But, agreed, I'd rather not go another six months or more in the opposite direction."

"What other temples were you unsure of?" Kita asked.

"Many of them. But the worst were AKAF's and Shadow Master's. And since we got both those clues from other sources, I may have been wrong in one or both cases."

"In any event," Sir Jors cut in. "You've done a marvelous job so far. I'm sure you are right, once again."

Or maybe not. It was the thought on everyone's mind, even if no one would say it as they tried to explore the shambles that had once been a grand temple. While Kita could somewhat see where the clearing for the temple grounds had been, the forest had come back as if taking revenge. Long abandoned from any caretaker, roots had unevened the mosaic floor and vines ate at the walls. The centerpiece of the temple, either a table or an altar, held a cup that wouldn't have fetched even a bronze duc and at least a few decades worth of grime and dust.

"Um, should we light some candles?" Kita asked, looking for a sconce or candle holder. She had dropped coins in a healing shrine on occasion before, but never actually been in one of Aloses's temples.

"While that might help to see, that's not how Aloses was worshipped here," Lakara said. "This is the *oldest* temple of Aloses. Maybe the oldest temple still in existence. Worship was different then."

"Not a sacrifice, surely," Sir Jors said, lighting candles and passing them around. "Aloses never demanded bloodshed, as I recall."

"No, in fact, violence to any creature within the shadow of the temple was strictly forbidden," Davorin said, as he touched a metal outcropping, only for it to fall off in his hand.

Kita winced slightly at the echoing sound, and moved deeper in. If she didn't spot a glow, who knew how long they could be searching? Lakara was talking, saying something about a serum or potion they would have to make from local plants. Maybe that's why the cup.

One corner of the temple seemed different. The dark had texture. She walked closer, candle out, only to stop in shock, as the flame was reflected back in a set of faceted eyes. Then two sets. Five sets. Many sets.

Kita fell back with a scream, candle flying from her hand as she hit the ground, swarmed. Like she was underwater, she could hear her name being called, knew they were running to her, even heard Whisper screech from outside. But all her focus was on the creatures surrounding her. "Oh! You're beautiful."

Tiny lizards, from six inches to a foot long, black as ink with wings like butterflies in blues and purples. After she didn't scream, flail, or attack, they calmed and started to race up and down her and the floor, cooing like doves. "What are you?" Kita asked the bold one that settled in her palm. It gave a trilling purr.

"Woodvryns," Lakara barely breathed out. "I thought they were a myth."

Kita looked over to see her companions being investigated by the curious flying lizards. "Are they dangerous?"

"Only if you mean them harm." Sir Jors slowly and carefully sheathed his sword. "Legend says they can breathe healing or disease."

"I think the concoction is supposed to appease them." Lakara beamed at the one balancing on the back of her arm.

"They seem pretty appeased." Davorin winced slightly as one landed on his head, tugging at his hair.

"Let's keep it that way." Kita carefully put her hands on the floor and shifted to see if the woodvryns would let her stand. Instead, she suddenly had at least three more in her lap and another chewing on her shoe. She relaxed. "I think I've been captured."

"It would appear." Sir Jors stroked at his beard, not quite hiding his smile, as he bent to retrieve her candle and handed it back to her. "Then we better make the required ransom to free you."

"What? Oh!" Lakara started bustling about. "Right. The potion. Okay, if we split up, we should be able to get the ingredients quickly. Kita, if they do let you up, find me, and I can tell you what to look for." She divided up the assignments, based on who would be sure to recognize the plants in question.

When the others left, Kita tried twice more to get up, to no avail. They weren't cruel or malicious about it, but there seemed to be no dislodging the woodvryns without using enough force that they might consider it an attack. If they could breathe *disease* if they felt threatened, well, Kita decided there were worse things than being a living pillow. "Just watch the claws. I don't need any scratches."

She winced as one of them scrabbled about her ankle. "Like that. That is exactly what I mean. Claws. Bad on skin." She lay back with a huff. "You don't know where the clue is, do you?"

"Who are you talking to?" Davorin asked as he came in, carrying several plants.

"My captors. I'm negotiating my release. Ow! Careful, lizardlings."

Davorin dropped his bundle on the altar and knelt by her. "Are you alright?"

"I'm fine. They just need to watch it with the sharp, pointy parts." One of them leaned a head up to her face, sniffing her mouth. "Yes, you. And your siblings." It cooed at her. "Yes, you're adorable. And fierce. And clumsy." It huffed at her. "It's fine. I'm clumsy too, sometimes."

"You are quite possibly the *least* clumsy person I've ever met," Davorin said with quiet assurance.

Kita blinked at him. She hadn't expected something like that. "Oh, um. Thank you."

"Do you need help?" Davorin asked. "I could *try* to move them."

"Better not. They're being friendly right now, and I don't want to rile them. It's not their fault those claws are sharp."

He didn't seem convinced but didn't argue. Nor did he move from her side. "At least it isn't pack lizard claws."

"Very, very true." Pack lizards could eviscerate a man in leather armor. "These shouldn't even scar."

"We're in a temple of *healing*. I'm pretty sure we can come up with a way to help you. Besides, one of the ingredients I picked up was yarrow root. We can make another tincture if need be."

She hadn't even thought of infection, and she should have. Those claws were probably filthy. "At least there's a stream nearby." She could wash the cuts out.

Lakara came then, Sir Jors barely behind her. The scholar spread everything out on the altar, sorting and muttering as she compared it to some list. "Good, we have everything." She looked back at Kita. "Still alright?"

"Fine." Anything else was cut off as the closest woodvryn again sniffed her mouth, then licked the tip of her nose. Biting her lips together, Kita shook with muffled laughter.

"Right. Should be ready in a few minutes." With Sir Jors

holding a torch for her, Lakara quickly prepared the potion. The further she got, the more the woodvryns took notice. First, they looked in her direction, eyes tracking her moves. Then there were darting head motions and leaning towards the altar. This gave way to shuffling and tense poses as if they were preparing to pounce. As Lakara stirred the cup, one woodvryn took off, flying towards her. Half a blink later, a dozen were flying. By the time Lakara was finished and pouring out the offering, every woodvryn in the temple surrounded the altar.

As soon as the woodvryns had abandoned her, Davorin had his hand out to help her up. She didn't *need* his help, and they both knew it. But it was kind of him to offer, so she took it. Other than a few scratches she wanted to get a good look at in daylight, Kita didn't think she was any the worse for wear. If they had breathed disease on her, she didn't feel sick yet. That said, as beautiful as the woodvryns were, she was not upset that they weren't climbing over her anymore. It seemed the way of fewer injuries.

The woodvryns finished the offering quickly, before turning their attention to the people who had invaded their home. One of them looked at Kita and huffed on her ankle. The stinging pain went away with a whoosh of warm air. "Oh, thank you." Soon all her scratches had been healed. "You are handy little creatures, aren't you? I don't suppose any of you want to come with us, do you?"

"Oh, it's strictly forbidden to remove them!" Lakara protested. "Aloses has cursed people for that in the past."

"I was kidding. Mostly. Certainly, I wouldn't try to take one by force." She eyed them swarming about. "Besides, they're clearly colony animals. It would be cruel to separate one."

"Now that we have that settled, and the woodvryns have been appeased," Sir Jors said, "perhaps we should go back to looking for the clue."

With that reminder, they scattered. The woodvryns didn't go back to sleep but went about as if exploring. Kita ignored them until she heard a shriek from Whisper. Alarm sped her feet as she dashed to the door of the temple. But nothing was wrong. Whisper flew in darting patterns, playing aerial tag with the woodvryns.

The pack lizards seemed to enjoy the visit from their smaller cousins too. Trouble seemed jealous that they could fly, and he couldn't. She chuckled as she discouraged the lizard from climbing a felled tree trunk. "You don't have wings. Don't even try it." The lizard grunted but didn't climb back up. "I don't blame you, though. Flying is amazing."

Perhaps it was risky, but Kita thought maybe it would be safe enough to share this joy with Whisper, just for a minute or two. Closing her eyes, she mentally called to the hawk, who happily let her in. They were joy. They were freedom. They were winning the game of tag. Sort of.

They swept a large circle, high above the building (*temple*, Kita's mind supplied), watching the winged lizards fly with them (*woodvryns*, thought Kita; *friends*, thought Whisper). A dive to take the breath away, under the playing woodvryns, before swooping up, scattering a swarm. Then back down, to…

Wait, what was that? At Kita's request, they flew another slow circle, eyes scanning the roof. A square topped by a diamond surrounded by a circle. That was the symbol! Some of the woodvryns were pulling away vines, revealing shapes that made no sense to Whisper and barely any to Kita.

She retreated back to her body too fast, wincing as the pain slammed into her head. Two hands; two feet; skin, not feathers; arms, not wings. She held back a groan and went back inside.

"Maybe I was wrong. Maybe this isn't the right one,"

Lakara spoke, tears in her voice.

"Well, we could—" Whatever Sir Jors planned to suggest, Kita never found out.

"It's the right one. The clue is on the roof!"

"The roof? Why would...?" Lakara apparently decided not to question things they didn't have answers to as they hurried outside. Then they stared at the building.

"Huh." Kita eyed the crumbling structure. No convenient, or even inconvenient, hand holds. No trees close enough, tall enough to see the top from. And honestly, Kita didn't trust the roof was in good enough shape to hold any of them. "Any ideas?"

Lakara bit her lip nervously, studying the temple. Sir Jors walked the perimeter, only to come back shaking his head. Davorin sighed.

"Um, well." Lakara winced. "How did you know the clue was there?

Kita didn't flinch, but only because she had known it was coming and was determined not to react. Instead, she watched her companions, her friends. They knew. All of them. Yes, they had previously established that they knew Kita had *probably* been Borrowing Whisper, and Sir Jors had even promised not to report it. But she hadn't actually admitted it. As long as no one actually *said*... But that wasn't going to work this time. "You know how."

Lakara smiled weakly, trying to hide her ingrained reaction to someone blatantly breaking the law. Sir Jors nodded gravely. Davorin surprised her. "Then that's how we'll get the clue," he said as if it was obvious. "Can he tell you the letters, or do you need to be Borrowing him and see for yourself?"

"If that's something you are comfortable with," Sir Jors

said as Kita gaped at him. "If not, then maybe we can come up with another option."

"I'm not sure there is another option," Davorin pointed out.

"He's right," Kita groaned. "I need to see them myself. Whisper can't identify something like that. But it won't be easy. I can't read it either."

Lakara sighed. "I knew I should have taught you the Vesrop alphabet." She pulled out what seemed to be the same scroll they used before. "Point out the letters you recognize? In a minute." She found the scroll she used to take notes and prepared a pen. "Ready."

"It's not that easy. I can't Borrow him and talk to you at the same time. I'll have to," she paused and tried to figure out the best way to handle this. "Have to see a few, come back to show you, and go back in. I've never Borrowed like that before. It's... risky."

Stories abounded of those who went too far, who could no longer remember which body was theirs, or who lost themselves in the between. She didn't know how true they were, but even the Queya had warned her about not losing herself when Borrowing. They could tell by looking at Whisper.

"Let's make camp," Sir Jors said, ending the charged silence.

"Here? Now?" Kita eyed the area. Not exactly the best spot for breaking for the night, and there were still at least three hours of daylight. Maybe more, as summer came closer.

"Here and now. Then we can take as much time as we need in order to get this clue. However we end up doing so." Sir Jors started moving debris out of the way, making a smooth place to set the tents.

They all fell into their normal routine. Ground cleared, Kita pulled the grass, and lined a ring with stone and brick to build a fire. Davorin handed her branches and kindling they had moved from the clearing. Lakara said something about fetching water, taking the cooking pot and water skins with her.

"Considering Aloses's rules about not harming another creature, it might be wise to forego meat tonight. But we do have bread, and I seem to recall seeing blackberries." Sir Jors picked up a leaf basket, like the Queya taught them to make. "I'll see if I can find them again."

Kita nodded but kept most of her focus on the fire. The first spark didn't catch. The second smoldered but didn't ignite. "Come on, light," she muttered. Third through fifth weren't any more successful. Sixth seemed promising. "That's it. You can do it." Nothing. She leaned in, trying to see if her spark had gone out. Then her kindling ignited with a woosh.

She rocked back so quickly she almost fell, only to have a hand in the middle of her back steady her. Kita spun in surprise. Davorin reddened and dropped his arm. "Sorry."

"No, it's fine. I... I didn't realize you were still here."

Davorin brushed down his robe as he gingerly sat on the ground. "How risky is it? Borrowing?"

Kita grimaced. "I don't know. No one ever actually taught me. I just, kind of, picked it up. Honestly, the first time I Borrowed Whisper, I was scared out of my mind." She realized what she had said and laughed wryly. "Literally. I didn't know what I was doing, how I had gotten there or how to get back. I still don't know the limits. I know there *are* limits, and that it's dangerous to break them. But I don't know the warning signs."

"Pain is usually a good one, I've found. At least with necromancy."

"I didn't know your powers hurt."

"They don't. Most of the time. Does Borrowing hurt?"

"Not usually. Coming back too fast does. But I've never Borrowed more than twice in a day. And that's rare."

Davorin looked at the roof of the temple. "I take it this would take multiple trips."

"I'm certain. I doubt I could keep more than three to five letters in my head at a time, and that's pushing it. Depending on how long the clue is..."

"Could Whisper tell you?"

"Birds can't exactly count. With my help, we can get up to five. More than that, it's a slew. From what I could see, before coming back, this is a slew. And I don't think it was all revealed. The woodvryns were still pulling vines back."

She leaned back, brushing against him to eye the building. "It doesn't make sense!" The complaint tore from her teeth unwillingly. "Why the roof? No one can see it there! What were they thinking?"

"You saw it," Davorin pointed out.

"Yes, but that's because I was Borrowing Whisper. If I couldn't do that, or even hadn't thought to try, then we'd have never known. How many others would or could have done that?"

"Maybe that's why. Maybe..."

"Maybe what?" Kita leaned away, rejecting the thoughts that sparked.

"Maybe the gods knew *we* would be here looking."

"No. Only AKAF is all-knowing. Aloses could never know that we'd be here hundreds and hundreds of years later. We aren't significant enough. No." She wasn't shaking. She *wasn't.*

"Perhaps AKAF told him?"

"That a group of... crazy idiots would be on a muddy quest from a filthy greedy king and would come after the temple was a ruined mess, looking for the impossible?"

Davorin pondered her words as if he wanted to object but eventually decided were fair. "It's possible."

Kita pushed herself to her feet and started pacing. "No. The gods don't... We aren't that important. *I'm* not that important. I don't *want* to be that important. Can't be. No!"

"Kita? What's wrong?" Lakara asked, back with the water. She looked around the campsite. "Did something happen?"

Sir Jors was almost on her heels. "I heard shouting. Is everyone alright?"

Davorin stood and looked at Kita. Words filled her throat and died there. Davorin nodded. "We're fine. Just discussing the clue."

Lakara and Sir Jors exchanged a look, but neither asked any questions. "I found the blackberries." He set the basket down. "How about we eat?"

Chapter Sixteen

Sacrifice and Risk

Or

"Is it worth it?"

Lakara knelt by Kita, scroll ready. No better options had arisen. They would have to try this. "When you're ready." If Kita was willing to take the risk, however reluctantly, then Lakara would make it as easy as possible.

"Remember, we have time. It doesn't matter if we can't get the whole thing tonight," Sir Jors said.

Davorin sat on Kita's other side, saying something about helping to ground her. Kita, still looking a bit ashy, nodded, closed her eyes, and leaned back. At first, she looked asleep. But the closer Lakara looked, the more she seemed... empty. Not dead, but uninhabited. Creepy.

A minute or two later, there was life in her face again. Her eyes blinked open, still blurry, and Kita sat up. Perhaps she hadn't completely broken the connection. Sleepily, Kita scanned the first scroll. "That one first. Then two of that one. I think this one came next. And..." Her hand trailed slowly, hovering over the paper. "That one?"

Lakara wrote them out hurriedly. "Alright, I have it."

Kita gave a half nod and drifted back. When she came up again, her voice slurred, and her hands trembled as she pointed out symbols and a space break.

"Perhaps that's enough for tonight," Sir Jors suggested.

"One more," Kita drawled, not looking up at him. Before anyone could object, she was back under. Lakara found herself barely breathing, then holding her breath as Kita didn't come back. After an eternity, her eyes pried open. Davorin had to help her sit up, as she gave Lakara the next few symbols, two words. "You've got them?"

"Yes, I have them."

"Good." Kita groaned and let herself slump to the ground. "I'm done for the night. Nothing else."

"Are you going to move to the tent?" Lakara asked.

"I'm done for the night. Nothing else."

Sir Jors chuckled. "You are going to be very sore if you sleep all night in that position."

"Done for the night." She didn't even twitch.

Davorin shook his head. "Lakara, help her straighten her legs. Kita, I'm putting a pillow under your head. Don't sit up or you'll hit me."

Lakara wasn't sure Kita even heard him, she seemed to be completely asleep. Carefully, she arranged the other woman in a more comfortable position while Sir Jors draped a blanket over her.

"With luck, she'll wake up in a bit and at least be able to move to her bedroll. If not, we can help her." He sighed, softly. "She was supposed to take the middle shift at guard duty tonight."

Lakara winced. "I don't think she can tonight. Um, maybe I can take a longer shift?"

"No, it's fine," Sir Jors said. "I think that as long as Kita is doing this, we can't reasonably expect her to hold a watch shift. I'll take it tonight."

As the sunset faded and night encroached, Kita did rouse some, but only enough to be persuaded to drink some water and move to her bedroll in the tent. Not enough to be lucid. No one mentioned anything about her taking watch and she seemed to sleep through the night.

In fact, Kita didn't rouse until after everyone else woke up, prepared breakfast, had a quiet but spirited debate on the merits of waking Kita or just saving her some, decided on the latter, and were almost done with the clean-up. She looked something like Lakara had felt the morning after drinking Queyan wine.

Whisper didn't look much better, Lakara noticed. His feathers looked ruffled, his eyes were glassy, and he almost seemed sick. "This is too much for you, both of you. Isn't it?" Davorin asked as he examined the bird. "He's in pain. You both are."

Kita gave a hum that sounded like agreement, eyes closed even behind her dark glasses. "I think that was too many times. Or too close together. Or something. I'm not doing it again until my head stops splitting. Not even then, if Whisper isn't ready." She took some water and quietly ate her gruel. At least her hands stopped shaking.

When the bowl was almost finished, Kita looked up. "Wasn't I supposed to take watch last night?"

"Not while you're doing this," Sir Jors spoke up immediately. "We may not be able to take this burden from you, but we can limit the rest of them."

"I probably shouldn't agree to that," Kita said, as she held a dampened cloth to her head. "But I can't remember why right now, with my head trying to split open. When I can remember, we'll discuss it then."

"Fair enough." Sir Jors stood, collecting water skins. "I'll get some more water."

Davorin offered Whisper more food, frowning as the hawk only accepted half of it.

"Leave it. He's probably almost as nauseous as I am." Kita slowly rotated her neck, wincing as it cracked loudly. "When this is done, I'm never Borrowing more than twice in a day again. If that." Whisper called softly, as if agreeing with her.

Lakara sighed, then looked at the woodvryns that started to show up. "I don't know that you can eat gruel, and we need that," she said as they gathered by the pot.

"Huh? Oh, hey, little lizards." Kita put her bowl down. "You can have mine. I'm done." As soon as she set it on the ground, three were swarming it. She stroked the nearest one. "Do you have anything for headaches?"

One flew up and hovered in her face. Kita put out her arm for a perch. The woodvryn sniffed at her, then breathed. She groaned as lines of pain were erased. "Wow, you are better than any medicine I've ever had."

Whisper got similar treatment and was soon flying about with the swarm. "That's amazing," Lakara said. "Why didn't we think of that earlier?"

"Wouldn't matter," Kita said. "We can't force them to do anything. They'll help or they won't. I'm grateful, but we can't count on them doing it again." She put the cloth down. "At least they did it this time. I feel much better."

"You look much better too," Sir Jors said, coming back with the water. "What happened?"

"Woodvryns. Well, if we can't force them, which we obviously can't, maybe we can encourage them? We fed them. That's why they helped us yesterday, and they healed you after you gave them your breakfast," Lakara pointed out. "If we keep sharing food, maybe they'll still help?"

It was a better idea than anyone else had. Kita also

declared she wasn't going to keep Borrowing, coming back, and Borrowing again. "I'll try it once in about an hour or so, then rest. Again in the afternoon, and maybe once more before dark. That's it."

Since Kita was the only one capable of Borrowing, and the one suffering the consequences of it, no one argued. Davorin, in particular, insisted Kita follow her instincts. "Magic is good at teaching you how to use it if you listen. If it feels wrong or dangerous, it probably is."

"Like when a muscle tells you it's time to stop using it," Kita nodded in agreement.

"Do you have any idea how much more there is?" Lakara asked.

Kita gave a half shrug. "Enough. It's hard to keep track. I have to focus really carefully to figure out what I've already done. Whisper doesn't have the concept of writing. Or much of one for numbers. That reminds me, you're copying down what I gave you; can I see it before Borrowing again? I want to make sure I'm not repeating myself. Last night was hazy."

"Of course." Lakara hesitated. This was a terrible time for it. Or was it? "Would it help if you knew the letters better? Maybe if I taught you a few of the most common letters?"

"It might. Right now, they're just strange shapes to me. Makes it hard to remember them." Kita straightened up. "Are they hard?"

"Maybe, maybe not. You picked up on the Graldian letters quickly."

It was a little like the initial reading lessons, though Sir Jors decided to join in this time. Instead of trying to teach the sounds the letters could make, Lakara focused on the names. Kita drew pictures in the dirt as she tried to keep them straight.

"That's *galis*. Don't forget the tail."

"And *radut* has the funny loop?" Kita scribbled something that would make the Head Archivist cringe.

"*Radutis.* Yes, but the loop has to go to the left. If it goes to the right, it's part of *tansi.*"

She didn't try to teach the whole alphabet, certainly not in order, but the five or six most commonly used symbols, maybe ten if Kita were a quick study. It could help. Certainly couldn't hurt. Besides, it gave them something to do while they sat around waiting for Kita to be willing to take the risk again.

As far as Lakara was concerned, her efforts were a brilliant success. When Kita did Borrow again, which Whisper didn't seem happy about; she came back with seven letters, three of which she could recognize.

"Think I've got more than half of them. Two more tries might be enough."

"If we have to stay an extra day, or more than that, we'll be fine," Davorin said. "I don't think we have a particular time limit. Not one that would be affected by a few days, anyway."

"Couldn't help it even if we did." Kita pushed herself to stand. "I need to walk around for a bit."

Lakara sighed at her friend's restlessness and settled in to read. If they were going to have a rest day, at least for the non-Borrowing part of the group, then it only made sense to enjoy it and actually rest. Reluctantly, she stopped reading long enough to eat. Kita was back. She didn't seem to be in pain, but she was clearly hesitant to try Borrowing again.

Whatever any of them might have feared, it didn't go too badly. Kita made two more attempts, hours apart, claiming she got the whole of it. She also denied any headache but didn't want to try Borrowing for a while. Kita fell asleep in the middle of eating dinner and didn't stir this time. Davorin and Lakara helped Kita into her bedroll and let her be as they tried to translate the clue.

"Not to shortchange Kita, I'm sure she did marvelously. But... are we sure she got this right?" Davorin asked when he and Lakara compared translations.

"Are we sure *we* got it right? I mean, we could have mistranslated," Lakara said.

"Both of us? The same way?"

"Well, put that way, it does sound unlikely. And what kind of clue is, 'the shadows are the key,' anyway?"

"Well, what if she mistook a *ritol* for a *zerif*? That's easy to do."

"Then we have... 'the ruby is the cane'. I don't think that makes any more sense."

"Not to me, it doesn't," Sir Jors said. "Though I admit to having no expertise in the language."

"Or how about... No, that's something about apples. Or ghosts." Davorin frowned at his parchment. "I think it's ghosts. Could be ghouls."

Lakara shuddered. "No ghouls. I really hope we don't have to deal with ghouls."

"Ghouls aren't real," Sir Jors said with a soft smile. "They're just a scare story."

"Maybe, maybe not. Some say the Dead Lands have ghouls. The aftermath of *lots* of necromancy." Davorin looked ill. "If anywhere has ghouls it will be there."

"*Which means* that when we *don't* find them there, we'll be safe," Sir Jors said, as if he could make it so.

Well, worrying about it now wasn't going to help anyone. Probably Sir Jors was right, and they didn't exist. She hoped.

Kita shivered as the forest thinned. While she had never been in a forest before the Forest of Gloom, she had enjoyed it; especially after meeting the Queya. They had taught her so much about how to navigate it, how to read the lay of the land, how to feel the welcome and life that abounded there. But beyond the forest, a land she couldn't even see yet; there was no life, no welcome. The Dead Lands radiated death and blood and destruction. It didn't want her there. She wanted to be there even less.

"Please tell me that the temple of Skoses is close to the border. Really close," Kita said.

"Um, shouldn't be too far. Two days, I think." Lakara's hand went to her pack before she withdrew, probably realizing it would be too dark to read any of her many, many scrolls and books.

Davorin, to Kita's surprise, looked almost as sick as she did. "Two days," he moaned. "That's... It's..."

"Tainted. Wrong," Kita supplied.

"Dying. Draining." He shook his head. "This is going to be nasty."

No one argued with him. If anything, he had understated it. The rich living earth of the forest gave way to gray, rocky, barren land. "Is there even water here? Or food?" Lakara asked, eyeing the emptiness. Even the Ocean of Sand hadn't seemed so lifeless.

"I don't know that I'd trust it if there was," Kita answered, trying to tug on Trouble's harness. The lizard refused to move. "Come on, you can do it." One paw touched the wasteland, and the lizard retreated back to the forest with a squeal, quickly enough that Kita was almost dragged off her feet.

Stripes and Longtail refused to get even that close. There was no persuading a five-hundred-pound lizard to move when they didn't want to. Kita threw a branch in frustration. "We'll have to leave the lizards. They simply won't come."

"Might be for the best," Sir Jors said. "Like you said, I'm not sure we can trust food or water in that land. Carrying enough for ourselves, that's doable. Carrying in enough for them and us?"

"Will they be safe in the forest?" Lakara asked.

"Should be. The largest predators are forest cats and even Trouble's almost twice their size. If we can give them a wide tether or a big pen, they should be safe enough to catch prey and get water without running off." Kita bit her tongue to keep from offering to stay with them, just in case. No, as much as she absolutely didn't want to step foot in that filthy heap of a wasteland, they were at the point where they would all be needed. "And we will be back in a couple days, right?"

"That would depend on what the clue says, wouldn't it?" Davorin carefully stroked Stripes' head. "Hopefully not more than a week though."

They found a good spot for the lizards. Not far from water, and close to a path the Queya used sometimes. Kita marked the trail to show that something interesting was near, and the tethers were designed to wear out eventually. If they didn't return, the lizards shouldn't be trapped forever, but they would still be there in a week or two. Hopefully.

After that came the sorting. Since they would have to carry everything themselves instead of having the lizards carry it, they had to be ruthless in their selection. Even the tents didn't make the cut. Too bulky to carry easily and it would make it harder to detect any threats. Their bedrolls would have to do. Food enough for a week per person. One spare cloak. Each person took their preferred weapon and a sling. Kita insisted on her personal pack. "It has all my tools in it." Not to mention pretty much everything else she owned in the world.

Sir Jors took his armor and an extra pair of daggers as well as his sword. Lakara dithered for what felt like hours before restricting herself to two books and three scrolls. Davorin took a small box that glowed with his magic and a book that probably cost more money than Kita had seen in her life. In addition, they made sure to have three water skins a piece, before filling the cooking pot with water. They would have to take turns carrying that.

"What about Whisper? Is he coming or staying?" Davorin asked.

Kita put her arm out, the hawk coming to light on it. "I don't know. What are you going to do? I won't force you, either way." She wasn't Borrowing. It would be a little while longer before she was comfortable doing that. But she did try to be receptive. He gave a shriek, flew to a branch, looked out, and looked back at her. She felt like he was scolding her for even thinking he would leave her. "He's coming. Better grab some food for him too."

"How long before the Queya come up this path again, do you think?" Davorin asked.

"Not sure. Probably not soon, but it looks like a semi-regular path," Kita said. "See that hollow? It's deeper than it looks, and there's magic. Like the healing cave had."

"So close to the Dead Lands?" Sir Jors asked, sounding surprised.

"Can you imagine a place that would need it more?" Kita asked.

No one could. "Right." Lakara took a deep breath. "Well, the sooner begun, the sooner back, right?"

Sir Jors gave a somber nod. "We go on."

Kita was the last to leave the forest, shivering sharply as soon as her foot touched the Dead Lands. A strange voice seemed to whisper in her ear, as if saying that if she left the forests now, she might never see them again. Swallowing hard, Kita forced her apprehension back and followed.

***

To Davorin's utter relief, the temple of Skoses was visible in the distance before dark fell on their first night. Unfortunately, that was the *only* thing going their way. The Dead Lands were more than aptly named. Plants didn't grow here. Not anything he recognized as plants, at any rate. Here and there would be tufts of gray or bone white material that looked like they had tried to be plants once upon a time. Kita had been the only one who dared touch one. It crumpled under her hand, while somehow also drawing blood. She gagged twice and visibly avoided any more exposure.

No birds flew. No signs of insects. No signs of life. Except that they all could hear or sense movement just out of sight. But Davorin *knew* nothing was alive nearby, except them.

It was an unsettling feeling. As a necromancer, he could sense the dying. Everyone who lived was, to some extent, dying. Normally, he couldn't tell unless that death was close. *Normally*, he was so surrounded by the living and dying, by people, animals, insects, maybe even plants; that he could only tell when death was days if not hours away.

But now, they were the only ones. Four people and one bird. Living and dying, hopefully not anytime soon. His senses, always so bombarded, didn't know what to do with the quiet. Instead, they screamed at him at all times. But if he relaxed them at all, he would hear the dead. And oh, there was so much death. The whispers were almost shouts. The shadows seemed to flit here and there without settling on anything. Better than them settling, though.

If he slept, if he dreamed, he would see it. See the battles that converted the Flower Fields to the Dead Lands. Could he stay awake until they left? Would he dare to sleep?

"Whisper found something. Water, I think." Kita's voice pulled him from his musings as she shaded an eye to look up. Even the sky seemed gray. Whisper shrieked as he circled. Kita whistled a four-tone scale. The hawk gave a swoop and dive in response. "Yes, water. Do we check it out?"

"How far out of the way?" Sir Jors asked.

"Should be close."

Despite attempts to ration, they had used up more water than was strictly wise. If it was safe, that deadly *if*, then more water would be welcome. But it was not to be.

The water, which actually was close to their path, was an almost rusty red and smelled like iron or some other decaying material. "Right, I am definitely not drinking that." Kita might have been the one to say it, but no one disagreed with her. By tacit agreement, they walked even further to get away from the creek of blood.

"It wasn't really blood, was it?" Lakara asked, after Davorin made the mistake of calling it that out loud.

"Don't know. Don't care. It certainly wasn't drinkable." Kita climbed a rock scrabble, spent a few seconds looking around, and scarpered back down.

"It might have been. Drinkable, I mean," Sir Jors said. "Not pleasant, or even recommended, but I remember campaigns where we were forced to rely on mineral springs, many of which were better for bathing than drinking. Strong smells are common, and sometimes discoloration. While it would certainly not work for long term, drinking a little might be less dangerous than dehydration."

Davorin shivered. "It wasn't blood. I'm sure of that. I'm equally sure that I would not risk drinking it unless I were on the verge of dying of thirst. And I'm not sure that dehydration might not be the better option. It was…"

"Wrong."

"Yes, wrong. Thank you, Kita." He shivered again. "Water… Water is life. I know death, and to a lesser extent, life. That water, it wasn't death, but it definitely wasn't life."

That ended the conversation. That, or Kita's cry of, "There's something over there!"

She pointed at an uneven section of boulders about a mile or two in the distance. Maybe. The unrelenting gray and field of rocks made it hard to judge. Davorin cupped his hands around his eyes to focus in the dying light. All he saw was rocks.

"I don't see anything," Sir Jors said, hand still resting on the hilt of his sword. "What did you see?"

Lakara gasped, suddenly pointing in the same direction. "Something moved! Something big!"

'Big' was a relative term, but the smudge of gray that rippled through the boulders might have been as big as a wolf. Definitely much bigger than they wanted to deal with.

"I don't know what that is," Davorin admitted, "But it's definitely not alive."

Kita drew her dirk, while Sir Jors gripped the hilt of his sword, but didn't draw yet. Lakara assembled the quarterstaff, that she had gained some talent with during their journey, with trembling fingers. Davorin didn't select a weapon. If they were actually attacked, his powers would probably be more effective than any common weapon, especially with his lack of skill. So his hands needed to be free.

"It will be dark soon," Kita noted. "We need a fire and

now."

"Wouldn't that be telling it where we are?" Lakara asked, holding the staff like a walking stick. She was shaking.

"Maybe, but—"

Sir Jors was cut off by Kita. "Better than being picked off one by one in the dark."

One advantage to the ground being covered with rocks was that they didn't have to worry about the fire spreading out of control. Using boulders and rock piles for cover, they were able to set up a half decent shelter for part of the way. Or at least, some warning if something tried to come from that direction. A few grass logs and branches from the forest made a small but steady fire. They would have to keep it going all night, because there really wasn't any visual warning without the firelight.

Davorin swallowed the sour taste of fear, even as he tried his best to see in all directions at the same time, hear the slightest sound of movement, and be aware of any sign of shadows of death. Kita, having finished making the fire, leaned against a large rock pile, and kept scanning the horizon, especially where they had seen movement. Whisper perched on her shoulder, evidently not wanting to go far as dark swiftly descended. Sir Jors sat on a large rock, sword laying in his lap, positioning himself close to where the known potential threat was. Lakara busied herself with passing out food, and keeping an eye out on the other directions, even as her eyes skittered to the north, where Skoses's temple and something not alive but moving, lay.

"Isn't fire supposed to be a deterrent to the undead?" Sir Jors asked.

"According to legend, yes," Lakara said. "Davorin?"

He grimaced. "I've not been in a position to find out

before. Nor do I know the sources of those legends. I *do* know that not all those types of legends are accurate. Honestly? I don't know."

"Rig…" Sir Jors trailed off as his body went limp.

Kita jumped to her feet and climbed their rock wall, searching for threats. Lakara hesitantly leaned towards the knight, checking his breathing and his pulse. Davorin closed his eyes, trying to sense anything out of the ordinary.

"He's asleep. Do we… Should I take his sword?" Lakara asked.

"Are you kidding? Do you remember the imps?" Kita remained on top of the pile. "I think we should leave it. Besides, most of the time he doesn't move. Unless he tries to walk into the fire, I think we should leave him alone."

"I don't sense a current threat, but that doesn't mean much," Davorin said.

Sir Jors suddenly sat up with a jerk. "Calmite!"

"What?" Kita asked, coming down from her perch.

"Calmite. Burn calmite to keep away the dead." Sir Jors shook himself. "Sorry, I'm not sure what that… I heard it. To burn calmite. But what is calmite?"

"Calmite?" Lakara muttered, half under her breath. "I know that word. Calmite, calmite. Right! It's an herb. Also known as death's daisy. Grows in defiled spots. But I haven't seen any of that."

"I have some. It's useful in a few rituals. It won't last more than tonight, though," Davorin warned as he rummaged through his magic supplies. The fact that the herb cost more than its weight in gold went unsaid. Gold certainly wasn't going to save them right now.

"Try to save a piece, if possible. Whisper and I can look

for more tomorrow. If any place is defiled, this is," Kita said.

"Um, a little speed would be appreciated." Lakara stood, staff held in quaking hands. Sir Jors rose as well, sword in hand, facing the same direction. Where empty eyes reflected the light of the fire. Then another pair of eyes shone. Was that a third set?

Davorin snatched a pinch of the herb and tossed it into the fire. The flames sparked green and purple before resuming normal colors, while the smoke thickened enough to choke. But when he looked back, the eyes were gone.

No one slept that night. Every hour or two, Davorin sacrificed a little more of the plant, keeping the unseen hosts at bay. He would feel self-conscious about the way he jumped at every noise; except they were all doing the same. Kita and Sir Jors took occasional slow patrols, as if they could see anything in the dark. As far as he could tell, there was no rhyme or rhythm to when they circled the camp, just when they got too edgy to stay still.

Dawn broke slowly, almost reluctantly, just as Davorin began to run out of the calmite. Wrapping himself in his robe, he took the offered breakfast, and tried to convince himself that surely whatever might have populated the night would leave them alone in the day.

"Did you manage to save any of the magic weed?" Kita asked.

The Davorin who began this trip would probably have yelled at her for failing to respect his craft. After all, even the pinch he had saved was probably worth more money than she had seen in her life. This Davorin saw the minute trembling of her fingers as she rubbed at the handle of her dirk, the flash of her eyes as she searched for any movement, and the exhaustion that hung like a shroud. Some things weren't worth fighting over.

She took the stem, a fuzzy thing with tiny white flowers that almost bordered on purple. "Kind of pretty. Smells horrible, though."

"It's called death's daisy for a reason." Davorin watched as she carefully showed it to Whisper. "Will he be able to find more?"

"If it's here, he'll find it." The bird took wing with a shriek as if agreeing.

"Now that we have that settled, I think it's best we try to get to Skoses's temple. If nothing else, it would probably be safer to sleep there than out in the open," Sir Jors said.

No one objected to that. "Maybe there will be a decent water source," Kita said, scrabbling to the top of a rock pile to look around.

"Anything?" Lakara asked.

"Nothing I can see." She skidded down, hitting the ground with a bounce before grabbing her pack.

At least they had something visible to aim for. Even better, Whisper came back after an hour with another sprig of calmite. "He says there's a nice big patch near the temple," Kita translated. "He also said something about holes in the ground and dead moving things."

Davorin shuddered. Lakara grimaced and gagged. Sir Jors took a deep breath and tightened the hold on his sword. "Anything about numbers?" He asked, ever practical.

Kita shook her head. "He can distinguish up to three on his own, with my help, we can get to five. Anything larger is just a blur to him. Could be four, could be a thousand." She sighed, throwing her head back to the sky. "Last chance to run for it and join the Queya forever." She gave a wry half-smile like she knew they wouldn't take her up on it.

No one answered her. In Davorin's case, he didn't trust

360

himself not to agree. Kita shook her head, pushing hair from her eyes. "Right. We go on." She started walking as they filed behind her.

***

Sir Jors called a rest break. Three or so hours since they broke camp, such as it was. A few hours until they reached the temple. At least eight hours until dark. So far, nothing amiss. He didn't trust their luck to hold. No one did. But the longer it held, the better, so no complaining.

Lakara made a face. "That's my second water skin out."

"There's still half of the cooking pot," Kita said, as she took the time to shake her own waterskin. "I've got maybe a quarter of mine."

"That's more than me," Davorin said.

Sir Jors checked his water again. "I'm about the same. Maybe a pinch more. You're sharing with Whisper, aren't you?"

"Yes, but he drinks less than you'd think."

He didn't question her ability to ration water. But if there *wasn't* a water source at the temple or nearby... No, considering the dangers, dehydration was probably far from their biggest threat.

"Well, if there are flowers by the temple, there must be water, right?" Lakara asked.

"I don't actually know. They're magical." Davorin shook his head. "*I* didn't bring half my collection of books just in case they might be useful, so I can't check."

"I did *not* bring half my books! In fact, for the most part, they aren't mine. They belong to the library. I was granted permission to borrow them." Lakara sighed. "I hope they don't get damaged. They need to go back."

Kita choked. Sir Jors looked over in alarm, but it was

quickly evident the younger woman was trying to smother laughter, with little success. "Sorry, just... sorry."

"What? What's so funny?"

"Never change, Lakara."

"But..." She sputtered. "It's important. Granted, none of my books are irreplaceable, that would be wrong. But it takes *forever* to copy a book. I should know, I've done it. That's probably... almost a century's worth of work in my pack left in the forest. Work that could be damaged by rain, or... um." She blushed.

"Mud?" Kita smirked.

Lakara took a breath to compose herself. "Well, yes. Essentially."

Kita didn't make a sound as her eyes closed and her shoulders shook. Until her eyes snapped open as she shot to her feet. "Ware!"

Sir Jors had been halfway to his feet even before her warning. "What are we dealing with?" His hand rested on his sword, but he didn't draw it yet. No use tiring out too quickly.

"I don't know. But something's close."

He allowed himself a quick circle, trying to memorize everything. Kita was flanking him on his left side, about two persons width behind and beside him, dirk out, other hand lightly touching the talons of an agitated Whisper perched on her shoulder. Lakara was five persons width almost directly behind him, gripping her staff in white fingers, casting nervous glances behind them. Davorin was halfway between them to his right, hands extended, eyes closed, sweat dripping from his wan face. In the center of them was the iron cooking pot and most of the packs they had taken with them. They hadn't built a fire.

Sir Jors turned back to face the direction Kita seemed

most anxious about. Rocks strewed around, some small enough to get stuck in a boot, some taller than him. But no sight of movement. No sound. Just as he was wondering if maybe Kita was wrong this time, he heard it. Something sliding against stones, pebbles dislodging from their paths.

He drew his sword.

The wind picked up. Something moved. He was pointing his sword before he recognized that he was currently threatening the remains of some plant. A ball of some dead-looking plant matter rolled past. Sir Jors took in a breath. He was useless if he lost his nerve.

Slightly calmer, he was able to notice the very strange sound the dead plants made as they scraped the ground. "Is that what you heard?"

Kita didn't answer.

"Could that..." Lakara swallowed hard. "Could that be the 'dead moving things'? Maybe?"

Sir Jors found himself willing Kita to agree. That they had been spooked by a dead moving bush and everything was fine. But she hadn't relaxed. Then Davorin groaned, "Shadow Master's hazy hall. What is *that*?"

A smell filled the air. A smell that Sir Jors realized too late, had been slowly percolating the area. Now, it was blinding in its intensity as he fought to restrain gags. From the corner of his eye, he could see Kita step back, eyes closed, waving a hand around her face as she choked. He wanted to check on the others as he heard coughs and gagging, but there wasn't time.

Something moved. Gray as the rocks, movement like a spider, if that spider was twice the size of a man and the same relative shape. With a howl that left Sir Jors' ears ringing, the ghoul, it had to be a ghoul, jumped at its nearest target. Kita.

With a cry of alarm, she jumped back two feet, dirk

swinging in a wide arc, nicking the creature's arm. So, ghouls bleed black.

Sir Jors intercepted before the monster could pursue or find a new target, stabbing it deep in the side. Another howl reverberated. Were his ears bleeding? No time to check. Sir Jors pulled back his sword, trying for a blow to the neck.

Injured or not, the ghoul moved fast. Quicker than he could swing, the creature jumped at him. All air rushed from his lungs as he hit the ground. His sword, where was his sword?

The ghoul roared in his face, black scaly eyes on him, yellow fangs dripping saliva onto his skin. One three-fingered hand forced his head back, exposing his neck. Sir Jors kept struggling, even as his eyes shuttered closed, waiting for those teeth to rip open his throat.

SMACK! Another howl of pain, and the hand moved. Sir Jors opened his eyes in time to see the wooden pole collide again with the ghoul's head. To his horror, the monster pulled away from him to target Lakara.

"Oh, no. She's not a threat." Kita threw a large rock, hitting it in what Sir Jors suspected was a shoulder. "I am."

The ghoul turned to the newest annoyance, only for Whisper to rake claws across its face and land on Davorin's shoulder. Davorin, who had his eyes closed and was whispering quickly and quietly in Restor.

Two steps towards Davorin, and the ghoul got distracted again by Lakara slamming her pole into its ribs. Before it could fully target her, Kita was stabbing it and dancing away.

Sir Jors forced himself to his feet, ignoring how everything hurt, and picked up his sword. The creature hadn't tried to jump again. Too injured or not bright enough? There was a lot of black blood on the ground, and it was definitely moving awkwardly. Sir Jors drove his sword deep into one arm and backed away.

Ignoring Kita, the ghoul lumbered after him. Until a pole thudded into its side with the crack of broken bones. "No, over here," Lakara said in a shaky voice.

Kita let the ghoul move about a foot before throwing two more rocks. One hit the monster in the head, causing it to cover one eye with a misshapen hand. Black flowed down freely. The other hit a leg, causing the ghoul to stumble. "Ignore her. I'm over here."

It staggered towards her, snarling in pain and fury. They had to end this and soon. Sir Jors aimed for the neck. And missed. Before he could step back or try again, the ghoul grabbed him with its free hand, claws stabbing into his shoulder, dragging him close enough for the stench of its breath to penetrate through the miasma of death surrounding it.

Kita and Lakara both attacked the creature but were ignored. Sir Jors stabbed again and again in desperation. Even if it wasn't enough to save his life; if he could take the creature down with him; ensure the party's safety. It would be enough.

His feet left the ground as he was raised up to the creature's mouth. Despite it all, he would be eaten anyway.

"Run!" He tried to shout, but it wouldn't leave his throat. He tried again, but barely a gargle escaped. The women tried attacking again. Why weren't they running? The ghoul wouldn't be satisfied with him for long.

"*ZITHOMOS!*"

The ghoul froze. The hand holding Sir Jors spasmed, causing him to fall. He hit the ground at the same time as the ghoul and with about as much grace.

Lakara ran to Sir Jors' side, checking his injuries, while

Kita prodded the now lifeless ghoul with Lakara's discarded staff. "Is it dead?"

"Yes," Davorin rasped out. He was white as milk and shaky. Sir Jors couldn't tell if it was fear, release of nerves, or the aftermath of whatever spell he had cast. "Or," he gasped for breath, "more accurately, it's... extinguished."

When they tried to question him, the necromancer held up a hand. "I can't do that again right now. No energy. We need to get to that temple. As quickly as possible."

"Then we better hope we don't run into any more of them." Kita moved to gather up their discarded supplies. "Don't even think about taking that pot! You can't carry it right now." She glared at Davorin when he stumbled over to help her. When Sir Jors moved to take it instead, she shifted her glare to him. "You either. Not only are you injured, but you need your hands free for your sword."

"I'll take the pot. I'll feel better knowing I can swing it at someone if I have to. You should probably take point. You're both uninjured and the fastest." Lakara stepped forward, taking her staff back.

"Fair. But we should still stick together as much as possible." Kita eyed the group with a frown before stepping forward, Whisper taking to the air ahead of them.

Sir Jors was too tired to argue, especially with what seemed to be good sense. Instead, he made a point of walking with Davorin, who still looked like he could collapse at any moment. Taking a mental inventory of his injuries, he concluded that he would be sore all over, should probably get someone to look at and hopefully clean his shoulder when they were safe, but he should be able to manage until they got somewhere safe. Next, he tried to survey the rest of the group.

Davorin's stumbling walk got neither better nor worse during his evaluation. The minute tremors could be fear, exhaustion, or both. At least his color seemed to be improving. Lakara and Kita were both clearly on edge, but neither had acquired injuries, and both seemed to be holding up well. Good, someone had to be.

Whisper shrieked out a warning. "Stay here, I'm going to check it out," Kita said, disappearing before anyone could object.

Five minutes passed. Ten. "Should we go after her?" Davorin asked. "She might be hurt."

"Whisper is still hovering above. I think if she ran into trouble, he'd react," Sir Jors said, hoping he spoke the truth.

"I don't want to mess up whatever she's doing, but this is taking too long," Lakara said, even as she eyed the bird above.

"We—" Davorin cut off as Kita slithered around the rock pile in front of them.

"There's three of them up ahead. At least two of them are bigger than the one we faced already. And there's something else, too. Looks a little like a snake mixed with a wolf. Don't even ask." Kita shook her head, then took a deep breath. "I think I've got an idea, but I need help. And I need you to trust me."

Chapter Seventeen

Dancing with Death

Or

Shadow Master calls the tune

Kita hugged the ground, peering out from the top of the second-highest ridge overlooking the way ahead. Still three ghouls and some kind of snake wolf. And if she was reading the terrain right, once they were past these monsters, they should have a mostly straight shot at the temple, perhaps less than two hour's travel. But the dips and rises in the land could be deceptive. Almost anything could be hiding just a few feet away. Or nothing, like the deep crevices that could appear without warning.

Blowing air through her teeth, Kita took one last second to hope that this plan she bullied the others into despite their objections actually worked. If it didn't, probably not one of them would see that temple. She certainly wouldn't.

Before she could lose the last of her courage, she pressed hard against the rocks and jumped to her feet. "Hey, you! Creepy monster things! Over here!" She waved her hands in case she didn't have their attention yet.

Whether it was the movement or the shouts that did it, they focused on her immediately. Faster than she would have believed possible, they charged towards her. Well, the ghouls did. The snake wolf moved in a more skittery motion. Not that it was any slower, if anything, it might be a little faster.

Her mind screamed at her to run, even as it pointed out that these creatures moved far faster than she could. "Don't move. Don't move," Kita muttered under her breath. Not yet. Not yet.

The first ghoul got almost to the base of her hill before falling into the crevice Whisper had spotted, that she couldn't see from the ridge. The second fell in as well. The third stopped and looked down, possibly in confusion. The snake wolf skittered on its two legs, climbing down the side.

"NOW!" Kita shouted, loading her sling. Two boulders rolled down from the next hilltop, with a third following swiftly. The first one skipped across the crevice, missing the puzzled ghoul by less than a foot, leading the ghoul to cry out in alarm. The other two fell in the crevice, hopefully injuring or killing the monsters inside.

With a ringing howl, the ghoul leaped across the hole, reaching ground at the same time the snake wolf climbed out. No sizable boulders on her hill. She had known that when she chose it, but was really regretting that fact right now.

"SLINGS!" Sir Jors shouted. Rocks flew through the air, focused mainly on the ghoul, larger and easier to hit. Though, the snake wolf might be a bigger threat. But if they could kill *one*, then they could focus on the other!

The ghoul gave a snarled roar and leapt, suddenly only feet from her. Kita tossed a handful of pebbles at the ghoul's eyes, before throwing herself to the ground. She rolled down the hill, wincing at the bruising rocks. More stone rained from the sky. It wasn't going to be enough.

Twice her size, faster than she could hope to be, stronger than any person, the ghoul was an opponent she had little chance against. It was blinded, that might give her just enough of an edge. Unable to see, harried by flying rocks, the ghoul lost balance and stumbled down the same hill.

Back on her feet, Kita swung her dirk desperately, managing a long but shallow cut in what was probably the belly region. Idiot! A dirk was a stabbing weapon. It could be her last mistake. With a growl, the ghoul swept out its arm. It just clipped her, hard enough to send her sprawling.

Wiping away blood, the ghoul laid eyes on her and snarled. Swallowing hard and holding out her dirk, Kita tried to adjust her weight so she could at least stand before she was killed. A large three-fingered hand, dripping black blood, reached for her hair.

Then the snake wolf dove at the ghoul, canine head ripping into the ghoul's injured torso. Having neither need nor desire to see how this ended, Kita jumped to her feet and ran.

"Where's the crevice?" She screamed, running around the hill. From the top, they should be able to see it, as she would if she slowed. But slowing down wasn't part of the plan.

"Move to your right! Two feet, no more than three!" Sir Jors called back. "Don't stray! There's two of them!"

A spot of light appeared on the ground in front of her, lining the way Sir Jors indicated. A reflection from his sword probably. Clever. Had to be Lakara's idea. Kita followed, not stopping until the light disappeared. Catching her breath, she spun a circle around. No signs of monsters. The rest of the party were climbing down from the other hill. Hopefully, that meant that the ghoul and snake wolf weren't interested in following them. Maybe they killed each other.

"Are you alright?" Lakara asked as soon as they were past the crevices.

"I think so. Bruised, but..." She stopped to evaluate. "I can still run."

"I pray we won't need to run. If we do, we won't see a dip until we fall in," Sir Jors said.

Davorin shivered. "Let's try to avoid that, please."

"I agree." Kita sighed. She hadn't wanted to do this, but there wasn't a choice. Whisper seemed as reluctant as she was, but he let her in. A moment later, she came back to herself. "Only one more large pit between us and the temple. He'll call out if he sees any other monsters moving."

"Should I take point now?" Lakara asked, uncertainly.

"No, I can still handle it." Lakara might be the only one still uninjured, but she didn't know what to look for or what to do if something happened like Kita did. She was certainly better than when she began, but Kita was sure Lakara would agree she wasn't the best choice to take point.

"We have to get to the temple. If we can do that, we have a chance. Only if we get there," Davorin said, sounding exhausted. "Skoses, as god of earth, is also intrinsically linked to life. The ghouls won't be able to enter the grounds."

"Then let's go. Keep an eye on the ground." Kita stepped forward, following her own advice.

Skoses's temple lay ahead. Could it be a sanctuary, or would it prove a fool's hope? Life or entrance to Shadow Master's hall?

***

Lakara wanted to cheer when she could clearly see the patch of calmite by the temple, because that meant they were almost there. The only thing that kept her from trying to run for it was that she wasn't sure her legs would carry her. Well, that and they hadn't found the last pit yet. That was a good reason not to run. She couldn't help but pick up her pace a little, though. So did her companions. How much longer? Ten minutes? Twenty?

Kita stopped suddenly, arms out to her side as if to ward everyone back. "Here's the pit." She backed off a few steps.

Looking up to Whisper, she whistled two high notes followed by a low one.

The hawk screeched back, flew a little higher, circled, and came to hover over a point about twelve feet to the left. "This way," Kita said, immediately walking in that direction. Everyone followed.

"I'm so glad you have Whisper," Lakara said. "I don't know that we would have managed without him."

"You *do* realize that the only reason that he can help us like this is because I'm, what's that word you taught me, 'brazen', that's it; *brazenly* breaking the law?" Kita looked back just long enough for Lakara to see her smirk.

Lakara jolted with the realization. Kita was completely right. If she weren't Borrowing Whisper, he would be, at best, a bird that could maybe help them hunt. Not one that could be a lookout or help them acquire the clue they needed.

"Maybe the law is wrong," Davorin said. "Or at least, unnecessarily harsh."

Her knee-jerk reaction was to argue. After all, there was a definite reason for the law. But really, all the law had done was to condemn a group of people who had a different ability that those in control couldn't use. Yes, it had been used to devastating effect during the Wars, but before that, there was a history of the Queya using the ability to help people. Finding the lost, rescuing the endangered, etc. And it wasn't like enchanters, healers, and necromancers couldn't do horrible things with their powers, no one said all of them were bad. After the Wars, the Queya had more or less refused to have anything to do with Graldish or Salardis anyway. Perhaps they were all poorer for it. "Maybe it is."

"Never thought I'd hear you say that," Kita said, voice light. "Now all we need is Sir Jors to agree and I'll know I'm dreaming."

"They have a point," Sir Jors spoke up from the back. "I understand the purpose of the law, but I do not believe it actually aids anyone. Those who are likely to use their ability maliciously are unlikely to care about the consequences of the law and those who would use it benignly are being punished without reason."

"Then why is it the law?" Kita asked, sounding sincerely curious.

"At a guess? Because they were afraid. But the law only reinforces the fear and makes people more afraid of the Queya. Who, from what I could gather during our stay, are far more interested in being left alone than trying to conquer others," Sir Jors said.

"Oh, they taught me about some of their conquerors and warriors, but at the moment, I'd say you're right," Kita agreed. "In fact, many would like to be allowed to integrate a bit more. For trade, at very least. But people react so badly when they leave the Forest of Gloom. Did you know they actually get along better with the Trovians than they do people on this continent?"

"What contact do they have with the Trovians?" Lakara asked.

"Because they don't attack the ships whenever they see them, and don't accuse everyone on a ship of being a pirate, the Trovian merchants will meet up with them sometimes. They have regular trading spots. That's apparently how my grandmother met my grandfather."

"They aren't all pirates?" Davorin asked, edging a little further from the pit that they were almost past.

"No, apparently most are merchants and fisherfolk. But Graldish and Salardis started imposing steep tariffs, like a tax, I think. When the Trovians couldn't or refused to pay, they say that Graldish and Salardis tried to declare the ships forfeit.

Which is apparently a major taboo for the Trovians, and they fought back. And got declared pirates. That's what the Queya said anyway. Though they admitted that many Trovians hold a grudge and will attack non-Trovian ships in fear or anger." Kita shrugged. "I get the impression it's more complicated than that."

"Most things in life are," Sir Jors agreed.

Lakara pondered that. While some of the histories she had read had made certain issues seem simple, other sources often held other views. She had always known that books depended on who wrote them, but it was still hard for her, sometimes, not to treat them as infallible.

"I didn't realize we were so near the ocean," Davorin said, as coming down from a rill revealed the wide expanse of water. "The temple must be almost on top of it."

"According to Whisper, it is. Or would be if the ground were flat." Kita shaded her eyes, despite the glasses, to watch the hawk. "But it's on a rise."

"The waves look rough. Good thing we didn't try to get here by water," Sir Jors said.

"I wonder." Lakara was surprised to hear herself say that.

"Wonder what?" Davorin asked.

"Well, this is, or should be, the last clue. But previous clues seemed to imply or mention a tower and something about water. 'By the light of the full moon is the black sea still.' That could be a metaphor, or we may need to go somewhere by water."

"What if we find this last clue and we *still* have no idea where the filthy jewel is?" Kita asked.

No one answered her. In part because Whisper screeched out a warning. Kita spun to look, her eyes going wide. "Run! To the temple! It's our only chance." The words hadn't fully left her mouth before she was demonstrating a possible reason why people speculated the Queya were related to deer.

Deciding that this was one time that her curiosity didn't need to be satisfied, or at least could wait, Lakara took off after her. Davorin was almost keeping pace with Lakara, while Sir Jors, probably deliberately, slowed just enough to ensure he was last.

Should she drop the cooking pot? It had to be slowing her down. But if she let go, there went half their water rations and her only accessible weapon at the moment. She had disassembled her staff when they had to climb hills and use slings, and it would take almost a minute to put it together again. As she had learned, anything could happen in a minute. Not to mention, if she abandoned the pot now, they'd probably never get it back. But was it worth it?

Before she could decide which option had less risk, the doors were in front of them. Davorin slumped against the closed door, as if all the energy had been drained out of him. Kita barely spared him a glance as she struggled with the gigantic wooden carved door. It would probably be beautiful if it weren't keeping them from a potential sanctuary.

Pulling the door did nothing. Pushing did nothing. Slamming into the door while crying, "Hey! Let us in!" unsurprisingly, did nothing. Kita backed up a step, glaring at the door while rubbing her shoulder.

"Wait a moment," Lakara said, eyeing the intricate border under the rings of the door.

"We don't have a moment!" Kita argued, looking ashy. Davorin groaned in fear or agreement.

"What do you see?" Sir Jors asked, standing so close that Lakara could feel the heat radiating from him.

"I think... I think it's a puzzle or key." Lakara traced her fingers over the triangles, finding the one that didn't seem quite so attached as the others. "Ah-ha!" Manipulating the piece so it was two places to the right and upside down, the new picture vaguely resembled the first letter of Skoses's name in Vesrop. The door pushed forward about an inch.

With four people putting all their weight on it, that inch quickly gave way to several feet. They rushed in, and almost as quickly, turned to push it shut again. Lakara got only a glimpse of whatever they were running from, but that was more than she ever needed. Some things should never be seen or spoken of.

The doors were shut and quickly barred. As no one had been in the temple for lifetimes, it should have been dark and unclean. While there was some truth to the unclean part, there was more light than Lakara had expected. High up windows let in sunlight that bounced off geodes to fill the room. Unless she was imagining it, some of the geodes were glowing.

"We're safe. Nothing dead or undead can enter the grounds." Davorin slumped on the wall, wincing slightly as the glow from the nearest geode intensified briefly.

"Doesn't look like it's doing you any good either," Kita said.

"I feel vaguely ill and very tired. A much better state than I would be in if I remained outside."

"Were you aware this would happen?" Sir Jors asked.

"I knew it was possible. I wasn't sure. But what was the point in mentioning it?"

Whisper flew in from one of the windows and landed on Kita's shoulders. Good. Lakara hadn't gotten around to worrying about the bird yet, but she would have as soon as she realized he was missing.

"We need some torches or something. It's still far too

dark to try to find a clue in this," Sir Jors said, after apparently being satisfied that everyone was as well as could be expected at the moment.

When the temple was abandoned, during the Necromancer Wars, it was short notice. Lakara had known that, it was in the books. It wasn't the same though, as finding discarded food and clothes that were in the process of being mended. Anything considered unnecessary was left behind. Fortunately for them, that included torches.

Soon the entire temple gleamed. For the god of earth, Skoses's temple was built primarily of packed earth and rock, with most of the decorations being clay or stone, or the geodes. Now that she was safe to appreciate it, Lakara found it beautiful in its own way. While not the most colorful of temples, the variations of textures and shine between stone and clay were interesting in their own right. The geodes, in addition to apparently being an antithesis of death magic and a light amplifier, glittered and shone in white and purple. The floor was stone in most places, with a large section that was opened directly to the earth.

Her favorite feature, and she would bet every book she had that at least some of the others agreed with her, was the spring that bubbled through the corner of the temple. Clean, drinkable water. Lakara didn't think any water had ever tasted better.

"Is it sacrilegious to spend the night in a temple? Like, if you aren't a priest or something?" Kita asked, as she carefully held some water in her cupped hands for Whisper to drink.

"I think it depends on whose temple. AKAF has always demanded that his temples be shelters for those in need. Some are a little more particular," Lakara said, trying to remember where Skoses fit in that spectrum.

"I think Skoses will understand," Sir Jors said. "After

we've paid our tribute. Has anyone seen any incense?"

"Oh, back then, Skoses wasn't worshiped with incense. There were sacrifices of crops and um," Lakara blushed. "One could take some of the... earth and combine it with water to make... wet earth. This, um, mixture was painted upon the skin until it dried, while the supplicant either knelt or lay down on the ground in silence. It was meant to encourage stillness and patience."

"So, we're supposed to get covered in mud? How does that honor Skoses?" Kita asked.

Lakara winced slightly, but Kita was technically correct. "Appreciation for Skoses's gifts. A reminder that one must wait for Skoses's blessing. And a reminder that we all return to the earth in the end."

"I've read that some learned special dances to honor Skoses while they were so... bedecked," Davorin said. "But since none of us know any of those, we would probably be better off with the kneeling or lying down."

"How thoroughly are we supposed to do this? Does it go on our clothes? Or just exposed skin?" Sir Jors asked.

"Or are we supposed to remove our clothes?" Kita asked.

Lakara had to be scarlet. "Exposed skin is fine. I've not heard of people disrobing except under the most extreme circumstances."

"And afterwards, we wash in the stream?" Kita asked.

"Precisely."

She shrugged. "Then we should refill our water supply first. No telling how long it will take the water to clear again if we have to make that much mud and then wash it off."

They did exactly that. Lakara winced at the cold, squelchy feeling of the mixture as she deliberately rubbed it on her skin, something she had never done before in her life. It seemed wrong to deliberately make herself unclean. It was even worse covering her face. Especially her eyes. "Make sure you cover your eyes. Skoses gave specific instructions for that."

Like her, Davorin showed clear distaste for the task, though he didn't hesitate or complain. Sir Jors worked in deliberate, unhurried movements. She couldn't tell what his thoughts on the matter were. Kita actually smiled a touch as she played with the mixture and seemed the least bothered by smearing wet earth on herself.

When they were all done, they took various positions, trying to find the most comfortable way to wait. Silence reigned and Lakara let her thoughts drift.

How would they find the last clue? What if Kita was right and they found the clue and still didn't know where the jewel was? Thousands had tried to find the Jewel of Ishni before, many of whom had the same starting information Lakara had. No one had found it. Perhaps this would be a dead end for them. Then what? If it was, would they even survive long enough to leave the Dead Lands? And what if they did get an idea of where the jewel was? How much further would they have to go on?

Were the pack lizards alright and still waiting for them? Had anything happened to them? Would it be safe to ever leave this temple? It would have to be. They didn't have food for more than a few days.

Was this just a nonsense quest? Did they stand even the slightest chance of finding the jewel? What was King Zikkar doing now? Had war broken out already? Would there be a chance to either prevent it from happening or stop it if it had started?

Lakara had almost drifted to sleep when someone moved. Carefully twitching her face, arms, and hands; Lakara decided the earth had dried and it was time to clean up.

Once everyone was clean, wet, and shivering; they spent a few minutes taking care of Sir Jors and Kita's wounds. Nothing was serious, but better to clean them and treat any open sores with yarrow. After that, they split up to search for the clue. Which would be a lot easier if there was some consistency to where the clues were. But no, the clues had been in lots of different spots. Floor, walls, decorations, even the roof. Maybe they would get lucky, and Kita would spot it because it was glowing or something. Of course, considering how much of the temple was glowing even to *her* eyes, that might not be so simple.

Whisper called out. Lakara mostly ignored him as she tried to search the closest wall. It didn't sound like a cry of alarm, and Kita would have a much better idea how to handle it than the rest of them would.

"What is it, bird?" Kita asked, eyes scanning the ceiling. He called out again. "Yes, I hear you. What do you...?" She trailed off, seeming to almost fall asleep on her feet before coming back to herself. For a moment, she didn't move, only to start shaking suddenly. Lakara came closer in alarm, only to suddenly realize the other woman was laughing. "It's the floor! The entire floor!"

Lakara backed up to a wall, using a torch holder and pillar to lift herself up slightly. Sure enough, she could just make out the outlines of the symbol carved into the ground of the temple. "Merciful deities. Who dreamed that one up?"

"The writing is at the border," Davorin said, indicating a stripe on the floor all around the main room, that looking closer, did appear to have letters carved into the ground. But centuries of disrepair had left the imprints partially filled in.

"Right. Well, the clue probably starts at one of the corners. Most likely that one." Lakara pointed to the northmost corner. "With earth being associated with the north, that makes the most sense."

Soon they had a system going, with Kita and Sir Jors attempting to clean the debris from the carvings while Lakara and Davorin followed behind them copying the letters they saw. Once they finished, they settled down to eat some of their provisions while Lakara and Davorin attempted to translate the last clue.

Lakara quickly became frustrated with her translation. "This one doesn't make any sense at all! 'Below the earth, over the sea, above the clouds and back again.' What does that even mean?"

"What do any of them mean?" Kita asked, tossing a small piece of jerky for Whisper to catch. "Have any of them made sense?"

"Well, we did come past the dead that we may live," Davorin said. "And if you were right about the meaning of a single coal being that one person can't do it alone, we've certainly proven that."

"Maybe, but what about the eye and the needle? Or the tower? Or the fire and ice? Here we are in the Heart of Earth, and we still don't understand," Kita said.

"No," Lakara answered slowly. "We *aren't* in the heart. The heart of a temple is never where the common people pray, it's further in. Deeper. Usually reserved for the priests. If we want to find the 'heart of earth', we need to find the central part of the temple."

She pushed herself to her feet. "Come on, I want to check something." There was some grumbling, but everyone followed her as she moved past the main worship area into the priests' living quarters.

It was in the kitchen she found what she was looking for,

a stone staircase down. Realizing she would look extremely foolish if it just led to a root cellar, Lakara gingerly descended the stairs, one hand wrapped around her torch while the other trailed down the wall. At least the steps were in good shape.

When she reached the bottom, for a moment, all she saw was signs of a kitchen cellar. Barrels and casks, baskets and jars. But a stream ran through it. As she followed the stream, it led to a cave.

In the cave, there was a small boat. It couldn't fit more than ten people, but it would fit their crew fine. "Under the earth, over the sea. We have to use the boat to go to the next location."

"But where is that? And how can such a small boat survive the ocean?" Davorin pointed to the cave entrance, where they could hear the tumultuous waves.

"Um, probably here." Kita pointed to a spot on the wall. Lakara had ignored it at first because it looked like erosion in the wall. But looking closer, it appeared to be a crude map.

"If this is a map, and I'm reading it right; neither of which I'd be willing to stake much on," Sir Jors said, "There's a small island not far out. But the path is mostly closed by rocks."

"The eye of the needle." Lakara shook her head. "It's all actually there."

"I repeat, the waves are far too much for a boat of that size. Or *any* size when you consider our joint lack of skill," Davorin said.

"Isn't the full moon tomorrow?" Kita asked.

"Yes, why? Oh! 'By the light of the full moon is the black sea still.' That's it. We have to do this tomorrow!" Lakara suddenly let out a terrified breath. "We have to do this *tomorrow*."

"Which means," Sir Jors cut in with a calming voice, "We

should probably all get as much rest as we can now. Tomorrow will be difficult enough on its own without adding to it."

***

If asked, Davorin would be willing to wager that he slept less than an hour. Maybe two.

"No, you slept," Kita denied as she helped him repack their provisions into some of the waterproof chests they found in the cellar.

"How do you know?" Davorin grumped. She was in far too cheerful a mood. Why was she cheerful? They were in the Dead Lands and tonight they had to go on another boat. She did worse on boats than he did! Initially, at least. Gods preserve them from needing to be on the water for more than a day.

"You snore."

"I do not!"

"Oh, you definitely do." She smirked. "Lakara!" The scholar looked up from where she was checking over the ropes. "Tell Davorin he snores!"

"Oh, no. I'm staying out of this. I'm… busy." She went back to the ropes, ignoring them.

"Sir Jors?"

He chuckled but didn't look up from where he was investigating the boat for leaks. "Well…"

"I do not snore!"

The knight smiled. "A bit. I'm afraid that I can snore worse. Kita hums in her sleep, and Lakara occasionally talks in hers."

"I do?" Lakara asked.

"You do," Kita answered. "I remember once you told me something about putting a book in an apple. I tried to ask you about it but all you said was that there were mice in the library."

"I don't remember that at all." Lakara shook her head.

"I didn't hear that one, but I do know that you once said to put out the fire because the unicorns would steal our bread." Davorin had spent about a minute trying to argue with her before realizing she was solidly asleep. He had also heard Kita hum in her sleep, but only when they were close by and didn't have the tents to separate them. Whisper did the same. Probably one of them picked it up from the other.

"Why would unicorns want our bread?" Lakara sounded completely bewildered. "I'm not sure they can even eat bread."

"I have no idea. You were the one dreaming it."

"And even if the unicorns did want our bread, putting out the fire wouldn't help. We'd want the fire to keep them away. That doesn't make sense."

"It makes about as much sense as putting a book in an apple because there are mice in the library," Kita said.

"But that's... silly." As if dreams should be logical.

"Many dreams are," Kita pointed out.

Lakara huffed and moved to the next rope pile.

"Maybe you heard Sir Jors snoring," Davorin said.

"No, he sounds completely different. Much deeper. It was you."

Davorin grumbled under his breath. Why was she so cheerful? He couldn't think of anything to be so happy about.

"Since we can't leave until tonight anyway, once we're certain everything is ready, anyone who wants to, can take a nap," Sir Jors said. "I can't say the night was kind to me either, and I think we should be as well rested as possible for this."

"We are all going, right?" Lakara asked.

Davorin froze. He didn't have to get on the boat. There was no need for him to brave the battering waves and the wall of rocks. He could just...

"And what? Wait here in the Dead Lands?" Kita asked. "Even if the creepy things can't enter the grounds, there's food for what, three days? Waiting to see if the others made it back? And if not, then what? Go back through all that again? No, if someone was going to stay, the time to do it was when we left the pack lizards."

She was completely right. "Kita may have a point."

"*May* have?" In the first month of the quest, she probably would have been insulted by his words. Perhaps she wouldn't have bothered to say anything, but she would have read insult there. And she probably would have been correct. Here, she smiled with just a pinch of warning.

He smiled back. "We're in a temple. Miracles can happen."

"Oh, really?" The next thing Davorin knew, he was lying on the ground, Kita pinning his arms in place with her legs, hands resting on his shoulders, her braid brushing his forehead. Eyes, so very like her hawk's, glinted playfully at him. "What say you now, Master Necromancer?"

Her hair hadn't been washed since they left the Queya at best, and the harsh sun and wind had left it frazzled and dry, wisps escaping the braid. Her face and arms were smeared with earth. Months in the sun had darkened her complexion, much more noticeably than any of the rest of them. Her hands were calloused, and her arms showed the muscle of one who worked hard.

By the standards of the palace, the standards he had lived by his whole life, he should be appalled. Aghast that she had dared touch him. Repulsed by her very appearance. But at that moment, all he could think of was how beautiful she looked. Words froze in his mouth.

When he didn't respond, Kita frowned and tilted her head. "I didn't hit you that hard."

"... Knocked me speechless," Davorin tried to smile back.

She huffed at that and rolled her eyes. "Well, if you apologize for your remark, I might see my way to letting you back up."

"You would be so gracious?"

"Of course. I'm not doing all the packing by myself."

Davorin chuckled. "I apologize. You are as wise as you are kind, and undoubtedly every word you speak is well worth hearing."

"Now you're making fun of me." Kita made a face at him.

"Not at all. I have been enlightened."

"Making fun." Kita flicked at his ear and pushed herself to her feet. "Come on, the packing won't do itself."

There wasn't much more to do. Within an hour, everything had been double, and triple checked, the boat was loaded, and they had eaten lunch. The only thing left to do was wait until moonrise.

Davorin decided to take advantage of the offer to sleep. Perhaps it would leave him in better shape when they did brave the sea. If only sleep came easier than it did the night before.

Sleep came easily. Too easily. One moment Davorin was trying to get comfortable on the stone floor, the next he found himself standing in front of a door. A door so black that it seemed to repel all light. No handle on this door, it would open of its own accord or not at all. The door to Shadow Master's domain. He had seen it before in his dreams. Never had it heralded anything good.

Davorin

"Yes, Shadow Master?" Had he died?

You have not come to me, either by choice or accident. You shall, though, in time.

Well, yes. He wasn't immortal. Hopefully not for a long time though.

You leave tonight for AKAF's island. No deity but AKAF can step foot there. Your group will journey on alone.

A shiver ran through him. "Does that mean we have the right place? Where none of the gods can go?"

Perhaps. This is not the only possibility, though it is the most likely. But only the All Knowing All Father would know for certain.

Why was Shadow Master telling him this?

Many have tried, throughout the centuries, to find the Jewel of Ishni. Some gave up. Others died. No one gathered all the clues. No mortal has stepped foot on AKAF's island in centuries.

"Mortals *have* gone there?"

Someone had to build the place.

Well, that made sense. "Do you know what we'll find?"

No. None of us do. You will be hidden to all but the sight of AKAF.

Would it be too forward to ask if Shadow Master had any advice for them?

Mind the rocks. It would be a shame if the most interesting thing mortals accomplished recently ended before we even found out if you were right.

The door vanished, and someone was shaking him awake. It was time.

Sir Jors took an oar and the prow as they maneuvered the boat to the mouth of the cave. He trusted the team with his life and had no doubt that Lakara and Davorin were far and away the best equipped to both translate the clues into Graldian and interpret what they meant. Nor could he think of a better interpretation of 'By the light of the full moon is the black sea still.'

Despite all that, he paused at the cusp, watching waves that would swamp them in a heartbeat if they tried to go out there, and wondered. What if they were wrong? What if this was suicide? What if…?

The moon shone on the water. Slowly, as if someone had stopped a clock and the mechanisms inside failed, the waves began to cease. Until the water was as still as glass.

"How long will it last?" Asked Kita when they had all just stared at it for a moment. "I don't want to be in the middle when it starts up again. Or stuck somewhere for a month waiting for another full moon."

That got them moving. Sir Jors hadn't even considered the time frame. If they only had one night, then they had absolutely better hurry.

They rowed out, maybe fifteen minutes, maybe twenty, when Lakara called out. "Look! A tower! That has to be where we go."

"If that's the tower, where are the rocks? We do *not* want to find those the hard way," Kita said.

Sir Jors shielded the top of his eyes and looked around. He couldn't see any. Which did not, for a second, mean they were safe. "Can Whisper see them?"

"I see better in the dark than he can. And I can't see them at all."

"Well, what if—"

Davorin was cut off. "The shadow is the key! The moon is casting a shadow of the tower. We just have to follow it!" Lakara said.

"Um, the moon will be casting a different shadow in an hour. How do we know it's this one?" Kita asked.

"Because we have to do something, and that's the best idea we've got," Davorin said.

"We'll go slow. If anyone sees anything, sing out. But I think this might be our best option. It's that or turn around now." Sir Jors waited a moment to see if anyone would object or offer a better suggestion. No one did. "Then, we go on."

It was nerve wracking. Every moment he expected to hear the scrape of wood against stone signifying they had made their last mistake.

"Rock. I think. About a foot to your left." Kita said. She pointed to what could be a rock or just a dark spot on the water. Sir Jors tried to direct away from it.

"Not too far," Lakara said. "Pretty sure there's a rock there on the right." She indicated the barest sliver of a point that rose from the water.

"They were right about the eye of a needle," Davorin said. "If the boat were any bigger, I don't think we would stand a chance."

"I'm inclined to agree." Sir Jors did his best to watch both sides, praying the rocks weren't wider than they looked.

"Another rock. Three feet to the left. And a little beyond that is a rock about a foot to your right."

Sir Jors shook his head and thanked the gods that at least Kita had good night vision. "But nothing straight ahead?"

"Nothing I've seen yet. Lakara, you may have been right

about following the shadow."

It took almost an hour, with numerous minor course corrections, but apparently following the shadow was a safe path, as they pulled on to the island without capsizing or smashing their boat. Sir Jors and Davorin pulled the boat further ashore while Lakara and Kita went to examine the tower.

When they caught up, Kita was rubbing her hands together, seemingly with nervous anticipation.

"What's the matter?" Davorin asked.

"This is why I'm here. The whole point of sending a thief. Here I am so out of practice that I don't even know that I can trust my fingers to remember what to do. But if any place would need me to be at my best, it will be here."

"You will do fine," Lakara said firmly. "We all will."

"Right. Of course. So, did anybody happen to spot the key to open this door or is picking the lock going to be my warm-up?"

Chapter Eighteen

The Unanswerable Question

Or

"Why???"

Lakara had stopped thinking of Kita as a thief long ago. Honestly, she couldn't even remember the last time it had mattered to her. Nor had Kita, to the best of her knowledge, made any attempt to steal anything or act in a criminal manner during the entire quest. So, it was with a bit of nervous excitement that she watched the other woman use strange bits of metal to manipulate the ancient lock. While certainly not a skill that Lakara was interested in learning, well, perhaps a little, it was definitely one she wanted to see done at least once.

Kita worked with smooth, unhurried movements; sometimes placing an ear to the door, other times pulling back as if to look into the lock. "I've never seen a lock of this design before. I don't really have a lot of experience picking locks to begin with."

"You don't? I thought—" Lakara cut off, suddenly realizing that her words could sound insulting or judgmental.

"There may be some good stuff locked up tight, but there's a lot almost as good that no one ever bothered to secure so tightly. And stopping to pick locks is a good way to get caught. Anything that slows you down for more than two minutes probably isn't worth it." Kita didn't sound upset, at least.

"But you do have *some* experience? And tools? And I'm going to stop talking now." Lakara really needed to learn how to keep her mouth shut.

Kita shook in silent laughter. "There are exceptions to every rule. Besides, if I had these on me when the King threw me in the dungeon, then I would have been long gone before he even mentioned this mu... silly quest."

"We would certainly all be the poorer for it," Davorin said.

"And you would be stuck here, staring at a locked," with a small click, the door moved inward a fraction of an inch, "door." Kita collected her tools and gave a small bow.

"Very good. I'll take point," Sir Jors said.

"Bad idea. There's almost bound to be traps. Is that something you're trained for?" Kita asked.

"I know how to spot a potential ambush."

"Little different." Kita waved everyone back, picked up a stone and tossed it at something Lakara couldn't see. A moment later, there was a loud crash. "Make that, there are definitely traps. I don't usually bother with this kind of work, but I have done it. Twice. Still alive, all body parts intact."

Sir Jors chuckled. "Well, with a ringing endorsement like that..." Then he got serious. "Just be careful. From what Davorin said, even the gods can't help us here."

"If they ever did."

Lakara winced at Kita's sacrilegious statement, but decided it wasn't worth arguing over. Especially since Kita didn't seem to be paying attention as she gathered stones and pebbles of varying sizes and a few sticks.

"What are you doing?" Davorin asked.

"We don't know what we're going to run into in there.

I don't have as much supplies as I would like, but these could prove helpful. Or not. Hey, what's this?" She picked up something that Lakara had initially mistaken for a large branch. But when Kita held it up, it appeared to be a cane. "Huh." She rotated it, spinning it in a slow circle. "Yes, this could be handy." She tapped the stone on the top. A small, red, almost flat piece. "Looks a little like ruby. I don't think it is though." Kita laughed. "Wouldn't it be funny if this was the famed Jewel of Ishni?"

"Amusing, but unlikely," Sir Jors said.

Kita nodded and used the cane to push the door the rest of the way open. Lakara and Davorin made eye contact. Maybe the ruby was the cane, after all. But what did that mean?

While rowing, only one person had a lit torch. It was necessary to ensure that as many people as possible could steer the boat and that they didn't accidentally set the boat on fire. Before entering the tower, everyone but Kita took a torch. Kita walked ahead of them, insisting they stay back at least a foot or two.

Cane held out in front of her, Kita used the stick to test various things. The ground in front of her, the walls, the ceiling. Even the large boulder not far from the door that was probably the cause of the crashing sound.

"Trick stair. Don't touch it," Kita said, hopping over the indicated spot.

"Tripwire. Don't know what it does, but there's magic nearby."

"Oh, a pit. We don't want that." She led them long ways around an area that Lakara would have guessed to be perfectly safe. Which was why Kita had point, and not Lakara.

Another time, she forced everyone back and rolled a handful of pebbles down an incline. Three javelins hit the far wall before bouncing off the stone. "That should have disarmed it but let me check." More pebbles. No javelins. "Fine, try not to touch them, just in case they're poisoned."

"I think that maybe you were right about taking point," Sir Jors acknowledged as he stepped over the wooden missile. "I can't even see half of what you warn us about until you point it out."

"Being able to see magic helps, but honestly, I'm mostly thinking of things I've seen, or how I would lay down traps for a treasure."

"You can also see better in the dark than the rest of us," Lakara pointed out.

Kita stopped. "I can?"

"Yes, you can. It's a Queyan trait. One you clearly inherited. Didn't you know that?" Davorin asked.

"I thought everyone saw like this."

"The only thing I can see more than seven to ten feet out is dark," Lakara admitted. "I can see a bit of what may be stairs over there, but that's it."

"It is stairs. Looks like they go to the top." Kita sighed. "Maybe I should go up alone then. I *can* see, and it might be easier for one person not to set off traps than a group."

"Not a chance!" Lakara denied. "If something happened to you or you got hurt, we might not be able to get to you. We might not even know!"

"Besides, it could take more than one of us to get it," Davorin said.

"You each have a point," Sir Jors said. "For now, I believe we should stick together. It may come a time where we have to consider your idea, but until then, we've accomplished the most while working together in the past. It might be best to remain so."

Kita nodded. "Fine, but if I say fall back, then you had better do it."

The steps were wooden. Wood that had been left unattended for centuries. The entire stairwell creaked and shifted as they slowly climbed. The silence was unbroken except for warnings to avoid certain sections, and twice the fall of part of the staircase or railing.

It seemed to go on forever. Lakara had long ago lost any sense of time. Was it still the same night? Was it the next day? Had a month gone by and it was another full moon? Who even knew?

Then they reached the top. A wide empty room with a pedestal in the middle. On the pedestal was a red stone about the size of Lakara's fist. "Hold," Kita said. "Don't move."

"What is it?" Davorin asked.

"I don't know. But there's no muddy way it's going to be this filthy easy." Kita looked around and sniffed the air. "There's a trap. I know it. But I don't know what or how to avoid setting it off."

She took a step forward. Then another. Part of the floor opened, revealing coals. A heartbeat later, the coal was aflame. Two other sections of the room did the same, also combusting as soon as exposed to air. Everyone held still, but that seemed to be the extent of it. "That's... that's fine. We're still. Still good. Stay there. Whisper, stay with Davorin." Kita carefully edged between the two closest fires.

"I can do it," Sir Jors offered. "You don't have to brave the fire."

"'Brave the ice, brave the fire.' That was one of the clues," Lakara said.

"I'm fine," Kita said in a way that made it clear she was

anything but. "Just need to…" She approached the podium and examined it carefully. "Huh, it's surrounded by something." Kita sniffed it. "It's like incense or something. But it's hard." She poked at it with her cane. Nothing happened. She tried her dirk, but it just skittered off.

"If it's incense, will the heat of the fire melt it?" Davorin asked.

"Not close enough. I would have to have the fire like right on the incense." She winced and rubbed her forehead. "Of course. Of all the dirty tricks."

"Kita! Whatever you're thinking, I think you'd better let —" Sir Jors cut off as a ring of fire sprang up, separating them. Lakara jumped back with a yelp. Whisper, still perched on a pale Davorin's shoulder, kept shrieking and shifting from foot to foot like he wanted to fly but there was nowhere to go. Even Kita cried out.

"No," Kita answered shakily, like she was trying to sound brave. "I think it has to be me." Moving a little closer to the fire, she poked the cane into it. Lakara relaxed. Like a torch. She could use that flame to melt the incense and get the jewel. How she would get out of the ring of fire was a question for later.

But when Kita pulled the cane out, it hadn't ignited. She tried again, longer this time. Still nothing.

"I don't understand. Why won't it light?" Lakara asked.

"Because the gods are sadis…" Kita cut off, biting her tongue. Then she took the cane to where the coals were and leveraged one away from the pile until it rolled to the pedestal. Running over, Kita grabbed the coal, ignoring the cries of dismay and horror, and dropped it next to the jewel. Blowing on her hand, she waited.

"Is your hand alright? Is it working?" Davorin asked.

"Yes and… no." Kita huffed. "One's not enough. 'A single

coal burns out quickly.' Utter filthy, muddy rot!"

"We can figure something else out!" Sir Jors called. "You don't have to—"

"We *need* this jewel. If we don't get it, there will be war. And we'll have no leverage against being executed!" She took a few deep breaths and her face set into a blank look.

"Kita, don't!" Lakara cried out.

She didn't listen. Not to Lakara or any of them as they tried to persuade her to stop. Lakara didn't even try to keep track of how many times Kita scooped up a live coal with her bare hands to put it on the pedestal.

At first, she tried to knock them from the pile first, but before long, she was all but reaching into the flames to snatch the glowing coals. Once her sleeve caught fire. Kita didn't even try to put it out until she had moved the coal.

The smell of the air changed. Not just decay and heat, but the sickeningly sweet smell of incense and charred meat. Whisper screeched like he was being tortured. Davorin was muttering something under his breath. Possibly prayers. But what good would that do? For the first time in her life, Lakara felt absolutely abandoned by the gods.

She didn't realize she was crying until a tear ran into the corner of her mouth. Her mouth that she hadn't known was open. Her throat hurt. Why?

An arm wrapped around her shoulders and pulled her away. Lakara struggled but Sir Jors was too strong, and she didn't really want to win. "Don't watch. Don't look." She buried her head into his chest and sobbed.

A crack resounded. Lakara turned to look. Kita used the cane to knock the coals away. The jewel had been uncovered. As soon as she picked it up, the floor closed up again, stopping the fire.

Kita swayed on her feet, far too gray, smudged with soot and smoke. Tear tracks evident, but a smile on her face as she waved the famed Jewel of Ishni. Possibly the first mortal to ever hold it. "I've got it!"

Then her eyes rolled up as she passed out on the floor.

***

It was fortunate that Kita was the smallest of them, Sir Jors mused as he carried her downstairs, trying to remember every spot she had warned them about. Lakara had taken point, using Kita's cane to test every step before going down. She had been the one to insist on grabbing the cane, both because Kita had put it to such valuable use and because she might want it when she woke up.

Sir Jors would far have preferred to take point himself, but he couldn't do that while carrying Kita, and light as she was, he was the only one who could do that long enough to get out. Besides, Lakara's memory was better than his.

"Shouldn't she be awake by now?" Davorin asked, hovering at his shoulder.

"If she were awake, she'd be in pain. And if we linger here too long, we could all be stuck. We need to get her back to the temple," Lakara said. She cast a quick look back to the unconscious woman in his arms. "She is breathing alright, isn't she?"

"A little slow, but that's to be expected. Steady. Regular."

Lakara nodded firmly, clearly trying to convince herself. "We'll get her to the temple, cleanse her injuries thoroughly, and treat them with yarrow. She'll be fine. Then we all get to yell at her."

"Perhaps the Queya will have a good treatment for burns," Sir Jors said, hoping. "They did for snake bites."

"Right. And if we're careful, lucky, and fast, we could

probably catch up to the Queya again in about a week or so. Or if we went the other way, we could try Aloses's temple. The woodvryns liked her," Davorin said.

Sir Jors tried to ignore the fact that they all knew they were being overly optimistic. Her hands were black. Granted, some of that was soot. But some of that would be burns. Probably serious burns. Burns that should have been treated immediately. But they had neither supplies nor time. If any of them were to stand any chance of survival at all, then they had to get off this island. If it wasn't too late already.

Lakara did a good job taking point. She only set off one trap by accident and they had all managed to avoid the flying metal spikes. Somehow, they ended up outside the tower, alive, and still in the same night. Judging by the moon, they had only a little over an hour until moonset.

"We have to hurry. If the waves start up while we are still in the water, we're finished." Sir Jors lay Kita in the boat in a position where she would hopefully be comfortable and out of the way. "Let's go."

The lightening of the sky and perhaps a lower phase of tide, meant they could actually see the rocks, which helped a lot. Still, it was a close race. They had barely reached the inlet when the waves started to stir again.

Kita woke up while Lakara was trying to clean her hands, and immediately started struggling. "Easy, you're safe now. Just let her work," Davorin soothed, gently pushing her back into a resting position.

She blinked up at him. "Did we get it? Is everyone alright?"

"We've got it and you're the only one who got hurt," Sir Jors said. "Lakara is examining your burns now."

"Right, so let me know if I'm hurting you too much,"

Lakara said. "And try to hold still."

She hummed an affirmative. "I'm fine."

"You *will* be fine. *If* we take care of them properly." Lakara grimaced, rubbing lightly at the hand she had immersed in a bowl of water. "I can't get your hands clean. That's important." She rubbed a little harder, then pulled back suddenly as Kita's hand twitched in her grasp. "Sorry! I know I'm hurting you."

"No. It doesn't hurt."

Lakara hissed slightly. "Doesn't hurt at all? Or doesn't hurt too badly?"

Kita shrugged and her eyes fluttered. "I'm fine. Tired."

"Right," Sir Jors said before Lakara could get more upset. "You've had a long night. Why don't you get some sleep while we finish your wounds?"

No one spoke until she drifted off, Whisper perched by her head. "How bad?" Sir Jors asked.

"*Bad*. If there's *no* pain, then she's damaged the nerves. That will probably never come back. And the chances of infection..." Lakara swallowed hard. "Burns are such a high risk anyway."

"Maybe it's just because she's so out of it?" Davorin offered, sounding like he didn't believe it himself.

"Maybe." Lakara let out a huff. "We don't tell her. Not yet. Not until we know something for sure."

Kita was much less compliant the next day when she realized her hands were bandaged in such a way that she couldn't use either of them. "I can't do anything!"

"You shouldn't *be* doing anything! If you re-open the skin, if you make the wounds unclean, if you open blisters; you risk infection. And permanent damage!" Lakara answered with the fierceness that only came over her when she was acting as medic and her patient was being difficult.

Kita went ashen. Whether it was because of Lakara's uncharacteristic harshness or the prospect of permanent damage, Sir Jors didn't care to speculate. "Fine. Don't do anything with my hands. But I have a question."

"What?" Davorin asked.

"We actually found the Jewel of Ishni. I still don't quite believe it, but unless you lied to me, or there was some other fancy paperweight in that tower, we have it. What do we do with it?"

Silence reigned. Kita hadn't been the only one to privately suspect they would never actually get that far. Sir Jors hadn't even tried to figure out how they could use it to bargain.

"Well," Lakara said. "We could... I have no idea. We could ask Vicaw for a military victory, but that's more fighting. We were trying to avoid that."

"Maybe ask Skoses for earth-based riches, enough that King Zikkar doesn't feel the need to expand his territory?" Davorin suggested.

"There's not enough money in the world for someone when they get that greedy." Kita leaned back; eyes closed. "Well, we could go with my old plan of demanding magical powers and turn the king into a pigeon."

"We'll consider that a back-up plan," Sir Jors said, trying to hide his smile.

Finally, they decided that the best plan was not to make any decision yet. Not until they had more information and a better idea.

"After all, it took us months and months to get here, it's not going to be a quick trip back," Lakara pointed out.

"It won't be *as* long. For starters, we won't have to winter over somewhere. And once we've caught up with the Queya, they can introduce us to the Trovian merchants they know. If they'll give us a ride, it could be only a few weeks."

"You *hate* boats!" Davorin pointed out.

Kita shrugged. "It beats four months of walking. Or I could stay with the Queya, while whoever wants to go, goes save the land."

"No point making plans just yet," Sir Jors said. "We still have to get out of the Dead Lands first."

They spent one more night in the temple, carefully gathering as much calmite as they could before leaving their sanctuary. Well, all but Kita who had been strictly ordered not to do anything at all with her hands. A demand that clearly chafed the independent woman, but she followed if only because the possible consequences were unthinkable.

"I want to clean your hands one more time while we have access to fresh water," Lakara said. "And while I have light."

With Davorin and Whisper keeping lookout, Sir Jors tried to help the women. Kita stared into the sky, not even looking. Which might have been for the best. He grimaced as he saw how black her hands looked, even after being cleaned. And blisters, so many blisters. Lakara winced as one of them burst during the process. "I'm so sorry. Did that hurt?"

"Did what hurt?"

Lakara carefully placed a finger on the least burned part of Kita's right hand. "Does this hurt?"

"No."

"Can you feel it?"

"No."

She tried another spot. "How about this?"

"No? Maybe?"

She hovered a finger close but not touching. "Can you feel that?"

"I think so?"

"Give me your other hand and close your eyes." Kita did so. "Let me know what you feel and where?"

Lakara pressed at various spots on both hands. But it wasn't until she got to the wrists that Kita was able to identify anything. Lakara met his eyes. Nerve damage. Extensive nerve damage. And burns, especially bad ones, could keep causing damage even after being removed from the source. It had been hours before they had been able to put her hands in water. "Right." Lakara sighed. "Well, remember not to move your hands. We are going to keep them clean and covered. Everything will be fine."

He suspected that even Kita knew that was a lie.

***

It wasn't until they camped for the night, when Lakara went to reapply yarrow on Kita's hands, that Davorin noticed the shadows. Infection. It had to be. He swallowed hard. "Make sure you're thorough."

Yarrow could fight infection. The Queya probably had all kinds of secret tricks for it. Mud, there had been one of those healing caves just outside the Dead Lands. Surely, if they could get Kita there, she'd be fine.

True, none of them knew the ceremony or whatever Malni had done to save the boy, but Kita was strong and resilient. Maybe the Queya were close. Close enough that they could help as long as they could get her to them.

"I will." Could Lakara tell? Or was the infection still too

minor? The shadows were wispy things, still easily dispersed.

The next morning, they were darker and completely surrounded her hands. Kita didn't seem to notice a problem, just grumbling about having to be fed like a child.

"What if..." Davorin hadn't meant to speak but couldn't help but continue. "What if we ask Aloses to heal your hands?"

Sir Jors and Lakara looked interested. Kita scoffed. "How selfish would that be? We're trying to prevent a war and I'm worried about my hands? They don't even hurt."

"That's..." Lakara bit her lip. "Um, we should probably keep moving." She sent a significant glance to both Davorin and Sir Jors. The Queya. They were their best hope.

By noon, the shadows had completely surrounded her, though they were light yet. Equally as alarming, Kita's legs went out underneath her. "Why is it so hot?"

Lakara put a hand to her forehead, withdrawing it immediately. "You have a fever!"

"No, I'm fine. We have to... keep moving."

Sir Jors picked her up. "And we shall."

"You need your sword. If we come across the creepy things..."

"The ghouls?" Davorin asked.

"Them."

"If we come across ghouls, I'll put you down," Sir Jors said.

There was a long silence as they kept walking. "Faster if you weren't carrying me."

"No," Lakara said. "It would be slower, because you can't walk quickly."

"Faster."

"We're not leaving you, and that's settled," Sir Jors said sternly.

Davorin wasn't sure if Kita planned to argue more or not, but she was asleep before she could say one way or another. Night fell, and they had managed to avoid any encounters. But Kita was definitely worse. For the last few hours, she had been passing in and out of consciousness.

As they went to eat dinner, she seemed to be in a lucid state. Davorin decided to take a chance. "We can save you. We have the jewel."

Kita shook her head. "Without the jewel, we all die. And you know it."

He sighed. "We have one more chance. If we can get you to that cave, the one on the border. You might have a chance there. So, you have to hold on. It's less than a day."

She smiled weakly. "I'll be fine. Figure out how you plan to save the world. I want to know."

Davorin stroked her hair and helped her swallow some water. He tried not to wince at how much heat she was putting out. "Well, I think I like this plan I heard about a clever woman. One brave enough to challenge the gods and generous enough to risk everything for her beliefs. Well, she demands magical powers, and turns the king into a pigeon. Then she heals herself, transports us all back to the palace, and what do you think? Sir Jors as the new king?"

"He'd be a good king. Better than King Zikkar," Kita agreed.

"*Whisper* would make a better king than King Zikkar."

She snickered; her eyes drifting shut. "Yes, I like it. King Whisper." Davorin let her fade to sleep.

He woke in the morning to the sound of Whisper shrieking like he had been stabbed. Lakara jumped to her feet, eyes on the hawk. "What is it? Are we under attack?"

Sir Jors also leapt to his feet; sword drawn. "I don't see anything."

Davorin ignored them both, all attention on the cooling body beside him. Kita was gone. Shadow Master had claimed her.

***

***

Chapter Nineteen

The Duel between Despair and Hope

Or

Doors open both ways

Sir Jors didn't realize until he heard the sob from Lakara. Then he saw Davorin carefully close Kita's eyes and gently place her hands in front of her in the customary burial position.

"No," Lakara whispered. "No." Barely louder, tears evident. "She can't be d... She can't be!"

His own eyes watered even as he saw the tremor of the necromancer's hands and the shake of his shoulders. Lakara fell to her knees beside them. Sir Jors moved to stand next to them, mind running through the prayers for the dead that he had used far too many times in the past.

Putting a hand on Lakara's shoulder, Sir Jors forced himself to remain alert, even as he wanted to join them in their grief. Kita deserved to be mourned decently, but if they were to strive for all the proper rites and rituals, then there was too high a chance none of them would survive the Dead Lands.

"We shouldn't bury her here," Davorin said, at last. "Can we... Can we get her to the forest, at least?"

It would increase their risk, but not an insurmountable amount. No more than carrying her alive would have. "We will."

They wrapped her as best they could, Davorin and Sir Jors taking turns carrying her as they traveled. Lakara tried to console Whisper, who had lapsed into silence and refused to fly. Sir Jors didn't know much about birds, but when he saw Whisper refuse to eat anything, he suspected the hawk would follow his mistress shortly.

If they had faced as many run-ins and threats as they had on their way to the temple, they would never have survived. But for whatever reason, they only encountered one ghoul. That one was far enough away that Davorin was able to use his powers to extinguish it before it was close enough to attack them. Then he needed to lean on Lakara for almost an hour while Sir Jors carried Kita.

Sir Jors was willing to attribute it to a miracle when they actually made it back to the Forest of Gloom, and even found the pack lizards who were none the worse for their time unattended in the woods. Trouble seemed particularly glad to see them, but even Stripes and Longtail looked interested. His heart felt heavier as he remembered that Kita had named the lizards. Of all their group, she had been the one to like the lizards the most, and they definitely reciprocated.

He set her down gently, not too close to the lizards. Trouble, of course, came over to investigate, nudging at her and trying to nuzzle. "No, Trouble. Leave... leave her be." He took the lead and led the lizard further away. It wouldn't take long for the lizards to consider her a potential food source and there was no way he could let that happen.

They had brought her back to the forest. But now what? "Did the Queya have any particular funerary rites? Do either of you know?" Both shook their heads. It wouldn't be easy to bury someone in the forest. Too many roots and they had no shovel. It wouldn't have been easy in the Dead Lands either, but they could have built a cairn. Here, there weren't even enough rocks for that. "We need to figure out what we should do."

"Why didn't we use the jewel to heal her?" Lakara asked. "We could have healed her, and she'd be fine!"

"I offered. Twice. She turned me down." Davorin didn't even look up as he spoke. "We could use the jewel to bring her back, and she'd be furious with us."

Lakara's head came up so fast that she hit Sir Jors' knee. "We could bring her back?"

"Well, presumably. If Shadow Master were willing to make the bargain," Davorin said. "But that doesn't change her wishes."

Her eyes narrowed. "Right now, I don't *muddy* care what she wants! She shouldn't have died!"

Sir Jors choked at the first swear word he had ever heard Lakara utter. Possibly her first ever. "As much as I sympathize, Davorin has a point. She said no. Because she knew that we needed the jewel. Stop a war? Remember?"

"I *remember* that not one of us figured out *how* we could do that. Do you think we're going to be any more successful if we get back to Corvis? Maybe some brilliant idea will show up? Who knows? Maybe we got the jewel *exactly* so we could bring her back!" Lakara glared. "And I think I put our chances higher at coming up with a solution with all four of us and no jewel than with the jewel but only three of us."

"I think," Davorin spoke slowly. "I think Lakara may have a point. Maybe I'm just being selfish about wanting her back. But when I visited the temple of Shadow Master, I was told that I would come of my own free will in time. That was also hinted at in my dream, but I didn't realize it at the time. What if the coming of my own free will was to bargain for her life?"

"She'll be furious."

"She'll be alive," Lakara countered.

"We're trying to prevent a war," Sir Jors said.

"And Kita is our best help in enlisting the Queya, and possibly even the Trovians for help," Davorin answered. "Not a guarantee, but…"

Sir Jors gave a huff. He would never be comfortable with this, but he was honest enough to admit that he would selfishly choose to have Kita back, even if she were angry with them. Even if it did make their whole goal harder. That tipped it for him. Their goal would be harder, but not impossible. "Then I guess the only question is, are you willing to do this?"

***

Davorin took his time preparing, double and triple checking every element. This had to be perfect. It certainly wasn't every day that one challenged the Deity of Death. There weren't many stories of that in legend. Even fewer where things didn't end in tragedy.

Incense was lit, ritual symbols were in their proper places, the runes were drawn in front of him, and the Jewel of Ishni rested on his ankles as he sat cross-legged on the ground. He exchanged one last glance with Lakara and Sir Jors, who gave him a hopeful, worried smile and a grave nod respectively; took one last look at Kita, the reason he was doing this, before closing his eyes and starting the chant that should leave him in a trance.

As the last word left his mouth, Davorin could already tell it had worked. The sound was different. The whispers of the dead were louder, echoing strangely. He was in front of the door again, Shadow Master at his side.

You came.

"You knew she would die."

No. Not until the infection set in. That surprised even me. Her lifespan wasn't supposed to end then.

"Then why did it?" She wasn't supposed to die?

Because when one handles hot coals with bare hands, bad things happen.

"If you didn't know she would die, how did you know I would come?"

I am a deity.

Right, no provoking the gods. Shadow Master had all the power here. "I've come to bargain for Kita. The Jewel of Ishni for her living out the rest of her natural lifespan." Hopefully, that would be decades and decades yet. Didn't the Queya sometimes live for more than a century?

That could be tomorrow. Or it could be eighty or ninety years.

"I don't suppose you would say which?"

No.

"It was worth a try."

Do you really think this will work?

"What do you mean?" The jewel had been argued over by the gods until AKAF hid it. That had to be decent leverage.

Some of the gods argued and bickered over it, even playing tricks on each other. Personally, I never saw much use myself.

"You... you don't *want* the jewel?"

It's been centuries. I'm not sure anyone cares anymore.

That... was not good.

Then again, you have provided us with more entertainment than we've had in a very long time. And perhaps some of them still want the bauble.

What was that supposed to mean?

I mean, that it might still be possible to leverage the jewel to save your kingdom and rescue the rest of you from certain death. If you don't use it here, trying to save a thief who even you suspected would save herself at the expense of the rest of you.

"She wouldn't! Not anymore, anyway. She didn't have to move hot coals with her bare hands. If she were willing to abandon the jewel, she'd still be alive."

Perhaps it was a love of riches.

"Then she wouldn't have argued against using it to heal her. Twice."

Then why are you here?

"Because... Because we'd rather have her with us, trying to find a possible solution, than have a sure solution without her."

Shadow Master gave a grin or grimace that made Davorin shudder. *I will make a bargain with you, Davorin, my necromancer. You can leave now, with the jewel, and I keep Kita. Or you can test your claims. Succeed, I release Kita, you, and the jewel. Fail, and I keep all three. What say you now?*

***

There was nothing but dark. She hated it. Light had existed once, hadn't it? She had walked in it. Shadows had been her friend, not her adversary. There were people. She hadn't been alone. Not in years. She had a companion. Who was her companion? Not a person, she didn't think. But there had been people. For some time, there had been people with her. Hadn't there been?

Her very essence seemed to be thinning. Fading? Or being called away? Changing, perhaps? How long had she been here? Hours? Days? Years? Millenia?

A jolt ran through her, and then she was elsewhere. A person stood before her. She knew him. Who was he?

"Kita?"

She knew that word. 'Kita.' That was her!

I should have anticipated this. Here, this will make things easier. A figure she couldn't quite look at tapped her forehead. Memories flooded in.

"Davorin? What are you doing here? Are you dead? You can't be dead!" They weren't supposed to die, they were supposed to live!

"I'm not dead. I came to bring you back."

Hope flowed. She could leave? Leave this place of dark and loneliness? "Back?"

Davorin smiled nervously and nodded. "We have a plan."

She tried to step forward. What would she be willing to give to live again? A lot. Another movement forward. Then cynicism kicked in. "What plan?"

"We're offering Shadow Master the jewel in exchange for your life."

Muddy *fools.* "And then I get executed when we go back to that scum sucker of a king! No, you're supposed to *use* the jewel."

"We are."

"Not for *me!*" Kita wanted to gesture but she still didn't feel like she had a body. "I'm just a thief. Born on the streets, dies on the streets. No one mourns us. Even if you did bring me back, what about my hands? No one would tell me, but I know it was bad. I'd never be able to rely on them the same way again. A thief who can't steal?" She shook her head, she thought, and hoped it came across. "It wouldn't be long before I was back here."

"You are worth far more than your hands. And yes, you were a thief, and may be again, but you are not *just* anything." Davorin moved towards her. "I don't know where you were born, nor do I care. I don't even know where *I* was born. You didn't die on the streets, and even if you had, that doesn't make you any less of a person. Yes, your hands were bad. But we didn't make the deal for a thief. We all agreed to this for Kita, our *friend*. Our companion. A brilliant thinker who has unusual outlooks on things that we hadn't thought about. The loyal woman who risked everything for a quest she didn't believe in and didn't want any part of. The one... the one I think I may have fallen in love with."

"What?" It was strange to gasp without air.

"I expect nothing from you and will not even mention it again if you wish. But it's true, even if I didn't realize it until Skoses's temple. And you deserved to hear it."

Kita paused. "I think... I think I could love you too. But you *can't* use the stone to save me. We'd both end up back here before the year was out. And so, so many others, too." It took everything in her, every bit of strength she had, but Kita stepped back, her head up, and spoke. "I refuse."

To her surprise, Davorin turned to the shadowy figure. "Will that be sufficient?"

It shall. A skeletal hand reached towards her and brushed her face.

Kita pushed herself with a gasp. Air inflated her lungs. Lakara and Whisper rivaled each other for the loudest shriek, but it was Lakara who embraced her, sobbing. "You're alive! It worked!"

"Perhaps, better than worked," Sir Jors said. When Kita looked towards him, he was helping Davorin stand. The Jewel of Ishni was in his hand.

"Shadow Master didn't care about the jewel." Davorin shook his head and gave her a small, wry smile. "So, a test was proposed. Honestly, I think Shadow Master knew what would happen, but wanted an excuse."

"What kind of test?" Kita asked. As happy as she was to be alive, which was a lot, she didn't like being a pawn, even for the gods.

"Supposedly it was to see if you deserved to be resurrected, I think. I made the offer and had to try to persuade you to take it. If you accepted, knowing we could all suffer if you did; then Shadow Master kept you, me, and the jewel. I tried to get him to let you go either way, but... you can only bargain so much with gods. If you refused, then, well, here we are."

Lakara gasped. "I didn't realize you'd be putting *yourself* at risk! But I'm so glad it worked."

"Talking to gods is rarely safe," Davorin admitted. "There is one more thing." He waited until he had everyone's attention. "Even for the gods, it's been a *long* time. Shadow Master said that it's possible that *none* of the gods care about the jewel anymore."

***

Possible wasn't certain. Maybe one or more were still interested. Especially since Davorin said that Shadow Master advised them to wait before trying to use the jewel.

"There was no explanation on why?" Lakara asked. Some degree of being cryptic was to be expected when dealing with the gods, especially face to face, may she ever be spared that, but this seemed particularly odd.

"No. Simply that something more opportune may present itself. Opportune *what* I wasn't told."

"Well, then we aren't really any worse off than we were before, we just aren't as well off as we were originally hoping." Lakara sighed. "Hold still! I'm sure your hands aren't still infected, but we still have to check them."

Kita huffed and leaned back against a tree. "Maybe they were healed all the way? They don't hurt. Don't feel hot either. They did yesterday."

"That would have been the infection." Lakara removed the last of the bandages. Kita's hands definitely looked better than yesterday, but that was about as much as could be said. No open sores or blisters, the burns appeared to have advanced to scars. But her hands, especially the palms, were still a blotchy mess of too pale and too dark spots. "Close your fists?"

Kita did so, frowning. "That feels weird."

"How so?"

"I'm not sure. Numb, maybe?"

"Close your eyes, tell me when you feel something and where."

Final result seemed to be that Kita could feel when Lakara pressed firmly almost anywhere on her hand, though she had more trouble in the center, and could feel a light touch on most of the fingers of her right hand and the last two fingers of her left hand. When Lakara tried with a blade of grass, only a couple spots caused her to react at all. Back of the hands were completely fine. Perhaps most importantly, Kita could manipulate each finger individually, but when she did some finger exercises, common to thieves, she was only about seventy percent successful.

"Well," Lakara took in a deep breath. "We'll figure something out."

"Like what? I'm a thief. That's all I've really known; all I have training for. I can't do that anymore. And I don't think they're going to get better. This feels... final. Like it's the best I'll get." She glared at her hands only to turn away with a wince. "And they're hideous."

"They aren't," Davorin said. "Your hands are proof of

your bravery, your selflessness, and your," he smiled. "Your stubbornness." Kita looked to be biting back a snicker or at least a smile. "And once you're a lady, you can wear gloves all the time if they bother you that much."

"But..." Kita gaped at him.

"We'll figure something out." He shrugged and pushed himself to his feet. "So, how are we getting back?"

"He's right," Sir Jors said. "I know it's frightening, but we'll help you find a new path even if your old life is closed to you. You were promised a ladyship. Perhaps we'll even find a way to make that work. I don't know how yet, but maybe. Even if we can't, I have seen many soldiers have to adapt to new circumstances as the result of injury. I have complete faith in you to do the same."

Kita nodded slowly. "I'll try to keep that in mind."

As they traveled through the forest, it had become evident that Kita was probably correct about the permanence of her injuries. No changes in responsiveness or sensitivity, no changes in color. The only change was the development of occasional spasms or tremors in her hand, and that was probably less a change and more something they hadn't had a chance to see before. According to Kita, sometimes she didn't even realize she had a spasm until she dropped whatever was in her hand.

Kita's mood about her injuries varied almost as much as the injuries remained unchanged. Sometimes she acted optimistic, that maybe they would get better, and she'd regain full function or at least close. Other times, she was angry. At Shadow Master for not healing her hands all the way, at AKAF for setting up the jewel so she had to burn herself in the first place, at herself for not figuring another way to get the jewel. And, while she was careful not to say it, Lakara knew there were a few times that she was angry at them for bringing her back. Sometimes she didn't have enough energy to be angry. She would be so depressed that even Whisper couldn't cheer her up. It was exhausting to watch, and Lakara couldn't imagine how difficult it would be to actually be going through it.

In an attempt to retrain her hands, Kita had taken to trying to braid strips of leather during their rest breaks. While staying with the Queya, Lakara and Kita had learned several elaborate plaiting techniques used for both practical purposes and decoration. It had taken practice, but both had gotten quite good at a few different types. Lakara's favorite was a six-stranded braid known as 'Winter's Knot' for reasons she didn't have enough of the language to ask. Kita had excelled at an eight-strand plait called 'Bird in Nest'.

Now, even her three-strand braids were lumpy and uneven. No one mentioned it, but Kita didn't need them to. The last time Lakara had tried to say something encouraging about it, Kita had thrown the braid at her face and told her not to lie. She apologized soon after, but it became an unspoken rule. Never say anything about Kita's injuries or anything that her injuries changed.

She was braiding now, frustrated as her fingers didn't do quite what she wanted them to do. Then her hand twitched and she dropped the project entirely. "Filthy rot! This is useless!" Kita buried her head into her knees. "If I can't even do this... What good am I?"

"Stop it," Davorin said, firmly. "You are more than your hands. To all of us."

She looked at him, barely peeking up. "You said that before."

"I meant it, too. I meant *everything* I said down there."

"*Everything*?" Lakara got the strangest feeling that there was quite a bit more going on than she understood. When she looked at Sir Jors, he seemed just as confused.

"*Everything.*"

Kita nodded slowly. "I... Can we talk about it later? When we know... when we know we have a later. When I manage to adjust to the new normal."

"As long as you need. Just say the word." Davorin nodded, before standing and grabbing the cooking pot. "I'll get some water."

He got about three steps before Kita called after him. "Davorin?" He turned. "It helps, a little. To know that."

"Good. I'm glad." He left then. Sir Jors went a moment later to gather wood.

Lakara bit her lip, wanting to ask Kita what was going on, but not daring to. It felt so private, and as much as they had learned so much about each other and seen each other in so many conditions, Lakara didn't feel she had a right to this.

Kita eyed her hands again. "Great loss and greater gain."

It took her a moment to place the semi-familiar line. "The prediction at Cryswayr's temple?"

She nodded. Well, Lakara certainly couldn't deny Kita had suffered loss. Her hands. Even her life temporarily, even if she said she couldn't really remember anything about it until she was talking to Davorin. Davorin said that was normal. The living were not meant to know what happened after death. Even a necromancer couldn't get a ghost or shade to tell anything but what they had known in life. Kita did admit to remembering being desperate to escape when presented with an opportunity. That told them enough.

"Do you know what the gain is?"

Kita looked in the direction of the river. "I might be starting to."

Chapter Twenty

Endings and Beginnings

Or

"Now what?"

Kita had mixed feelings when they reunited with the Queya. She was happy to see them, of course. Coming in contact with people who were pleased to see her was still an unusual occurrence for her. Most of her time before the quest was spent largely self-isolated. Sometimes she encountered people multiple times, but it wasn't common and those she did usually knew exactly what she was. Even thieves weren't usually glad to see another thief. Folks like Jalen were the exception, not the rule; and even with him, she had never felt completely safe.

It was amazing to find out parts of her past and heritage that she never knew existed. Almost as wonderful as having people who completely accepted her. Even when they found out about her injuries, the Queya were as welcoming as could be. Unfortunately, none of the Queyan traditional remedies were more effective than what they had already tried. Any progress made now would be from practice and stubbornness.

Her braids were a little better than they had been, though she was still prone to dropping things without warning. She'd never be as good as she was, and certainly not enough to make her livelihood through anything that required skilled handiwork. A thought that would bother her less if she had any idea what else she could do.

She hadn't particularly enjoyed being a thief. Oh, it was a thrill sometimes. The excitement of risking getting caught. The pleasure of a perfect palm or pick. Having money to use or spend. Sometimes, when the mark was particularly well-off or obnoxious, it was even a little like revenge. But Kita couldn't say she had missed it while traveling. Most of the time, she hadn't even thought about it.

Davorin said he loved her, but what did that mean, exactly? The king's necromancer could hardly marry a street thief, even if he wanted to. And Kita refused to be anyone's mistress or bedwarmer. Of course, if King Zikkar had actually valued him, he wouldn't have sent Davorin out on this suicide mission. So, he probably didn't care who Davorin married. But would Davorin even think as far as marriage? He wasn't as concerned with status as he had been months ago, but it was still a far leap.

For that matter, did she want to marry *him*? Kita had never actually considered getting married. Who would want to marry a part Trovian street thief who couldn't stay in one place for long? As much as she cared about him, could potentially fall in love with him, marriage might be a step too far for her, too.

But it really wasn't worth thinking about now. Someday, they would talk over what exactly they both wanted. But that could wait until they knew they weren't going to be executed the moment they set foot in Corvis. If they went to Corvis.

The problem with rejoining the Queya was that it left her in a quandary. Absolutely no one would blame her if she chose to stay. The Queya would be pleased to have her join them on a permanent basis. Even Davorin admitted he could possibly see himself settling here. Well, as settled as a semi-nomadic people could be.

But Lakara and Sir Jors were adamant about finishing the quest. Get to Corvis and figure out how to try to save the kingdom and the continent from an unnecessary war. Both had made it clear publicly and privately that she didn't have to go with them.

She could stay here, her part done. No one would argue that she hadn't done her fair share. Maybe even more than her fair share. But was that right? They were willing to sacrifice the Jewel of Ishni just to bring her back to life. How could she abandon them now? If she stayed with the Queya, she would probably never even find out what happened to them. The Queya got so little news from that far south that they hadn't even known the name of the current king. Or cared, for that matter.

So, perhaps her best option was to go with them. Find out what their solution was, make sure everyone survived. After that? Well, it wasn't impossible that she could find a way back up to the Queya afterwards. Or one of a million other possibilities could present itself.

Malni was not just supportive, she already knew. "I have seen a vision of your path. It is a long one, but it will cross ours many times. When you walk with us, we will rejoice. When you separate, we will hope for your return."

"How could I come *many* times? It took months to get here with a group. I don't know that I could actually make it here on my own. Maybe, but not guaranteed."

"Perhaps you'll come by water. We are to meet up with our merchant partners in three days' time. You could come to some arrangement with them. Perhaps you will even meet more relatives."

That was an interesting thought. The Queya had accepted her as family as soon as they recognized her dirk. She didn't look much like the Queya, who had a gray tinge to their skin and almost all of them had brown hair. Though her eye color was actually pretty common here. But anyone looking at her came to the automatic conclusion that she had some Trovian in her ancestry. Perhaps that would be all she needed to convince some to help her. Or maybe they would decide she wasn't Trovian enough and was therefore a traitor. Most likely, she would run into both.

Then there was the fact that it would mean traveling by boat. She had far more than enough of water travel to last her the rest of her life. But if it could save her months of foot travel? The last few trips hadn't been terrible. Yes, she still got seasick, and it frightened her. But she managed and even the storm hadn't been as bad as it could have been.

Meeting the Trovian merchants went well, despite their nervousness. None of them had met a full Trovian before, and it quickly became apparent that only half the merchants spoke Graldish. In fact, a few were highly disdainful of the language and those that spoke it. But scorn was nothing she wasn't intimately familiar with. So long as it remained on the level of looks and words, most of which she couldn't understand, then she didn't care.

One merchant captain, who called herself Layvra, offered to give them a ride to Talisna when she heard their story. "Don't know how long land travel would take but it should be close."

"I made it from Talisna to Corvis in about five days once. Maybe a week with this group and the pack lizards," Sir Jors said. "How long would it take to get to Talisna?"

Layvra smirked. "In a hurry? If the seas and waves behave, I can get you there by the feast of Sovitz."

"Two weeks?" Davorin asked, almost aghast. "You can get us that far in two weeks?"

"Like I said, if the sailing is good. Don't know how you

groundwalkers manage, myself." Layvra looked at Kita. "So, you're Haldor's whelp? I never met the man myself, but I heard about him. He was from my clan. Think he and my mother were cousins or similar. When he died, Kalina was offered his ship, but she chose the land. Did you know her?"

Kita shook her head. "According to my father, she died young. But my father was gone by the time I was five, so I don't remember much." She wasn't going into his being declared a Never-Was. That wasn't Layvra's business. The whole thing probably had a lot more to do with his background than any crime he may have committed. Possibly. Her mother never told her any details.

Layvra shook her head. "Well, then it's time you learned the Trovian way to sail." Her grin looked almost evil. What were they getting themselves into?

**

Davorin did not like boats. He hadn't from the first time he had stepped foot in one, and not a single experience had changed his mind. The Trovian remedy for seasickness helped. It tasted like an old stocking boiled in lizard brains and smelled worse; but it worked. Within ten minutes of swallowing the mixture, Davorin didn't have any stomach issues. Of course, he spent at least fifteen minutes gagging. Kita, the coward, said she'd pass. She was only ever sick the first day anyway.

Despite his dislike, he had to admire the speed of travel and the views. Not having to wind their way around landscapes or visit particular places allowed them to save a lot of time. So far, the trip had been quite smooth. According to Captain Layvra, this was one of the best times for sailing. The storms of fall hadn't started, the cold of winter was still a way's off, and spring was almost as volatile as fall, even if the storms weren't as severe.

The boat was also more comfortable than the fishing

boat they had taken refuge on before and certainly smelled better. The crew lived on the boat, more or less full-time, unlike the fisherfolk who usually had homes they went back to between trips. As a result, more time and space had been devoted to living quarters. The fact that the merchant's stock took up less room than fish probably helped. Captain Layvra and her crew, while willing to take advantage of opportunities that came up, specialized in cloth and jewelry. Including dark glasses like Kita's. Both Kita and Davorin were in separate negotiations to earn or buy a pair before they finished the voyage. Kita because she wanted a spare, and Davorin because there were times it was useful to cover his eyes.

Cloth and jewelry required dry, comfortable storage spaces. They also, to the amusement of the quest crew, did a thriving sub trade in spices. Fortunately, they hadn't tried to claim Davorin was a spice merchant.

As far as the Trovians and Queya knew, they had been on a pilgrimage, which was mostly true. Davorin suspected that the Trovians and Queya thought they were a little crazy, but pilgrims did strange and foolish things sometimes. The group had been in complete agreement that they weren't going to mention the Jewel of Ishni or that King Zikkar either planned to or had already started a war.

Twice, the boat met up with another boat and joined together to exchange news and, if agreed, supplies. Once, they disembarked in Salardis for a day of trading. Despite listening carefully, Davorin couldn't hear anything that suggested a war had started. In fact, from the rumors he heard, soldiers at the border were heading further inward, towards the capital. When he asked Sir Jors about the strategy behind that, the knight was puzzled.

"Unless he's expecting a threat to hit the capital, it doesn't make sense. Even then, he's leaving the borders too open. Mobility counts for everything sometimes. It will take weeks to put those troops back. If Salardis were to attack right now, they would certainly win, and could potentially take miles of territory before meeting organized resistance strong enough to slow them down. Even if he wants to make them seem the aggressors, this is a strange strategy."

It wasn't until they almost reached Talisna that they got an answer. Another ship met up with them, buzzing with rumor. Rumor that Captain Layvra made sure to tell them directly.

"I don't know if this is true, but word is that King Zikkar is choosing his successor. He has called forth his knights and nobles to Corvis to compete for the right to be considered."

"His successor?" Kita asked. "He's never cared about that before."

"Rumor is, he's dying. And since he has no heir…"

"That… explains a few things," Sir Jors said slowly. "Leaving the borders less defended makes a little more sense if those who would be there think they have a chance at the throne. I assume he's brought back the Palace Games."

"Three kings have been coronated through the Palace Games in the past," Lakara said. "Brain, brawn, and courage. They were considered the necessary qualities to rule well and wisely."

"So, whoever wins this, becomes the next king?" Kita asked. "And it's open to nobles and knights?"

"So I hear," Captain Layvra said.

"*All* nobles and knights?"

"I think so. But you'd have to get to Corvis to find out. And I'm going to go elsewhere now, so I don't hear this." She left them. Kita walked over to the door of the cabin and listened, before nodding and coming back.

"What are you thinking?" Lakara asked.

"Davorin, do you count as a noble?"

He had to stop to think about it. "I don't believe so. As the king's necromancer, living in the palace, I almost might as well have been one. I certainly had similar rank. But I have no title, no lands, so technically, not a noble."

"Okay, Lakara?"

"What?" She paused, then choked. "What? No, I'm a scholar. Definitely not a noble."

"I didn't think so, but I wanted to check. So, that puts it all on you, Sir Jors. I know you're a knight."

"Well, yes, but..."

"But nothing. She's right," Davorin said. "If *all* knights can compete, then you're eligible."

"But if the king discovers us, he'll remember how he sent us on the quest. At which point he could easily have us executed for treason for not obeying his orders."

"Not if it's the Palace Games. Tradition is that all contestants are to be kept anonymous until the end, to be fair. Each participant is given armor that conceals the face, and their identity is only revealed at the end," Lakara said. When everyone looked at her, she shrugged. "I had to recopy the primary book on the Palace Games two years ago."

"Then we've got this," Kita said. "Did the book say what kinds of tasks there were?"

"Certainly. There was a detailed list." Lakara closed her eyes and waved her hand, trying to recall details. "Yes, I can remember them all. Even," she smiled as she opened her eyes again, "come up with possible future tasks, based on past ones."

"Worse comes to worse, we can try to barter for you to

win," Kita said.

"No. We aren't going to do that. If I am to win, then it shall be fair. If I lose, and whoever the successor is proves not to be more amenable, then we shall revisit our options." Sir Jors stood firm on this point.

"Then we had better get to Corvis in time," Davorin said.

***

Sir Jors tried to hide his apprehension. Rumor had proved accurate so far. The Palace Games began tomorrow. It wasn't quite official that the king would pick his successor from the results, but that was what everyone claimed.

They had made it to Corvis about one hour before the gates closed on the last day of registration. Part of that was probably because of their visit to the temple of Aloses in Talisna. Kita's injuries remained unchanged, but Sir Jors couldn't bring himself to regret the delay. Perhaps she would try again here in Corvis. Or perhaps she had become resigned. She wasn't talking about it.

King Zikkar had made an address tonight to the crowd who flooded the streets, wishing the contestants luck and honor. Knowing that the king was unlikely to notice anyone in particular, especially at a distance, they had dared to come and listen at the outskirts. Even to Sir Jors, at a distance, he didn't look well. Kidney disease, maybe? Probably his heart wasn't healthy either.

"The shadows have almost completely overcome him. Three days. At most." Davorin helped him apply the borrowed cuirass. Every contestant was given a set of armor and a small tent, tall enough to stand in, but not able to hold more than five or six people comfortably, for their use during the event. Every suit of armor is a little different, and Sir Jors wanted to make sure that he knew all the quirks of this set before he had to do anything strenuous in it.

"Most of the Palace Games competitions lasted two days in the past." Lakara held out his scabbard. "The first day is for the mental challenges. There is always at least one, sometimes as many as three. Since the ability to listen to good advice is valued, you are allowed to consult others. To prove that you can recognize good advice from bad, you are required to pick who your advisors will be ahead of time. You can have up to three, and they will also be hidden from the crowds."

"Well, that works perfectly for us. Especially if we can get Kita to leave the pack lizards," Sir Jors said. Coming into Corvis had made Kita very agitated. She hid it well enough to fool someone who hadn't shared a hundred fires with her, but it was obvious to them. She wasn't willing to abandon the group, but nor was she comfortable getting any closer to the city or the king than she had to.

"She'll be here. I'm sure she'll want to see you perform." Lakara started to hold out his shield before pausing. "You want *us* as your advisors?"

"Who else would I pick? We've managed to travel half the world together; clearly, we are stronger united. Besides, I've been gone almost a year. I don't even know who else I could consult who would be in Corvis right now. And if I did tell anyone I was back, then word might get back to the king."

"Maybe. I saw one of my fellow scholars today. He didn't recognize me. But I didn't try to talk to him."

"It's been a long time. You look different. Travel will do that. I *certainly* look different." Davorin moved to look out the tent, before rejoining them at the center.

"True in both cases," Sir Jors admitted. Davorin had lost a fair bit of weight, while Lakara had gained some visible muscle. Both had become tan, Lakara more so. She had left for the quest wearing the shoulder-length hair that had become fashionable by ladies of the court about five years previous.

429

Now it was considerably longer and usually braided back. In fact, since meeting the Queya, she had experimented in some very elaborate braids. Davorin hadn't managed to remain clean-shaven, something he had grumbled about considerably in the beginning. When asked why he hadn't shaved when they got to Corvis, he said that it was part of his disguise. "Were you close friends?"

Lakara had talked a great deal about her time as a scholar, but seldom mentioned individuals she worked with. He suspected he would have remembered if she had said anything about a special friend, but there were all sorts of degrees of friendship.

"No. We rarely spoke. We had worked on one project together, but that was a few years ago. I'm not surprised he didn't recognize me. My parents wouldn't recognize me, either." Lakara shook her head. "You know, I'm not sure *anyone* would remember me well enough to have a chance to recognize me now. I wasn't close to anyone before we left. If I were wearing my scholar's robes, maybe. But I don't have those anymore." The robes in question had been deemed unsalvageable while they were in Winterwatch and burned. He couldn't remember exactly what happened, but he thought Trouble was involved.

"You might be the most inconspicuous of us, then," Kita said, sweeping in suddenly. "Davorin has to watch his eyes or wear his dark glasses, and knights are better recognized than scholars. I've got people looking at my skin or my hands."

"How are the lizards?" Davorin asked, not bothering to comment on her remarks.

"Fine. They're stabled close to the temple. People are less likely to try anything close to AKAF's chosen place."

"Are you willing to be one of my advisors for tomorrow's challenge?" Sir Jors asked.

Kita raised her eyebrows. "Um, sure? What challenge?"

"Tomorrow is the puzzle challenge." Lakara quickly filled her in on the rules.

"What kind of puzzle? Like riddles? Or rearrange shapes? Solve a problem?" Kita asked.

"That is an exceptionally good question. Lakara?" Sir Jors asked.

"It varies. Each tournament is a little different. I suppose we'll have to find out tomorrow."

As such, the next day found a disguised Sir Jors standing in a group with about twenty other contestants for his group. The best few from each group would move on to the next ranking. The best from that ranking would move on to the next day's contest.

An advisor in an elaborately embroidered blue tunic came out to announce their challenge. "You will be presented with a possible issue that could plague the kingdom and required to provide two possible solutions and the likely consequences of those actions. Your answers will be evaluated by the King's Council for judging, based on originality, how accurate your predictions are deemed to be, and the feasibility of your ideas. You have two hours." A scroll was passed to each contestant.

Sir Jors went back to his tent before breaking the seal and unwinding it. "Shall I read it out loud?"

"What's a cat-ras-poph-ic?" Kita asked, reading over his shoulder. Sir Jors couldn't help a smile at how far she had come, and how she butchered the word.

"Close. It's 'catastrophic'. It means a terrible event," Lakara said. "Yes, please read it out loud."

"It says, 'A catastrophic famine is gripping the land. You believe the answer to this famine is a new crop from across the sea. But the peasants reject the strange vegetable. How do you get them to plant this crop?' Well, that is a challenge."

"Don't force them. Even if you can make them grow it, you can't make them eat it. They have to want it," Kita said instantly.

"Agreed. Perhaps a tax relief for those who grow it?" Davorin suggested.

"Plus, free seeds. Provide the food free, or at least cheap, and money to grow it? Some will," Lakara said.

"Or tell them they can't have it," Kita said. "Grow it in the royal gardens, put up a fence, not a good one. Hire guards and tell them to do a lousy job, like missing people or taking bribes. 'Accidentally' leave some in places where it can be stolen. Anyone who is caught stealing it is given basically no sentence. Maybe make them work in the field where it grows. Make a big deal about it being served in fancy banquets. Before you know it, it'll be all over the kingdom."

"Two solutions. Now, consequences?" Sir Jors summarized each of the options in separate paragraphs, making sure there was enough space to finish. "The first one would encourage some people, and if we are right about the crop helping to end the famine, then seeing their success would encourage their neighbors. Cons?"

"It is an expense when the kingdom may not have the best budget," Lakara admitted.

"Some people would take the seeds but might not grow it. Or grow it badly either because they don't know how or don't want it," Kita said. "Assuming that it even grows here."

"We *have* to assume it grows here, or the scenario is completely useless. As for the second, people will try it, but it's hard for them to grow the crop if it's technically illegal." Sir Jors re-dipped his quill for more ink.

"But after a year or two, now that people want it, you can legalize it," Kita said. "Worse problem would be guards who choose to arrest or beat people who are caught."

"That could be an issue, but perhaps a program among the guards for accountability. If they knew they'd be reported, hopefully, the guards would be better behaved," Lakara said.

Kita scoffed.

"I'm afraid I would have to agree," Sir Jors said. "As a soldier, you find that the loyalty you feel to your fellow soldiers sometimes outweighs the loyalty you feel to those above. Guards would probably be similar. I'm not saying it's impossible, but I wouldn't expect a lot from such a program unless the punishments are frighteningly strict. But some overseers might not be amiss. Any other consequences?"

"While the peasants can get food in this manner, it will take longer for them to be able to grow it, since they will be stealing it when it is already grown for immediate consumption," Davorin said. "Also, one garden, no matter how big, can't possibly provide as much support as multiple smaller fields."

Sir Jors noted that under the cons list. "It would require getting various nobles to do the same thing. Both ideas revolve around a different aspect of people. The first one appeals to the desire to follow the law, while the second appeals to the desire to break it."

"There's always been a bit of joy in the forbidden. Trust a thief, we know."

Sir Jors read through what he had written. "This will have to do. I have to present it in a few minutes." He used some sand to dry the ink, then blew on it. Once dry, he re-rolled the scroll and tied it. Nodding to his companions, he stepped out to face the judgment of the council.

Waiting was nerve-wracking. Each of the twenty scrolls had to be read and discussed by the council who were far enough away and speaking quietly so they couldn't be heard. Occasionally, they shared one with King Zikkar who sat on his throne, looking practically dead. One, which Sir Jors had a sick feeling might have been his, actually made the king laugh. Was that good or bad?

Good, apparently. He and another contestant were chosen to go on to the next round. But that wouldn't be until evening as other groups were winnowed through. Sir Jors went back to his tent for lunch and to re-group.

An eternity and a blink later, he found himself among thirty other contestants. "For this contest, you will be given a list of laws. You will be required to recognize which are and which are not actually laws of the kingdom. The twelve contestants who do the best in time and accuracy will move on to tomorrow's round."

To no one's surprise, Lakara was a master at this, often even able to tell what year the law was enacted. Sir Jors left that part off, except when it came to one that had been the law and was later repealed. He included the years from both of those. Twenty minutes later, Sir Jors was handing in his answers. If he got them all right, and he certainly wasn't going to wager against Lakara's knowledge, then he would definitely be in the top twelve. Only one person finished before him.

As he expected, his number was listed as one to continue. To his surprise, the person ahead of him wasn't called. Perhaps they hadn't been accurate enough.

"Tomorrow's contest is the sword. You will be chosen in pairs to compete in a scored match. Chasley's rules apply. The winner of each pair will move on to the next match until only one is left. Pairs will be chosen by random draw."

"What's Chasley's rules?" Kita asked when Sir Jors went

back.

"Tournament rules to prevent injury. The swords are blunted, and everyone is wearing armor. A hit to the arm or leg is worth two points, a blow to the torso is five, disarming your opponent is seven points. The head is off-limits. First person to ten points wins as long as they are at least two points ahead of their opponent. If they aren't, then the first person to be five points ahead of the other wins," Sir Jors said.

"Huh. That sounds safer than to third blood," Kita said thoughtfully. "More complicated, though."

"It's also exhausting. So, we had better sleep," Sir Jors said.

***

Lakara tried to remain calm, but it was hard. The first match hadn't been bad. Sir Jors and his anonymous competitor had played a skillful but fair match, with Sir Jors winning twelve points to five. Afterwards, both bowed to each other and took their seats. It had lulled Lakara into a false sense of security that everyone would treat the challenge that way. As a contest that one desired to win, but that must be played fair, with honor and respect to the competition.

The second match, involving two others, was a frenzied battle that barely escaped ending in tragedy. Neither competitor was able to continue. One was disqualified for breaking the rules, while the other was too injured to continue. Apparently, the chance of a throne was too much for some to resist.

None of the other rounds were quite so fierce, the threat of being disqualified being enough to hold them back. But most rounds looked closer to the second than the first. Sir Jors' second round, while it did end in his victory, also seemed to injure him. And now he was going for his third.

"He'll be fine," Kita said, not looking at Lakara, eyes on the pitch.

"He's hurt. He was rubbing his arm after the last one," Lakara said.

"Ribs, too," Davorin said.

"And his opponent is limping. I was watching. This one's strategy is more speed than force. And he, maybe she, can't tell, doesn't have the speed anymore. Sir Jors can win this one fine." Kita kept her eyes focused. "Three dou says he wins in less than two minutes."

Neither Lakara nor Davorin took her up on her offer, but the man in the seat on the other side of her did. Two minutes later, Kita was three dou richer and Lakara tried to be relieved. "He's not bleeding, is he?"

Kita shaded her eyes to look. "A little bit. Most of it will come down to the next match. If his opponent is in even worse shape when they begin…"

The next match was brutal, and the winner would be up against Sir Jors in the final. "If Eight wins, Sir Jors has the advantage. If it's Four, then the match will be a lot harder," Kita said. Four won, and Eight had to be helped off the green.

"Four has shown a great deal of finesse and the ability to be quite forceful. This could be close," Davorin muttered.

"He's trying to hide it, but his arm's bothering him," Kita said. "It will be close, but if Sir Jors realizes he's weak there, his odds are better. Even if he doesn't, it will be a lot harder for Four to be as vicious as he was in this match."

The match began as steel met steel. "Are you sure his arm is bothering him?" Lakara asked, as Four swung as if he were trying to cut Sir Jors to pieces. He had already managed to score seven points to Sir Jors' five.

"Positive. One way or another, this will be finished in a

minute."

Sir Jors managed to block and his next attempt at a strike was equally blocked. Four aimed a blow far too close to Sir Jors' head, that he managed to block. Lakara was about to say something about her being wrong, but when Four tried to swing again, the sword flew from his hand.

"Winner, Six. Twelve points to seven!" The announcement rang out. Sir Jors was led to the front of the low balcony where the king sat with his council. "Remove your helmet and state your name!"

Lakara gasped. They hadn't prepared for that. What would King Zikkar do? She grasped Kita's hand who squeezed back either reassuringly or also afraid. Davorin patted her shoulder, so she grabbed his hand too.

In the field, Sir Jors removed his helmet, stepped forward, and spoke in a loud voice. "I am Sir Jors of Vaslisina."

Lakara didn't dare look away as King Zikkar grew pale and then purple. He jumped to his feet, hand outstretched, pointing at Sir Jors. "You!" Strangled grunts emerged, before he fell to the ground as if boneless.

"He's dead," Davorin whispered to them both.

It took the officials a few minutes to come to the same conclusion. Then they whispered together for another few minutes before the one who had been doing the announcing came forward.

"King Zikkar is dead! Long live King Jors!"

Epilogue

Sometimes, Lakara still couldn't believe how things had worked out. Sir Jors becoming King Jors was surprising, but not nearly as surprising as him asking her to be his queen.

"Me? You want me to be queen? Why me?" Surely, he should be looking to the ladies of the court. Or the nobles. Even the royalty of nearby countries to help solidify his grasp on the throne.

"Who else could I possibly ask? I've shared a hundred fires with you, and it has only given me the desire to share thousands more. I want you, and Davorin, and Kita, to be part of my life. To help me figure out what I'm doing and remind me that I'm still the second-born son with Aloses's sleep curse. From a strategic standpoint, I've learned to depend on your knowledge and practical thinking skills. I know you would make a good queen. And I can't think of anyone I would rather share my life and the throne with."

"Presenting Necromancer Davorin and Lady Kita," the courier announced. Lakara sat up sharply. Kita and Davorin had been away for a year, working with the Queya and Trovians.

A peace treaty was still being formed with the Trovians, but the waters were becoming safer as pirates decreased and merchants increased. Between that and the building of new roads, and some negotiations with Salardis, it was actually possible for the average traveler to reach the Forest of Gloom in about two months. Most still weren't inclined to try, but interest was slowly building. Almost all of that had to do with Lady Kita and Davorin's work as ambassadors. But Lakara, and she knew, Jors, missed them when they were gone.

"Enter and approach, friends," King Jors said with a smile. "You will join us for a private supper?"

"We would be honored," Davorin said. Kita never bothered to hold her tongue in private, but mostly stayed silent in court settings. Probably because for all her skill as an ambassador, she never completely learned to speak in what was considered an approved manner.

They were looking well. Probably they had reached Corvis the night before and taken the time to clean up first. Davorin had lost the beard that he inevitably grew whenever he traveled, and while he wasn't wearing his embroidered necromancer robes, his clothes were of good quality. Kita was using her staff with the flick of a ruby at the top, something she had insisted on keeping for her pains. Both almost seemed to glow. Lakara could barely wait to hear their stories.

Dinner came soon, if not soon enough. Kita presented them with the standard gifts they had accrued during their journeys. While some of the goods were highly valuable, Lakara's favorite was the slightly imperfect six-stranded belt. "You've come far," Lakara said, recognizing Kita's work.

"Still get numbness, and I know I'm missing sensitivity, but..." She shrugged, rubbing her omnipresent gloves together, as Whisper tried to tug at her hair.

Lakara's next thoughts were interrupted as she noticed Jors slip into sleep. As a precaution, she gently tugged his knife from his hand. They kept up a light conversation while watching him until he came back to awareness. No one mentioned anything.

"You plan to stay at least the winter, surely?" Jors asked.

Kita and Davorin exchanged a look. "Actually, your Majesty, with your permission, we'll be staying considerably longer," Davorin said.

"Granted, of course. We'll be glad to have you. But why?" He asked.

Kita rubbed at her stomach. "We want to wait until our child is able to travel with us."

Lakara put a hand to her mouth. "That's wonderful! I'm so happy for you both." Later, after she had a chance to inform her husband in private, she would be able to tell her friends that she shared their news.

In the meantime, she sat back and listened to their tales of lands and people, much of which she had firsthand experience with, and how the four of them were changing and shaping the world for their future children. Even without using the Jewel of Ishni.

THE END

About The Author

H. J. Harding

H. J. Harding is the author of the Moonlit Memories series and the Hyde Chronicles. She lives between the states of Chaos and Confusion and occasionally updates her website at www.hjharding.com.

Comming Soon

Ring of Blood

Book Three in the *Moonlit Memories* Series.

Liska and Todd have been through many challenges in their relationship and lives, but surely things will get easier soon, right? All they have to do is get Todd to graduate, get his family to accept their engagement, plan a wedding , and try to get through a normal school year without anyone targeting them.

They make it about two weeks. Outside threats, family complications, and school problems, of course. They can face it all if they have each other. Can't they? *Do* they?

Winter 2024

www.ingramcontent.com/pod-product-compliance
Lightning Source LLC
Chambersburg PA
CBHW072334020726
47506CB00004B/885